★

Where Donovan was he had no need of a mug. Neither hunger nor thirst troubled him. Time passed without leaving any wake, and the only sensation he knew of was a terrifying lightness, as if he might float away and be lost. Once, just once, he opened his eyes and the fairy was there again. Except of course that he didn't believe in fairies.

A thought struck him. Maybe it wasn't a fairy: maybe it was an angel. He looked again, critically. It didn't look much like an angel, though he wouldn't have claimed to be an expert. Another, and worse, thought struck him. It looked like an imp.

He shut his eyes again, and thought that this was one of those occasions when playing dead made a lot of sense. In fact, it was quite possibly the only game in town.

★

"Lovers of police procedurals will appreciate the good detective work that relies on intellect as much as muscle power."

—*Publishers Weekly*

"Jo Bannister continues to expertly write tales that are some of the sub-genre's best novels."

—Harriet Klausner

Previously published Worldwide Mystery titles by
JO BANNISTER

A BLEEDING OF INNOCENTS
CHARISMA
A TASTE FOR BURNING
NO BIRDS SING
THE LAZARUS HOTEL
BROKEN LINES
THE HIRELING'S TALE

JO BANNISTER

CHANGELINGS

WORLDWIDE®

TORONTO • NEW YORK • LONDON
AMSTERDAM • PARIS • SYDNEY • HAMBURG
STOCKHOLM • ATHENS • TOKYO • MILAN
MADRID • WARSAW • BUDAPEST • AUCKLAND

CHANGELINGS

A Worldwide Mystery/February 2002

First published by St. Martin's Press, Incorporated.

ISBN 0-373-26410-0

Printed in U.S.A.

I

ONE

STACKING SHELVES at the Castlemere branch of Sav-U-Mor was the best job Tracey Platt had ever had. It was regular, it paid well—well, better than most jobs available to an unqualified sixteen-year-old—there was overtime, and as long as you didn't actually do the damage yourself there were perks in the form of dented cans and battered boxes. Plus, Sav-U-Mor was an American supermarket, so shelf-stacking here was the closest Tracey was ever likely to get to working abroad.

Moving steadily along the cool cabinet, bringing forward the unsold goods and stacking the new ones behind them as she'd been taught, Tracey Platt didn't see much wrong with the world. For a girl from The Jubilee, who had neither the ambition nor—Tracey believed in being honest with herself—the intellect to succeed as a criminal, she thought she was doing pretty well.

Until, reaching mechanically to bring to the front the last of the weekend's unsold yoghurts, she saw something that shouldn't have been there. Tracey stopped in her android progress and, frowning, leaned forward for a closer look.

Tracey's vocabulary didn't stretch to the word 'botulism', but if it had been a regular ingredient of yoghurt it wouldn't have been written in thick black letters on a sticky label. Tracey could recognize a threat when she saw one. She took a rapid step backward and called for help. 'Mr Woodall. Mr Woodall! Mr Woodall!!' she cried, shriller and shriller until he appeared at her shoulder.

The under-manager leaned forward until he could see what was bothering her. Then, too much a gent to shake her, he squeezed her hand and said, very calmly, 'That's enough, Tracey. Now, let's both walk away—very carefully...'

IT WAS OCTOBER now so the photographs in the tourist brochures were no longer legally binding. The canal was brown. The buildings on Broad Wharf were brown, and brown clouds lowered out of the sky and dropped their cargo like celestial tankers dumping toxic waste while God wasn't looking. Even the swans, those without the foresight to swallow a fish hook and get themselves sent to a sanctuary for the winter, had a khaki tinge.

It was ten o'clock on a Monday morning so the last unwilling schoolboy had trudged through the gates of Castle High and on all the long stretch of towpath between Mere Basin and Cornmarket only three living souls were in sight. Undaunted by the weather or lacking the wit to get out of the rain, depending on your point of view.

Detective Inspector Liz Graham, who was one of them, inclined to the latter. She saw nothing admirable about defying something as relentless as the British autumn. It was weather for staying inside whenever possible; for fighting over the parking space nearest the door; for sending lower ranks out for the morning doughnuts.

It was not a day for taking your house for a drive.

For as long as she'd known him Donovan—the second living soul—had done this at intervals: disconnected his power supply, coiled up his warps and taken his narrowboat *Tara* off into the inland waterways. It was the only kind of holiday he took. He was a canal buff: he knew where all the locks were, how they operated and how long it took to negotiate each one. He came back with photographs of sluices and windlasses which were so devastatingly boring they acquired a kind of fascination.

This trip, though, he was avoiding locks as much as possible. He was still creaky from the bullet that carved a finger-deep trench below his ribs four months earlier: he didn't need to pit himself against tons of black timber every few miles. Also, he had a cold. With the black hair hanging in rats' tails in his dark angular face, his bony shoulders shrugging the collar of his black oilskin coat up around his ears and a cough rattling in the depths of his chest, he was as good an advertisement for the joys of boating on the Castlemere Canal as Yul Brynner was for hair tonic.

'You need a sou'wester,' Liz observed judiciously.

Donovan barked a laugh. He wasn't into headgear. He wore a motorcycle helmet because he had to; Liz couldn't remember seeing him in any other kind of hat. It was a small grief to her that she hadn't known him as a beat copper in a woodentop. Frank Shapiro reckoned Donovan was transferred to CID precisely because he was so unconvincing in uniform. CID was the only branch of the force in which not looking like a policeman was an advantage.

'All I need,' said Donovan heavily, blowing his nose and swigging fiercely from a little brown bottle marked 'Philbert's Cold & Flu Remedy: Use Sparingly', 'is for the frigging rain to stop.' His voice was thick with phlegm, but thicker still with the mid-Ulster accent he was determined to carry to his grave.

'Have you seen a forecast?'

He nodded grimly, raindrops splashing from his nose. 'More of the same.'

'Well, for heaven's sake,' said Liz, running out of patience, 'tie the damn boat up and try again later. You're supposed to be looking after yourself. They won't clear you for work until you're fit.'

'They cleared the chief,' growled Donovan.

Liz hid a smile. Donovan had been deeply offended that Superintendent Shapiro—fat, fifty-six and recovering from a bullet in the back—had been considered fit for duty by the same doctor who had rejected him. 'The chief does his best work sitting down. You do yours at the run. It makes a difference.'

The other difference, that she didn't mention, that she wasn't sure he'd been told about, was that no question had arisen over Shapiro's psychological state. Division was concerned that Detective Sergeant Donovan had taken too many injuries in too short a time; that if it wasn't a psychological problem getting him into all this trouble he must have one as a result of it. Either way, they wanted him a hundred per cent before they'd let him tackle so much as a second-hand car dealer suspected of clocking. Take a trip, said the doctor, try again when you get back.

Liz thought the break would do Donovan good too, but not for that reason. She had no reservations about his mental well-being. Donovan was passionate about his job, would go on doing it day in and day out until someone made him stop. Sometimes it was her, sometimes Shapiro; sometimes Fate dropped a heavy hint in the shape of a broken bone. It wasn't a psychological problem, it was just the way he was: a natural extremist. He did everything to excess. Division had him down as a loose cannon; Liz knew that the only thing wrong with Donovan was that he tried too hard. But in a grindingly hard and dangerous situation there was no one she'd sooner have at her back.

And because she wanted him back where he belonged she was here to see that he did as he was told and took his holiday. She'd rather have been waving him off on a charter flight to Greece, but sun and sand weren't Donovan's native habitat. If cruising the fens was the jolliest thing he would contemplate then it would have to do.

But she still didn't know why it had to be today, in drenching rain and with a man-sized habit in paper handkerchiefs.

Of course there was a reason, even if it made sense only to Donovan. If he started today he could have his holiday and get over his cold at the same time; then he could say he'd been on a cruise, pass his physical and be back at work by mid-October. There was nothing magical about October, he just didn't want his sick leave dragging on into another month. He didn't know how Queen's Street had managed without him this long.

But Liz Graham was his superior officer; they had an easy relationship these days but not easy enough for him to say as much aloud. 'Get on your way, boss, there's no point both of us getting soaked. Er...'

When he didn't finish Liz looked at him through the veiling rain and saw embarrassment on his gaunt features. 'Sergeant?'

'Look out for the chief.'

She didn't actually need telling. Three months earlier there'd been some doubt if Frank Shapiro would walk again. He'd made an excellent recovery, but this first week back at work was bound to find weak spots that hadn't bothered him at home. There would be a period of readjustment, and if he needed some-one to lean on Liz's was the shoulder of choice.

'I will,' she said softly. 'I'll look after him, you look after yourself, and I'll see you next week.'

'If you need me before that,' Donovan began hopefully.

'It'll be just too bad,' Liz finished briskly.

'I'll be going up the Castlemere canal to Posset, by the Thirty Foot Drain as far as Sinkhole Fen, then across by the Sixteen Foot Drain to join the Arrow at Foxwell Dam and home by the river. You can leave a message at the Posset Inn, at Sinkhole engine house or at Foxwell lock.'

He might have been speaking in Sanskrit. 'Or I could dial your mobile number.'

He scowled. 'It's on the blink again. I don't know why every-one else's works and mine's always acting the lig.'

Liz glanced around but refrained from stating the obvious: that they weren't designed to work under water, that if he lived in a house and drove a car his phone would work as well as hers. 'Donovan, I shan't need you; but if I do I know where to find you. If you're going, go. But for pity's sake, don't be too long before you tie up, dry out and get a hot meal. You won't pass your medical if you come back with double pneumonia.'

He gave her his saturnine grin. Then he whistled to the third living soul out of doors that inclement morning, and the great black dog bounded back up the towpath and hurdled the rail on to *Tara*'s forepeak. Leaning down Donovan engaged the engine and the note deepened as the screw bit into the brown water. Liz stood back and watched him steer the unwieldy craft out into the canal like Charon setting off across the Styx. But after a couple of minutes *Tara* was no more than a blur viewed through the closing curtains of rain, and she turned away and strode up the walkway to where she'd left her car in Brick Lane.

Even when the time came for looking back, she had no sense of premonition—no awareness as she saw him off that she might not see him again.

SUPERINTENDENT SHAPIRO, back in his office at the end of the second-storey corridor, looked up at the sound of her step and beckoned her through his open door. 'Come and look at this.' He was studying a yoghurt pot in a plastic bag.

She looked. 'Lunch?' she hazarded.

His rumpled face, uncharacteristically brown from having the time to sit in his garden, spread in a grin. He'd missed her. He'd missed the job, but also the relationships that went with it. His friends were all police officers. 'Do I look like a healthy eater?'

The simple answer was no: he looked like a man who snacked on chip butties. 'I thought perhaps you were coming out.'

Shapiro shuddered. All he knew about health food was that it was brown. 'It isn't my elevenses, it's a Clue.' Somehow he managed to pronounce the capital letter.

Liz's interest quickened. 'To what?'

'Ah,' he demurred. 'I haven't actually got a crime yet; but I expect one'll be along soon.'

He'd succeeded in confusing her, which was an achievement for his first day back. 'Perhaps if I go out and come back in again...?'

Shapiro waved her to a chair, passed her the yoghurt pot. The plastic bag was marked 'Evidence'. 'A shelf-stacker at Sav-U-Mor found it this morning.' He also managed to invest the name of Castlemere's biggest supermarket with his disapproval of its spelling.

Liz took it carefully. 'Is the yoghurt still inside? In fact, was it yoghurt inside?'

'No,' said Shapiro. 'And yes, but not exclusively.'

The pot contained—or had done—natural unflavoured yoghurt with a sell-by date three days hence. The foil top had been partially lifted. 'Forensics did that,' said Shapiro. 'When we got it the lid was intact.'

Turning it in her hands Liz found what had alarmed the shelf-stacker. An address label tacked to the back of the pot bore the legend, in large black felt-tipped letters: 'This could have been botulism.' She put it down, a little more quickly than she meant to. 'Could have been?'

Shapiro nodded. 'In fact it was lime jelly. All it would have given you was a nasty shock.'

Liz frowned. 'But if the lid was intact, how...?'

'You tell me.'

She kept looking. Finally she saw it: a pin-prick hole in the bottom of the plastic pot sealed with a bead of clear material. 'Hypodermic?'

He nodded. 'And?'

'Superglue.'

He nodded some more, approvingly. 'I don't know why we need a laboratory. A good eye can tell you as much as anyone in a white coat.'

'It couldn't have told you if the lime jelly was contaminated with botulism,' said Liz. The thought of it made her shudder. Every week—twice if she couldn't get Brian to do some of it— she brought home a car-boot full of groceries. It never occurred to her that any of them could have been tampered with. A hypodermic of lime jelly had destroyed that confidence for ever.

Which was, presumably, the idea. 'Blackmail?'

'No demands yet,' said Shapiro. 'It could just be somebody messing around—making a point, proving how easy it is? Perhaps a disgruntled former employee out to embarrass the supermarket.'

It was certainly possible; but it wasn't safe to assume it was merely a bad joke. 'If it is blackmail, what does the store want to do?'

'The manager will do what head office tells him. It's a big multinational, apparently, head office is in Seattle. For himself, he'd rather pay than risk injury to his customers.'

It was the compassionate response. But it would make blackmail the easiest, safest, most profitable crime in the book: everyone who asked for money as an alternative to doing something unpleasant would be paid. It had to be resisted, even if there was a price.

'What are we doing?'

'Dick Morgan's looking through the security tapes. Scobie's going over the supermarket's employment records with the manager, looking for someone who left in a huff. Mary Wilson— when did she join CID, anyway?—is on the computer, looking for anyone in the area with a bit of previous. What else can we do? Patrol the aisles, challenge customers who take too long choosing between mango and fruit-of-the-forest?'

Liz couldn't think of anything he'd missed; nor did she expect to. He'd been off for four months: it was maybe just long enough for his acuity to drop to where the rest of them were on a good day. 'Mary came upstairs while you were trying to convince the doctor that if Ironside could crack cases from a wheelchair you could certainly do it on crutches. It's early days but I think she'll do well. She always had more gumption than the other Whoopsies.'

She heard herself saying that and cringed. After the effort she'd put into storming the male citadel of criminal investigation, Liz of all people should have found a better shorthand for Woman Police Constable. But habit dies hard; and she'd been called a lot worse when she was one. And indeed since.

'No fingerprints, I suppose.'

'Only the shelf-stacker's.'

'What about the writing?'

'Done with a stencil. You can buy them at stationers, for writing posters and the like. Stencil, marker-pen, address labels—all standard lines, unless he's carrying them round with him we'll never trace them to one individual.'

'When did all this start?'

'Eight-oh-seven this morning. I was on the job by twenty past.'

Liz glanced over and yes, he looked as smug as he sounded. She smiled. 'Welcome back, sir.'

Shapiro beamed. 'Thank you very much.'

THE INFURIATING THING about the security tapes was that the culprit was almost certainly on them. Sav-U-Mor's undermanager Tony Woodall was able to identify the yoghurt as part of a batch which arrived on Saturday morning. The earliest it could have been on the shelf was 10.15 a.m., and the damage had been done before the store shut on Sunday. Tapes covering the entire period, with the cool cabinet clearly visible, were still available.

DC Morgan watched them all, then he watched them again. Then he watched just those sections where somebody was hovering over the yoghurt. In the end, square-eyed, he trudged round to Shapiro's office and shook his head glumly. 'I've seen it. I've probably seen it half a dozen times. But I can't spot it.'

The snag was that the cabinet was against the wall and the camera was in the middle of the ceiling, so anyone looking at the yoghurt had his back to the lens. Morgan had never realized how popular yoghurt was. Half the population of Castlemere must have helped themselves from that cabinet over the weekend. Those who knew what they wanted, took it and left could probably be discounted because of the time needed to do what was done.

'How long, do you suppose?' asked Shapiro. 'To inject a yoghurt pot, seal the hole and hide it at the back?'

DC Morgan was not an ambitious police officer but he was a thorough one. He'd mimed it out, against a stopwatch. 'Depends whether he did it on the spot, sir. If he did, not less than twenty seconds and probably more like half a minute. And that depends on there being no interruptions. The other possibility is that he bought a pot, left the store, tampered with it, then returned and put it at the back of the shelf. In that case he could do it very quickly but he'd appear on the tape twice.'

Shapiro was impressed. 'And does anybody?—appear twice.'

'Oh yes,' said Morgan wearily. 'Men; children; women with prams, women without prams; old age pensioners, Rastafarians, and a man in a beret with only one arm. We can probably discount him—unless he got a mate to hold the pot for him.'

Shapiro breathed steadily. 'You're telling me we have pictures of an incident taking place, we just can't isolate them.'

'That's about it, sir. Of course, if we get a suspect we can look back at the film and see if he's there.'

'And in the meantime...?'

'Maybe Scobie's having more luck.'

WHEN DETECTIVE Constable Scobie played rugby, which he did until the ENT surgeon said that if he broke his nose once more he could set it himself, he specialized in tackling. Teammates theorized that he didn't even want the ball, he just liked knocking people over. Opponents suspected he was on week-end leave from Broadmoor.

It was a style of play he used in his professional life too. By the time Sav-U-Mor's under-manager had spent half an hour answering his questions about present and former employees, those who left under a cloud and those who might have wanted a payback, he was beginning to feel like a suspect himself.

'Constable, if I knew who was responsible for this I would tell you. I don't. I can't think of anyone who might be.'

'Someone is.'

'Obviously. But I don't think it's a member of staff; not current and not recent. There's always some turnover but we haven't had to sack anyone for months.'

'How many months?' asked Scobie.

'Three, maybe four; and that was an elderly cashier who was getting too forgetful to manage the till.'

'It's not manual strangulation we're talking about, it's injecting jelly into a yoghurt pot. My old granny could do it, if she had enough of a grudge.' The faintest of bells tinkled in the back of Scobie's mind.

'The cashier I'm talking about couldn't hold a grudge for three months: she'd forget what she was angry about. And it's hardly rocket science, is it?—it didn't take three months to set up. If she'd wanted to embarrass us she could have done it the day she left.'

'All the same,' said Scobie doggedly, 'I'll pay her a visit. To eliminate her from our inquiries. Name and address?'

Tony Woodall shrugged, looked back his records. 'Mrs Alice Marsden, 27a Cambridge Road.'

Scobie blinked. 'Ah.'

Woodall stared at him. 'You don't mean she's done this before?'

'No—no.' Incredibly, the detective was blushing. 'Actually, Mr Woodall, Alice Marsden *is* my granny.'

DC MARY WILSON HAD done a course on using the Police National Computer. But though the various databases gave her a list of criminals operating in the Castlemere area, and another list of people who had committed this kind of crime in the past, no names appeared on both lists. The computer didn't know of anyone living in or around Castlemere with a history of corporate blackmail.

She shook her head apologetically. 'Sorry, ma'am, nothing. Maybe if we get some more information about him?'

Liz nodded resignedly. She hadn't expected any more. The computer was a tool of criminal detection, not a substitute for it. 'One thing, Mary—there's no need to call me ma'am. The boys call me Guv, Donovan calls me Boss, the people downstairs call me Mrs G—at least, they do when I'm there. Any of them's OK by me. Ma'am makes me feel like minor royalty opening a swimming pool.'

Wilson grinned. 'And we call Mr Shapiro the chief.'

'That's right.'

'Even though he's no longer a Chief Inspector but a Superintendent?'

'Now he's the other sort of chief. Sitting Bull. Geronimo.'

'Crazy Horse,' offered Wilson.

Liz shook her head. 'No, we're saving that in case Donovan gets promoted.'

Wilson chuckled. 'Does that make me Minihaha?' With her frank blue eyes and her blonde hair cut in a pageboy bob there was something engaging about Mary Wilson. But people who worked with her quickly found she was a much tougher proposition than she looked.

Which was as well, because she'd need to be. Liz remembered being at this stage of her career. It had seemed to go on for ever. The glass ceiling had seemed to be made of rock quartz. The sense of relief when she went as Detective Sergeant to DI Shapiro, and finally found herself treated as a fellow professional, was almost enough to make her cry.

Wilson said, 'They all seem to be men.'

Liz was still thinking about detectives. Then she realized the conversation had moved on. 'Oh—blackmailers, you mean? What, all of them?'

Wilson shook her head. 'Not blackmailers in general, but

those who try to extort money from big companies. According to the computer anyway.'

Liz considered. 'Still, don't jump to conclusions. It could as easily have been a woman.'

'Well, maybe not,' ventured Wilson; and Liz knew it took courage for a new DC to contradict her DI and respected her for it. 'Physically, yes—but what about mentally? Even now, most women have families and most women shop for them. You don't muddy a pool you want to drink from. I'm not sure anyone who buys food for her children could bring herself to contaminate food for some other mother to buy.'

Liz nodded slowly, digesting. 'Good point. Perhaps it would be rash to rule out mothers as suspects, but it might make sense to concentrate first on any single men who come up.'

A pleased blush warmed Wilson's cheeks. She'd been here a month and already she was being taken seriously by senior officers. Today the glass ceiling looked like cellophane.

TWO

BRIAN GRAHAM wasn't single but he had no children—or else he had five hundred of them. As head of the art department at Castle High he taught solemn eleven-year-olds how to mix poster paints and lectured on the Pre-Raphaelite Brotherhood to seventeen-year-olds who would soon be at art college and know more about the subject than he did. In between came 3b and their preoccupation with the wobbly bits in classical art.

'Sir, sir—sir! They haven't got no hair!'

'Sir—*why* haven't they got no hair, sir?'

'Sir, sir—didn't people have hair then?'

They were not, of course, referring to the intricate coiffures in the Old Master they were studying.

Graham glanced at his watch but found no help there: it was ten minutes to close of play. Besides, two decades in the class-room had taught him to face the enemy without blinking.

It was not the first time he'd been ambushed like this. Pupils always thought they'd come up with some new way to embarrass their teacher; but anyone who survived the first two years had seen, heard and dealt with it all. He gave a long-suffering sigh.

'Yes, Maureen, people had body hair then the same as they have now. It's a matter of artistic convention. Just as a modern artist might choose to be tactful about my hairline, your cold sore or Darren's teeth'—Darren grinned, pleased, showing off the overbite with which he impersonated Dracula so successfully and so often—'so the classical artists turned a blind eye to what they considered the less beautiful aspects of the human form. Today we find that rather coy, go for the warts-and-all approach.

It doesn't mean we're right and they were wrong, just that we have different priorities. People who study art in another three hundred years will find our ideas equally odd. They might see nothing worth painting in any of us.'

The bell rang for the end of the school day but Graham was not yet free to go home. He'd been manoeuvred into helping the sports department. The first XV were playing rugby on one pitch while the under-fourteens were playing hockey on another, stretching the supervisory resources of the PE staff to breaking point. Brian Graham knew nothing about rugby so he was allocated to Miss Simmons to help with the hockey match.

He was planted on the line and told what to watch for, but he didn't think he was doing it right or why did girls of both schools keep coming up to him mouthing obscenities? He was glad when the whistle went. It came as a terrible disappointment to find it was only half-time.

The second half seemed to go quicker, and Castle High lost by two goals—which seemed only fair to Brian, who considered it rude to defeat one's visitors. Victors and vanquished departed towards the showers.

Brian might have known nothing about sport but he knew a fair bit about schoolgirls. He knew that schoolgirls coming together in any numbers without adult supervision would eventually begin to scream. He thought nothing of the hullabaloo coming from the showers until the girls started coming out too, in various states of undress, shrieking and pointing and stamping their bare feet in hysterics. Even then he wondered if it was part of the normal celebrations of a win, until one of the girls, steelier-nerved than the others, managed to get out some recognizable words.

What they were was, 'It's blood, sir! Everywhere. Coming out of the showers. All over everyone. Everywhere!'

IT WASN'T, IN FACT, BLOOD. It was raspberry jelly. There were gallons of the stuff, too dilute to set, in a white drum beside the attic water tank, connected to the system by means of some hose, Jubilee clips and a plastic tap. When the showers were turned on the jelly was syphoned into the pipes.

'Well now,' said Liz thoughtfully, as the last of the crimson tide was swilled down the drains by the school caretaker, 'I hope no one's claiming this was a coincidence. That two people have independently lit on the idea of using jelly as an offensive weapon.'

Dick Morgan was halfway into the roofspace, perched on top of a ladder with the drum, now almost empty, in his arms. 'Not me, Guv. There's a note on this one too.'

When he got it down they studied it. The same square black letters, the same gummed paper. This time the message was: 'This could have been acid.'

And it could have been. It might have been harder to buy than several packets of raspberry jelly, although there are many legitimate uses for acid in industry and a minimum of research would enable anyone so inclined to acquire some. After that, apart from using a glass carboy and rubber hoses, the installation would have been the same.

'So he doesn't actually want to hurt anyone,' said Liz. 'At least, not yet.'

'But if he wants money,' frowned Morgan, 'why doesn't he say so? It's no use being shy if you're a blackmailer.'

'Maybe he wants us to think about it. Think about the consequences if it had been acid.'

'Us?—who?' asked Morgan. 'Exactly who is he planning to blackmail?'

It was a good question. Liz hadn't realized as quickly as her DC that targeting the school was a different proposition to targeting a multinational supermarket chain. She found that slightly worrying; but everyone knew that Dick Morgan was brighter than he let on. He lived in fear of being promoted and given more responsibility.

'OK,' said Liz, 'so it's not Sav-U-Mor specifically. Is it the town as a whole? You can't blackmail a school—who'd pay? But you could conceivably blackmail a town. Threaten its children, through the food they eat and the schools they attend, and maybe you'll scare people enough that they'll drum up the money somewhere: from the council; from local businesses; from a whip round in the streets. It might be quite a clever move.

If he was going for a particular store we could stake it out. But this makes him much harder to find. His only connection with Sav-U-Mor may be as an occasional customer; his only connection with the school may be that he found an opportunity to come here with his drum and his bits of hose. If he wore overalls and seemed to know what he was doing, nobody'd challenge him.'

Though somebody may have noticed, just thought that the arrangements were made by someone else. The caretaker was the best bet. His name was Duffy, and he was swabbing the pink stuff off his tiling as if he'd suffered a personal insult. Liz had not overlooked the fact that the school's janitor was ideally placed to interfere with the school plumbing; but his whole manner argued against.

'Mr Duffy.' She nodded, and he nodded back brusquely. They knew one another well enough not to need introductions: Duffy knew Liz was the art teacher's wife as well as a detective, she knew he was formerly a merchant seaman. He was in his mid-thirties, and though he probably had a first name no one at Castle High knew it. 'Someone's got a funny sense of humour.'

'He'll be laughing on the other side of his face if I catch up with him,' growled Duffy, swabbing furiously.

'Any idea when it was done?'

'It must have been today. This afternoon, even.'

'You were up there earlier?'

He nodded at the drum now sitting in the middle of the changing rooms while the Scenes of Crime Officer went over it with a fine-tooth comb. 'There's no kind of timing device. The stuff would be drawn up the first time the showers were used. They were used before lunch, and again at about three. He must have been up there after that.'

Liz was impressed. Now they had a time window: whoever did this was in the roof space between three and six p.m. 'Did you see anyone suspicious in that time?'

'There are twelve hundred bloody kids here,' he spat, 'every one of them a criminal in the making. That's just our kids. After four o'clock two buses rolled up containing another thirty thuglets from two other schools. And that's only the kids. You should have seen the teachers.'

Liz wondered what had induced him to work in a school if that was how he felt. Or perhaps he only felt that way as a result of working in a school. 'What about before the buses came? Did you see anyone round the changing rooms who could have done this? Have you had any workmen in the school?'

He spared her a frankly incredulous look. 'Mrs Graham, if I'd seen anyone I thought might have done this I'd have said so by now. No, I didn't see anyone carrying that drum into the shower block and leaving without it. Yes, there have been workmen in the school—there always are, this is a big complex. But I didn't see anything suspicious. If I'd seen someone somewhere he shouldn't have been, or doing something he shouldn't have been doing, I'd have stopped him.'

Liz nodded. 'Of course. I'm sorry, I have to ask—people forget all sorts of important details until they're prompted. These workmen: do you know what firm they're from and what they're doing?'

'Well, the overalls say Sidgwick & Mellors,' said the caretaker heavily, 'so that might be a clue. They're strengthening the floors in the chemistry block and refitting the library.'

Both were on the far side of the campus from the sports field. 'And you haven't seen any of them wandering round here?'

'No.'

He wasn't going to say any more because he hadn't seen any more. Liz believed him: if he'd seen anything suspicious he'd have done something about it. Not to protect the children but to preserve the sanctity of his little kingdom. Mary McKenna might be the principal of Castle High, but even she knew who was the boss. Liz left Duffy to his swabbing.

'Well, we know when,' she told Dick Morgan. 'If we can find a suspect that'll come in useful.'

Morgan sniffed apologetically. 'Actually, he didn't have to carry the thing up there this afternoon. He could have put it there days ago, linked up the hoses, left it ready to go. All he had to do today, and he didn't even have to do this in person, was turn the tap. Half the pupils of this school would have done that for him for a fiver.' Morgan had the same opinion of children as Duffy, perhaps because he had three of his own.

'Terrific,' growled Liz. He'd cast doubt on the only useful bit of information she'd garnered so far. She turned to the Scenes of Crime Officer. 'Can *you* give me anything to work on?'

It was too early for Sergeant Tripp to make even an interim report; all the same, the pained look was mostly from habit. 'There aren't going to be any fingerprints,' he said judiciously, nodding at the smears of aluminium powder. 'He used gloves. The hoses and clips you'd find in anybody's shed, the tap's probably off a rainwater butt. The drum held cooking oil, probably came from a caterer.'

'So he could work in a restaurant?'

'Or he could have salvaged it from their bin.'

Liz breathed heavily at him. What he was saying was No, I can't give you anything to work on. 'How about Forensics?'

'Ah now,' said Tripp respectfully, 'Forensics. They'll be able to tell you what brand of cooking oil, and what brand of jelly.'

As a piece of science it was undoubtedly impressive; as an aid to detection it was negligible.

'I'm going back to Queen's Street,' Liz told Morgan. 'Tidy up here, then you can call it a night.'

Brian, who was sitting on the wing of her car, looked up resignedly. 'You'll be burning the midnight oil, I suppose.'

Liz lifted one shoulder in an apologetic shrug. 'Don't wait up.'

CRIMINAL DETECTION is like most forms of creativity: ten per cent inspiration, ninety per cent perspiration. At nine twenty she and Shapiro were still pushing the thing across the desk between them like a very slow game of table tennis.

'None of the items he's used so far can be traced to an individual,' the superintendent observed. 'Anyone could have got hold of any of it. We can't get at him that way. So what about the targets he's chosen?'

Liz shrugged. 'High profile, good scare factor. Large numbers of people coming and going, even at the school. Though he'd be safer if he had a right to be there—a teacher, a parent, ancillary staff, even a pupil.'

Shapiro was doing mental arithmetic. 'Assuming you're right, that narrows it down to'—he sucked his teeth—'maybe fifteen hundred people.'

'You could rule out the smaller children,' said Liz helpfully. 'Lifting that drum into the roof space took a certain amount of strength.'

'Fine,' said Shapiro glumly. 'That gets us down to, oh, five or six hundred, and no guarantee he's one of them. Or maybe he's a she.'

'Not according to Mary Wilson.'

Shapiro elevated a gently ironic eyebrow. 'Who's been a detective—what?—four weeks?'

'Who's been browsing the PNC for similar episodes. All of them perpetrated by men.'

He accepted the rebuke. 'It's getting time we heard from him. He's shown us what he can do. He can think up a nasty, sneaky way of extorting money, and he can carry it out so slickly we've no idea who we're looking for. If it really had been acid in the drum we'd have twenty-odd schoolgirls in hospital—all of them hurt, many of them scarred, some with their sight or even their lives in danger—and we'd be no closer to catching him than we are now.

'So we know he's a serious threat to this town. No one's going to underestimate either what he can do or what he's prepared to do. And we know nothing about him: we could flood the town with patrols and never be more than a minor inconvenience to him. He's done enough. So what's he waiting for? It's been over three hours. Surely the time to hit us with his demands is while we're reeling with shock, inundated with hysterical half-naked schoolgirls.'

Liz gave a little rueful shrug. 'Maybe he's letting us stew first. He's got us rattled: maybe he reckons that twelve hours to think about it, about what could have happened and what could happen next, is a good investment. By then this town could be scared enough for the money to start looking unimportant. Assuming money's what it's about.'

'What else?'

'A sick joke? A power trip?'

Shapiro shook his head. 'One incident could have been, but two? That's twice he's risked being caught committing a serious offence. A joke he could have played by post or over the phone: that he took the risk of doing it in person suggests he has something to gain beyond mere satisfaction.

'What worries me, Liz, is that he's building up to something. Something unforgettable. What if next time it's for real?'

'Do you want me to get Donovan back?' Liz asked quietly.

Shapiro thought for a moment, then shook his head. 'If he isn't fit it wouldn't do us any good—he'd just be sitting on the sidelines glowering. Besides, another pair of hands wouldn't be much help right now. Let him have his holiday. If the situation deteriorates so much that we need him fit or otherwise, we can get him back here in a couple of hours. Leave it for now. Let him enjoy himself.

'I think we should wrap things up too. If there were going to be any more developments tonight they'd have happened by now. First thing in the morning set up a meeting with the Mayor and Chief Executive of the council, the chairman of the Chamber of Trade—and since they were directly affected, Ms McKenna from Castle High and the manager of Sav-U-Mor. We can bring them up to date, tell them what we'd like them to do and get some feeling for whether they're likely to do it. Get Mr Giles involved as well: if we're going to catch this man the best chance is Uniform spotting him acting suspiciously.'

But nothing that had happened so far suggested this was a man who went around acting suspiciously. So far the only proof of his existence was a wake of frightened people. And so far no one had been hurt. If that changed, fear would turn to panic and panic could cause more injuries even than acid.

'I'll be in by seven. Call if you need me sooner,' said Liz. She collected her coat and left by the back stairs. The rain which had eased briefly during the afternoon was once again hammering out of a pitch-black sky. There had been no sun all day, now there was no moon. No illumination of any kind: not in the sky, in her head, or at the end of the tunnel. In spite of what

Shapiro said she wished Donovan was here. A major crisis without the gloomy Irishman was like a pantomime without the dame.

WHATEVER SHAPIRO THOUGHT, Donovan was not enjoying himself. Barely ten miles into the Castlemere Levels, the familiar vista of flat land and endless sky lost in the murk of scurrying rainstorms, with the surreal feeling of being suspended in water like a deep-sea diver, he'd decided to take a break from his holiday. He'd turned up a quiet backwater, moored *Tara* to the bank and gone to bed with his cough bottle and a hot whiskey. When the need arose Donovan could rough it with the best; but one of the advantages of living on a boat was that you didn't have to abandon home comforts to have a change of scene. Tomorrow, when the rain stopped and the Philbert's Remedy had knocked his cold on the head, would be soon enough to start having a good time.

THREE

THE OFFICIAL ORGAN of Castlemere society was the *Castlemere Courier,* but it came out on Thursdays. Until then, information about Monday's events would have to rely on hearsay and jungle telegraph to get about. In a small town it's a pretty reliable system: everyone at the meeting in the Town Hall on Tuesday morning knew what they were there to discuss.

Superintendent Giles got the ball rolling. 'Gentlemen, Ms Mc-Kenna, I don't think I need tell you why we've asked for this meeting. Some of you were directly involved, and I imagine the rest have heard a fairly comprehensive story by now.

'Just in case anyone got the embroidered version, I will recap on the facts. Someone adulterated a pot of supermarket yoghurt and the shower system at Castle High's sports fields with coloured jelly and left notes indicating that he could as easily have used more dangerous contaminants. I want you all to be clear, nobody was hurt. But the obvious inference is that it could come to that.

'We're not yet sure what he wants. We're assuming it's money but he hasn't said. Apart from the notes he left with the jelly, he hasn't made contact. He will. One of the purposes of this meeting is so that we can discuss the possible responses before we're under pressure for an instant decision.'

There were hawks at the table, and there were doves. The Chief Executive of the Borough Council, who didn't need re-electing, was a hawk; the Mayor was a dove. Mary McKenna was a hawk: she'd had thirty years' practice at dealing with thugs and terrorists, even if most of them were children.

Donald Chivers, chairman of the Castlemere Chamber of

Trade, was a hawk. He knew that any ransom would come directly from his members' tills or indirectly from his members' rates. The Mayor might talk as if he had funds of his own but they were creamed off other people's incomes. If Castlemere decided to pay blackmail the traders would pick up the lion's share of the bill.

Tony Woodall, under-manager at Sav-U-Mor, was a dove. He knew that cheap milk and the massive savings on own-brand products were entirely beside the point if he couldn't keep his shelves stocked with consumer confidence.

'No offence, Mr Woodall,' said Shapiro mildly, 'but I'd have thought your manager—Mr Surtees, is it?—would have been here.'

Woodall sucked in a breath. He was a man in his mid-thirties, stocky and athletic under the suit. 'Mr Surtees had a fit of the vapours after the thing with the yoghurt and is off sick. I'm afraid I'm the best you're going to get.'

Shapiro wasn't complaining. There was enough hysteria around the town without importing it into this meeting. The phones at Queen's Street had been blocked for two hours last night by the parents, grandparents, uncles and some quite casual acquaintances of the children who'd gone home damp and tearful and not entirely sure what had happened to them. Some thought it really had been acid in the drum in the attic. Some of them had been hurried down to Accident & Emergency at Castle General, even though there wasn't a mark on them, in case they'd suffered some subtle form of burning that would only become apparent later.

'And the other purpose of this meeting,' continued Superintendent Giles, 'is to ask for your co-operation in controlling this situation and bringing it to a safe conclusion. There are things we can do to protect our fellow citizens, and you people can organize a lot of them. When you leave here, I'd like you to call meetings of your own staff, update them, and tell them what to be on the lookout for.'

'Like what?' demanded Chivers. 'Speaking for my members, I think most of us would notice if somebody was going round tampering with the stock in plain sight. But we haven't got eyes in the backs of our heads. Don't think you can shift responsibility for stopping this man on to the traders. It's a crime: preventing it is a police matter. Don't think you can make us your scapegoats.'

Shapiro thought the meeting was already getting out of hand. 'Nobody's looking for scapegoats, Mr Chivers. We want to stop this man, and then we'd like to find him. But he isn't going to be pursuing his campaign at Queen's Street, he's going to be in your shops, in the council's facilities, in public places. Like it or not, you people and your employees are more likely to encounter him than we are. We just want you to consider how you can minimize the damage he can do.'

'I've done that,' said the Mayor. 'We can pay up.'

'It may not be money he wants.'

Chivers elevated a heavy eyebrow. 'What else?'

'It might be political. We might be pawns in a bigger game: animal rights, overseas aid, political prisoners, Free the Tamworth Two. Is anyone aware of anything controversial looming in this town? A new road planned over the last redoubt of the Lesser Spotted Godwit? We haven't many trees to cut down, but how about orchids?—does someone want to build executive homes on top of some? Is a local business supplying aid and succour to one of the world's less admirable governments? Or nothing of the sort, just something that could provoke strong feelings in someone who might react this way.'

Put like that it sounded so vague he couldn't imagine getting a useful response. And from the long silence it seemed he hadn't managed to ring a single bell even very faintly. But as he went to move on, Mary McKenna said pensively, 'There's BioMed.'

Shapiro should have thought of them himself. It was years now since there'd been any trouble at the laboratory, but it was still there in the quiet countryside of The Levels, still doing commercial research with a Home Office licence for animal experiments.

It was burned down by animal rights activists in the mideighties. It was called BioMedical Technology then and did a lot of work for industry. After rebuilding the name was subtly altered and so was the thrust of the work. It may not have concerned itself exclusively with the development of medicines, but a good PR man made sure that was the bit that people knew about.

'Have you heard something?' asked Shapiro.

McKenna shook her dark red hair. 'But it's a hardy perennial on the kids' hate-list. There isn't as much enthusiasm for stringing up the director as there was ten years ago but only because today's bright, go-ahead teenager is more concerned with his grades than the morality of big business. I wouldn't be amazed to see it hit again.'

'Because of the animals?'

'The animals; the rainforest; business here supporting corrupt regimes abroad. Don't look at me like that, Superintendent, I'm not saying it is so—I'm saying that among idealistic students it is perceived as being so. And let's be honest,' she went on, warming to the subject in the face of the dismissive expressions around her, 'there's more than a grain of truth in it. We British are an ethical people until our principles start costing us money.'

They were veering off the point; but it was useful background to Shapiro because what mattered on this occasion was not whether BioMed had skeletons in its cupboard but whether someone in an indignant frame of mind could think they had.

Superintendent Giles intervened. He was a tall fair man, an officer of Liz Graham's generation, and he had the unnerving knack of going straight to the heart of a matter. 'An eco-warrior,' he said crisply, 'wouldn't have contaminated the yoghurt. He'd have gone for the veal.'

Liz was nodding. 'So maybe it really is just about money. We haven't heard from him because he doesn't think we're ready to pay yet.'

'Speak for yourself,' muttered His Worship the Mayor.

'Let's try and keep things in proportion,' said Shapiro. 'So far no one's been hurt. That wasn't luck, it's how he planned it. He didn't want to hurt anyone. But if he asks for money and doesn't get it, that will change. A threat is only credible until it's called and nothing happens.'

Derek Dunstan had only been mayor for six months. He'd thought it would be about opening fetes, kissing bathing beauties and unveiling portraits of himself, and six months into the job they sprang this on him. All he could think of was the avalanche of complaints he was going to get if it all went wrong. 'Surely we can agree,' he said pompously, 'that nothing is as important as safeguarding the citizens of this borough.'

'We can agree on that,' nodded Superintendent Giles. 'The question is how we can do that most effectively. Will they be safer if we pay off this thug and let all the others know where to find us? If we hold out now, someone could get hurt. If we don't, we could have a succession of similar incidents; and as Mr Shapiro says, it's the nature of these things to become more violent. The people of Castlemere will be safer if we can deal with this once and for all.'

'That's easy to say now,' said Woodall worriedly. 'But can we hold the line if people start going down with botulism and seeing their skin peel off?'

'Botulism?' echoed Ms McKenna.

Woodall nodded. 'That was the secret ingredient in our yoghurt special. At least, it wasn't, but that was the threat.'

Shapiro was looking at the teacher, his grey eyes keen. 'Why?'

'Because commercial applications are being developed for the botulinum toxin. I'm a chemist,' she explained to those of the gathering who were not old acquaintances, 'I was reading something in the trade press. BioMed is involved.'

It was probably a coincidence. There was no botulism in the yoghurt: anyone could have picked a toxin out of the dictionary, he didn't need access to it. Still, it was reason enough for someone to visit BioMed.

'Secrecy isn't an issue,' said Shapiro. 'The incident at the school was so public there can't be anyone left in town who hasn't heard about it. But I'd like to discourage speculation. It would help if we could agree on our response to enquiries, and to refer anyone who wants more detail to my office.'

There was a momentary pause but they were all happy with that. In a difficult situation it's always nice to have someone to pass the buck to.

'So finally,' he said, 'we need to decide how to respond to this threat. Pay or hold out. There are risks both ways. Mr Giles explained the police position: that terrorism has to be fought even if there are casualties. But we can't stop you paying a ransom if you think it's the right thing to do. Whatever you decide, we'll keep trying to catch this man. But I can't guarantee we'll catch him before he does some harm.'

There was some muttering around the table, an exchange of glances. Donald Chivers was the first to speak up. 'Can we have a show of hands?—I think it would be more appropriate in the circumstances than a secret ballot.' He stuck his own broad hand up in favour of fighting.

So did Mary McKenna; so did Dick Travis, the council CE; and so, after a moment's vacillation, did the Mayor.

Tony Woodall shook his head. 'I don't think it's the right decision. I don't think you have any idea what this man can do to us or how we'll cope with the panic he'll cause. But I'm not going to persuade you, am I?—and it's important that the vote's unanimous.' He raised his own hand and made it so.

'Thank you,' said Shapiro, meaning it. 'We'll do all we can to make sure this doesn't backfire on you.' The meeting broke up. Nobody stayed for tea and biscuits.

LIZ DROVE OUT by the River Road to BioMed's laboratories. Ostensibly the reason for her visit was to establish how difficult it would be for someone with malicious intent to obtain and handle samples of the toxin. It would be interesting to have the information, though events might prove it irrelevant. Unofficially it was an opportunity to size up the people working with the material. The threat could have come from anyone; but if his demands were resisted he had to be able to back them up with action. Which made someone with a background in pharmaceuticals a more credible suspect than someone with a library ticket and access to the *Encyclopaedia Britannica.*

The facility was tucked so discreetly into the landscape you could pass it and never notice. Even if you spotted the corporate logo, down at knee-height beside the gravel drive, the same PR man who'd abbreviated the name had redesigned the badge with stalks of corn shooting out of it. Only when you turned down the drive and ran into enough security to defend the Pentagon did you begin to suspect that raising a better barley was not the prime function of the place.

Liz ploughed patiently through the layers of security, answering some of her questions as she went. Nobody wandered in here under the guise of delivering a parcel. The systems were tight, efficient and practised—even producing her warrant card didn't earn her a free pass. These people were serious about security, and whether they were more concerned with terrorists or industrial spies they'd done enough to deter both. Security can never be total: someone with enough incentive can always find a way in. But Liz had seen enough to know that illegal entry here would involve arms or explosives and have sirens wailing all over the site.

The alternative was infiltration. A firm with this kind of security would certainly check out new employees. On the other hand, someone who was prepared to blackmail an entire town would have no scruples about pressurizing an individual scientist or technician. If the blackmailer had to be ready to prove his seriousness, and if botulism was his weapon of choice, and if BioMed was the only place he could get it, then coercing a member of staff seemed the likeliest way.

It was an awful lot of ifs.

Dr Black was not, at first sight, promising coercion material. Intimidating BioMed's director would challenge a bull buffalo primed for the rut. He was very short and very broad, and appeared to have been carved by the same sculptor as the Rock of Gibraltar. He had dark, crinkly hair and black marbles for eyes, and he walked with the slight swagger of one who knows exactly how valuable his time is. But he greeted Liz affably and took her to his office.

'If you hadn't called I was going to call you. I wanted to assure you that if this man really has got hold of botulinum, he didn't get it from us.'

'You can be sure of that?'

'Absolutely,' said Dr Black, nodding vigorously. 'Our systems would show any shortfall. They could not be suborned by any one member of staff.' He smiled, showing massive white teeth. 'Even me.'

'That's reassuring,' said Liz. 'So really you're saying it isn't a credible threat.'

Dr Black rocked a stubby hand. 'I don't think he has or can get botulinum toxin from us. I couldn't rule out him acquiring some elsewhere.'

'Such as?'

'A hospital path lab. Botulism is fortunately not common in Britain, but there has been an increase in many forms of food poisoning—ask Castle General if they've had a botulism case recently. If they have, that's two places you could get it—the hospital, and wherever the patient picked it up.'

'How transmissible is it? I mean, is it catching?'

He shook his head. 'The vector material would have to be ingested. You could get it from a contaminated yoghurt, you couldn't get it from standing beside someone who ate a contaminated yoghurt.'

'But if you did get it, it would be bad news?'

'Oh yes,' agreed Black fervently. 'The toxin attacks the nervous system. Botulism kills by paralysis.'

Liz frowned. 'Then what on earth are the commercial applications? I thought we'd gone out of the biological warfare business.'

The director chuckled. 'Even Porton Down is cleaning up its image these days. Actually, I believe they're working with cosmetic botulinum too.'

'*Cosmetic?*' Liz heard her voice rocket.

Black was enjoying himself. 'Face cream. The toxin is scaled down and ring-fenced until its effect is merely to suppress the layer of cells implicated in causing wrinkles. And tics, in fact.'

Liz was staggered. Never a massive consumer of cosmetics, from now on she would be downright abstemious. 'Can I see where you're doing this work?'

'Of course.' He conducted her through a maze of corridors, pausing to use his swipe card at regular intervals.

In fact, seeing the laboratory told her nothing more. It was people in white coats working mostly with computers. Dr Black pointed out a locked refrigerator marked 'Caution: Bio Hazard' but that was about as scary as it got.

'Most of the preliminary work is done with computer models,' admitted Black. 'Which makes it even harder for someone to steal actual biological material.'

Liz didn't know enough about biology or chemistry to learn anything by looking for longer. She signalled her readiness to leave, began thanking Dr Black for his help.

One of the white coats came over, a young man with a ginger moustache and a petulant expression. 'Dr Black, if Miranda is absent again tomorrow we're going to need another technician. I'm being held up.'

'All right, Dr Soames,' said the director, the faintest edge on his voice. 'I'll find you someone.'

Mostly to make conversation as they walked back Liz said, 'Staff problems?'

Black shook his head. 'Dr Soames enjoys a little drama. Ms Hopkins' absence from work for one or two days can have no long-term effect on his research. When a valued member of staff doesn't feel free to take a couple of days off to cope with a family crisis, that's when you start losing your valued members of staff.'

'Crisis?' Certain words, that cue discretion in the rest of us, make police officers prick up their ears.

'Only a little one. Her daughter was playing hockey at Castle High yesterday afternoon. I don't think she was hurt but she was upset. Miranda wanted to stay home with her till she was over the shock.'

'ANOTHER COINCIDENCE?' Liz's tone was so ambivalent Shapiro wasn't sure if he heard a question mark or not, if she was telling him or asking his opinion.

He hedged his bets. 'Hard to know. I mean, if there was botulism in the yoghurt it would have been very interesting—a woman with two distinct connections to this, with access to the contaminant through her work and to the school changing rooms through her daughter. But it was jelly in the yoghurt. I dare say she had access to that too, but it's hardly grounds to arrest someone.'

'Should I pay her a visit? I could say I was checking that all the girls were OK. It'd give me a chance to weigh her up, see if she's suspect material. Though from what Dr Black said I doubt it. He called her a valued member of staff.'

'Perhaps she never mentioned her plans for germ warfare over the coffee and croissants.'

FOUR

MIRANDA HOPKINS answered the door at the second knock. In her mid-thirties she was a few years Liz's junior, a faintly exotic-looking woman with her long, slightly metallic fair hair crimped and held back by a bandeau. She wore a dark ankle-length skirt and, despite the weather, no shoes. 'Yes?'

Liz introduced herself and asked after Saffron—she'd got the name from the school before coming. Ms Hopkins stood back from the door to invite her in. 'We're playing Scrabble.'

A less exotic-looking child than Saffron Hopkins would be difficult to imagine. She had her mother's fair hair but it hung very straight, shone with health and was chopped off at shoulder level. Broad bones gave her a square face, a love of sport gave her scrubbed ruddy cheeks, and for a moment Liz thought she was looking at herself at the same age.

She'd been a plain child, but she hadn't spent enough time looking in mirrors to worry about it. As long as her pony attracted its share of admiration she was happy. It came as a genuine surprise when, in her late teens, she started attracting admiration as well. She still did. No one but immediate family had ever called her beautiful, but she was both handsome and striking: tall, strong and fit.

She introduced herself again, to the girl. 'I just stuck my head in to see how you were feeling.'

Saffron shrugged. 'I'm all right. But Mum said I could stay home if I wanted, so I did.'

Liz nodded. 'Good choice. What do you get on Tuesdays—geography?'

'Double maths.'

'Eeugh!' They traded a companionable grin.

Liz turned to Miranda. 'It must have given you a hell of a start when you heard what happened.'

'Heard about it? I was there. I was more hysterical than Saffron was. It seemed forever before we could be sure that, actually, no one was hurt. Until then we all thought something terrible had happened. The place was a mad house, with parents trying to find their children and children trying to find their clothes.'

'Did all the girls have parents there?'

'Not all. There were probably five or six of us cheering from the sidelines. Or not, in fact, because it was a pretty pathetic performance.' This time she and Saffron swapped a grin.

'If the game wasn't worth watching, maybe you had time to look around a bit. Did either of you see anything odd? Anyone acting strangely; anyone round the changing rooms who didn't seem to belong there?'

They thought for a moment but remembered nothing out of the ordinary. 'Of course, there was a lot going on,' said Miranda, 'with the rugby match as well. There were a lot of people, adults and children, who didn't look familiar and were wandering round as if they weren't quite sure where they were going.'

'The jelly was in a white plastic drum about so big.' Liz demonstrated with her hands. 'Did you see that at any point?' But they hadn't.

'I was over at BioMed earlier today,' Liz volunteered. She thought it best, since someone was bound to mention it when Miranda returned to work. 'The previous threat mentioned botulism, and I heard the laboratory was working with it.'

Miranda Hopkins nodded. 'I work with it myself.' She frowned, concerned. 'Does that make me a suspect?'

'Not for the moment,' smiled Liz. 'Right now we're concentrating on people with access to raspberry jelly.'

THE REST OF THE DAY passed without incident. Close of play found Liz and Shapiro sharing a last pot of coffee in his office. Like most police stations, Queen's Street ran on coffee and angst.

'What do you make of it?' asked Shapiro. 'Has he had enough? Made his point and called it a day?'

It was a nice thought but Liz wasn't convinced. 'Made what point? If he was a disgruntled ex-employee taking a swipe at the supermarket, what was the business at the school about? And if it was about showing he can strike at this town anywhere and any time, why call it a day before he's got a penny out of us? He can't be scared we're on to him—he hasn't given us enough to work with. So why go to the trouble of setting it up and then lose interest? I'm sorry, Frank, but no. He hasn't gone away. He has something else in mind.'

Shapiro thought so too. 'So what's he been up to this last twenty-six hours that's more important than making his next move?'

'Maybe he's caught a cold,' said Liz, not altogether seriously. 'There's a stinker going round: Donovan had it.'

Shapiro wasn't concerned with his sergeant's well-being so much as the mindset of the man they were dealing with. 'He could have caught a cold,' he conceded; 'or he could have been knocked down by a bus; or he might have had to attend his aunty's funeral. But the likeliest explanation is that he's working on something that requires a bit of time. Something more dramatic than terrifying twenty-two schoolgirls. He's planning something nasty, I'm sure of it. One good sock in the teeth, then he'll hit us with his demands.'

'And we'll tell him to get lost,' said Liz. 'Then what's he going to do?'

'I don't know, but I bet he does. Maybe that's why he needs a day off: to set up the next two attacks. The one he doesn't expect will scare us into compliance, and the one he does.'

'We're still talking about he,' Liz noticed. 'You agree with me, then—Miranda Hopkins isn't much of a contender?'

'I doubt it. Though I may change my mind if suddenly the town's full of botulism. No, I think it probably is just a coincidence.' He gave a little self-deprecating grunt. 'That has the ring of somebody's famous last words.'

'Whose?'

He thought for a moment. 'Quite possibly mine.'

Liz chuckled. 'Go home, Frank. Give Angela a treat.'

Shapiro's eyebrows rocketed. 'I know my back's a lot better, but the rest of me's still fifty-six!'

'That's not what I meant!' giggled Liz. 'Though far be it from me to discourage you... I *meant*, if you'd got home by eight o'clock more often she'd probably never have divorced you.' The visit Mrs Shapiro made after her ex was shot had stretched to a longer visit while she saw him settled back in his cottage and by now was acquiring an air of permanency.

Shapiro bent a quizzical eye on her. 'And what about Brian? Is he supposed not to mind that you work most of the hours God sends?'

Liz blinked. She honestly hadn't seen that she was subjecting her own marriage to the same abuse that had ended Shapiro's. 'That's different. Brian's—'

'Brian's a patient man,' said Shapiro, 'but he didn't get married for the privilege of snatching breakfast together. It's a job, Liz. Remember that. Whatever your ambitions, however hard you're prepared to work for them, remember it's still just a job.'

What he said was true. But—as he also knew—it wasn't a job you could throw half of yourself into. Either you did the best you could, taking the consequences of that on your home life, or you marked time—kept an eye on the clock, kept your spouse happy and kept your children under the same roof. There were people who managed the juggling act of throwing themselves with equal vigour into both family and work, but not many; and fewest of all halfway up the promotion ladder. Of course, Liz had no children to worry about. Less stress on the marriage; and also less glue in it.

'I know I neglect him,' she admitted. 'I think he's resigned to it. He knows I love him.'

'Contrary to the words of the popular song,' intoned Shapiro, proving—if anyone had wondered—how out-of-touch with popular music he actually was, 'love is not all you need.'

She would have brooked such criticism from almost no one else. But she'd known Shapiro a long time, owed him a lot, both personally and professionally. She knew he had her interests at heart. They enjoyed a relationship that was more than purely

professional, and the bit that was extra was not so much friend-
ship as family.

It came of doing hard time together, of seeing each other at
their best and their worst; of having to depend on one another,
occasionally for their very lives. People whose idea of a work
crisis is a downturn in the sales figures, a new-broom boss or a
tax on office car-parking cannot be expected to understand how
frustration, exhaustion and occasional deep terror combine to
forge relationships that can shatter like glass or endure like iron
but nothing in between.

'It may have to be,' she said quietly.

Shapiro nodded slowly. He hadn't meant to criticize, just
wanted to be sure she recognized the problem as he had not.
Almost the first he knew that he had been a failure as a husband
and father was Angela coming downstairs with a suitcase. 'Have
you thought any more about going for your promotion?'

'Yes. I want it. I've earned it, and I want it.' When they'd
first discussed this she had sounded uncertain; now she was sure.
'Not right now, but soon. Somewhere in the next four years.'

'It would be the ideal solution,' agreed Shapiro. 'They won't
let me go on doing this for ever, and there's nobody I'd sooner
see in this office after I've gone. But it won't be my decision.'

'I know. All the same, it's pretty obviously a good idea. Unless the powers-that-be decide I'm not up to it.'

He shook his head firmly. 'That's not what I've heard.
They're under pressure to promote good women officers: it
would solve a lot of problems to move you in here.' For a
moment he said nothing more, considering. 'I know you won't
ask, so here's my position. I can retire any time in the next four
years. I'll stay on as long as it's helpful to you, and leave as
soon as you need me to. Don't think of it as a favour. I want
to leave the place in safe hands. If I can do that by careful
timing, I'll be happy whenever it comes.'

Her hand reached across the desk and folded over his. 'You're
the most generous man I've ever known.'

He smiled and squeezed her fingers before releasing them. 'It
isn't generosity. If you like, it's the last really useful thing I'll
be able to do for this town. I'd like to get it right.'

Liz said, 'I'll try to justify your confidence, Frank. Assuming it works out the way we hope.'

'It will,' promised Shapiro. 'Or I'll damn well stay where I am, and visit crime scenes in my bath chair.'

NOTHING HAPPENED overnight. But at ten fifteen on Wednesday Sergeant Bolsover phoned from the front desk in a state of panic. He had a young woman and a baby in reception, both of them were screaming, he gathered one of them was hurt and it was something to do with a bottle of baby lotion, and that was the most sense he'd been able to extract from the situation.

Liz went down to sort it out.

The mother was not much more than a child herself. She might have been seventeen, she could have been less. She was angry and tearful, and at first Liz too had trouble making out what had brought her to Queen's Street. 'Try to calm down and tell me what's happened. First, are you all right? And is the baby?'

'No thanks to that!' She picked up the plastic bottle she'd placed on the desk in order to slam it down again, emphatically. Then she whined in pain and held out her hands like a boxer waiting to be gloved. 'Look at them!'

The palms were bright pink. Scalded? 'What did that?'

'Caustic soda.'

Liz frowned. 'What happened?'

The girl picked up the bottle once again, this time upended it. An address label was attached to the bottom. In large, regular black letters it said, 'This *was* caustic soda.'

Liz deferred any further questioning while she sent for the police surgeon. 'Have you done anything about it yourself?'

'I washed them in lots of cold water,' said the girl, a tremor in her voice. Now she was being treated seriously the anger was giving way to shock. 'I couldn't think what else.'

'How does it feel now?'

'Going off a bit. Hurt like hell half an hour ago.'

Dr Greaves was there within five minutes, swabbed her hands with some solution to take the heat out of them, injected an antibiotic to guard against infection. 'I think that's all we need do,' he said. 'Go to your GP tomorrow, tell him what happened, but I think you'll be on the mend by then. The burns haven't gone very deep. Cold water was the right idea. It's the best thing for all burns. Cold running water and plenty of it.'

Her name was Sheila Crosbie, and she couldn't believe she was getting a First Aid lecture right now. 'Yeah, right, I'll remember that next time some freak tries to burn me!'

Dr Greaves beat a tactful retreat. 'Let me know if there's anything more I can do.' Liz nodded.

'Where did you buy the lotion?' she asked.

'Simpson's, in Brick Lane.' She lived in a block of council flats opposite The Jubilee; Simpson's would be the nearest chemist.

'When?'

'Yesterday. About five thirty, on my way home. You get through a lot of stuff with a four-month-old baby.'

'But in fact you didn't use it on the baby.'

It was the mildest of observations but it was enough to set Sheila Crosbie off again. 'You get through a lot of other things with a baby, too,' she snapped, 'and one of them's washing. My hands were dry, all right? I put some on my hands and a minute later I was climbing the walls. If I'd put it on the baby first he'd be in hospital!'

'Doesn't bear thinking about,' agreed Liz. 'I don't suppose you feel very lucky right now, but it could have been so much worse.'

'What kind of freak does something like that?' demanded Sheila. 'Puts caustic soda in something you slap on babies?'

'The same one who threatened to poison a yoghurt eater and burn twenty schoolgirls with acid. The notes are identical. When did you notice yours?'

'After I washed my hands enough so the sting was easing off, I was going to take it back to Simpson's, along with a piece of my mind. When I picked it up again I saw there was something on the bottom. So I came here instead.'

Liz had manoeuvred the bottle into a plastic bag. Even as she did it she knew she was wasting her time. It would have Sheila Crosbie's fingerprints all over it, and Kenneth Simpson's, and those of anyone who may have considered buying it in the last couple of days. The only one being careful to keep his prints off it, in fact, was the blackmailer. But she had to go through the motions.

Forensics would also be able to say how much caustic soda was in the bottle and how it got there. Probably the same way the jelly got into the yoghurt: it was a plastic bottle, stronger than a yoghurt pot but still capable of being pierced with a sharp needle. When they removed the label they'd probably find the hole.

'What's the baby's name?' she asked absently as she sealed the bag.

'Jason,' said Sheila Crosbie, defiantly.

Liz couldn't think of anything else she could usefully ask. She doubted Mr Simpson would be able to tell her much either: when the baby lotion arrived in the shop, perhaps, which would give the earliest date it could have been tampered with, but nothing more. It was a standard mass-purchase line, even a small local chemist would sell them by the gross. He wouldn't remember whom he sold them to.

Shapiro, when she brought him up to date, went back to something Dick Morgan had said. 'He thought it might be easier to do in two visits. Buy the stuff, take it home and tamper with it, then come back later and slip it back on to the shelf while buying something else. Ask Simpson if he remembers anyone coming in twice since the jar went on the shelf.'

But he didn't; or rather, there were too many people who came in on a daily basis for someone to arouse suspicion by returning too quickly. People forgot things, bought the wrong things, simply had nothing better to do than wander round any shop they passed. Kenneth Simpson remembered Sheila Crosbie buying her baby lotion; could name half a dozen other local mothers who'd bought the stuff in the last few days; couldn't remember anything remotely suspicious about any of them. Partly because he'd never thought of it as a problem line. He watched those who turned up for their daily methadone prescription like a hawk. He didn't pay the same sort of attention to purchasers of basic nursery products.

'Are all your customers locals?' asked Liz.

'Most of them are. We get the whole of the Jubilee trade,' he said, his tone acknowledging this as a mixed blessing. 'But we're close enough to the town centre to get those who're having trouble parking. I guess three quarters of our customers are from this end of town.'

It was a stab in the dark, and she knew as she asked the question that the answer could mean very little in the circumstances he described. It was like treating all Sav-U-Mor's customers as suspects when she knew perfectly well that Brian did his share of the shopping there every week. But she had nothing else to ask. 'Is Miranda Hopkins a customer of yours? A woman in her mid-thirties, long fair hair, teenage daughter—she lives in Rosedale Avenue.'

'Oh yes,' Kenneth Simpson nodded readily, 'I know who you mean. Nice woman. Has a bit of trouble with her hands—the chemicals, I suppose, she works at BioMed. I get her a special dermatological handcream.'

'Do you,' said Liz thoughtfully, nodding in concert. 'Do you really?'

'*STILL* A COINCIDENCE?' she asked Shapiro.

He chewed on the inside of his lip. 'Damned if I know. Quite possibly yes. But it is odd, the way she keeps being there or thereabouts.'

'Yes, but so does Brian.' When his eyebrows rocketed Liz explained. 'No, I'm not considering him a suspect, I'm using him as a control. He uses Sav-U-Mor and he was at the school when the incident there occurred; I bet he goes into Simpson's from time to time. That's all we have on Miranda Hopkins: that she was at the school, with a perfectly good reason, and that she uses a local shop.'

'Brian doesn't have access to botulism.'

'We don't know the blackmailer does either.' Liz thought for a moment. 'Still, maybe I should bring him in for questioning.'

Shapiro chuckled. 'That's going to be the problem—that almost anyone who attracts our attention for any reason is going to have had perfectly legitimate reasons for being in all the places involved. They're all more-or-less public areas, and this is a small town: you're always bumping into the same people. It means nothing.'

'Miranda Hopkins is a chemist—she'd have access to caustic soda.'

'I'm a Detective Superintendent and I have caustic soda under my sink! I'm sorry, Liz, you're clutching at straws.'

'Thor Heyerdahl crossed the Atlantic on a boat made of enough straws,' she commented perceptively. 'While straws is all we have, I think I'll keep an eye on people who seem to have more than most.'

'Miranda Hopkins.'

'And Brian,' she said with a ghost of a smile.

FIVE

ALTHOUGH THE DAMAGE was in fact minor, the escalation from threats to an actual physical attack had a marked effect on Castlemere. Half the town knew what had happened to Sheila Crosbie, what had almost happened to baby Jason, within an hour of their visit to Queen's Street. Within two hours women were leaving work to go home and check the contents of their cupboards before the children got out of school.

In situations like this, only one thing may be counted on absolutely: that those who respond to the crisis will overreact in inverse proportion to the amount of good their contribution will do. Thus, while the traders who might have been able to limit the blackmailer's activities were still debating whether an attempt to do so would be tantamount to accepting liability, every bar, every turf accountant's and every street corner soon had an ad hoc committee of those who knew how to handle the situation better than the police. By common consent, vigilante patrols were the way to go.

The other task to which they applied themselves was allocating blame—not to the blackmailer himself, a pointless exercise since his identity was unknown, but to easier targets. At noon someone hurled a brick from a speeding car through the window of the Sav-U-Mor supermarket, with a note attached saying, 'Pay up, you mean bastards.'

As soon as he'd cleared up and called the glazier, Tony Woodall was round thumping on Shapiro's desk. Shapiro let him thump. It was mostly reaction, adrenalin provoked by the incident now swilling round in his system with nothing to do but make him twitchy. Shapiro's desk had taken the brunt of Donovan's temper before now, it wasn't going to collapse under the ire of a supermarket under-manager.

'Do you know something you're not telling us?' demanded Woodall. 'Has he made contact? Has he asked for money and been told to get lost?'

'No, no and no,' said Shapiro with measured calm. 'Mr Woodall, sit down before you impale yourself on my Pending spike. There was another incident this morning. A girl burnt her hands with caustic soda in a bottle of baby lotion. But she's not badly hurt, and there was in fact a warning on the bottom of the bottle. It's worrying, but it's not Armageddon.

'And no, he still hasn't made contact. I still expect him to at some point—if it isn't an attempt to extort money I don't know what it is.'

'Then...?' Woodall waved the note attached to his brick in wordless fury.

Shapiro spread his hands. 'Mr Woodall, they're making the same mistake you did—assuming somebody must know what's going on, assuming there must have been a demand for money by now and a decision has been taken to hold out against it. Which it has, though so far there's nothing to hold out against.'

'So what are you going to do about this? Anything? Or do I just collect the things until I've got enough to build a privy?'

Shapiro tried not to smile. 'If anyone saw who did it, I'll go round and charge him with malicious damage; if not I'll endorse your insurance claim. I'm sorry but a broken window is the least of our problems right now. Obviously people are anxious; regrettably, some anxious people lash out at the nearest target. It won't just be the glaziers who are busy today, it'll be Women's Aid, the NSPCC and the RSPCA.'

Relenting, because Woodall hadn't asked to be stuck in the middle of this, he added, 'It might be a good idea if we gave a press conference. Set the record straight as to exactly what's happened and what hasn't. That should take the pressure off you. I don't know why you've been singled out as the villain.'

Woodall sighed. 'Because Sav-U-Mor is the only organization involved which is big enough to pay off a blackmailer. We're a multi-national, that makes us a bunch of callous rich bastards to start with. If the attacks continue it must be because we were asked for money and wouldn't stump up.'

'If it's any comfort, it won't go on being your fault for long,' said Shapiro wryly. 'It's only a mater of time before it's mine.'

Woodall was about to leave. Then Shapiro saw him waver, and think about something else he might say but wasn't sure he should.

'What is it?'

The under-manager turned back. 'You'll know soon enough but you might like to know now. My head office are taking this pretty seriously. They're sending their troubleshooter. Apparently he's had some experience with corporate blackmail in the States.'

Shapiro breathed lightly for a moment, avoided saying anything he might later regret. None of this was Woodall's fault. He wasn't even the manager, his influence in Seattle must be minimal. 'I see,' he said, levelly. 'They do understand that, even if their troubleshooter finds the culprit before we do, they won't be allowed to hang him from the flagpole?'

'Mr Shapiro, I've never met Mitchell Tyler. I have no way of knowing if the rumours about him are true, half-truths or urban myth. But if only half of them are true, he'll turn this town upside down looking for someone who dared to threaten the great god Sav-U-Mor. Anything you can do to settle this matter before Mitchell Tyler arrives in Castlemere, you want to do it.'

Shapiro blinked. 'When's he due?'

'The weekend. He'd have been here sooner but he's up in front of a Grand Jury.'

He didn't want to know, but he needed to. 'Fiddling his tax returns?'

'Homicide. Manslaughter.'

SUPERINTENDENT GILES called the press conference for 3 p.m. By then Shapiro had more to say than he'd expected, because the ransom demand had finally turned up.

It didn't come by post, or by telephone. It was found in a brown envelope, addressed to Detective Superintendent Shapiro and marked 'Urgent', tucked under the windscreen wiper of an area car that parked in Brick Lane for ten minutes while Constable Stourton bought some throat lozenges from Simpson's. It wasn't buying them that took the time, it was checking the packaging for messages. He found none; but when he returned to the car, sucking, he found the blackmailer had been and gone while he was in the shop.

When Shapiro opened the envelope and saw what it contained, he sent Stourton and every available officer back to Brick Lane to knock on doors. But no one had seen anything and there were no security cameras covering the scene—which might have been a coincidence but which Shapiro was beginning to feel was characteristic of his adversary. That wasn't a lucky break: he'd sized up where the various CCTVs were located around Castlemere, worked out their fields of view, and looked for a police vehicle parked outside one. It was the work of a moment to slip the envelope under the nearest wiper; he could have done it without breaking his stride. The chances of him being spotted were remote.

Inside the envelope the note was written in the same square stencilled letters as the warnings, and equally succinct. '£1m or people die. Get it and wait.'

'One million pounds,' whistled Shapiro. 'Not a bad return for some groceries and stationery.'

'And nerve,' said Liz. 'That's really what he expects to be paid for: having the nerve to ask. Setting it up, making us sweat and then telling us what he'll take to go away.'

'It's a nice round figure,' said Shapiro.

'It's probably about the right figure. If this goes on until someone gets hurt, sorting out the insurance will cost a million pounds. It could cost local businesses a million pounds in lost confidence. In purely financial terms, it would probably pay Sav-U-Mor to divvy up rather than send in their specialist and risk him starting more trouble than they can handle. It's a lot of money to us common folks, but even a million pounds doesn't buy what it used to. Half a mile of motorway, three houses at the better end of Cambridge Road? A Van Gogh sunflower, the fetlock of a Derby winner or a third of a footballer. Times change, Frank—we're the only coppers still in circulation.'

Shapiro was nodding pensively. 'He's done his homework, hasn't he?—he's thought about this. He knows where he can take risks—like at the supermarket, like putting this on the area car—without much danger of being caught. He knows how to disguise his writing without telling us what papers he reads. And he knows how much money is worth his time and the risk to his liberty without pricing himself out of the market. I don't like this man. He's too clever, he's going to be hard to catch.'

'If we don't catch him he'll really hurt someone. He could have done this time—it's pure luck the Crosbie baby wasn't burned. You don't strip the nappy off a grizzly baby to see if you've just slapped caustic soda on its bottom! She might have put up with his crying for hours before taking him to the doctor. By then he'd have needed skin grafts.'

Shapiro checked the time. 'Nearly half two.' The digital watch had come too late for him: he automatically translated its precision into a cosier analogue approximation. 'We've half an hour to decide how much we tell the Press.'

In the end it took fifty minutes and the Press had to wait. Then Detective Superintendent Shapiro, flanked by the Mayor and the chairman of the Chamber of Trade, rose to explain exactly what was going on. That was what had taken the extra time: agreeing to hold nothing back. In a situation like this, where the police couldn't hope to protect everyone, people needed to protect themselves. To check their purchases for tampering; to act immediately on any notes they found; to watch for suspicious behaviour in others.

'I *don't* mean I want the people of this town turning vigilante. That isn't necessary, it wouldn't be helpful, and it would result in more innocent people getting hurt than if we left the blackmailer to do his worst. I mean, we need to be aware of what's happening around us. If someone's spending longer than seems reasonable hovering over the cooked meats, have a look at them. Be ready to give a description. Then tell the retailer so he can check the produce. If he has any doubts, he'll call us and we'll go all the way to a laboratory analysis if we have to. There'll be a lot of false alarms, but hopefully we can minimize the risk of serious injury.'

Gail Foster from the *Castlemere Courier* was first on her feet. 'Mr Shapiro, can you confirm that Sav-U-Mor are sending a specialist from America to help find this man?'

Shapiro pursed his lips. 'I understand that, as an international organization, they have specialists in a great many things we don't see much of in Castlemere. I dare say if we were threatened by a tornado Sav-U-Mor would know just the man to deal with it.' There was a tiny, appreciative chuckle. 'There's been a feeling in town that they haven't done enough to protect their customers. I don't share that feeling, I think it's most unfair to blame the victim of a crime for not preventing it, but they're anxious to do all they can to help and this is what they proposed. Mr Tyler arrives at the weekend.'

'Assuming he isn't in San Quentin by then,' murmured Ms Foster, attracting curious glances.

Tom Parker, a local freelance representing some of the nationals, was doing sums in the margin of his notebook. 'A million pounds. Am I right in thinking that isn't actually beyond the ability of local businesses to pay? And therefore that the decision has been taken on principle?'

The chairman of the Chamber of Trade went to take that one but Shapiro wasn't yielding the floor. 'This isn't about money, it's about protecting people. If we pay up, this man may very well take the money and run. But since it worked so well, he may come back for more. Or someone else may. You're right, it's a policy decision. You start paying blackmail, you never get the door closed again. Maybe we could afford to pay him off, but we're not going to. Him, or anyone like him; not now, and not ever.'

As the press conference dispersed Liz sidled up beside him. 'That was very generous.'

'Generous?'

She eyed him knowingly. 'Frank, I've known you a long time, I know what that was all about. It was about making yourself the target. If this goes wrong, if people get hurt, they won't blame the Town Hall or the traders, they'll blame you.'

He shrugged and didn't deny it. 'I've got a broad back.'

'That doesn't mean you have to paint a bull's-eye on it!'

When they were alone he turned to face her. 'Liz, there's every chance this'll go wrong. Or not wrong, because what we're doing is right, but messy. The best way to limit the damage is to make sure all the flak is going one way.'

'And you think that, since your career is coming to an end anyway, it might as well be you that everyone's aiming at.'

'Better me than you, anyway.'

Liz stopped in the corridor. After a few paces, reluctantly, Shapiro stopped too.

'It's not that I don't appreciate the thought,' she said quietly. 'But I don't want to build my career on the ashes of yours. If a scapegoat's needed, at least I'll have time to put it behind me. You may not have. You've been too good a copper to go out under a cloud.'

He shook his head. 'I've nothing left to prove. Anyone who matters knows that, regardless of the outcome, this was the right decision. If a bunch of frightened people need someone to blame when things get nasty, that's something I can do. After the dust settles they'll see things clearer.'

Liz wasn't convinced. But she knew there was scant chance of changing his mind if he was doing what he believed to be right and necessary. She wished she could call on Donovan's support. Donovan's powers of persuasion were not legendary because logic wasn't his strong point. He fought with his heart rather than his head. You could always poke holes in Donovan's reasoning, but you couldn't deny the strength of his feelings. He'd walk barefoot over coals to prevent Shapiro ending his days at Queen's Street as a ritual sacrifice.

But Donovan wasn't here. He'd be back in a few days, and this wouldn't be resolved in a few days. When he discovered what Shapiro intended he could be relied on to go ballistic without any prompting.

LOCAL RADIO RAN it almost immediately; the television stations had picked it up by early evening. Everyone in Castlemere knew what had happened and what the official response was going to be by the time they'd had their tea. That meant the blackmailer knew too.

Shapiro waited for his phone to ring. He'd primed the switchboard to start a trace as soon as anyone called him: if it turned out to be his wife, no harm done. He was sure the blackmailer would contact him, if only to place the blame for what might follow. It was another reason he took the lead at the press conference. He didn't want the call to go to Tony Woodall at Sav-U-Mor or Kenneth Simpson the chemist, he wanted it to come to Queen's Street where the systems were already in place.

Not that he expected to trace it all the way to the blackmailer's sitting room. If he got a fix at all it would be on a public phone that would be swinging from its wire in an empty kiosk by the time they got there. But someone might have seen him using the phone. A full description was a lot to hope for but even a passer-by might remember age, size, colour, style of dress. Just knowing he was a middle-aged, middle-class white man with no distinguishing features would rule out a lot of people who were none of those things.

So he sat by the phone, catching up on his paperwork, and waited. And no one called. Not only the blackmailer but everyone else in town seemed to be giving him a wide berth. At one point he asked the switchboard to make sure his line was working. It was; still no one wanted to talk to him.

At seven o'clock he called Angela to say he was sending out for a sandwich and didn't know when he'd be home. She knew why, asked no questions, wished him luck. Though the exchange took hardly a minute he was oddly cheered by it. Six months ago he'd had no one to tell he'd be late home, no one who cared if he went home at all. Ten years ago there'd have been a tight-lipped intake of breath as if he'd done it on purpose. Perhaps it had been a mistake getting married in the first place. Perhaps if they'd lived in sin for thirty years Angela would never have left him. Married people expect more of one another, and he'd never been in a position to give her all she was entitled to.

Mary Wilson was going out so she brought him a round of cheese and pickles that was at least as kosher as he was. Actually, he quite enjoyed the odd ham sandwich when there was someone new on the desk. He sat by his phone and ate his tea, and tried to think of something—anything—that he knew about his adversary and somehow hadn't registered. But there was nothing.

At ten fifteen the phone finally rang.

Liz had given up and gone home half an hour before. Just long enough, Shapiro thought ruefully, to get into her pyjamas and start making some supper. Oh well, it wouldn't be the first time a police officer had turned out with pyjamas under his clothes. He called her home number.

'Meet me at Castle General. They have someone in ICU they think we ought to know about.'

His name was Martin Wingrave, he was thirty-six, he was a joiner, and he wasn't up to answering questions. He was in an isolation ward awaiting transfer to Cambridge Fever Hospital.

Shapiro frowned. 'And this concerns me because...?'

Dr Gordon was a man in his early thirties with an expression of earnest scholarship behind thick glasses. 'Because he has cholera, and he didn't get it from an unwise ice-cream in Karachi. He got it here, in Castlemere, from a bottle of cold remedy.'

Shapiro shut his eyes. So that was it: that was the next move in the game. The blackmailer had done with empty threats and minor injuries and gone straight up the scale to life-threatening communicable diseases. He'd said people would die if he wasn't taken seriously: this was him proving it.

'Is he in any danger?' asked Liz through clenched teeth.

Dr Gordon gave an awkward shrug. 'He's certainly sick. And people do die of cholera—even with modern treatments you can expect to lose about one per cent of patients. Worldwide, *Vibrio cholerae* kills five million a year; but most of them are children and Mr Wingrave's a fit man at the peak of his strength with access to good medical treatment. I can't offer a guarantee, you understand, but I'd be surprised to lose him.'

Behind the shut eyes Shapiro had been thinking. 'You know where he got the bug. Does that mean you have the bottle it came in?'

Dr Gordon took them down to the pathology department in

the basement. In a sealed plastic sleeve in a fridge with a warning sign on the door was a small brown bottle of the sort that wait in expectant ranks in every chemist's shop in the land every winter. 'Philbert's Cold & Flu Remedy,' proclaimed the label. 'Because Granny knew best.'

Also in the sleeve were the square cardboard box the bottle came in and the white address label that had fluttered out of the box when the paramedic picked it up to see what his patient had overdosed on.

The label read: 'This was cholera.'

'Which took the guess work out of it,' said Dr Gordon. 'Is he behind this? The man you're looking for?'

'Oh yes,' said Shapiro with heavy certainty.

It occurred to him then that he wasn't getting much input from Liz, and he looked round to see what she was thinking.

Her brow was furrowed as if she were trying to remember something. She started to say, 'I've seen one of those somewhere before.' But halfway through the sentence she remembered where. Shock hit her like a slap in the face and her eyes flew wide.

'Donovan was swigging that stuff like a soft drink when I saw him off at the wharf!'

SIX

SHAPIRO LEFT LIZ to discover what she could at the hospital and returned to Queen's Street. Soon news of Martin Wingrave's misfortunes would get out. This was a frightened and angry town already, when people realized the lengths this man was prepared to go to... Well, Shapiro needed to be in his office. Eighty thousand scared people are a mob in the making. He wanted to be on hand to forestall what trouble he could and deal with whatever he couldn't.

On the way back to the police station he called at his house. He left the engine running while he let himself in, located Angela and kissed her firmly. Then he went back to work.

Liz forwarded the Philbert's bottle to Forensics in the probably vain hope that it would yield some clues. Dr Gordon was called away while she was doing this; when she was finished she hunted him out again.

'Cholera,' she said. 'Tell me about it. What's the incubation period? What are the symptoms?'

Dr Gordon looked pensive. 'Of course, this isn't a classic case. If he really has got cholera from a specimen cultured for the purpose, the usual timings may not apply. If you get it from dirty water you could expect to be feeling ill within twelve to forty-eight hours. Most people are still on their foreign holiday when they succumb. It lasts anything from two days to a week.'

'It's fairly dramatic, then. I mean, you're not likely to confuse it with some ordinary run-of-the-mill sickness. A cold, for instance.'

Gordon blinked. 'I wouldn't have thought so.'

So it was a coincidence. The blackmailer couldn't have contaminated every bottle of Philbert's Remedy in Castlemere; he probably only tampered with one. That was what he'd done before: a specimen act to show what he was capable of. Donovan had had a cold. If the Philbert's Remedy was as good as Granny thought he should be over it by now.

'How long before we can talk to Mr Wingrave?'

'You won't get any sense out of him tonight: he was febrile, I gave him a sedative. Tomorrow, maybe. But I'm hoping to have him transferred to a fever unit by then.'

'Because of the risk of contagion?'

'It's not a nice thing to have in a hospital at the best of times, and we don't know what to expect of this due to the atypical vector.' He saw her waver and repeated it in patient English. 'With him drinking it neat instead of as a few bugs in a contaminated ice-cube. Concentrated like that, it could be a lot more virulent. I don't want it getting into the air conditioning while we're waiting for the lab results.'

If she couldn't talk to the patient, perhaps she could get her questions answered elsewhere. 'How did he get here? Did somebody call an ambulance?'

'He did, apparently. And not a moment too soon. If he'd waited any longer I don't think he'd have got to the phone.'

So he lived alone: no family who might know where he bought his cold remedy and when. 'Do you have the address?'

It was a flat in one of the big red-brick villas in Rosedale Avenue; the paramedics had lifted his keys when they collected him so she wouldn't have to break in.

Something occurred to her before she left. 'Do I need to take special precautions in there?'

'Rubber gloves and a face-mask would be a good idea.' Gordon found some for her. 'Otherwise, do what you do abroad: don't drink the water.'

'I'll need to talk to Wingrave as soon as he's making sense. Will someone call me?'

'Of course.' He gave her the number of the fever hospital in case Wingrave was transferred before that.

Liz needed to know when and where Wingrave bought his cold remedy, although she had little doubt it would have been from a local shop in the last few days. That was what the black-mailer needed: an alarmingly sick victim at just the right time to swing the vote. Which suggested someone familiar with his material. A doctor, a medical scientist? Her thoughts strayed back to Miranda Hopkins. She worked with botulism: perhaps she also worked with, or at least had access to, *Vibrio cholerae*.

And she lived in the same street as Martin Wingrave. Coincidence? Quite possibly: there were a lot of houses, and a lot of them were in flats. There was a good chance they knew one another, at least by sight. But then, if Hopkins were involved, why draw attention to herself by poisoning a neighbour?

But whoever did it, and precisely how they did it, it must have taken a little time. Time to doctor the bottle; time to plant it on a shelf; time for Wingrave to buy it, take it and become ill. It was hard to see how it could all happen in less than a day. So this wasn't a response to what Shapiro told the press conference eight hours ago: it was a response prepared one or more days ago to what the blackmailer knew Shapiro would be saying about then.

Oh yes: this was a clever man. Cold, and clever.

The flat confirmed that Martin Wingrave lived alone. There were no feminine traces, just tweed and wood and leather. A neat man, careful and particular; and the last time he'd been here, a desperately sick one. Even through her mask the smell was overpowering. She went to open the windows, stopped herself just in time. She didn't know enough to be sure she wouldn't release a plague on the town like a hungry tiger. She put on her mask and bore the discomfort.

Liz tried to visualize the sequence of events. Martin Wingrave caught a cold and bought a bottle of Philbert's Remedy. He couldn't have had it in his bathroom cabinet from the last time he had a cold or it wouldn't have been tampered with. He brought it home and started taking it. But as his cold got better Wingrave got worse. Maybe he thought it wasn't so much a cold as flu, in which case he'd keep taking the medicine.

He hadn't had the bottle more than a couple of days. The chemist's bag should still be around, either in the rubbish or—

he was a neat man, organized, a place for everything and everything in its place—in a kitchen drawer.

She tried the drawers first. And there it was, top of the pile—a blue plastic bag emblazoned with an official-looking crest and the name of Kenneth Simpson, Dispensing Chemist. She went to knock Mr Simpson out of his bed above the shop in Brick lane.

It took the chemist a minute but then he remembered: Mr Wingrave bought the remedy, along with a bumper pack of paper hankies and something soothing for his nose, on Monday afternoon.

Liz nodded. 'That fits. I'm sorry, Mr Simpson, this sod has it in for you. He probably planted the cold remedy at the same time as the baby lotion.'

Simpson regarded her glumly. 'Aren't there any other chemists in town?'

'I suppose it was safer for him than visiting two different shops.' Something occurred to her. 'You fill prescriptions, don't you?' He nodded. 'That could be how he did it: brought in a prescription, and while you were in the back he doctored a couple of items from your stock. Martin Wingrave came in on Monday afternoon, Sheila Crosbie on Tuesday: can you get me a list of prescriptions you filled since, say, Friday?'

'I can,' nodded Mr Simpson, 'but there'll be a lot of them.'

It was the signature tune of this investigation: at every turn, either there were no suspects or there were too damn many.

WHEN SHE FINALLY got home Liz found Brian still up and with a fresh attempt at supper ready to heat. She leaned on him as an old horse leans on a gate while he finished off. 'Bless you.'

'Do you want it in bed?'

'Mm.'

She told him where she'd been, what she'd discovered, all the blind alleys she'd marched up and then had to shuffle back down again.

'Poor old Simpson,' said Brian when she finished. 'He's not the jolliest shopkeeper in town at the best of times. He'll be crying into his toiletries after this.'

'You know him?'

'Of course I do,' said Brian. 'It's a useful shop, and you can always park outside. I was in about this time last week, stocking up. I got some Philbert's Cold & Flu Remedy...'

They regarded one another levelly for a minute, then Brian got up and went into the bathroom. He came back with the little cardboard box held between finger and thumb.

They inspected it from all angles but there was no warning, not in the packaging and not on the bottle. 'Even so,' said Brian, 'I think I'll ditch it. The last thing you need if you have a cold is the worry that you might get cholera as well.'

Then he put his head on one side as something occurred to him. 'You say he injected contaminants into the other products with a hypodermic? Well, not this one he didn't.'

He was quite right. It was a glass bottle with a tin lid sealed with a plastic strip. Any attempt to tamper with it should have been obvious.

'UNLESS WINGRAVE WAS too preoccupied with his cold to notice,' said Shapiro the next morning. 'If the seal was removed it might not have struck him there should have been one.'

'To remove the seal the blackmailer must first have opened the box,' said Liz. 'And if the box had been opened Kenneth Simpson would have noticed. He sells these things all the time, anything abnormal would hit him in the eye.'

'You're suggesting our friend has found a way of penetrating a sealed glass bottle inside a shut box? He's not just a blackmailer, he's a magician as well?'

She wasn't suggesting anything, could offer no explanation. 'Sorry, Frank, right now magic seems the best line of inquiry. We could haul in the usual suspects—Paul Daniels, Tommy Cooper, Harry Houdini...'

'Cardboard boxes aren't supposed to be hermetically sealed,' said Shapiro, ignoring her. 'They're folded together or glued together. Given a little time he could have opened the box carefully enough to close it again without it showing. Simpson only saw the outside. Wingrave saw the bottle as well, but he wasn't familiar enough with the product to know it should have had a seal round the lid.

'He didn't do it on the premises,' he concluded. 'He bought the stuff, took it home, doctored it, then put it back on the shelves under the pretext of looking for something else. Tell Mr Simpson not to waste his time with the prescriptions, his name isn't on the list.'

They weren't looking for someone who had spent a lot of time in the shop, rather for someone who had gone in twice.

Or possibly not. 'Actually,' said Liz apologetically, 'he may not have bought them from Simpson in the first place. He could have bought standard lines like that anywhere: he didn't have to risk showing his face twice.'

'They'd have somebody else's labels on,' objected Shapiro.

'He peeled the labels off. When Wingrave bought his cold remedy, and when Sheila Crosbie bought her baby lotion, Simpson would just think his labelling gun had misfired and check the price on an adjacent item.'

She became aware that Shapiro was watching her oddly. When she caught his gaze he cleared his throat, a reticent sound. 'Frank?'

He was looking downright embarrassed. 'Did you call Donovan?'

She frowned. 'Call him?'

Shapiro was practically squirming. 'You know. Just to make sure he's all right. With him using the same stuff Wingrave had. You said you were going to call him.'

She hadn't, but she wasn't going to call Shapiro a liar. 'I'll do it right away.'

The mobile rang—the gremlins must have been on holiday too—but Donovan didn't answer. That meant nothing. Probably he just wasn't within reach. Halfway through a lock was a bad time to knock off for a chat. Liz thought she'd try again later, if she got a spare moment.

Then she thought she'd make a spare moment.

DONOVAN HEARD the phone ring. It wasn't that it didn't suit him to answer, more that he couldn't get his head round what

it was. He knew he should recognize the sound. It was coming
from his jacket, draped over a chair. He wondered what it might
be, and why it was ringing bells in his mind as well as in his
ears. Then it fell silent and he forgot it.

His slowly roving eyes recognized the saloon, making him
wonder why wasn't he in bed. Well, because it was day—he
could see the chair with his jacket on it. But he hadn't *been* to
bed, he'd spent the night here; he thought he might have been
here longer than that. He thought it was probably time he moved.

But thinking was as far as he got. Gravity must have been
turned up a couple of notches during the night: when he went
to sit up it spread a firm hand against his chest and pressed him
back into the sofa.

And he had the uneasy feeling of having forgotten something—possibly, something important. He thought about it, hunting it doggedly through his consciousness until he had it. The
pain. Remembering brought it back, rested, refreshed and eager
to get on with its day; in spite of which he managed a wan
smile. How could he have forgotten that? It had clung to his
side like Prometheus's eagles, talons fixed in his flesh, hooked
bills tearing at his innards, for as long as he could recall. Weakly
he pawed the T-shirt away from his ribs, was surprised not to
see blood.

Another sound touched the edge of his consciousness—not
the ringing, perhaps a voice? His eyes travelled the saloon again,
slow and disorganized, seeking clues. They passed over the
stove, the table, the companionway, the chair—and then went
back, blinking, knowing *that* couldn't be right and fully expecting it to be gone when he looked again.

But it wasn't. There was a fairy sitting on the steep wooden
steps down from the deck. It had pale kapok hair, so fair as to
be almost white, as susceptible to combing as candyfloss. It had
long eyes guarded by pale lashes, and a small sharp triangular
face. It sat on the steps with its pointed chin in one long-fingered
hand and regarded him with calm, inhuman interest. It spoke
again, and though he couldn't understand the words the voice
was high and light, musical like a tapped crystal.

He tried again to rise, pushing his long legs off the sofa. But between them gravity and the eagles defeated him. The talons redoubled their assault on his flesh so that the breath caught in his teeth and he sank back helpless, knowing he couldn't leave this sofa to save his life. Detective Sergeant Cal Donovan had exposed himself to a variety of assaults in his life, confident in his ability to defend himself against most of them. Today he was at the mercy of anyone, or anything, that thought to pass some time by wandering in here and slitting his throat.

The realization grew on him that he was sick. He hadn't been well for days; sometime yesterday, maybe the day before, the deterioration had gathered pace. He'd tied up somewhere and lain down on the sofa with a hot drink and his little brown bottle, and waited for the worst to pass. He was distantly aware that may have been a mistake. Particularly if now he was seeing things.

He shook his head—fractionally, every movement hurt. 'Who are you? *What* are you?' Even to himself his voice sounded frail and breathy, incapable of reaching across the room. So he wasn't surprised when the fairy made no answer but, raising itself on long limbs, turned and sprang up the steps and vanished, the hatch banging behind it.

Donovan went on watching the steps for some time, expecting it to return, possibly bringing with it something even odder and less welcome. The fairy didn't; but the darkness did. It had never entirely gone from the corners of the room: now it began encroaching again, like dusk falling. Even in his current state he knew another whole day could not have passed. The gathering dark was more to do with his illness. He retained enough sense, just, to be afraid of it. He tried to fight it, push it back into the corners, hold it off until the day returned. Whimpering with the eagles in his side, the weight of the world on his chest, somehow he managed to raise himself on shaky arms, at least to face the danger sitting up.

The darkness wasn't impressed. It wasn't just creeping out of the corners now, it was pouring out of the walls, flooding the saloon. He was going to drown in it. He fought to stay afloat, to stay conscious, but he hadn't the strength to fight for long. Exhaustion intervened. His last conscious thought despair, a last desperate obscenity on his lips, he let it take him.

SEVEN

WHEN DANGER THREATENS people stay indoors. Even if the threat is of earthquake, vulcanism or nuclear fallout, enemies before whom walls might as well be made of paper, people feel safer in their own homes than anywhere else.

But if the enemy is one which strikes in the home, which lurks in the larder or bathroom cabinet, which can come through the plumbing or—who knows?—up through the gaps in the floorboards, where dwells safety then?

For the people of Castlemere, at least those not gainfully employed so that they had the choice as to how they spent their day, it dwelt in numbers. A force like magnetism, that they felt but didn't recognize as fear, drew them together, gradually combining the knots on street corners and the groups that formed outside the pubs and bookies into a crowd that filled Castle Place and made it difficult for the buses to get through.

Anywhere there's a crowd there's someone ready to address it. This time it was a brickie's labourer called Ron Budgen, father of five children and a familiar face around The Jubilee. He wasn't out to make trouble today, though he'd made enough in the past: he was genuinely concerned about the safety of his family.

He blamed the police. All the taxes people paid—well, a lot of people paid—and the only time you ever saw them was if the Road Fund Licence on your van inadvertently fell off and got replaced by a beer label! When you needed them, when people were getting hurt and people's kids were being terrorized, where were they then? They were doing their shopping while

homicidal maniacs left notes under their windscreen wipers,
that's where!

The crowd had spread out by now, swelling into Queen's
Street, so that a taxi on its way there had no choice but to halt
behind the snarl of buses and cars in the north end of the square.
The passenger waited a minute, tapping broad fingers in staccato
impatience on a worn leather briefcase. He glanced at his watch,
which like the briefcase was old but good. Then he got out of
the taxi, hefting a battered suitcase behind him, and set off to
walk.

'Oi!' complained the cabbie. 'What about my fare?'

'I didn't hire you for half a journey,' growled the passenger.
He was an American.

''S not my fault the square's blocked!'

'Or mine. But if I'm walking I'm not paying.'

'I'll get the police!'

Mitchell Tyler looked back at him with contempt. 'If you
were capable of getting to the police you could have earned your
goddamned fare!' Carrying his luggage, he shouldered his way
into a crowd that, without appearing to notice him, still somehow
contrived to keep out of his way.

In the same way Bert Fry the taxi-driver decided against pursuit. He was as tall a man as the American, and as bulky; still
the quiet voice of reason in his head told him you couldn't buy
a lot of orthodontistry with a three-pound local fare. Perhaps
he'd see the American again later, when he had his mates with
him. But the same whisper of sanity suggested that they, like
this crowd, would move out of his way as the Red Sea parted
before Moses, and leave Bert standing there with egg, or more
probably blood, on his face.

Tyler carried the heavy case as if it contained only a change
of underwear. An astute observer would have noted that the bulk
filling his light grey suit was almost all muscle. The crowd
hardly impeding him, he crossed Castle Place and turned down
Queen's Street, looking for something like a Seattle precinct
house.

What he found was two large Victorian villas knocked into
one, with a blue lamp on a wrought iron bracket above the front

door. Nice touch, he thought sardonically. That must put the
fear of God into the local Mafia. The thought that the Mafia
might not have heard of Castlemere didn't occur to him.

He climbed the steps and found himself in a hall bisected by
a counter with a fat, elderly man in uniform behind it.

'Can I help you, sir?' rumbled Sergeant Bolsover in his deep
thick peaty Fenland voice.

It took a lot to surprise Tyler these days, but back home the
guy would have been working in the police museum. As an
exhibit. 'You know you've got a riot brewing out there?'

Speaking slowly was in Sergeant Bolsover's genes; so was
thinking quickly. 'That's not a riot, sir. That's the populace ex-
ercising its democratic right to free assembly.'

The American grinned without much mirth. He was a man in
his late forties, but though he was gaining forehead at an
alarming rate nobody ever called him Baldy. 'Mitchell Tyler.
For Detective Superintendent Shapiro.'

Shapiro sent Mary Wilson downstairs for him. She looked at
Tyler; he looked at her. She offered to carry his suitcase. He
laughed like a bull elk belling and dropped it in a corner before
following her upstairs.

When the two men met, each was exactly what the other was
expecting and yet still, somehow, a surprise. Shapiro struck Tyler as an academic, quite possibly hot stuff on the theory of
crime but maybe less conversant with its hard realities. Tyler
reminded Shapiro of Donovan's dog.

They didn't so much exchange pleasantries as mark out their
territories.

'I'm not here to tell you how to do your job,' said Tyler
briefly. 'I'm here to protect Sav-U-Mor's interests.' Long practice allowed him not to flinch as he said his employers' name.

Shapiro nodded gently, hypnotically. 'Good. Since that's
pretty low down my list of priorities we should hardly get in
one another's way at all.'

Tyler barely flickered an eyelid. 'And the other thing is, I like
to get things moving.' The unspoken inference was clear: You
won't get in my way, I'll be out ahead of you.

Shapiro sighed. 'Mr Tyler, I'm sure I don't need to tell you all the things you won't be allowed to do during your stay here. *We* don't carry guns as a matter of course, you certainly won't be able to. You won't be able to question anyone who doesn't want to answer. If you have any information, or any suspicions, you will bring them to me and I will investigate them. I understand that you have a job to do, but I won't tolerate private armies, even very small ones. Lay a finger on anyone in this town and I'll have it off at the knuckle.'

Tyler smiled coldly. 'Superintendent, I'm a businessman. That's all. I deal in information. When I find out who's threatening my company you will be the first to know. I have no interest in your judicial procedure: all I'm here to do is find him and stop him. The sooner I can do that the happier we'll all be: me because I can go home, you because you'll be rid of me, Sav-U-Mor because they'll still have some customers. We're on the same side here, Superintendent. It would be a pity to waste effort disliking each other when we could be looking for this bum.'

Shapiro blinked. But perhaps now wasn't the time to point out that slang doesn't travel well. 'I think we understand one another, Mr Tyler. Do your job and good luck: you find him before I do and I'll be delighted and relieved. But don't expect me to turn a blind eye if the way you do that contravenes our law. I won't. This police station may be small by your standards but I have more than one cell at my disposal.'

As Shapiro saw him out he couldn't resist alluding to the delay in Tyler's arrival. 'Sorted out that business with the Grand Jury, did you?'

Tyler bared his teeth in a pit-bull grin. 'They decided it was self-defence. I showed them where he got me with the blowtorch.'

Liz was coming up the front steps as Tyler, reunited with his case, was going down them. They didn't exchange a word. But their eyes locked, momentarily, and Liz was taken aback by the sheer physical presence generated by the man.

In Shapiro's office she said, '*That* had to be Mitchell Tyler.'

'Oh yes,' said Shapiro heavily. 'Interesting man. I think he was saying, if I watch my step he'll let me stay on the case.'

Liz chuckled. 'You must be doing something right then.'

He thought for a moment. 'Find out where he's staying. I'd like to be able to get hold of him at short notice.'

'You mean, if we need his help?'

'I mean, if people with broken fingers start turning up at Castle General.'

SHE TRIED DONOVAN'S mobile again. Now it was unobtainable; so he'd turned it off in the last couple of hours. At least he wasn't lying unconscious in the bilges of his boat. She'd try again later. Maybe she'd get him next time.

She called Sergeant Tripp. 'Any word from Forensics on that bottle we sent them? The one Wingrave got cholera from?'

Even on the phone she could see him roll his eyes. 'There's been a little slip-up.'

'How little a slip-up?'

'They seem to have confused our little brown bottle with somebody else's.'

Which meant the chain of evidence was already broken, rendering it useless in any court case which ensued. For now, though, she'd settle simply for the information it contained. 'Get on to them, Sergeant, chase them up. Get them to find the damn thing and analyse it.'

'I thought we knew what was in it.'

'We do; probably. But I want it confirmed. I don't want to be chasing all over the country looking for a source of cholera if it turns out the label was just another threat and actually Martin Wingrave overdosed on curry.'

TYLER WAS STAYING at the Castle Arms in the square. (It wasn't really a square, it was a diamond, and the signs said Castle Place, but locals referred to it as The Square.) The Castle Arms wasn't the most expensive hostelry in town but it was the classiest. Tony Woodall had reserved a room as soon as he knew his company's troubleshooter was on the way. He thought if he had the room booked he wouldn't be asked to put Tyler up at his house.

The big American checked in, had a shower and ordered a steak sandwich. He'd been travelling for fourteen hours, his body clock had no idea what time of day it was, but it never said no to a steak sandwich. The vegetarian revolution had passed Tyler by entirely.

Then he called Woodall. 'We need to talk.'

'Of course. Do you know where we are?'

'No. But I expect you know where the Castle Arms is.'

The last time Tony Woodall knocked on a door with such trepidation was when his high-school headmaster summoned him to discuss a missing poodle.

They went over the same ground he had with Shapiro; perhaps a little quicker because he knew what the questions would be and how much detail would be helpful. Also, he hadn't had the same sense of urgency about getting out of the Detective Superintendent's office.

'So basically,' Tyler summed up when he'd finished, 'the yoghurt in the store could have been tampered with by a member of staff or a customer. The baby lotion and the flu remedy could have been doctored by a member of staff or a customer, and the school showers could have been fixed by a member of staff, a student or a parent there for one of the matches.' He looked up from the notes he'd taken and the teeth were showing again. 'And you're a member of staff at Sav-U-Mor, a customer at the pharmacy, and a parent at Castlemere High who was present during the shower incident because your son was playing—rugby.' He had to read that out. It might have been jai alai or buz kashi to judge from his expression.

Woodall heard himself blustering. 'That's the kind of town Castlemere is. There are only eighty thousand inhabitants: of course we all use the same shops, have kids at the same schools. It's not significant. I could find you half a dozen other people in the same position.'

'Name one.'

For a horrible moment he thought he wasn't going to be able to. When inspiration struck he beamed with relief. 'Brian Graham. He's a teacher at the school, he was supervising the hockey match that afternoon. Hockey—that's a girl's game,' he explained, daring a little impertinence. 'He shops at Sav-U-Mor once or twice a week, I know him to nod to. And I've seen him in Simpson's the chemist.'

Tyler nodded. He might have been satisfied, he might just have been saving his powder. 'Maybe I should talk to Brian Graham.'

'Maybe you should,' agreed the under-manager. 'You can get his home address from Detective Inspector Liz Graham, Frank Shapiro's second-in-command. He's her husband.'

Tyler looked at him sharply. 'Tall woman, about forty, long blonde hair? I saw her at the station house.'

Woodall was definitely feeling braver. 'Round here it's called a police station.'

Tyler eyed him unblinkingly for ten seconds, long enough for Woodall to feel his own eyes starting to water. Then he did the smile again. 'So Tony—Tony? that's right, is it? So tell me about the poodle.'

WHEN WOODALL FINALLY escaped from the Castle Arms he sat in his car, shaking, trying to determine his best course of action. Flight had much to recommend it, except that Tyler would follow. That left going home and locking himself in, or telling the police.

The latter course had two things to recommend it. It would break Tyler's hold on him, and was the obvious thing for a law-abiding citizen to do. Also, he could walk to Queen's Street from here, which was safer than driving when he was as edgy as a ginger cat at a Boxing Day hunt.

He was going to ask for Shapiro. At the last moment he had a better idea and asked Sergeant Bolsover if Detective Inspector Graham was in her office.

She was trying Donovan's number again, again without success. When she looked up and saw Sav-U-Mor's under-manager as white as a sheet in front of her she thought something else had happened.

She put the phone down. 'Mr Woodall? Have there been—developments?'

'In a manner of speaking,' he said, and she could hear the

tremor in his voice. 'I need to tell you what happened to my old headmaster's wife's poodle.'

WHEN HE'D GONE Liz and Shapiro eyed one another over her desk, neither keen to break the silence. They really didn't know whether to treat this as a joke or not.

'We were looking for someone with a bit of previous,' said Liz. 'This is the closest we've come so far.'

'I'm not sure poodles count,' said Shapiro, straightfaced. 'I'm almost certain that people who come in here telling us about their previous don't count.'

'That could be a clever move,' countered Liz. 'He knew Tyler was on to it. What better way of making sure we dismissed it than coming in here in a muck sweat saying he had to confess or we might think he was the blackmailer?'

'A fifteen-year-old boy holding an apricot poodle to ransom. It's not exactly crime of the century.'

'Nobody starts off with the crime of the century. They start with little crimes. If they get away with them they try something more ambitious.'

'He didn't get away with it.'

'No, he didn't,' agreed Liz. 'He was beaten bloody by his headmaster. But he almost succeeded. But for a bit of apricot wool in the hinge of his locker, he'd have walked away with a hundred pounds—and a hundred pounds was a fortune to a teen-age boy twenty years ago. He may have failed, but he learned two valuable lessons. That it's your own mistakes that betray you: if you're careful enough you can stay ahead of the game. And that people will pay good money to protect their families.'

'Families!' snorted Shapiro. 'It was a poodle!'

Shapiro had never had animals; Liz had always had them. She shook her head. 'It was small, fluffy and utterly dependent—as far as that woman was concerned it was her baby. A hundred pounds?—she'd have mortgaged the house to get it back. And young Tony knew that. He knew she wouldn't mess him around while her baby was in danger.'

'It's still a hell of a long way from hiding a poodle to infecting a town with cholera!'

'Of course it is. But he's all grown up now with money of his own: he can afford to think bigger. Invest a thousand, even a few thousand pounds, against a return of a million.'

Shapiro frowned. 'You think he *bought* cholera? Where?'

'I have no idea. Frank, I'm not saying he did this. I'm saying somebody did, and it could have been him. Where can you buy cholera? The same places we thought of before, only this way he doesn't have to work there, he only has to bribe someone who does.'

'And he came in here,' he said, warming to the theory, 'because once someone knew about his youthful prank it was better that we know too. So he couldn't be accused of hiding it. Hell, we might assume that he wouldn't come in here to tell us about it if he was involved in the current situation.'

'And *do* we think that?'

'Beats me,' confessed Shapiro. 'He had a couple of opportunities that we know about, he might have had others. He had the same motive as anybody else: a million pounds. And by his own admission it's an idea that's occurred to him in the past. Whoever did this probably tried something similar, on a smaller scale, first. At this point in time Tony Woodall is the only person we know who fits that profile. I think we have to treat him as a suspect.'

'I wonder how Tyler knew about the poodle.'

Shapiro gave a pontifical shrug. 'There wasn't a court case; even if there had been, a juvenile's record is expunged once he's adult. It had to be from either the headmaster and his wife, or from Woodall himself. My guess is Woodall's been at a company bash sometime, drunk more than was good for him, and told someone the story as a joke. And the other party filed it away in case one day it came in useful.'

'Tyler scared the living daylights out of him,' commented Liz.

'I have news for you,' said Shapiro heavily. 'Tyler scares the living daylights out of *me!*'

EIGHT

HARANGUING A CROWD is thirsty work. Fortunately, a couple of Ron's more thoughtful friends supplied him with cans as he spoke. Inevitably, as the pile of cans mounted the quality of his thinking diminished and the volume with which he expressed it rose. By one o'clock the gathering had heard everything he had to say three times over and was beginning to drift away in search of some lunch. Suddenly lunch seemed a good idea to Ron too. It wasn't so much the fish and chips he fancied as something to wash them down with. Leaving a little pyramid of beer cans in the middle of Castle Place he and his mates made their way towards Fast Edna's in the shadow of the castle.

Ron considered himself a man who could hold his drink; and a helpful tip in that regard is always to let it away when it's done its job. He left the others to order and disappeared into the Gents discreetly located under the wall of Castle Mount.

He was not a particularly fastidious man. He'd seen all sorts of unsavoury spectacles in these public conveniences, contributed his fair share, was mostly content to live and let live— except of course for queers. A man had to have some standards.

A young man in a long raincoat came down the steps behind him, cast him a furtive look and disappeared into one of the cubicles. 'Best place for you, you queer,' muttered Ron with routine vindictiveness, and returned to the task before him.

Until there was a sharp intake of breath behind him, a desperate imprecation and a soft plastic clatter, and something rolled out from under the door and lay on the tiles. Ron blinked but it was still what it looked like the first time: a hypodermic syringe.

Ron didn't do much running these days but he could cover

the ground when he had to. He raced up the steps to street level
and his red-faced yell travelled a great deal further than Fast
Edna's. 'Everybody: I've got him! The bastard son of a bitch,
he's down here. The blackmailer! I caught him in the act.'

Ron wasn't the sort of man who inspired confidence even in
his friends. Most of the two dozen people who gathered round
the Gents were only there to see what sort of a fool he was
making of himself now. Even those who dashed down the steps
for a closer look didn't do so because of their faith in his judgement.

Then they saw the man he'd apprehended. He was about
twenty-three, with long hair and a wisp of beard framing a pale
and dirty face. He was wearing a long coat that looked as if
he'd decoked an engine on to it, and trainers that had been white
about the last time Ron went for a run. He didn't have 'Blackmailer' tattooed on his forehead but he did have a hypodermic
syringe in one hand and a large block of chocolate, still in its
wrapper, in the other. Ron had him by the wrists, holding up
his hands for all to see.

For a second there was silence. Even the feet on the steps came
to a shocked standstill. The men stared down at him and, hunched
in terror, saucer-eyed, the man with the syringe stared back.

They fell on him like a breaking wave. Fists flew, boots
swung. A couple of them found Ron and he bellowed furiously,
redirecting them to the proper target. The young man disappeared under the onslaught and only a thin wail marked where
he went down. After that there were just the bent backs of his
assailants, the grunts of anger and triumph, the sough of heavy
breathing.

Then someone at the back of the pack, already suffering the
frustration of being unable to get a kick at the ball, gave a
startled squawk and flew backwards up the steps, landing in a
heap on the pavement. He wasn't hurt, except where his collar
had bitten into his throat, but he had barely a moment to puzzle
over how he had got here before someone else landed on top of
him. A few seconds later the pile grew to three.

By now the scrum inside had lost interest in the man it was
attacking and was trying, quite urgently, to work out who was

attacking it. Those who still had their feet under them crowded
back towards the door: when a fourth body hit them, more or
less chest high, they panicked, broke and ran, trampling those
lying bewildered on the pavement.

Thirty seconds later, when PC Jim Stark arrived at a run, he
found the public conveniences all but empty. The last three men
were emerging up the steps. One had a second, bloody and unconscious, over his shoulder and the third by the scruff of the
neck.

'Do you realize you're losing control of this town?' gritted
Mitchell Tyler, thrusting one of his burdens into Stark's hands
and laying the other down carefully on a handy bench. 'He's a
heroin addict. You can see the needle tracks on his arms. The
chocolate's for if he can't get a fix. They thought he was the
blackmailer. They kicked him half to death. This one'—he
jerked Ron by the front of his jacket, looked as if he'd have
liked to do more—'started it.'

Stark radioed for an ambulance and a car. While they waited
he looked at the man on the bench. He was breathing, which
was the main thing Stark needed to know. If the casualty was
breathing it was better to wait for professional help; if he wasn't,
even inexpert intervention could only better his chances. Three
minutes isn't long enough to scramble an ambulance, and after
three minutes people who aren't breathing start dying.

There was a lot of damage—superficial, skin and flesh torn
away by the force of well-aimed boots, and also structural. One
cheekbone was certainly broken, and both collarbones, and nobody's wrist was designed to bend that far. There might also be
internal injuries. But he was alive, and if it had gone on five
minutes longer he wouldn't have been.

'He's lucky you came along,' said PC Stark.

Mitchell Tyler regarded him with only a little less venom than
he reserved for Ron. He shook his head. 'No, son. He's unlucky
you didn't.'

'I OWE YOU AN APOLOGY,' said Shapiro. 'I warned you not to
lay a finger on anyone in this town. If you hadn't ignored me
we'd be dealing with a murder now.'

Tyler gave a negligent shrug. 'You don't owe me a thing. We're on the same side. Your town and my employers need the same thing: an end to this business, quick, before anyone else gets hurt.'

'If you've any suggestions—?' murmured Liz. She was perched on the windowsill of Shapiro's office, the canal at her back.

Tyler turned towards her. He had the unsettling habit of moving just a little faster than he looked like he should. 'I've got one for you, Inspector. Tell your husband to watch his step. I've heard his name in connection with this.'

He couldn't have surprised her more if he'd ducked behind the bentwood coat stand and turned into Superman. Her voice cracked in astonishment. 'Brian? You're joking!'

'No.'

One way it was funny, but another it wasn't at all. A young heroin addict had just been kicked half to death in a public lavatory because someone had put two and two together and come up with fifteen. A middle-aged art teacher might seem an improbable suspect, but he'd been there or thereabouts often enough for it to be noticed. What had occurred to one person would have occurred to others. In the current climate of fear and suspicion it could be enough.

She stood up abruptly. 'That's it. Frank, we have got to get on top of this! Before the whole bloody town spirals out of control.'

'I agree,' he said mildly. 'I too would welcome any suggestions.'

It's easy to insist that something must be done, harder to decide what should be done and how. They were already doing all they could. No avenues of inquiry had been overlooked, or dismissed as not worth the trouble. They were asking the questions, they just weren't getting the answers.

'Maybe, just for the moment,' hazarded Liz, 'it's more important that we're seen to be doing something than that *what* we're doing is productive. You're right'—she glanced at Tyler—'we need more presence on the streets. We need to be out there tackling this—talking to people, pulling them in if we've any reason to. Even if we let them go after ten minutes, the mere fact that we look as if we know what we're doing may be enough to stop people like the Neanderthal in the cells from going out and doing it themselves.'

'Possibly,' said Shapiro softly. 'And the other thing that might happen is that everyone we question shoots to the top of the hate list. It won't matter that we're just doing it for show if as soon as we send someone home a gang of vigilantes picks him up again. Do you want that to happen? Do you want it to happen to Brian?'

Her mouth opened and closed a couple of times and nothing came out. Her immediate reaction was that it was a monstrous thing to say. But it wasn't at all, it was a legitimate question. If what she was proposing was such a good idea, why was she worried about the fallout landing in her vicinity?

Tyler saved her the embarrassment of replying. 'Did Woodall call you?'

Shapiro looked at him over the glasses he didn't wear. 'Mr Woodall,' he said precisely, 'came in here. He seemed to think you suspected him.'

'I knew about the business with the dog. I wanted to see how he'd react.'

'He came here,' said Liz. 'I think he was looking for protection. Do you still suspect him?'

Tyler regarded her at rather greater length than was strictly necessary. A ghost of a smile seemed to hover round the corners of his lips. 'You can make a case. He had perfect access to the yoghurt pot in the first incident, good access to the school showers in the second, and limited access to the pharmacy where the other stuff turned up. Plus, he has a history of this type of crime. OK, it was a poodle, but the point is he was willing to terrorize someone for money.

'The other thing is, he's the loudest voice telling you to pay the ransom. Everyone else, as I understand it, was for holding out. Woodall was for paying.'

'Everyone else was talking about their own money,' observed Shapiro dryly.

Tyler was looking at Liz again. He seemed to enjoy looking

at Liz. 'You're right about one thing. You need more people on the street. It may make the blackmailer twitchy. It may have the opposite effect: make him cocky, get him to make a mistake. Whatever, it'll make everyone else feel safer.'

'I'll talk to Superintendent Giles,' said Shapiro. 'But I'm not sure how many more rabbits he can pull out of the hat. We don't have a huge deployment here.'

Liz caught his eye. 'I know where we can find one extra bunny.'

Shapiro chuckled. He'd heard many epithets applied to his sergeant—applied many of them himself—but bunny was new. 'Yes, all right. If this isn't an all hands on deck situation I don't know what is. But if he isn't answering his phone—?'

'It may be on the blink,' said Liz. 'Quickest thing will be to send someone for him. He told me which way he was going, but it didn't make much sense. Something about drains?'

'Ask Dick Morgan, he knows the canals. Then send Mary Wilson. Tell him to tie up where he is and come back with her.'

After she'd left the office Tyler said, 'Who are we talking about?'

'Detective Sergeant Donovan,' said Shapiro. 'He's off on sick leave. I think he'd be sicker still if we let him miss this.'

Tyler frowned. 'Then why hasn't he called in? He must know what's going on.'

'He's on a boat. He left on Monday, before it started.'

'He hasn't heard a radio or seen a paper in four days?'

Until that moment it hadn't struck Shapiro as odd. But Donovan wasn't rowing across the Atlantic, he was cruising the canals within twenty miles of home. He'd be stopping at locks, at pubs and at shops. He'd be talking to other canal users. And four days had passed without him knowing the town was in crisis?

Without a word he picked up his phone and dialled Donovan's number. A pleasant female voice regretted that it had been impossible to connect him and advised trying again later. Still without speaking he got up and went next door.

'Liz, don't send Mary, send Morgan. Tell him to take my car'—he handed over the keys without reservation: the new Jaguar hadn't come through yet, he was driving a middle-aged Vauxhall—'and not to come back until he's found him. He'll know where to look and who to ask.'

The beginnings of a puzzled frown fell out of Liz's face, leaving it smooth with concern. 'Something's wrong, isn't it?'

Shapiro shrugged awkwardly. His back still hurt if he subjected it to sudden movements. 'I don't know. Maybe not; maybe we're just on edge and jumping to conclusions. But it's four days since we heard from him, and the only way he could not know what's going on here is if he hasn't spoken to a soul since then. Which is just about possible. He had a cold, maybe he holed up somewhere and shut the world out for a few days.'

'And switched the phone off?'

Shapiro nodded. 'Maybe. If he didn't want waking up? Anyway, I want to know now. If I'm overreacting, fine, there's no harm done. But if he's in trouble I want to know.'

ARMED WITH WHAT Inspector Graham could remember of Donovan's itinerary, DC Morgan set off in the Vauxhall and confidently expected to have found *Tara* within the hour. Narrowboats travel at walking speed except when they come to locks or their crew come to pubs. Fifteen miles a day is Blue Riband speed for a narrowboat. In theory *Tara* could be fifty miles away, but she wouldn't be. She was travelling a loop that would take her barely twenty miles from Castlemere.

The furthest he could have got, judged Morgan, was the Foxwell Dam where the Sixteen Foot Drain locked into the River Arrow for the leg home. He started there, at the lock-keeper's cottage. The keeper knew both *Tara* and Donovan and hadn't seen either of them. So Morgan got back in the car and followed the line of the Sixteen Foot Drain back to the engine house at Sinkhole Fen. *Tara* hadn't been there either.

But she passed the Posset Inn late Monday afternoon. The proprietor recognized her livery of black and green. He'd expected Donovan to tie up further down the towpath and come in that evening, but he never appeared. When he walked his dog down the towpath the next morning there was no boat and no sign that one had been there.

So the narrowboat had turned up one of the spurs between Posset and Sinkhole Fen, and Donovan had tied up and gone below to nurse his cold. Three days later he was still there. Morgan hadn't given much weight to DI Graham's misgivings about the Philbert's Remedy, but now he was beginning to feel a twinge of unease himself. Three days was a long time to sit in the same dead-end spur, going nowhere and seeing no one; particularly in weather like this. The rain was more intermittent now but the landscape he was travelling through was so wet it was hard to be sure sometimes whether he was looking at the canal or a flooded field.

Morgan stopped the car and pulled the map out of the glove compartment. It was a good map, it showed all the minor roads, all the hamlets and a lot of the individual farmhouses. And it showed the canal in all its navigable reaches. It did not, however, show all the individual cuts and spurs dug by individual landowners two hundred years before to link their own properties with what had promised to be the transport network of the age. Many of them had disappeared entirely now, filled deliberately or by neglect. Others still existed as ghosts of their former selves, clogged by weed, overgrown by willow but still wide enough and deep enough to take a boat if the helmsman knew where to look. Donovan would know them all. Morgan grew up in Castlemere, knew the canal like an old friend. Donovan had been here nine or ten years and knew it like a lover.

If the road had run parallel to the water the search would have been much easier. But it didn't: largely they ignored one another, made their own ways even between the same points on the map. Occasionally the canal appeared as a line of willows separated from the road by a single field. More often they drifted apart by anything up to a couple of miles, and access was down side roads and farm lanes and often only on foot.

Searching ten miles of canal like this would take all day, and even then would leave large stretches uninspected. Morgan drove back to the Sinkhole engine house, and they provided him with a launch and someone to handle it.

It was cold and wet everywhere, more like November than early October; on the water it was especially raw with a dank chill that hung above the surface and penetrated the bones. Morgan wished he were more suitably dressed, eyed his companion's parka and oiled-wool sweater with envy. It was five o'clock: the afternoon was already over, soon night would fix its claws in the fens in a grip that would not relax for twelve hours.

'I hope we can spot him before it goes dark.'

'We have to,' said the boatman, 'we'll never spot him afterwards. Not if he's gone up one of the spurs. They're hard enough to find in daylight, we'd be wasting our time in the dark. Pass him ten metres away and never know he was there.'

Fate dealt them one small kindness: the rain stopped again, immediately improving visibility and with it the chances of success. Morgan felt the stirrings of hope.

In the middle of Sinkhole Fen, a couple of miles from the engine house, the boatman steered the launch close against the northern bank and slowed the engine to idle. 'Something's been through here.'

Morgan still couldn't see an opening. Bullrush and reeds the height of a man crowded the margin of the water. But there was a break in the trees behind them. 'Where does it go?'

'There's a bit of a lake at the back there. It helps keep the water level up. You can get up into it in something the size of this: I don't know about a narrowboat.'

'I bet DS Donovan knows,' said Morgan.

They turned into the cut, nosing through the reeds. Then Morgan saw what the boatman had seen first: that some of them were broken. The hollow stalks tapped against the sides of the launch like fingers drumming on the hull.

After about fifteen metres the reeds began to thin, the glint of light on water appearing through the waving heads. The launch emerged into the open. It wasn't a lake by normal standards: it was a mere, the shape of a teardrop, perhaps half a kilometre through its longest axis.

There were no jetties, no buildings, no farms within sight. There were no muddy trampled areas where cattle came down to drink. There was just the long teardrop of water, the blond sedges fringing it round, the pewter sky above. And ducks, and a pair of swans in the middle of the mere.

'There.' The boatman was pointing the length of the little lake. Against the far shore, half swallowed by the reeds, was a boat. She wasn't moored, she'd buried her stern in the bank and was peeping out of the vegetation like a child playing hide-and-seek. The hull, like the hulls of all narrowboats, was black; the superstructure was picked out in green.

'That's her,' said Morgan. The engine note deepened as the launch picked up speed.

Closing with *Tara* confirmed their first impression, that no attempt had been made to moor the boat. Her warps were still coiled neatly on the tiny foredeck. She'd drifted on the lake until the wind and the rain pushed her into the reeds.

The boatman helped Morgan aboard. At the sound of their feet on the deck the chain locker beneath them exploded with a paroxysm of furious sound. 'It's that bloody dog of his. No!' Morgan exclaimed urgently as the boatman reached for the hatch. 'Letting him out would not be a good idea.'

They moved aft over the cabin roof, dropped into the well with the great swan-neck tiller, and Morgan rapped on the cabin door. 'Skipper? It's Dick Morgan. Are you in there?'

There was no reply that he could hear. He opened the door. 'Skipper?'

Dick Morgan felt like the men who found the *Mary Celeste*. There were signs that Donovan had been here, but he wasn't here now. The bed hadn't been slept in but the sofa had: there was a mug of scummy cold cocoa on the floor beside it, cushions with the impression of a head piled at one end. There was also a small brown bottle, empty and overturned on the rug.

There was nothing else. Morgan searched the boat from stem to stern—well, all except for the chain locker and he knew what that contained—but Donovan was no longer on board.

NINE

THEY WERE RACING the day to make even a rough search of the area around the mere before the light went. Inevitably they were beaten; but not before those who had done this before had all reached the same conclusion.

Dick Morgan voiced it. 'I don't think he went ashore.'

Without wanting to, Liz was extrapolating from that conclusion to the next, which was as obvious as it was unwelcome. The effort to avoid it made her unreasonable. 'How can you possibly say that?' she demanded.

Morgan had no illusions about what he was telling her. He explained simply and without inflection. 'There's deep silt all the way round the water's edge. You'd churn the bank up clambering out so there'd be no missing it.'

'You missed the way in,' Liz pointed out nastily. 'A damn great narrowboat came through and you couldn't even see there was a channel.'

She was upset, Morgan didn't take it personally. He explained that too, patiently. 'The boat pushed the reeds aside: when it had passed they sprang back into place. But to get ashore you'd be trampling on them and you'd break a lot. You'd leave a scar of black mud and broken reeds that a child couldn't miss. There's nothing like that here.'

Liz blinked and nodded jerkily. She knew she was blaming him for something that wasn't his fault. She hoped they knew one another well enough for him to forgive her. 'I know, Dick; I know.' She closed her eyes for a moment. 'All right. He's not on *Tara*, and he didn't go ashore. So there's only one place he can be.' She looked around her where the mauve and orange twilight glinted on the water. 'First light tomorrow we'll put the divers in.'

They were already at the scene. Shapiro had asked for a team from Division. While there was still a chance of finding the missing man unconscious in the thick sedges around the lake they'd searched on foot with everyone else. But they'd worked in situations like this before, they knew before Morgan did that they weren't going to find Donovan on land. Quietly they'd dropped out of the search line and suited up.

Sergeant Warren, in her wetsuit and with her mask pushed to the top of her head, was sitting on *Tara*'s coachhouse roof while Liz and her constable talked in the well. Now she spoke up. 'There's no need to wait till morning, ma'am. There'll be no visibility down there: we'll be working by touch anyway. We'll get started.'

Liz nodded gratefully. They were talking about searching for a body, there was no longer any urgency. They were willing to go down in the cold and the dark and begin a job that might take days not for Donovan but for her. 'If you can do it safely,' she said. 'Don't take any risks. You can't save anyone's life here.'

Warren nodded. She was a slender woman in her late twenties, in the wetsuit she looked like an otter. 'We'll be careful.' She slid into the mere with hardly a splash. Three more sleek dark shapes followed her.

Liz said, 'I'll tell the chief.'

'We don't know anything yet,' said Morgan stolidly. 'Not for sure.'

She managed a sombre smile. 'Dick, we do. We know he came here on this boat, that he isn't on it now and that he didn't leave on foot. His jacket's over the chair in the saloon, and his wallet's in one pocket and his phone in another. Where do you think he went without them? We know he was ill, and he was swigging that poisonous damn remedy. We don't know when he left *Tara*, but we know that the last night he was here he slept on the sofa. There's only one way to read that: he was sick and getting sicker. Too ill to make the boat fast, too ill to look for help or even to get to bed. Sometime in the last three days, disorientated, delirious even, he stumbled up on deck, missed his footing and went over the side. He's dead, Dick. If we're lucky we'll find his body. Even that may be too much to expect.'

There was a long silence. Then Morgan, pragmatic as ever, said, 'What do we do about his dog?'

One thing was certain: Liz wasn't going to open the chain locker. 'Lucy Cole will take him. She feeds him when Donovan can't get home. I'll have her brought out here.'

'Will you tell her? About the skipper?'

She looked round again, taking in the desolation of the spot—the vast and barren sky, the bleached reeds keeping up their endless whispering campaign like malicious old women, the cold water still and brown as an oil slick. 'Dick, I think she'll guess.'

SHAPIRO WAS WHITE. Even though the stairs still gave him trouble he met her at the back door and ushered her up to his office, sitting her down and plying her with coffee without saying a word. For a couple of minutes they sipped in silence. It was hard, terribly hard, to break it. They both understood the situation. But they couldn't discuss anything else until they'd dealt with this.

'What a stunner,' said Shapiro eventually. His voice was hollow with shock.

Bemused and incredulous, Liz shook her head. 'I can't believe it. I mean, I *believe* it—I accept it, I know he isn't going to come walking in the door going Fooled you! But in here'—she laid one palm flat on her chest—'it isn't real. I can't get my head round it. He was on holiday, for God's sake! He was going to be back by the weekend.'

'It's the'—Shapiro struggled for a word—'banality of it I can't come to terms with. I mean, yes, Donovan was always going to die young. Was going to rush in somewhere that angels fear to tread; or come a cropper on his motorbike; or—you know. Something dramatic. Push his luck too far, take one risk too many. But this? He got sick, fell off his house and drowned? How does that *happen* to a man like Donovan?'

'It didn't.' She stared at him, her eyes behind the swollen lids glinting like mica. 'Frank, it didn't. He didn't get sick. Somebody poisoned him. He was murdered. This isn't a case of black-mail any more, it's a murder inquiry.'

Of course she was right. Somehow that was more likely; that he could believe in. 'We'll need the body to prove it.'

'They're looking. In the meantime we have the bottle. It's on its way to Forensics now.'

'Was there a warning?'

'Not on the bottle. I couldn't find the packaging. He must have thrown it away.'

'I'll ask Kenneth Simpson if Donovan bought it from him.'

'Simpson's is the nearest chemist to Broad Wharf. It's the obvious place for Donovan to shop.' The sound of his name on her lips brought her up short and choking. 'I can't *believe* what it is we're talking about. Donovan being dead. After all this time, all those close shaves—but this time it's for real. He isn't going to wake up with a crowd round him this time. He isn't going to wake up at all.'

Shapiro touched her hand, as much for his own comfort as hers. 'Until we find the body we can't be quite sure that's what happened. I know—how it looks is usually how it is, probably I'm clutching at straws and we'll have to get used to the idea that he's gone. Only, until we find him, there is still a tiny chance...'

She didn't fall for it. Neither did he.

A bit after ten Shapiro stuck his head through her door to say he was going home. Liz nodded. 'I shan't be much longer my-self.' But it was another hour before she could drag herself away from her desk and the mounting paperwork—witness statements, forensic reports, photocopies of the warning labels and the ran-som demand. By then she'd been staring at it for three hours and she hadn't had a single fresh, useful thought. Half the time she hadn't even been thinking about the frightened people of Castlemere.

She'd been thinking about the detective sergeant from hell. She hadn't chosen Donovan and she hadn't wanted him. He'd been wished on her, like a deceased relative's Labrador. She'd inherited him from her predecessor, which is rarely satisfactory. In this case Shapiro had been quite candid about his reasons:

Donovan would give him fewer problems as a sullen second fiddle to the new DI than as a loose cannon. She'd taken him as a favour, and for Shapiro's benefit alone she'd put up with his moods, his temper, his blatant disregard for the formalities of police service. She'd given him three months, promised herself more congenial assistance if her efforts to knock him into shape failed to bear fruit by then.

That was three years ago. She hadn't given up trying to knock him into shape, but somewhere in those first months she became aware that good policemen come in different guises and behind the bloody-mindedness, the grim determination to raise as many hackles as possible, was a man struggling to do the job well. He wasn't a natural, he didn't find it easy; but he cared so much that it was possible to understand and even forgive much about him that had seemed inexcusable. If he was short with the failings of others he was deeply intolerant of his own. If he lacked charm, he also lacked guile; without discretion, he was also without deceit. What you saw was what you got; what he said was what he meant. None of that made him easy to work with, but you always knew where you stood. He didn't agree with you to your face and undermine you when you weren't looking. He'd cover your back if the only thing he had to do it with was his own.

He was going to be a hard act to follow.

Brian was already asleep. Liz woke him crawling into bed. He asked, mumbling, still drowsy, how the inquiry was going. She told him how she'd spent the evening. She was astonished to find herself crying.

Wide awake now, Brian held her close, her body shaking against his chest, murmuring trite words of comfort into her hair.

'I don't know why I'm carrying on like this,' she sniffed as her sorrow abated. 'God knows it's something that happens. I've lost colleagues before. I don't know why it feels so—personal—this time.'

Brian stared at her. 'Liz, Donovan was more than just a colleague. You three—you, him and Frank—were a team. You didn't just work together, you looked after one another. You were closer than most families. Of course it hurts that you've lost him. It'll hurt a lot more once you're over the shock. Don't deny what he meant to you. You need to accept it in order to grieve, and you need to grieve in order to move on.'

'Grieve!' she exclaimed, almost managing a chuckle, almost managing to suggest that the death of her sergeant was just another bit of bad news in a bad news week. But then she heard herself, heard herself devaluing him. There weren't many people for whom the death of Detective Sergeant Cal Donovan would have been a personal loss, but she was one and she owed him better than to pretend otherwise.

'How's Frank taking it?' Brian asked gently when she'd allowed herself to cry.

'He was stunned,' said Liz. 'He didn't know what to say—neither of us did. It was so unexpected. You see someone off on a week's holiday, it doesn't occur to you they're not coming *back*.'

'So what happens now?' He meant, was there someone at Queen's Street who could do Donovan's job or would Division send them someone.

She misunderstood; but it really didn't matter. Getting her to talk about it, to face up to what had occurred and what it meant to her, was the important thing.

Her eyes glinted like winter sun on icicles. 'What happens,' she said in her teeth, 'is that we find this bastard before he decides to give us another demonstration of what he can do. He's a killer, Brian; more than that, he's an indiscriminate killer—he doesn't care who dies as long as someone does. He didn't know Donovan, probably never met him. All he knew, all he cared, was that someone would buy that flu remedy and get very, very sick at about the time he put in his demands. A lever: that's all Donovan's life meant to him. He wasn't angry at him, he didn't hate him, he didn't want to destroy him. He just wanted to damage somebody, and Donovan would do. It was the same with Sheila Crosbie's baby: he wanted to burn somebody and a baby would do as well as anyone. He's a psychopath, Brian, nobody's safe until we have him behind bars.'

He was nodding, his chin on top of her head. 'He'd be proud of you. Donovan. He'd be proud of you getting on with the job.'

She looked up at him. 'Brian, this is going to sound silly.'

He smiled sombrely. 'But?'

'But...I want you to be careful.'

His eyebrows rocketed towards where his hairline used to be. '*Me?* Why?'

'Because I need you to be. Because I've lost enough. Because this whole stupid town's jumping out of its skin, anyone could get hurt now just for being in the wrong place at the wrong time. Because if anything happened to you there'd be no one to hold me.'

He dusted a feather-weight kiss on to the top of her head. 'I'll be careful,' he promised.

II

ONE

ON FRIDAY MORNING Liz hitched a lift to Castle High with Brian because she wanted to hitch a lift from the school with someone else. She didn't explain this very well. Brian thought she was still concerned about his safety. It was forty years since he was last taken to school, by his mother.

After he'd gone inside Liz waited at the school gates.

Miranda Hopkins drove an under-powered white 4x4 that was fine for watching hockey matches from but would have been no good at pulling a sheep out of a ditch. Running late, she didn't bother to park, just pulled up long enough for Saffron to get out, trailing her books and her sports kit behind her.

But before she could drive off the passenger door opened again and Detective Inspector Graham climbed in. 'I hope you don't mind,' she said; but Ms Hopkins heard it in her voice that actually it didn't matter whether she minded or not.

'Er—no, of course not,' said Miranda, startled. 'But I'm going to work, I don't know how you'll get back.'

'I'll call a taxi,' said Liz shortly.

Miranda eyed her passenger sidelong as if to reassure herself it was the same detective she'd spoken to earlier, so altered was her manner. 'Has something happened?'

'Yes,' said Liz baldly. 'Somebody's died.'

'Oh no...'

Liz cocked an eyebrow at her. 'Why so surprised? It was always going to happen. You can't blackmail people without threatening them with something. If they won't pay up, you have to carry out the threat.'

'Will they pay up now?'

Liz's hazel-green eyes flared. 'Now there's an interesting question! Not who died, or how, but what about the cash?'

Miranda felt herself bridle. She wasn't used to being treated like this, and she didn't like the feeling that it was personal. She seemed to be being accused of something.

Miranda Hopkins looked like a faded hippy but under the cheesecloth and dirndl lurked a soul of steel. Being a single parent isn't an easy option. Doing it well, and at the same time succeeding in a demanding job, takes intelligence, application and inner resilience. She had the confidence to stand up for herself against tougher opposition than a CID officer having a bad hair day.

Her voice was clear and steady. 'Inspector Graham, are you under the impression that what's happening in this town has something to do with me?'

Liz declined to answer. 'Do you work with cholera?'

Miranda stared at her—for so long she almost crashed the car. She pulled into the side of the road. 'What?'

'It's a simple enough question. You work with botulism: do you also work with cholera?'

'No,' said Miranda, clinging on to her patience. 'Not at present. I have done.'

'So you'd know how to get hold of some.'

'I'd know how. That's not the same as saying I *could* get hold of some. There are security procedures, it's not considered a great idea to have people wandering in and buying a bag of *Vibrio cholerae* as if it was sweeties!'

'You're not just people,' said Liz roughly. 'You're a scientist employed by a reputable company working in the field. Are you telling me you *couldn't* get hold of the stuff?'

Miranda thought for a moment. 'Maybe I could. In the unlikely event of wanting to.'

'A million pounds is a fair incentive.'

The technician gaped at her. 'You do! You think I'm behind this. You think I terrorized half the town, my daughter included, and now I've killed somebody. Who, anyway? Who am I supposed to have killed in order to extort a million pounds from the good people of Castlemere?'

'My sergeant,' said Liz.

In Miranda Hopkins' eyes shock gave way first to understanding, then to compassion. The eyes of a murderer? Liz hoped so, because then Donovan would be avenged; but the cool spot in her head where she was still thinking rationally had its doubts. Anyone can lie. Someone who could plan and carry out a scheme as cold-blooded as this one could probably lie convincingly. But compassion is a hard thing to feign.

'I'm so sorry,' said Miranda Hopkins softly.

'Is that a confession?' demanded Liz. She regretted it as soon as the words were out. If she was talking to the killer it was a stupid thing to say; if she wasn't it was crass.

Miranda shook the cloud of fair hair. 'No. I really don't have anything to confess to. I'm sorry that you've lost someone who mattered to you.'

'Donovan?' said Liz, and it was half a word, half a snort. But in time she heard herself doing it again: trying to lessen the loss by denying what he'd meant to her. That's what they'd do at Division when the word got round. Shocking business, they'd say; but still...you know...Donovan? And then they'd add: I suppose, if it had to be somebody... She owed him better than that. So did Division, actually, but he wouldn't have expected much from them.

She shut her eyes a moment and breathed deeply. Then she nodded. 'Yes,' she said simply, the bitter edge gone from her voice. 'Yes, he did.'

Back on the road, Liz resumed her questioning. But the anger that had fuelled it was gone. She hadn't dismissed Miranda Hopkins as a suspect, but she was calm enough now to realize she didn't know enough to hold an opinion.

But if the woman was a less than persuasive suspect she might still be a useful witness. 'Since you've worked with cholera, tell me this. How easy would it be to infect someone?'

'Easy enough,' said Miranda, 'it's a resilient little bug that thrives anywhere there's warm weather and bad plumbing.'

'But not in Britain. You'd have to go abroad?'

'Or culture it, from samples taken from a patient or contaminated food or water. Give them a nice agar plate and just the

right degree of heat to make them comfy—and then stand back
because when these things take hold they spread. It wouldn't be
difficult. It wouldn't take a lot of technical know-how.'

'Could it be delivered in a flu remedy?'

'Depends on the recipe. Enough antibiotics would kill it, but
a basic fruit juice and sugar cough mixture would do fine.'

'How stable would it be? Could it live in the bottle for a few
days?'

'Inspector, cholera didn't get to be a major cause of sickness
in large parts of the world by being picky. It isn't a smart bomb
of a bug, more a howitzer: fill the air with shrapnel and some
of it'll hit something.'

Liz nodded slowly, absorbing and extrapolating. 'Dr Gordon
talked about a one per cent mortality rate. So choosing cholera
may not mean the blackmailer intended to kill—in the way that
it would if he'd used, say, arsenic.'

Miranda shook her head. 'It's easily treated and recovery is
fairly rapid. The main danger is in areas without modern facilities. In Britain today you'd have to try pretty hard to die from
cholera.' She stopped abruptly, catching her breath. 'I'm sorry,
that was—clumsy.'

It was, but it was important. It changed Donovan's death from
murder to manslaughter. Did that make it better or worse? It
made it partly his own fault; or at least a risk of the lifestyle
he'd chosen. Donovan's main weakness was the same as his
greatest strength: he was a loner. He lived alone, he took holidays alone. When he got sick there was no one to help. When
he fell in the canal there was no one to pull him out.

Liz had never been entirely sure how much of that was from
choice and how much was simply that he'd been no good at
relationships. He'd never seemed to have much time for people,
not as individuals. He'd do whatever was necessary to protect
The People because that was what he was paid for, but people
with a small p had never really interested him. Liz suspected it
was because he hadn't understood them very well. She wondered if he'd opted for loneliness because it was easier than
trying to play a game whose rules no one had explained to him.

'Inspector,' said Miranda Hopkins gently. When Liz looked

at her, momentarily surprised to see her there, she was proffering
a tissue.

'Damn it!' she said fiercely; but she took the tissue. She
hadn't realized that tears were spilling on to her cheeks.

'Don't be embarrassed,' said Miranda softly. 'We're women:
we cry more easily than men. We feel more. The price is worth
paying.'

When Liz joined the police force there were senior officers
who spoke openly against women taking a full and equal role
on the grounds that (a) they'd fall in love with the suspects and
(b) they'd keep bursting into tears. Success had meant proving
them wrong: showing she was not only as good as any of her
male colleagues but also as tough. In twenty years the only other
person she'd cried in front of—apart from Brian—was Frank
Shapiro.

And she was embarrassed. Perhaps Miranda Hopkins was no
more than the bystander she had at first appeared. But she was
still a stranger, and ambitious detective inspectors don't break
down in front of strangers. Lamely, by way of explanation, she
said, 'It keeps hitting me.'

'Had you known him long?'

'Three years.'

'Longer than some marriages.'

Liz managed a smile at that. She'd never thought of Donovan
as husband material; as far as she knew, neither had anyone else.
But it wasn't a stupid remark. This was a perceptive woman:
she understood people, how they felt and what made them tick.
A useful talent for a blackmailer, of course... But no. Blackmail
is of necessity a cold, ruthless and uncaring business, and in all
the English language it would be hard to find three adjectives
less applicable to Miranda Hopkins. She just wasn't a credible
suspect for this kind of crime.

Miranda said seriously, 'You need to talk about it.'

Liz shook her head, put the tissue in her pocket. 'Possibly,'
she said, 'but not to you.'

'I wasn't offering. And not to your husband either, or your
colleagues. A professional: a priest or a counsellor. Someone
you can shut the door on at the end of the session and never see

again if you don't want to. But you're hurting and you need to talk about why. You need closure.'

Liz shook her head again, stiff with resentment. 'Thank you for your tissue. But you can keep your advice.'

Miranda shrugged and gave up. 'Do as you think best. But this is where I work: can I go in or are you arresting me?'

She'd stopped outside the gates. Liz opened the door. Half in and half out she paused. 'Any arrest right now would be premature. I don't know who killed Sergeant Donovan, Ms Hopkins. But I'm going to find out, and I'm going to make them pay. That's *my* idea of closure.'

She called for a taxi. Waiting for it she wandered back up the River Road.

You need to talk to someone, Miranda had said. But keeping her feelings to herself was more than a habit now, it had become ingrained, as much a part of her as her fingerprints. Yet she was aware of a debt of honour owed to the dead man. If she couldn't tell anyone else what he meant, who he was, she could at least confront it herself. In the privacy of her own head as she walked she formulated words she would never say aloud.

He was a difficult man, bad-tempered, bloody-minded and mule-stubborn, she thought; and I'm going to miss him for ever. He wasn't the best copper I ever knew; he wasn't the best man. He just might have been the most honest. People always reckoned he was a maverick, but that wasn't it. He was just trying so hard to do a good job that sometimes he crawled out on a limb—so far, sometimes, he didn't hear the sound of sawing.

But his heart was so much in the right place you couldn't stay angry at him for long. He was never too tired to do his job, never too scared, and he never made a distinction between those who were worth the trouble and those who weren't. He was a good policeman and a decent human being. And I wish I'd said some of this to him while I had the chance.

The taxi hove into sight: Liz raised a hand to hail it. Oddly enough, her heart felt lighter already.

WHEN SHE GOT BACK to her office she collared Dick Morgan, who'd received by default the promotion he'd always avoided and taken over Donovan's desk. He was the only candidate: Mary Wilson had the makings of a sergeant but not yet the experience, Scobie had the experience but not the wit. The jury was still out on whether Scobie qualified as Homo Sapiens.

'The cholera bug could be cultured from someone carrying it,' she told Morgan. 'Get on to the hospital, see if there have been any cases through there in the last few months.'

'How many months?' asked Morgan, who didn't like being caught using his initiative.

'*I* don't know. See what they offer you and ask if it was recent enough to be relevant.'

He was going, ground to a halt in her doorway. 'Guv?'

'Mm?'

'Do I have to use the skipper's office?'

It sounded pathetic but actually Liz understood. She'd felt the same way about moving into Shapiro's office after he was shot; and worse about seeing his stand-in using it. 'It's only a room with a desk in it. Donovan's not going to need it again.'

'You'll need to bring someone in. Maybe we should leave it for him.'

Liz frowned. 'Dick, right now the last thing I need is a new sergeant. You won't get stuck with the job, I promise. But it'll be a weight off my mind if you'll do it till we're out of the woods. And yes, that means using the sergeant's office. Everything you'll need is in there, it's where your calls will be sent. Just—do it. It isn't haunted. You're not going to hear the faint ghostly hum of a motorcycle engine if you're working there late at night.'

He managed a wry grin. 'He won't come back as a bike engine. He'll be a disembodied voice by the coffee machine going, "Who's got me fecking mug?"'

Slowly, slowly, they were coming to terms with it.

Morgan phoned the hospital. But Dr Gordon was unable to offer him anything helpful. The last case of cholera they'd had was over a year ago: it was hard to think that was relevant.

'What about the Wingrave sample?' asked Morgan. 'Anything helpful there?'

Dr Gordon made embarrassed noises. 'Actually, there's been

a bit of confusion at this end. The path lab said they'd rerun the slides and get back to me. They'd done the wrong tests or something.'

To DC Morgan this seemed no more than par for the course. From the start this had been one of those investigations where anything which could go wrong inevitably would. Discouraged, he put down the phone and sat alone in his office—Donovan's office—and wondered what he could usefully do next.

'Coffee,' he decided. But he went next door to the squad room to fetch his own mug.

WHERE DONOVAN was he had no need of a mug. Neither hunger nor thirst troubled him. Time passed without leaving any wake, and the only sensation he knew of was a terrifying lightness, as if he might float away and be lost. Once, just once, he opened his eyes and the fairy was there again. Except of course that he didn't believe in fairies.

A thought struck him. Maybe it wasn't a fairy: maybe it was an angel. He looked again, critically. It didn't look much like an angel, though he wouldn't have claimed to be an expert. Another, and worse, thought struck him. It looked like an imp.

He shut his eyes again, and thought that this was one of those occasions when playing dead made a lot of sense. In fact, it was quite possibly the only game in town.

TWO

IF THERE HAD BEEN any clues to investigate, any suspects to chase, they'd have been out there doing it. It wasn't a good sign that Castlemere's senior detective and his deputy were both at Queen's Street at the same time.

But since they were they took the opportunity for a little brainstorming. It was a technique that they'd refined over the years, that had served them well enough in the past to be worth a try now. Any time they seemed to have exhausted all possibilities, explored all lines of enquiry and hit the buffers at the end, it was worth getting together and just batting ideas between them. Sometimes they found they knew more than they thought.

'Blackmail,' said Shapiro, going back to basics. 'At least we have a motive: he's doing it for one million pounds. So he's ruthless and he's greedy. And he's an arrogant bastard. He thinks he's cleverer than us. He thinks he can pull this off, and go back to whatever it is he does when he isn't blackmailing towns, and we'll never find him.'

'Can't think what'd make him think that,' murmured Liz.

Shapiro twitched her a smile. 'He mustn't know us, Inspector.' The smile died. 'Except that he will do, won't he?'

'He will?'

'I think he'll have made sure he does. He knew when he started this who the opposition would be. He's done his homework in every other respect, damn sure he's studied us too.'

It was an uncomfortable feeling, like being spied on. This man that they still knew almost nothing about had made a point of knowing about them. What they were capable of; what to expect from them.

Liz sniffed. 'Well, we may not have studied him in quite the same way, but we know something about blackmailers in general. They're loners. They may occasionally take a partner, they may employ peripheral players as hired help, but essentially they're loners. It's the safest way.'

Shapiro regarded her. 'Safest?'

Liz nodded. 'More than most criminals, the extortionist lays himself open to discovery. He can't hit and run: he has to deal with his victims. Approach them, talk to them, collect his ransom. Protecting his identity is vital to success, and no secret is entirely safe once it's been shared. Two blackmailers might keep a secret, because if it got out both of them would know who was responsible, but more than two and somebody's going to blow it.'

'Fair comment,' agreed Shapiro. 'So we'd prefer a single blackmailer but we're willing to consider a partnership of two. Does Tony Woodall know Miranda Hopkins?'

Liz blinked. She hadn't considered the possibility. She considered it now. 'Their kids go to the same school, they're both into sport, there's just a year between them...yes, it's quite likely they hang out together. And if they do the parents probably do know one another. All the same...'

'You don't like them for it.'

'I quite like Woodall,' said Liz judiciously. 'He could have produced the first two episodes very easily. He has form of a kind. And he was very keen to get the money handed over. I don't much fancy Hopkins.'

'But Hopkins could get hold of the cholera for him. It's hardly a standard line at the cash and carry.'

But Liz wasn't convinced. 'I really don't see Miranda Hopkins being involved. She's...not the type.'

Shapiro elevated an eyebrow. 'The type?'

Liz found herself blushing. 'I know, I know: in the right circumstances almost anyone can commit almost any crime. But the relevant word here is Almost. Blackmail is such a cold, calculated offence. I've known otherwise nice people who committed murder, but I've never known any who went in for blackmail. Blackmailers, when you finally track them down, you feel you should have known all along.'

'That's the ones that you *do* finally track down. What about the ones that you don't?'

Somehow, today it wasn't working. They weren't resolving anything; they weren't even thinking anything fresh. They went to break up.

But Liz hovered in Shapiro's doorway. 'Er...'

He shook his head. 'No, still nothing from the mere. It's a lot of water to search.'

She nodded. 'I know. I'm not even sure why it feels to matter. It's pretty obvious what happened. I don't know why it feels less real because there's no body.'

'Completion,' suggested Shapiro. 'You can't draw a line under the thing until you've had a funeral. It's not a religious ritual, it's a human one. You need an X marks the spot somewhere to show what happened and give you a point to move on from. Otherwise you're waiting for something that never comes and it's hard to get on with your life.'

'I hadn't even thought of the funeral.' Liz's eyes widened. 'Somebody'd better tell his family.'

'What family?' asked Shapiro dourly. 'There's a couple of dotty aunties in Glencurran, they just about exchange Christmas cards.'

Liz found herself smiling. 'No, they send him a postal order for his birthday as well. They'll have to be told, Frank. They mustn't read it in the papers. Speaking of which...'

He sighed. 'I prepared a press release earlier. I was putting it off, but you're right, we can't wait until the *Courier* asks Lucy Cole why she's walking his dog. I thought we'd stick to the basics for now—boat found drifting, Donovan missing. If we say we think he had cholera this town'll tip over the edge into hysteria.'

'What about the boy Tyler rescued? Is he going to be all right?'

Shapiro shrugged. 'He's a drug addict so the term's comparative. Yes, he'll recover. He's got five broken bones, they really laid into him, but he'll mend. He'll live long enough to die of an overdose.'

'And Tyler himself? Have we heard any more from him?'

Shapiro shook his head. 'Either he's jollied off for a day's sightseeing, which seems a little unlikely, or he's pursuing his own enquiries.'

'Perhaps he's cornered Woodall again.'

'If he has I expect we'll hear about it, from Woodall. He seems to think it's our job to protect him from his company's troubleshooter.'

'Actually, it is.'

'Perhaps that's why he was so keen to get the ransom paid,' mused Shapiro. 'Perhaps he knew that, if this went on long enough, he'd have Mitchell Tyler on his back.'

'But if Tyler scares him that much, why start a course of action that would inevitably have that result?'

'Maybe it's a double bluff. Maybe he isn't that scared—he just wants us to think he is so we'll rule him out.'

Liz sniffed. 'If we're getting into maybes, maybe Scobie's granny did it all along.'

WHEN HARRISON FORD woke up in similar circumstances, Donovan reflected philosophically, it was to the sight of Kelly McGillis who promptly began to disrobe. Why did it not surprise him that when he woke in a strange bed his guardian angel was old enough to be his mother?

This was sophisticated thinking for a man who'd been unconscious for three days.

The woman felt his eyes and turned with a smile. 'Mr Donovan. Back in the land of the living, I see.'

He took that as a good omen. He doubted it was something dead people said to one another. 'Looks like it.' His voice was a croak, a husk of a thing, dry and without strength.

'How do you feel?' She had silver hair curling over the collar of her checked wool dress, and the rosy cheeks of her youth had paled and shrunk a little, leaving the bones of her face prominent. It gave her a certain nobility which the clear gaze of her blue eyes did nothing to diminish.

Donovan felt like a clumsy stable boy being picked up by the owner of the horse that kicked him. 'I've felt better.'

'You've been ill. Do you know where you are?'

Unable to lift his head, he looked round by swiveling his eyes. Even that hurt. He was in a room of sprigged cottons and substantial furniture. Nothing about it looked familiar. He shut his eyes. 'No.'

She'd been about to explain but he was too weak to listen. 'Don't worry about it now. You're safe here. Go back to sleep, you'll feel better tomorrow.'

But he wasn't ready to return to the blackness. Somehow he knew he'd been there too long already, had found it hard to leave. He forced his drooping lids apart by sheer effort of will. 'What happened? Where's my boat?'

'Close by. Everything's all right. There's nothing that needs your attention right now.'

'Who are you?'

'I'm Mrs Turner—Sarah Turner. This is my house. You've been our guest for a few days, since Elphie found you. You've had pneumonia.'

It took time for him to absorb that. Pneumonia?—and he'd lost whole days to it? 'What day's today?'

'Friday. If you're not going to sleep, perhaps you should try to get some food inside you. Start with this'—she filled a glass with water, propped up his pillows so he could drink it—'and if you keep that down I'll make you some soup.'

He wasn't aware that he was hungry, but sipping the water made him aware that he was thirsty. He emptied the glass, passed it back for a refill. 'Elphie?'

'My granddaughter. Well—my stepson's daughter. She found you. It's as well somebody did.'

'Pneumonia?'

'People die of pneumonia, Mr Donovan. If they don't get help they do.'

'I think I passed out.'

'You must have been ill for days. Why on earth didn't you call someone?'

He thought back. But the past wasn't just a foreign country, it was a foggy one. 'My phone's up the left.'

Mrs Turner was obviously an educated woman but that education had not extended to Ulster vernacular. 'You couldn't get through?'

'Guess not, or the cavalry'd have arrived by now.' His eyelids were drooping again, his voice growing slurred. 'I saw a fairy...'

Sarah Turner smiled again. 'Go to sleep now, Mr Donovan. I'll explain properly when you wake up.'

THREE

WHEN DONOVAN surfaced again the fairy was back, perched on the window seat and watching as if she expected him to do something interesting. It was the sheer intensity of her gaze which roused him. He groaned and rolled over, shielding his eyes against the light, and she was sitting there cross-legged, a few feet from him.

'You're Elphie.'

Her bright gaze sparkled with delight. Donovan knew nothing about children but he supposed she was about six years old. 'You're a policeman.' The little piping voice chimed exactly with the pointed face, the slender limbs, the floss of ash-blonde hair. Even now he had more of his wits about him, he was still inclined to look for the gauze of wings tucked behind her shoulder-blades.

'Donovan,' he said. 'My name—Donovan.'

'Nana says I've got to call you Mister.'

Donovan gave a gruff chuckle. 'Nobody calls me Mister, and you're not big enough to start.'

She recognized it as a joke. The pale triangle of her face spread in a beam. 'I'll tell Nana you're up.' Wings or not, she flew from the room and down the stairs beyond.

Her departure gave Donovan the opportunity to explore his circumstances. A glance under the bedclothes confirmed his suspicion: he was naked, someone had been tending him like a baby. He had no recollection of it, none at all. He remembered being in the saloon on *Tara*, to weak to try the phone again, then waking up here. Nothing in between. The woman said it was Friday. He'd lost three days.

She said he'd had pneumonia. His chest felt bruised. He'd never really been ill before. Injured—he knew the Accident & Emergency wing at Castle General better than some of the people who worked there—but not ill. Pneumonia was an old man's disease!

Another, slower, footfall on the stairs and Mrs Turner—that was the name he'd been looking for—appeared with a tray. 'Elphie says you're feeling better.'

'I must be. I can keep my eyes open.' But he found it difficult to look at her. A man unused to dependency, to whom the very thought was anathema, he was appalled to realize he'd been utterly dependent on a stranger for three days.

But if Donovan was embarrassed, Sarah Turner wasn't. She smiled. 'Let's see if you can eat as well.' She put the tray in front of him.

He couldn't work out what time of day it was, had to ask. 'Three o'clock in the afternoon.' And, anticipating his next question: 'Still Friday.'

She'd made him chicken soup—what Shapiro called Jewish penicillin—and toast. He began sipping it to please her, found appetite came with the eating. It was four days since he'd had anything solid.

Satisfied, Mrs Turner left him to it. 'When you want a wash, the bathroom's next door on the left. Simon brought your shaving kit from the boat.'

'Simon?' Donovan mumbled through the toast.

'My stepson. Call if you need anything.'

The food put some life back into him. His chest still ached, his limbs felt heavy and his head light, but these were the aftermath of illness rather than illness itself. He'd slept his way towards recovery.

After he'd eaten he tried getting up. It took him two tries to reach the dressing-gown left thoughtfully at the end of the bed. Simon hadn't brought that from *Tara:* Donovan didn't own one. Mostly, if he wasn't asleep he wanted to be ready for whatever little surprises the day had in store.

So that, washed and shaved, his next priority was to track down his clothes. He found them in the wardrobe, washed, pressed and hung up. Almost, they looked too clean to be his. He put them on anyway and, already feeling more in control of his situation, headed downstairs.

The rattle of pots led him to the kitchen. Sarah Turner was baking. She looked round in surprise when he cleared his throat. 'Mr Donovan! You shouldn't be up and about yet. Sit down'— she pulled out a kitchen chair—'before you fall down.'

She was right: his knees were trying to bend both ways. He slid gratefully into the chair. 'Listen, I—er—' He tried again. 'Thank you for looking after me. I'm sorry to have imposed on you.' Since he didn't ask much from other people he didn't get much practice at thanking them. Even to himself it sounded an absurdly formal way to address a woman who'd stripped the damp clothes from his unconscious body and put him to bed.

It did to her too, but she was too well brought up to giggle. 'You're very welcome, Mr Donovan: I'm only glad you're all right. We were a bit anxious about you that first night. Then the antibiotics got to work, and after that it was really only a matter of letting you sleep it off.'

'Have I put someone out of their bed?'

She beamed. 'Heavens, no. This is a big house, we've more than enough room for guests. Don't even think of leaving to-night. See how you feel tomorrow, but stay as long as you need to. Elphie's enjoyed having you here. She doesn't see many new faces.'

He snorted. 'I can't have been too entertaining out cold!'

'Well, it's quiet out here. There are no children in the village now: she has to make do with me, her father and any stray puppies, sick lambs and orphan chicks she can find. I'm afraid she sees you as the ultimate in sick lambs, Mr Donovan.'

He scowled. 'I wish you wouldn't call me that.'

Her head tilted to one side. 'You prefer Sergeant?'

'I prefer Donovan.'

She shook her head crisply. 'I don't call my employees by their surnames, I'm certainly not addressing a guest that way. I presume you have a Christian name?'

He nodded, reluctantly. 'I never use it.'

'Why ever not? If it's good enough for God, it's certainly good enough for you. What is it?'

'Caolan.'

In thirty years, the only pleasure his first name had ever given him was the way it made Sarah Turner stop and blink. 'I beg your pardon?'

'Caolan. It's Irish.' He relented a little. 'People who insist on doing call me Cal.'

She looked relieved. 'Very well. Cal. Now, we have a sort of farmhouse tea at six. If you're well enough I suggest you join us, then have an early night. Or if you're tired before that I'll have Simon bring you up a tray.'

'I'm OK,' he grunted, embarrassed by her kindness. He chewed on his lip. 'Mrs Turner—can you tell me what happened?'

'Yes, of course.' She dusted flour off her hands and sat down facing him. 'On Wednesday morning Elphie found your boat moored on the towpath. She insisted she knocked; when she got no answer she peeped through the window. She saw you on the sofa, thought you were asleep, thought she'd wait for you to wake up.' She watched him, gauging his reaction. 'That must seem very rude to you. She doesn't mean to be, she just doesn't understand that people like their privacy. And in the event, it's probably just as well. You really were very ill.'

Donovan nodded slowly. 'I'm surprised they left me here. It wasn't your job to look after me, they should have taken me to hospital.'

'Who?'

'Well—the doctor, whoever you called. Did he think I lived here?'

'Dr Chapel lives in the village. He didn't think you needed to be in hospital, and I was happy to look after you. It was a dreadful night, and the road out here is so long and so bad we thought you'd be better tucked up in a warm bed than bouncing around in the back of an ambulance. Dr Chapel put you on antibiotics, he said that and a bit of care was all you needed.' She smiled brightly. 'And he was right.'

'What village? Where are we, exactly?'

'East Beckham. It's a bit pretentious to call it a village—there are a dozen houses and Mrs Vickery runs a general store in her front room. Everyone else works for The Flower Mill.'

Donovan was still thinking in terms of baking. 'You mill grain?' He knew East Beckham as a dot on the map north of the Thirty Foot Drain. He didn't know there was any industry out here.

'Flower with a W,' said Mrs Turner. 'It's a family business. We grow bulbs: cut flowers for the spring, bulbs for the garden centres.'

Of course, bulbs. Donovan had seen the fields in April, great splashes of primary colour like a child's painting. In many ways the fens are more like Holland than the rest of England.

'What happened to my dog?'

'He's all right. We left him on the boat but he's got food and water, he'll keep until you're fit to go and see to him. Tomorrow, maybe. Tonight you really should stay indoors.'

He didn't need persuading. The towpath had to be half a mile from here, he'd have collapsed in an abject huddle within the first hundred metres. He couldn't believe how weak he felt.

Mrs Turner smiled again, sympathetically. 'So Cal, what brought you out this way? We're a little off the hire-boat circuit. Surely you don't suspect a major crime in East Beckham?'

For a moment he sounded quite offended. '*Tara* isn't a hire-boat, she's my home. But no, I'm not here on business. I had some leave, I thought I'd get out of town for a week.'

'Sick leave?' Seeing his surprise she quickly apologized. 'I'm sorry, I saw the wound in your side. It's quite recent, isn't it?'

After a moment he nodded. 'I was shot.'

'In the line of duty?'

One dark eyebrow rocketed. 'Well, it wasn't a social occasion!'

'I don't mean to pry,' said Mrs Turner. 'But I read about it in the papers. I thought that was you.' She pursed her lips. 'You were very brave.'

Donovan shook his head. Like every born outsider, he both craved acceptance and couldn't take it when it was offered. 'That's not what it is. You do what you have to—what the situation requires. Afterwards someone says "That was brave" or "That was stupid", but at the time you're just trying to get through. To get home.'

'You could probably have got home without a hole in your side,' Sarah Turner suggested softly.

He never found it easy to talk about himself. He shrugged awkwardly. 'There never seemed to be a moment when there was a choice. Some things you don't ever do. You don't turn your back on people who need your help. Once you accept that, the rest kind of follows. If you can't walk away, you have to find a way through.'

Donovan remained uncomfortable with her regard. He'd been considered a hero before. But what he remembered of the events in question was feeling scared all of the time. It betrayed a curious naivety in the pit of his soul, a place where he'd never quite grown up, that he couldn't see anything remotely admirable in that.

He changed the subject. 'Your husband runs the business?'

Mrs Turner shook her head. 'I'm a widow—Robert died fourteen years ago. His son manages The Flower Mill now.'

'That's Simon? Elphie's father.'

'That's right.'

'You never felt like retiring to the south of France when the next generation took over?'

Sarah Turner hooted with mirth. 'What—lie on a verandah stirring a daiquiri? Not really my scene, Cal. I'm too old to circulate, too young to vegetate. Besides, who'd look after Elphie? No, my place is here. I mightn't have been born in the village but I fully intend to die here.'

Donovan wasn't much of a social animal either. He didn't understand the rules of conversation. He thought it was about exchanging information, didn't understand why the people he did it with tended to get a glazed expression and edge away. He made people feel they were being interrogated when all he was doing was passing the time until he could leave without causing offence.

He said, 'Doesn't Elphie's mother live here then?'

He saw at once it was the wrong thing to say. Sarah Turner's gaze turned from friendly to glacial, then back again, in less than a second. If he hadn't been looking right at her he'd have missed it. If he hadn't been a professional investigator, trained to see and experienced enough to trust what he saw, he might have thought he'd imagined it. But, however brief, it was intense enough to token some real, abiding grievance in the woman's life. Her anger wasn't at Donovan for prying, it was older and deeper and cast in concrete. Mere mention of Elphie's mother made her see red. It had for a long time and it always would. Probably people round here knew better than to provoke her, so his transgression had shock value as well.

But Sarah Turner was a civilized woman for whom good manners were not an optional extra. Seeing his puzzlement she felt obliged to explain. Salvaging a rather cool smile she said, 'Elphie's mother has never taken care of her. She abandoned the child when she was just a baby, as soon as it was clear she was going to need special looking after. I don't know where she is now, and I have no wish to know. We don't have a lot of time for Elphie's mother in this house.'

Donovan knew he'd hit a raw nerve. He didn't know if he'd make things better or worse by apologizing. He settled for a lopsided shrug and a grunt of 'Families!'

Sarah relaxed and nodded agreement. 'Families indeed. Oh well, I've been pretty lucky in mine. And I include Elphie in that. My life would be so much poorer without her.'

So there was something wrong with the child. But if she wanted him to know what she'd tell him: he had no right to ask. The sharp little pixie face, the piping voice, the fascination with people she didn't know and the lack of any discretion around them, that so far as Donovan knew could have been quite normal in a child her age, were in fact symptoms of something amiss. He felt an odd little pang and wanted to ask—and even he knew better—whether Elphie would be all right or if she was living on borrowed time.

He found something innocuous to say. 'What's Elphie short for?'

'Elizabeth.' Sarah laughed. 'But you have to admit, Elphie suits her better.'

'How old is she?'

'She's eight. She's small for her age, and she won't get a lot bigger, but that doesn't stop her filling the house.'

'I don't know anything about kids,' confessed Donovan. 'She brightens the place up, but.'

You don't get many compliments on a handicapped child. Sarah Turner recognized that as one and beamed, and didn't bother herself with the peculiar Ulster syntax. 'You're an only child, Cal?'

A blind dropped behind his eyes and for a moment he seemed unwilling to answer. Then he gave an ambivalent half-shrug. 'I am now. My sister died when she was twelve, in the car bomb that killed my mam and dad. My dad did a bread run, but he drove the same sort of car as the police reservist three doors up. The Provos offered their apologies, so that was all right.'

The irony didn't fool her: she felt his pain. Her hand crossed the table between them and closed on his wrist, feeling the tension in the long tendons like wires under the skin. 'I'm so sorry. When was this—how old were you?'

'I was sixteen,' he said. 'That's when I came to England. My brother was a woodentop with the Met, I went to live with him.' He saw her bewilderment and translated. 'A London policeman.' He gave a slightly shaky sigh. That surprised him: he didn't know these events still had the power to move him. 'Two years later he was dead too. In a car chase: he thought he was as good a driver as the guy in front, and he was wrong.' He forced a chuckle. 'And people say motorbikes are dangerous!'

Sarah Turner felt a surge of compassion for the gangling Irishman, long and thin as string, with his peculiar accent and his haunted eyes. When they brought him here she'd seen him as a burden; when they found his warrant card she'd been alarmed, wondered what it meant, what he was doing here. They'd agreed to care for him and she'd undertaken the task with application if no enthusiasm. But it had proved difficult to go on thinking of him as a threat as he lay sweating with pain and fever upstairs.

Still it was only now, talking to him, that she began to see him as a real person with a place in the world beyond the fen, a life of his own that sometime he'd want to return to. It raised fresh questions and made the solutions more difficult. Thus far they had acted in their own best interests. Now he was awake it was going to be impossible to continue ignoring his.

They could have left him on his boat. He would probably have died, but at that time his death would have come at no cost to Sarah or anyone in East Beckham. Two things made them intervene. One was the possibility of a reason for his being here beyond his untimely illness. The other was Elphie. Everyone else involved might understand the need to turn their backs on so problematic a stranger but Elphie never would. It was hard to explain, but Sarah understood instinctively that if they'd let Donovan die, something in Elphie would have died too.

Dr Chapel decided the matter, as he'd decided so many in the past. He was an old man now, his position in the community mostly honorary, but the years which had bent and weakened his body had not dulled his mind. Difficult decisions in East Beckham were always taken to Dr Chapel; and Dr Chapel advised keeping the stranger at the big house. That way no bridges had been burnt. If he was here on police business someone would come looking for him; if he wasn't there was time to decide their next move. If they let him die and in due course be found, the police would certainly come to The Flower Mill, whether or not they were interested in it before. They would be puzzled that no one from the village had investigated the boat tied so long to their towpath; and curious policemen wandering round the place was the last thing East Beckham needed. One policeman, glad of their help and too weak to be inquisitive, was a much safer bet.

Dr Chapel had not said, though the inference hung in the air like marsh gas, that if it turned out they would have been better to let him die after all, there would be another chance. A canal on the cusp of winter offered opportunities enough for a fatal accident. It wasn't only motorbikes that could be dangerous.

But Sarah found herself hoping, not only for Elphie's sake, that no such measures would become necessary. It was hard enough to have one death on your conscience; she didn't need another.

FOUR

'SIR, SIR—SIR! Isn't your missus a detective, sir?'

Brian Graham had been waiting for this, and it came as no surprise that it arrived courtesy of 3b. He reminded himself that patience is a virtue before replying. 'That's right, Darren.'

'Corr!' said the Dracula impressionist, impressed. 'Is she after him then, sir?'

'After who?' Brian knew it should be 'whom' but considered it pretentious. He also knew who Darren meant.

'Plagueman!' The boy's eyes were shining.

'*Who?*'

'It's what they're calling him, sir,' said Maureen long-sufferingly. 'You know, like Superman. Batman.'

'VAT-man,' offered Darren, to general derision.

'Yes, of course she is,' said Brian. 'Everyone at Queen's Street is trying very hard to find him, before anyone else gets hurt.'

'Taking long enough,' observed Chuck Burchill dourly. (He was Charlie until his voice broke during the summer holiday.)

Brian shrugged apologetically. 'These things do take time. If it was easy to catch criminals nobody'd ever take the risk of being one. But they mostly get caught in the end.' This was a somewhat generous interpretation of the crime statistics, but one of a teacher's duties is to try and prevent his pupils joining the Mafia.

'It can't be that hard,' sniffed Chuck. 'All they've got to do is find someone who was in them two shops and here at school.'

'*Those* two shops,' Brian corrected automatically. He put aside his box of slides, prepared a quick math lesson instead.

'All right, let's think about that. Stand up, everyone who's been in Sav-U-Mor since Friday.' Virtually the whole class rose. 'Yes, me too. Now, those who've also been in Mr Simpson's the chemist's since then, stay on your feet—the rest sit down.' Most of the class, just a little disappointed, took their seats. Brian remained standing with the others.

'Yes, I've been in there too. OK, now how many of you'—he counted quickly—'four were in school on Monday afternoon?' For a moment Darren forgot himself and sat; he rose again quickly, with guilt all over his face. Kindly, Brian pretended not to notice. 'Everybody? Excellent. So in fact, five out of twenty-seven of us meet Chuck's criteria of being in all three places at relevant times. If we did the same with the rest of the population of Castlemere, we'd find that an awful lot of them were in both shops, and some of them had a perfectly good reason for being at the school. A lot of people work here. Some parents came to the sports matches, others came to collect their offspring after class.

'Do you see what I'm saying?—everything that's known about this man also applies to an awful lot of other people. Five of us in this one classroom. It isn't enough that any of us *could* have done what was done. The detectives at Queen's Street have to find the one person who *did* do it. That's what takes the time. Not just finding someone, but finding the right someone.'

When he came out of school at five to four he found the paintwork dribbling off his car in bubbly streaks that smelled of acetone.

He knew teachers who had, but he'd never been the victim of real vandalism before. He'd had one class whitewash his blackboard, and another go through his art books stamping ink fig leaves in all the appropriate places. But those were just pranks fuelled by a juvenile sense of humour. This was malice fuelled by fear. The paint-stripper flung over his car could as easily have been flung in his face.

His knees started to quiver. He turned round and walked back inside, and sat for ten minutes in the now empty staffroom before picking up the phone and calling his wife.

'HOW THE HELL did this get started?' demanded Liz furiously.
'It wasn't one of your jokes, was it?'

This was monstrously unfair. Brian Graham wasn't one of
life's jesters. His humour was piqued by entirely more subtle
stimuli.

He was still shaking. He'd left the car where it was: Liz called
the garage and arranged for them to collect and repair it as soon
as SOCO had finished dusting for fingerprints. Brian thought
that was going a bit far. Almost certainly some of the kids were
to blame, and though he'd expect them to pay for their fun he
couldn't see himself pressing charges.

'Liz, you know as much as I do. I was at the school when
the shower incident happened. I use the supermarket and the
chemist where the other stuff turned up. We were talking about
it in school and I said as much. I was just pointing out how hard
it'll be to find the culprit when so much of what you know about
him applies to half the town. Yes, me included. I didn't see any
need to pretend otherwise.'

'Mitchell Tyler said I should warn you. Even he'd heard your
name mentioned. I thought he was crazy.' Her voice went
thoughtful. 'As far as I know, the only one Tyler had talked to
at that point was Tony Woodall. Why would Woodall try to cast
suspicion on you?'

'To divert it away from him?'

She pictured the American flinging strong men around like
dolls inside the Gents under the castle. 'That's understandable.
He knew Tyler's reputation, he was scared of him and anxious
to get him off his back. You can't blame him for that.'

'*I* can!' exclaimed Brian.

Liz gave a tight smile. 'Come to that, so can I; but I can
understand it. It may not be significant.'

Brian sniffed. Now his nerve was steadying he had the surplus
emotional capacity to feel resentment. 'On the other hand, if
Woodall *is* responsible, and he *did* want to divert attention away
from himself, that's what he would do.'

Liz groaned. 'Oh God, Brian, what's happening to this town?
One psychopath has turned a bunch of perfectly ordinary people—people we know, that we see in the street every day—into

a panic-stricken mob. They've done damn near as much damage as the man they're so afraid of. They nearly killed the boy with the syringe: if this goes on much longer they will kill somebody. Can't they see they're a bigger danger to one another than the maniac we're looking for?'

'You said it: they're frightened. Frightened people aren't rational. They cling together for the same reason fish shoal: there's more inside where they're protected than outside where they're exposed. They feel safer. They seem not to have noticed that nature responded to the shoaling instinct by producing the shark.'

Liz chewed on her lip. 'Brian—would this be a good time to visit some relatives?'

He stared at her; concentrating on her driving, she avoided looking back. 'What relatives?' Their Christmas card list was no longer than Donovan's: Liz's father was the only surviving parent and neither of them had siblings.

'Evesham's pretty in the autumn,' Liz ventured.

'Your dad thinks I stopped you making a good marriage. I never see him without being told the Master of Fox Hounds was after you.'

It was quite true. Two more different men than Liz's father and husband would be difficult to imagine. Edgar Ward, at the age of seventy-two, had only this spring retired as secretary of the hunt: now he walked puppies for it instead. Brian Graham wasn't a militant vegetarian but nor would he deny his principles in the interests of a quiet life. Meetings between them were always fraught: however pretty Evesham was in autumn, evacuating Brian to his father-in-law's probably wasn't a great idea.

'All right, then—what about these art history courses you're always on about?' They had great difficulty choosing holidays. Liz craved action, Brian sought culture. 'Couldn't you take one of those for a fortnight?'

'I can't go anywhere for a fortnight. Not to Evesham, not on an art history course. Liz, I have a job! I can't just walk out on it because somebody vandalized my car.'

'Your job is teaching,' acknowledged Liz tightly. 'And some of your pupils threw acid over your car, and they did that because they think you used them as ammunition in a campaign of terror. Just how effective a teacher can you be in those circumstances?'

'Slightly more effective,' he retorted, nettled, 'than if I get known as a guy who'll run a mile at the first sign of trouble. Damn it, Liz, I don't know where you get the nerve to suggest it! I have sweated blood over some of the things you either had to do or felt you had to do. Do you think, because I didn't ask you to stay home, that it didn't worry me? Do you think I could see you in danger, and hurt, and shrug it off because after all it was only part of your job?

'I've gone to bed and cried because of the things your job makes you do, the risks it makes you take. But I don't think I've ever reproached you for it. I've certainly never asked you to give it up. So what gives you the right to ask me? Do you think your job is more important than mine? Or that you love me more than I love you? Because if that's it, you're wrong on both counts.'

She let the car coast to a halt by the kerb because she couldn't drive and give him the attention he deserved. She felt a tremor in her forearms and gripped the wheel to still it. 'You're right. I'm sorry. I never, never meant to suggest that what you do is unimportant. As for who loves who most, I've never thought of it as a competition.'

Mollified, Brian touched her arm. But he wouldn't change his mind. 'I'm not going anywhere. If I'm not at school on Monday morning, that'll be it: every pupil and half the staff will think I've run because I have something to hide. Unless you catch this man they'll go on thinking that. They'll think I'm someone who'd threaten kids, who'd hurt unsuspecting shoppers, for money. I don't want that hanging over me. I don't want to spend the rest of my career being thought of as the man who got away with murder.'

She leaned her body into his. 'God Almighty, Brian Graham, I love you so much!'

His long arm extended around her shoulders. He wasn't a handsome man by any standards, hadn't been when he was younger. But he had the sweetest smile. It still made her heart melt. 'Bet I love you more.'

AFTER SHE'D TAKEN him home she returned to Queen's Street. Shapiro was waiting for her with a very strange expression. 'Come and sit down. I have some news.'

'About the blackmailer?'

'I'm not sure.'

Liz stared at him. 'How can you not know?'

'Sit down and listen, then you tell me.'

Lucy Cole had called him. Donovan's dog had been restless last night, which didn't particularly surprise her; but this morning he'd refused his breakfast and that did. Brian Boru wasn't a dog to let emotion come between him and a meal. Lucy watched him, and by mid-morning was convinced the animal was ill.

She didn't know who Donovan's vet was but Keith Baker was the sturdiest of the local men so she phoned him. Sure enough, he knew Brian Boru and, pulling on his motorcycle gauntlets and cricket pads, agreed to examine him.

The dog was severely anaemic and when he took a blood sample for analysis the needle hole kept bleeding. That was enough for Baker to start treatment, but he waited for confirmation of his suspicions before phoning Lucy. Realizing the significance of what he'd found, she immediately phoned Shapiro.

'The dog was poisoned,' Shapiro told Liz. 'Warfarin. Only sheer bloody-mindedness kept him on his feet that long.'

'Warfarin?' Liz couldn't get past the extraordinary fact to start seeing the implications. 'Rat poison?'

'It's an anticoagulant, formulated to destroy rats without doing much damage to anything bigger. For something as big as a pit bull terrier to go down it must have ingested a hell of a lot.'

'Could he have got it accidentally?'

'Not in *Tara*'s chain locker. That was the dog's kennel, Donovan wouldn't have left dangerous substances in there.'

It made no sense. If Donovan put his dog in its kennel before illness overwhelmed him, either it would have stayed there until it was found or died of starvation, or it would have broken out. What was inconceivable was that it would break out, go scavenging for food, find enough rat poison to blitz eighty pounds of pit bull terrier, then come back and shut itself in the chain locker again.

'Then someone poisoned it.'

'I can't see any other explanation.'

'Not Donovan.'

Shapiro shook his head crisply. 'No. Not after the trouble he went to rescuing the thing. If he'd lost control of it he might have had to put it down, but he'd never have poisoned it.'

'Then someone else was on *Tara*. Someone we don't know about.'

That was how Shapiro read it too. 'Yes.'

Liz looked up, her eyes widening. 'So what we thought happened—we don't actually know that's what happened at all!'

'No.'

Finally she understood that gnomic remark about the blackmailer. 'Something happened to Donovan, but it may not have been cholera. And if it wasn't cholera, he may not be dead.'

'Yes,' said Shapiro simply. 'That's what I thought too. I wasn't sure if it was just wishful thinking, I wanted to see if you'd come to the same conclusion.'

'If there was another party involved'—she was thinking on her feet, working it out as she spoke—'then where we found *Tara* may not be where Donovan left her. She may have been moved. Put somewhere she could go unnoticed for days or even weeks.'

Shapiro was nodding sombrely. 'That isn't necessarily good news. The reason the divers haven't found a body could be they're looking in the wrong place.'

'So where's the right place?'

He gave a helpless shrug. 'I have no idea. I've been poring over a map of the area, and all I can come up with is that if the boat was moved it must have started off somewhere that was inconvenient for whoever moved it.'

Liz leaned over the map too, reviewing the few facts they

had. 'He passed the Posset Inn late on Monday, may have stayed nearby that night. The boat was found yesterday afternoon. If somebody felt the need to hide it, maybe he wouldn't want to be seen doing it in broad daylight. Let's say he took her to that mere Monday night, Tuesday night or Wednesday night; and he threw the dog poison so his barking wouldn't attract attention. Have you ever had a dog, Frank?'

Shapiro blinked. 'The kids had one once. I didn't see much of it. Why?'

'Dogs live for the moment. Never mind jam tomorrow, they'll wolf the dry crust today. They don't think they'll have a bit now and a bit later. If somebody threw food into the chain locker, Brian Boru would have eaten the lot within ten minutes.'

'So?'

'If he'd eaten rat poison on Monday night he wouldn't have been taken ill on Friday morning. I'll check this with Keith Baker, but I don't think it would have taken more than a day. The boat was found about four o'clock on Thursday, yes? I bet it was left there, and the dog poisoned, no later than Wednesday night. Perhaps around dawn: enough light to steer by, and find that overgrown channel, not so much the man at the tiller would be recognized if anyone saw him.'

'So there are two days we know nothing about,' said Shapiro. 'Tuesday and Wednesday. But if Donovan was on schedule for those two days he'd have passed the engine house at Sinkhole Fen, and he didn't. Even if the people there missed him, they'd also have had to miss *Tara* coming back again. He should have got there mid-afternoon on Tuesday. Where was he instead?'

'Whether or not he had cholera, he was certainly sick. Maybe by Tuesday he'd had enough—he tied up somewhere and went to bed. Maybe he was all right, just not going anywhere, until whatever it was that happened on Wednesday.'

'What happened on Wednesday? Hazard a guess.'

She spread a hand. 'A robbery?'

Shapiro was unconvinced. 'It's a narrowboat not Onassis's yacht: nobody'd break in thinking they were going to find jewellery and large wodges of cash. Plus, even below par, Donovan should have been able to see off a burglar. And how many burglars would have tackled a boat with that dog on board?'

'Maybe that's why it was poisoned.'

'Well, it didn't work, did it? The dog was still on its feet when the boat was found on Thursday afternoon.'

He was right: a burglary really didn't fit the facts.

'Could there have been a fight?' wondered Liz. 'Between Donovan and someone else; or else he stumbled on a crime in progress and tried to stop it. For whatever reason there was a fight, and Donovan'—she saw too late where this was going, had no choice but to follow—'got the worst of it. At which point the other party realized he was facing serious charges and tried to dispose of the evidence. He hid *Tara* in a backwater. He hoped that when she was eventually found there'd be nothing to connect her to him. He hid her, dealt with the dog, and then he left.'

'How?' asked Shapiro.

Puzzled, Liz frowned. 'How?'

'We know he didn't climb up the bank and walk away. Unless he can fly there was another boat.'

Liz nodded pensively. 'Maybe just a rowing boat. He towed it behind *Tara* till he reached the mere, then got into his dinghy and rowed back the way he'd come.'

'If he had a boat of his own, either he lives on the canal or he works on it. A passing maniac could conceivably have overpowered Donovan and taken his boat, but where would he have got hold of a dinghy?'

'He certainly knew something about boats,' agreed Liz. 'He knew where the mere was, and he could handle *Tara* well enough to get her inside without leaving any obvious signs. Also, he had to be able to lay his hands on large quantities of rat poison at short notice. We're talking about a local man.'

'All right. The incident—whatever it was—occurred somewhere we could connect him to. So he moved the boat. He didn't dare move the dog so he poisoned it. He may have expected the rat bait to work faster than it did.'

Shapiro's expression was full of misgivings. 'Someone went to a lot of trouble to cover up what happened. He wasn't that worried because he'd given Donovan a black eye. I think he did all this because he was afraid he could go to prison for a long time. Liz, it may be when we get to the truth of it, the bottom line is Donovan's still dead. Somebody moved that boat to hide something, and Donovan wasn't able to stop him. I think we have to accept that, at the very least, he's in deep trouble.'

Liz stood up, brisk and businesslike; only Shapiro, and Brian, knew her well enough to hear the quaver in her voice. 'Then we'd better find him. Frank, I know it's asking a lot right now. But we don't have any leads on the blackmailer that you need every available body to follow up. Give me Dick Morgan for the weekend. If we can't find Donovan, or find out what happened to him, in that time we'll be back on the team first thing Monday morning.'

She had a point. The blackmailing of Castlemere was the most important issue, but just now there wasn't much for CID to do. Public order was a matter for Superintendent Giles and the uniformed branch. When the man got in touch again there might be new evidence to consider, hopefully new leads to follow, and then Shapiro would want her with him. But until either there was another incident or they heard from him there was nothing Liz could do here. And for heaven's sakes, she was only talking about the local waterways, none of them more than ten miles from town. And she had her mobile phone—Shapiro could call her in any time he needed her.

Of course, the same had been true of Donovan, and he'd vanished without trace.

Or maybe just without leaving a trace where they'd been looking. If they were reading the signs correctly this time, progress could come when they started asking the right questions in the right places.

'All right,' he decided, 'take Morgan and see what you can find. But for pity's sake, Liz, stay in touch. I don't want you disappearing into a black hole too.'

She thanked him with her eyes and left.

When he was alone Shapiro thought for a few minutes. Then he picked up the phone and asked for SOCO. 'Any word yet on the analysis of the flu remedy you took from DS Donovan's boat?'

'Just got it here, sir,' said Sergeant Tripp. 'Shall I bring it up?'

'Just give me the highlights. What was in it?'

'Cough medicine, sir.'

'Just cough medicine.'

'Just cough medicine.'

Shapiro put the phone down. He started to smile. It was too soon to celebrate, but at least now there was a little room for hope.

FIVE

ELPHIE WASN'T the only one in East Beckham who was fascinated by a strange face. One after another they wandered in and took a place at Sarah Turner's table as if they ate there every night: Dr Chapel, bent and elderly, a dry stick of a man; Mr and Mrs Vickery, he the foreman at The Flower Mill, she the local shopkeeper; Alan Hunsecker who maintained the machinery on which the business, like all modern agriculture, depended; three generations of Turners.

Elphie dragged her father over before he'd had the chance to wash in order to perform formal introductions. 'This is Donovan. You haven't seen him since he woke up.'

The square, solidly built man in cords and a Barbour extended a soil-grimed hand apologetically. 'Everything's urgent with Elphie. Simon Turner. I'm glad to see you on the mend.'

'I'm grateful for your help,' responded Donovan. 'I'll try not to impose on you much longer.'

'No problem,' said Turner. 'Stay as long as you want.' He excused himself and disappeared into the scullery.

Elphie stayed with Donovan, pressing her small hand determinedly into his. He gave her a startled glance but didn't shake her off. She led him to the table and sat him down, seating herself beside him.

Creakily, Dr Chapel took the chair on his other side. He leaned one elbow on the table and peered disconcertingly into Donovan's face. Then he delivered his verdict. 'You're lucky to be alive, young man. The canal's no place to be with pneumonia. A canny doctor and good nursing: that's all that stood between you and the Grim Reaper.'

Donovan launched once more, rather wearily, into his paean of gratitude; but Chapel cut him off with a cackle like sticks breaking underfoot. 'Don't want your thanks, young man; good to get a bit of practice from time to time; Elphie's asthma and Alan hitting his thumb with a wrench is about all the doctoring I do these days. Nice to know I can still tackle something more interesting if I have to.'

Elphie piped up, 'Donovan's a policeman.'

'Yes, I know,' nodded Chapel encouragingly. His eyes, pale with age, switched back to Donovan. 'Traffic branch?'

'CID.'

Simon Turner returned, clean, and took his seat at the table, which was Sarah's cue to serve. Donovan thought the guests must have surprised her no less than him: she'd added to the stew anything that came to hand.

'If anyone hasn't got enough,' she said, 'I'll butter some bread.'

But everyone made declining noises; and anyway, they weren't there for the food, they were there to check out the visitor.

Donovan was aware he was being checked out and didn't really know why. He couldn't understand what significance his presence here could have for these people. Except perhaps Sarah who'd looked after him and Chapel whose professional interest was engaged; and Elphie, who didn't need reasons for what she did and felt. But the others? He couldn't imagine why they were looking at him, covertly, over the stew, as if he'd arrived in a puff of blue smoke and they weren't sure yet whether he was the Demon King or the Fairy Godmother.

East Beckham was a bit off the beaten track, but surely no-where was that secluded any more? Didn't they have television? Surely he wasn't their only chance this year to see a face they didn't grow up with? He hung on to his patience and bore their scrutiny without comment, but in the privacy of his own head he was thinking this place needed a good bus service: they lived in one another's pockets too much to be healthy.

After tea Sarah chivvied them gently on their way. Only Dr Chapel remained at the big table, oblivious to her hints, propped on bony elbows and talking with Simon about the pests and diseases of commercial horticulture.

At length he straightened and turned his pale-blue gaze on Donovan. 'We must be boring you rigid, young man. But all our livelihoods depend on the flowers. When your whole way of life, and that of everyone you know and care about, is tied up in one undertaking, you have to get it right. You can't take any risks. You do what needs to be done.'

'I guess,' said Donovan, uninterested.

'I suppose it's the same with police work. People say ends shouldn't justify means, but to some extent they have to. Certain ends have to be achieved. Simon has to have a product to sell, and you have to keep the peace, and sometimes how you do that is less important than the absolute need to get it done. Am I right?'

Donovan shrugged. He didn't know why this desiccated leprechaun of a man made him uneasy but he did. 'Only so far. I don't know nothing about flowers, but what policemen can do is pretty well set out in law. We overstep the mark and we lose the collar. It fairly focuses your mind on the contents of the Police & Criminal Evidence Act.'

'Don't you find that frustrating? Don't you sometimes think the law should take account of the greater good of the greater number?'

'The greatest number is still made up of individuals. If you can't protect the individual, another name for the greater number is a mob.'

Dr Chapel gave a disappointed little snort. 'And I took you for a thinking man! You're just a tool of government like all the rest.'

There were days—there were whole weeks—when Donovan felt that way too. It didn't stop him stinging at the scorn of a man who, however deft he was with a hypodermic, hadn't earned the right to judge either him or his profession.

'Yeah? Well, you can thank your lucky stars that it's true. In a democracy, government is the agent of the people—that's you. You wouldn't want to live in a country where the police force isn't accountable to an elected government.'

With a last disparaging sniff Chapel lost interest in the conversation. He switched his attention back to Turner. 'About those weevils, Simon. They're your glasshouses, you must do what you think best, but I think you'll need to fumigate. I think if you leave it too long you'll have a problem you won't be able to contain. Better a deliberate sacrifice than to lose everything you've planted.'

It wasn't what Turner wanted to hear. His round, open face was worried as he raked strong fingers through his light brown hair. 'I can't believe that's necessary. There has to be an alternative.'

'Oh, there is,' allowed Chapel. 'It's to wait and see what happens. But if the buggers get out of control, it'll be too late—you'll have lost your one chance of dealing with them. You're too nice, Simon, that's the problem. You always think there's a nice, tidy solution. But there isn't. Sometimes the only answer to plague is fire.'

He'd had his say on that subject too. He pushed his chair away from the table and straightened as much as his old frame would allow. He called through the scullery door, 'Thanks for the meal, Sarah. See you tomorrow.'

She hurried out, stripping off her apron. 'Don't come out specially, Tom, they're dank old days and you want to keep the damp off your chest. As you can see'—she nodded in Donovan's direction—'your job is done.'

The dry-stick hands gave her shoulders an avuncular squeeze and Chapel cackled at her fondly. 'Being a doctor is like having the contract to paint the Forth rail bridge: you never finish, you just start again somewhere else. Don't worry about my chest: it's survived seventy fenland winters, I dare say it'll cope with one more. I'll see you tomorrow.'

She let him out at the back door. Donovan listened but didn't hear a car. 'He walked here?'

Sarah looked at him, momentarily distracted. 'What? Oh—yes. Nobody in East Beckham lives more than two hundred yards away. The whole village would fit into a good-sized football stadium.'

'It's as well to get on with your neighbours then,' he observed.

'Yes,' said Sarah sombrely. 'We depend on one another for everything out here. If you want a private life you have to live in a city: in a small village there's no such thing.'

Donovan wasn't quite sure how to put this. 'You do know Castlemere's only about ten miles away?'

That made her laugh. 'Only as the crow flies. The village mentality takes the scenic route.'

She returned to the scullery to finish the washing-up. Donovan followed and started drying. 'How long has The Flower Mill been here?'

'The business, about three hundred years; this house, a hundred and forty; my husband's family, four generations.'

'It's a good thing Simon wanted to take over,' said Donovan. He looked up from the plates, wryly. 'Or is that not how it works with a family business?—do you have no choice?'

Sarah looked round at him, her head a little on one side, slow to answer. 'No, there's always a choice. There has to be—even in a family business, not everyone is born with the same talents. Running The Flower Mill takes a knowledge of horticulture, but it also takes business acumen, an ability to manage people and salesmanship. Robert, my husband, had all of that, but there was no guarantee his son would.'

'You could always have got in a manager.'

'In fact,' she said, a thread of emotion breaking the surface of her voice, 'my son Jonathan was going to manage the place when Robert retired. He loved the business. He was tramping round in Robert's cast-off wellies within days of us coming here. While Simon was off seeing the world Jonathan was studying commercial horticulture in France. We thought the future was secure.'

Donovan wasn't sure if she wanted to be prompted, but the habit was hard to kick. 'What happened?'

She took an unsteady breath. 'Robert had a stroke and died. We'd only been married six years—he was fifty-four years old. I was so—angry. But at least I had Jonathan; and so did the Mill. We were going to manage.

'Then Jonathan turned his tractor over and drowned in a ditch.'

Donovan had always supposed his family was God's punchbag, for thumping when things were going badly in the celestial mansion. It came as a shock to learn that on alternate days He was thumping the Turners.

All he could say was, 'God in heaven!' and it was more an accusation than a prayer.

'Robert had been dead just six weeks,' continued Sarah Turner. 'We hadn't got the will sorted out or anything. I thought we were going to lose everything, I didn't see how we could continue.

'But Simon, bless him, after misspending his youth for five solid years, set about picking up the pieces. What he didn't know he found out; what he couldn't do he got someone to show him. Of course it was his inheritance, it was in his interests to look after the business; but it was a lot of work. He could have sold up, used the money to go travelling again. Everyone in East Beckham owes him a debt of gratitude. None of us would be here if The Flower Mill had been sold.'

'I nearly said something very stupid,' Donovan said apologetically. 'I nearly said You were lucky!'

Sarah gave a rueful little smile. 'It's all right, I know what you mean. It could have been worse.'

'How old was your son?'

'He was'—a fractional pause while she did the sum—'twenty-one, just a couple of years younger than Simon.'

Looking on the bright side wasn't something Donovan was good at but he felt it incumbent upon him to try. 'And now there's a new generation. Is Elphie horticulturally inclined?'

'Elphie would make a good Flower Fairy but I can't see her running the business. I keep telling Simon to find himself a big bruiser of a wife and start raising tractor drivers!'

'There's no chance,' hazarded Donovan, 'Elphie's mother and him might get back together?'

'None,' replied Sarah Turner crisply. It was an effective end to the conversation. They finished the pots in silence.

It was only half-past seven but Donovan was tired. He made

his excuses and hauled himself upstairs. Lacking the energy to undress he sprawled on top of his bed and fell asleep.

He was woken an hour later by the sound of a car in the yard. It was none of his business but old habits die hard: he got up and trudged over to the window. But he was too slow: it had already gone.

Elphie must have heard him moving: it was mere seconds before there came a light but still somehow peremptory knock at his door quickly followed by the child herself, all bustling intensity, carrying a photograph in a frame. She plonked down on his bed and waited impatiently for him to join her.

'This is us,' she said firmly. One narrow finger tapped the glass as she spoke. 'That's Nana. That's Grandpa Robert—I never knew him. That's Daddy. That's Dr Chapel—he was Grandpa Robert's bestest man. That's Uncle Jonathan: I never knew him either. That's my mommy. I *did* know her,' she said reflectively, 'but I don't remember. And that's the vicar.'

'Did you know him?' asked Donovan solemnly.

The child gave a wide beam. 'Don't be silly, I wasn't borned then!'

Donovan studied the photograph with the required gravity. It was the Turners' wedding day: the usual faintly bemused expressions of two families with little in common brought together in front of a church none of them would normally have ventured into, posing with a man in a long white dress they would usually have crossed roads to avoid.

Even without Elphie's assistance he'd have been able to identify both Sarah and Simon. Twenty years had passed, turning the bride in her pretty floral dress and hat into a woman in her late fifties and the round-faced youth beside her into a father and a businessman. Robert Turner was easy to identify too, if only by his enormous smile and the proprietorial arm with which he encompassed his new wife. He must have been ten years older than Sarah, Donovan surmised. Of course, it was a second marriage for both of them.

A process of elimination allowed him to name one more member of the party—Jonathan, Sarah's son, on the bridegroom's other side. Six years after this photograph was taken

he lay dead in a ditch. He stared out of the picture frame with
a certain wariness, less enthusiasm for the proceedings than the
other parties to them—almost as if (and this was Donovan's
Celtic feyness at work) he suspected this wasn't the best day's
work from his point of view. If his mother had married a postman he'd still be alive.

And that was Elphie's mother, was it? Donovan peered closer.
She was older than Simon—four or five years, which is a lot at
that age. Of course, it wasn't at that age that they got together.
If Elphie was eight it may have been ten years after this family
group was gathered, and five years between late twenties was a
very different thing.

So who was she? A bridesmaid, apparently, so presumably a
friend of Sarah's. Or perhaps a relative; which made the falling-
out between them more difficult than if Elphie's mother had
been a stranger when Simon brought her home. What was it all
about? Elphie's condition? A damaged child puts a big strain on
a relationship. Or just two people who found they didn't like
one another as much as they had loved?

Donovan caught himself trying to interrogate a bunch of people in a photograph and decided that even for him this was
obsessive behaviour. Their relationships were not only their own
affair, they were ancient history, no possible concern of his.

More to be polite than because he wanted to know, he said,
'What's your mammy's name?'

'I don't know,' said Elphie.

Donovan blinked. 'OK.' So she wanted him to see her
mother's photograph but not to know her name. That was all
right. The child was a law unto herself: he knew that already.

'Nana says I mustn't ask about her,' Elphie confided solemnly. 'She says she let us all down and isn't part of this family
any more. But she is pretty, isn't she?' There was a wistful note
in her high light voice that tweaked at Donovan's heart strings.

'She certainly is,' he agreed firmly. 'And you know, just 'cos
people can't be there any more, doesn't mean they're entirely
gone. There's lots of your mammy in you. That means, anywhere you go, you'll always have a bit of her with you.'

He was rewarded with a beam like sunrise breaking through

Elphie's sharp little face. ''S right,' she said with conviction; and hugging the photograph to her narrow chest she marched away.

IT WAS AFTER ELEVEN when Liz and DC Morgan called it a night. With the car's interior light on and the Ordnance Survey map spread across their knees they ticked off the black square that was the last house they'd visited and exchanged a discouraged glance.

'Well, it's perfectly obvious then, isn't it?' said Liz wearily. 'If none of the people living in any of these houses saw either *Tara* or Donovan, either on the canal or in the mere, there's only one logical explanation. Alien abduction.'

Dick Morgan thought for a moment, then shook his head lugubriously. 'Doesn't make sense.'

Liz was too tired to chuckle. 'None of it makes sense. Why pick on that bit?'

'They're aliens,' said Morgan, 'not masochists. If they'd abducted the skipper thirty-six hours ago, they'd have sent him back by now.'

SIX

SOMEHOW HIS BODY was aware that it had already slept too long. Donovan woke before six, while the sky was still dark and the house silent. He washed and dressed and quietly went down to the kitchen. Still there were no signs of life. He supposed flowers were less demanding of their farmers than dairy cattle, which even on a Saturday would be bawling to be milked by now.

As he sat at the farmhouse table, hands cradled round a mug of tea, gradually he became aware he was being watched. He didn't think Sarah or Simon were spying on him through the crack of the scullery door, and there was nothing sinister about Elphie however odd her behaviour. So he didn't understand the unease he was beginning to feel. He owed his life to these people: how could he feel threatened by them?

It had to be a hangover from his illness, like the ache in his chest and the lack of stamina. Normally he could go all day on caffeine and acrimony: having no energy was a strange, rather frightening sensation. The ability to keep going when others had stopped had got him out of a lot of trouble: he liked knowing that, as a last resort, he could always run like hell. Today he'd have had trouble staying ahead of Dr Chapel.

He sipped his tea and avoided looking at the scullery door, and observed aloud, in a tone of some regret: 'Well, if no one's awake, I suppose I'll have to find the boat on my own.'

He got up and headed for the back door, and when he got there Elphie was waiting, thrusting slender limbs into a bright red duffle coat and green Wellington boots.

He pretended surprise. 'I didn't know you were up. Can you tell me where my boat is? I need to feed my dog.'

'I'll show you.'

Donovan was glad of her company. The fen was a wet wilderness, a man could lose his bearings out there.

But they weren't ready to leave yet. Elphie regarded him critically and shook her head. 'You'll catch your death.' She went back to the scullery, returned with her father's coat. It was too broad for Donovan but he hadn't one of his own. They'd brought him here wrapped in a blanket, hadn't thought to bring him something to go back in.

Elphie set out across the yard, skipping in her giant boots and trilling a high, light, wordless ditty like birdsong. Donovan was too slow for her: she grabbed his hand and tried to hurry him along. Failure made her giggle. Her pleasure in the stupid game made him grin.

But they weren't going the right way. About the only thing he knew about East Beckham was that it lay north of the canal. Elphie was tugging him further north, towards the peaty heart of the fen. Donovan stopped and looked around, noting the rising sun, checking his references. Then he pointed. 'The canal's that way.'

Elphie nodded energetically, the floss of pale hair flying. 'The pond's this way.'

'Pond?'

'They moved your boat. Why's it called *Tara?*'

Her lightning changes of subject left him floundering. 'It's where the old kings of Ireland ruled.'

'Are you from Ireland?'

'Yeah.'

'Are you a king?'

He barked a laugh. 'I'm a policeman.'

'I saw the queen on the telly. Her horse did a poo.'

'They do,' agreed Donovan lugubriously. His grandfather worked with horses. The first paid job the young Caolan ever had was shovelling up after the damn things.

Elphie headed north-east, following a path that only her eyes could see. After two fields the plough gave way to a wasteland of reeds and sere autumn grasses, waving together with a constant faint susurrus like a convention of sotto voce gossips. The ground grew wetter underfoot: drainage was too expensive to squander on land that wasn't growing anything. There was no evidence that anyone had been here for months—except possibly Elphie, who could walk without leaving footprints.

Even looking for it, Donovan saw the pond barely soon enough to avoid walking into it. The high featureless reeds parted before his hands and there it was, an expanse of still water mirroring the silver sky.

If he'd been here thirty-six hours ago he'd have seen the bow of his boat sticking out of the reeds of the far bank. If he'd been here twenty-four hours ago he'd have found Sergeant Warren and her team still working methodically up and down the shallow mere in search of his drowned body. But yesterday, the best search they could conduct having proved fruitless and with a new slant on events that suggested Donovan may never have been here, they'd packed up and left. *Tara* too had gone. Only the broken reeds along the banks and at the channel hinted at recent activity.

'I'm looking,' said Donovan carefully, 'but I'm not seeing anything.'

'It was here,' said Elphie, eyes wide in her little pointed face.

'OK,' said Donovan, non-committal. 'Shall we try the towpath?'

She nodded energetically, and taking his hand once more steered him round the edge of the mere, finally heading south.

But they never got there. This had been a mistake: Donovan wasn't strong enough to tramp round the fen. When their way crossed a stony track with a bit of a bank beside it he sank down with relief, out of breath and shaking his head. 'I'm sorry, Elphie, I'm whacked. How much further is it?'

She considered a moment. 'Little long.' Which he took to mean more than a step, less than a trek. Half a mile? If she wanted him to go another half mile she'd have to carry him.

He was looking up the track, supposing it led back to the house, wondering how far that was, when rescue arrived: Simon Turner riding a quad bike and towing a trailer. 'Here you are. Mum was beginning to worry.'

'Sorry about that,' said Donovan, hauling himself to his feet. 'I was looking for my boat. I think we got lost.'

Elphie objected to that. 'It was there before. It's gone.'

Turner nodded. 'We took her down to Posset. She'll be safer there.'

Donovan couldn't remember where he'd finally tied up, maybe it hadn't been a great choice. Certainly *Tara* would be safe enough at the Posset Inn. 'What about the dog?'

'George is looking after him. We thought he'd be more comfortable in one of the old stables than shut up in the hold of your boat.'

Donovan nodded. George Jackson, the publican, knew Brian Boru well enough to treat him with respect and not fear: he was less likely to cause pandemonium in the back yard of the Posset Inn than at The Flower Mill. 'Can you give me a lift down there?'

'Of course. But not in this. Let's get back to the house. You look all in. Get in the trailer, the pair of you.'

Donovan was too tired to care about his dignity: he did as he was bid. Elphie climbed in beside him, and they bumped back up the track to The Flower Mill.

Sarah met them in the yard as if they'd been missing much longer than half an hour. 'Is everything all right?' she asked, scanning their faces in turn so Donovan wasn't sure whom she was asking.

Some sort of an explanation seemed to be required. 'I was looking for my boat. But apparently it's been moved.'

She looked at Turner, then quickly back again. 'Yes. It was— a little in the way. The men took it to—'

'Posset,' said Turner. 'I told him. I said I'd run him over later. When he's up to it.'

Sarah nodded quickly. 'When you're up to it.' She shepherded them inside, took their coats, exclaimed over Donovan's wet feet, sat them down at the table and began serving food as if the sheer volume of it would pin them in place.

'I'm sorry if I worried you,' said Donovan, eating and watching her face at the same time. 'I shouldn't have taken Elphie without asking.'

'I wasn't worried about Elphie,' said Sarah dismissively. 'She knows every reed and pool out there. I was worried about you. You're not strong enough to go wandering off like that. Not yet.'

He couldn't argue with that. 'I could call a friend, get someone to pick me up.'

'Or you could stay put until you're feeling better.'

She managed to make him feel ungrateful for trying to leave. 'I have to report for work on Monday. If I don't they'll send out a search party. Can I phone from here?'

'Of course you can,' she said negligently. 'Though the line's a bit unreliable—all those miles of wire stretching from the fen. Finish your breakfast. It's still early, there's no rush.'

Reunited with his coat, Turner went out as soon as the meal was done, taking Elphie with him. Donovan went on sitting at the table.

'I'm confused,' he said. 'That place Elphie calls the pond. If *Tara* was in there, how could she be in anyone's way?'

Again the sharp glance. 'She wasn't in the pond. You tied up at the towpath. That's where we found you.'

Donovan frowned. 'Then why—?'

Sarah Turner swivelled from the sink to look at him. 'Cal, you mustn't put too much stock in what Elphie says. She's a dear child but she's no more reliable than the phone. She's eight; she looks about six; mentally she is and will remain about four years old. You need to make allowances. I don't know why she took you to the pond. Your boat's at Posset.'

He changed the subject. 'She showed me your wedding photo.'

'Did she,' Sarah said evenly, stacking the pots.

'What was her mother's name?'

The steady clatter of plates broke momentarily before continuing. 'Her mother?'

'In the photograph.' Donovan frowned, puzzled that she didn't understand. 'Next to you. I thought she was your bridesmaid.'

Mrs Turner shook her head. 'That's what I mean about Elphie. The girl in the picture: she *was* my bridesmaid but she wasn't

Elphie's mother. Elphie never knew her mother. I think that bothers her. I think she just picked a pretty woman in a family photo and adopted her. It's not important, it's not worth arguing with her. Just don't take anything she says as gospel.'

Donovan could understand that. 'OK. Can I try the phone now?'

'In the hall.'

He knew as soon as he picked it up that the line was dead. Jiggling the bar didn't help.

Sarah stuck her head out of the kitchen as he put it down. 'No luck?'

'No.'

'Try again later.'

'I hope my dog's all right. He's—a bit funny.' He meant, if he wasn't fed on time he might make his own arrangements.

'I'm sure he's fine.'

SATURDAY MORNINGS in the Graham household varied enormously. If there was a push on—some sort of crisis, a crime wave crashing on the beach of Castlemere—it was a day like any other and Liz would be in the office or on the road by eight o'clock. If she had the day off—which is to say she not only had the day off officially but in practice as well—she'd feed her horse at seven and then disappear back under the covers until mid-morning. It was her chance to catch up on lost sleep.

Brian didn't have many late nights during the week but he too tended to lie in on Saturday mornings. It was his chance to make up for lost time as well.

Today, though, Liz fed Polly half an hour early and collected Dick Morgan from Chevening at seven. They'd visited every property on or within half a mile of the canal's north bank last night, and found no one who'd seen Donovan or his boat between Monday and Thursday afternoon. Now they were going to doorstep the southern bank, hoping for better luck.

It was slow work. The properties weren't arranged in neat rows along the canal, they were scattered in ones and twos separated by stretches of towpath that could be walked but not driven. Nor did the road run conveniently parallel to the water.

It wandered off through Chevening and Fletton, and hamlets half the size. They managed to tick off five addresses in the first hour, seven in the second.

At five past nine Liz's mobile rang. She pulled over to answer it, was surprised to find herself talking to Keith Baker, the vet.

'Thought you'd want to know,' he said. 'Donovan's dog died in the night.'

Liz shut her eyes and vented a soft little pant. It wasn't the loss of the dog that distressed her. It wasn't a nice dog, a dog you could pat and get a wave of the tail in return, a dog you could slip half a Rich Tea biscuit under the coffee table. It was a pit bull terrier in all but name, jaws on legs, a dog that only chewed slippers to get at the feet inside. But it was Donovan's dog, and losing it seemed to lessen the chances of finding him.

It was nonsense, of course, the two things were unconnected; still she felt knocked back by the news.

When she'd caught her breath she said, 'Was it warfarin?'

'Oh yeah,' drawled Baker. 'A lot.'

'When?'

'Can't be too precise, but probably late Wednesday or early Thursday. This is rat bait, yeah?—it takes both quantity and a little time to inflict damage on a big dog.'

Which was pretty much what she'd been hoping to hear, though she'd have preferred to hear it in other circumstances. 'It had to be rat bait? There's no other way he could have got it?'

'No likely one. People take it for circulatory problems, but even if Donovan had a dicky heart it would have taken more than the odd pill dropped on the carpet to do this. No, we're talking poison.'

'That just may be good news,' said Liz. 'Donovan didn't poison his dog, so someone else was on the boat. It may be that person knows where he is, what happened to him.'

Baker was reluctant to sully the silver lining she'd managed to find in the cloud of misfortune. But it needed saying. 'Inspector—if you're thinking that person may be holding him, I'm not sure that *is* good news. I wouldn't wish my worst enemy in the hands of someone who'd kill a dog with rat poison.'

SEVEN

SATURDAY MORNING'S post brought a letter for Shapiro.

It was a very short letter. 'I want my money. If you don't act soon I will.' He'd used the same stencil and felt-tip as before. The first-class stamp was franked in Cambridge the previous day.

While he was waiting for Sergeant Tripp to collect the letter, Shapiro found himself thinking not about the contents but the author. He was beginning to build up a picture of him.

He was a realist. A million pounds was the right sum to ask for. He could have asked for more but he'd have had less chance of getting it. Half a dozen major retailers could raise that money between them without difficulty. The insurers for just one big one might look at the demand, and the risk of litigation if someone died, and decide to pay up. For five million pounds they'd have fought; for one, in purely financial terms it might be cheaper not to.

He felt to be in command of the situation. He knew the effect he'd had on this town, knew the terror any further episodes would provoke. He believed that ultimately Castlemere would put its safety above its bank-balance.

He was watching developments. He knew no efforts were being made to gather the ransom, and he blamed Shapiro. That wasn't particularly perceptive: detectives are paid to catch criminals, not make deals with them. Everyone else involved was entitled to take a pragmatic view, but Shapiro would negotiate only if he believed the alternative was untenable. The one thing worse than paying ransom was seeing hostages die. By addressing his demands to the senior detective the blackmailer was saying he was willing to go that far.

And he was meticulous. The envelope was addressed to 'Detective Superintendent F. Shapiro, CID, Queen's Street Police Station, Queen's Street, Castlemere.' He prided himself on getting the details right.

If anyone had asked Frank Shapiro his opinion of psychological profiling he'd have sunk his double chin on his chest, smiled his avuncular smile and said that, while these new-fangled ideas had their place, it was hard to beat good old-fashioned police work as a means of bringing criminals to justice. He liked to think of himself as a good old-fashioned policeman.

But actually he'd absorbed a lot of new ideas and psychological profiling was something he did rather well. If Liz had been here he'd have bounced his ideas off her, but she was on important business too and up against the clock even more than he was. Today he'd have to bounce them off himself, like a solo game of ping-pong.

So what else did he know about the blackmailer? Well, he knew that he was a headcase. Obsessive, compulsive, megalomaniac. Clever, and proud of it. This man might not have a criminal record—not for blackmail, not for anything. He was clever enough and confident enough to go straight for the big one. He didn't need to start small and learn from his mistakes: he'd pride himself he wouldn't make any.

'And so far you haven't made many,' Shapiro murmured aloud. One of the advantages of seniority is that while people may doubt your sanity they don't often challenge it.

But there was someone out there who knew what the man was capable of. Family—not friends, he wouldn't have any, but acquaintances, workmates. They knew he was dangerous, even if he'd never done anything to prove it. They might feel silly for being afraid of him, but they knew instinctively that he was a man to avoid, not to cross. Rooms would go quiet when he walked into them. People would stand rather than sit next to him on buses.

'A socialized psychopath,' said Shapiro judiciously.

'Pardon, sir?' said Sergeant Tripp, standing patiently in the doorway.

'Just thinking aloud,' said Shapiro, defensive in spite of himself.

'What kind of psychopath?' asked SOCO.

'A socialized one. It means he knows better than to wear his hat sideways and claim to be Napoleon. He can conform to any standards of behaviour required of him, but it's an act. He has no sense of right and wrong. He wants something, he takes it. He has no sense of sharing the world: he thinks it's here for his convenience, that he has a right to use it as he chooses. He neither knows nor cares how other people feel. In a very real sense he's unaware of their capacity for feeling.'

'Really, sir,' said Tripp stolidly. 'So we're not looking for a minister of the cloth, say.'

Any time Shapiro felt to be rooted in the past, the history of police detection rather than its future, talking to Sergeant Tripp cheered him up immensely. 'Probably not,' he agreed. 'Or a doctor, a teacher, a writer or a musician. He could be an engineer or a scientist. He could be a financial genius. But he won't be a professional gambler because he can't read faces.'

SOCO pulled out a chair and sat down. He was getting interested in this. 'Not a family man, then. More of a loner.'

Shapiro nodded. 'He may live alone. Or some poor woman may have taken him at his own valuation long enough to come under his sway; in which case she'll be with him until he's tired of her because she'll be too afraid to make the break herself. So he could be a family man with a house full of children. But I bet he never goes to parent-teacher meetings, takes them fishing or cheers from the sidelines as they shoot past the post.'

That struck a chord with him; in fact, two. 'I must check with Castle High and see if any parents were attending matches for the first time.' What he thought and didn't say was: The sort of father I was, in fact.

A movement in the doorway made him look up. DC Scobie had joined them. 'Forensics on the phone for Sergeant Tripp, sir.'

Shapiro excused him with a nod. 'Tell them there's another

letter on its way to them. We might get lucky: he might have left something on the paper.'

'Or the stamp,' said Tripp.

Shapiro frowned. 'The stamp?'

Sometimes Sergeant Tripp wondered about the people they made up to superintendent these days. 'Probably he licked it,' he explained, as if to a child. 'If he's a secretor—if markers for his blood-group appear in his saliva—that's a physical link between him and the crime.'

'Will there be enough genetic material for them to work with?' asked Shapiro, impressed.

'Won't know that till they've tried, sir,' Sergeant Tripp said heavily.

Shapiro waved Scobie inside. 'Talk to the sports teachers at the school. I want to know if any of the parents shocked everyone rigid by turning up to watch.'

Scobie nodded pensively. Pensive was not something usually associated with the largest detective constable in Castlemere. 'It might not have been the first time. It might have been the second.'

Shapiro raised an enquiring eyebrow.

'He could have been at the last match too. To check the layout, the timings, whether he'd be noticed if he went near the shower block. And so he wouldn't stand out like a sore thumb when it mattered.'

'Good thinking, constable,' said Shapiro. But it was disconcerting to be out-thought twice in one morning. Tripp he could understand, the man was a specialist in his own field, but Scobie? Being out-thought by Scobie was like losing a game of Snap to Stevie Wonder.

Then he went downstairs to see Superintendent Giles, and after that he called another meeting. Same guest list; pretty much the same subject.

'He's getting impatient. He wants his money.'

The Mayor sucked in a deep breath, the Chief Executive nodded, the chairman of the Chamber of Trade sniffed. Kenneth Simpson looked at Tony Woodall who looked, edgily, at Mitchell Tyler.

Tyler said baldly, 'But he isn't going to get it, is he?'

Shapiro folded his hands on the table before him. 'My advice hasn't changed. But I promised to keep you apprised of developments, and this is one.'

'We're going to have to pay,' said the Mayor, looking round the table for support. 'Aren't we? Sooner or later we're going to have to pay. We can't let people die.'

'It really isn't that simple,' murmured Shapiro.

'Then let's *make* it simple,' said Tyler tersely. 'Sav-U-Mor will not contribute to any pay-off. It will instruct its insurers not to make a contribution on its behalf, and warn them that it will take its business elsewhere—*all* its business—if they make a contribution on anyone else's behalf. We won't pay ransom, or condone payment by any other party.' His teeth glittered wolfishly. 'That clear enough?'

A shock wave travelled round the table. These were important people in Castlemere, they weren't used to being mugged. A lot of throats were cleared, several sentences begun and aborted.

Though he wasn't wearing it, Derek Dunstan felt the weight of the mayoral chain pressing him to respond. 'Mr Tyler, there's more at stake here than Sav-U-Mor's profit margin. I appreciate that's why you're here, but you must appreciate that the safety of the people of Castlemere is what concerns the rest of us. If they can best be protected by finding the money, then find it we must.'

Donald Chivers was a successful businessman, he hadn't achieved that by virtue of his timid nature. He came to his feet like a disturbed bear. 'You may not be aware, Mr Tyler, that the Castlemere outlet of Sav-U-Mor is a member of the Chamber of Trade and as such is bound by decisions of the Chamber. If the traders of this town decide to pay up, Sav-U-Mor will abide by that decision. Don't think you can save your share of the cost by taking the moral high ground. If the police can't catch this man there's only one way to go, and the big players aren't going to walk off and leave the little men to foot the bill. Any attempt to shirk your obligations and we'll be obliged to take legal advice.'

Shapiro had to admire the man. Sav-U-Mor was a multinational; Mitchell Tyler was the man they employed to remove obstacles to their progress; and Donald Chivers, managing director of Chivers Sporting Equipment, with two stores and a pitch at the weekly market, was marking his card. He must have known about the Grand Jury hearing. Perhaps he thought the police station was the only place he could threaten Tyler with impunity.

As an officer of the local authority Dick Travis had spent much of his career throwing buckets of cold water over scrapping councillors. He did it automatically now, like a mother making peace between rowing children. 'I'm sure it's premature to consider the legal position. I'm sure we can find a consensus—in fact, we have to. The people in this room have to decide on the best way forward. It'll be unfortunate if we reach the wrong decision but worse if we fail to reach any decision at all. The people of Castlemere are looking to us for guidance.

'Last time we spoke we agreed to hold out. Recent events seem to have shaken that resolve. But I don't suppose anyone would want to pay if an arrest was imminent. So—Mr Giles, Mr Shapiro—can we ask, what are the chances?'

This was by its nature a CID matter. Superintendent Giles looked across the table, and even at that distance Shapiro could read his mind. Please, he was saying, whatever you tell them, don't tell them 'Two—small and none!'

Shapiro eased himself to his feet with a sigh. 'Mr Travis, I'd love to tell this man where to go on the grounds that we're going to have him in custody before he can do any more harm. But I don't want to mislead you. We have a number of suspects. We may have to eliminate them all from our inquiries as the evidence mounts; or we may be able to narrow the list down to one, clap him on the shoulder and say, ''Ah-ha, chummy, got you bang to rights''.'

Most of the men round this table had known each other for years. Shapiro's brand of gentle irony was as familiar to them as the 1950s B-movies on which it drew. But Mitchell Tyler only met him this week, had never known anyone like him before. One eyebrow climbed.

Shapiro waved an apologetic hand. 'I'm sorry, Mr Tyler, you

must think you've stumbled into an episode of the Keystone Cops. Actually, though Castlemere may be a hick town by your standards, statistically we have a good clear-up rate. We will get this man. I just can't tell you when.'

'And in the meantime,' said the Mayor, 'people are dying.'

Tyler turned towards him like radar. 'Oh?'

'Mr Dunstan exaggerates,' gritted Shapiro. 'People have certainly been hurt, and one man is missing. Initially we believed he was a victim of the blackmailer; now we're less certain. He may still be alive; and either way, it doesn't seem to have anything to do with this.'

Dick Travis's gaze was touched with compassion. 'That is good news, Superintendent. We'll all be hoping for the best.'

Tyler picked up a subtext and turned his searchlight gaze on Shapiro. 'Your sergeant?'

Shapiro nodded. 'Inspector Graham is investigating, I hope to know more later today.'

'Superintendent—I thought Inspector Graham *had* a case.'

Shapiro's voice dropped the half-octave that said he was running low on tolerance. 'Don't worry, Mr Tyler, nothing will take priority over the vital importance of protecting Sav-U-Mor's investment. But I also intend to use some of my resources to try and establish whether a young man who's repeatedly risked his life for this town has finally run out of luck.'

They stared at one another for long seconds and neither of them blinked. Travis edged, metaphorically, between them. 'Gentlemen, we have to reach a decision. Do we pay the ransom or not?'

'Pay,' said the Mayor. 'Or somebody's going to die.'

'Consult the insurers,' said the chairman of the Chamber of Trade. 'If they're agreeable, we pay. It'll cost less in the long run.'

Kenneth Simpson didn't move in high-powered company. But fate had singled him out as more than a bit-player in this, entitling him to as much of a say as anyone. He took a moment to organize his thoughts.

'I don't just sell combs, condoms and cold remedies. I'm a pharmacist. I trained for a lot of years so that when someone's

GP decides they need thyroxine they won't find themselves taking amioderone by mistake. People put their lives in my hands every day. I'm not boasting, I'm just trying to explain that taking responsibility for people's safety is fundamental to what I do. My shop is the repository of powerful drugs, all of them dangerous if used incorrectly, some of them lethal. I can't afford to make mistakes. I could kill someone.'

He took a breath and looked round but nobody was drumming his fingers. Most of them knew Simpson, but for the first time they saw him as more than just a fat man in a white coat with a nice line in toiletries. He was a highly qualified professional doing his best to find a way through the ethical maze.

'I hate this,' he said vehemently. 'I hate thinking that the next product I sell could put someone in hospital. I've been over my stock with a magnifying glass—that isn't a figure of speech, I actually did it—but I can't guarantee I didn't miss something. I could close the shop, but if he can't use mine he'll use another one where maybe they haven't been as thorough.

'So I'm going to stay open because I think it's the best I can do for my customers. For the same reason I'm not willing to pay a ransom. If we hold out this madman may hurt, may even kill, more people before Mr Shapiro finds him. But that'll be the end of it. If we pay we open the floodgates. Every greedy immoral thug in East Anglia will beat a path to our door because if we paid out once we'll do it again. I think we owe the people of this town better than that. I think we have to take risks now so as to protect them from worse in the future.'

In the silence that followed Dick Travis nodded gently, approvingly. 'We still seem to be in two minds. But if the police, the biggest retail outlet in town and the most directly affected small business are all opposed to buying this man off, I'm not sure those in favour can proceed. Finally it comes down to this: if the cash isn't there the ransom can't be paid.'

Tyler had expected to have to hold this line alone. By planting his standard beside that of Sav-U-Mor, Kenneth Simpson had given him the strength to compromise. 'What we need is time. Suppose we agree to hold out for a further, limited period to give Detective Superintendent Shapiro time to do his job?'

'And meanwhile anyone who buys anything in this town risks an encounter with acid, cholera or worse?' growled the chairman of the Chamber of Trade. 'I don't see why my members should be put in that position.'

'It isn't just the traders,' Travis pointed out, 'it's the whole town. You think an adulterated potion is a disaster? What if he manages to infect the swimming pool? Or a bus, or the water supply at the hospital? We could have dozens of casualties. This is not purely a financial matter.'

'All right,' said Tyler with mounting impatience, 'you want a solution? You want to keep people safe until the police find this man? Shut the town down. I mean it. Shut every business, every public facility, every school, every food outlet, every means of transport. If people have nowhere to go they'll stay home and they'll be safe.'

The others stared at him as if he'd proposed nuking the town. Then the heads started shaking. 'We couldn't.' 'We haven't the authority.' 'Imagine the *cost!*'

'Maybe you don't have the authority,' said Tyler. 'And maybe you don't need it. If the shopkeepers choose not to open, the shops will be closed. If the council keeps its facilities closed, no one can use them. If everybody co-operates you won't need powers you may or may not have.'

The two policemen traded a bemused look. Neither had expected this. They thought about it now. It was radical but it would probably work; as long as the blackmailer was in custody at the end of it. If he wasn't there'd be hell to pay. Shapiro suspected that the first sign of it would be a gold watch inscribed with his name.

Tyler looked round them expectantly. 'It isn't complicated, you don't need an expert evaluation. Round this table are the civic leaders of Castlemere: you have the right, and the duty, to make a decision. So make it. If it seems like a good idea, go for it.'

Still they hesitated.

Shapiro cleared his throat. 'You appreciate, the police don't actually have a say in this. We're a long way short of a state of emergency. But that isn't what Mr Tyler's proposing. He's suggesting a sort of Wakes Week—a town holiday. There will be firms that can't comply, where shutting down and starting up continual processes would just be too difficult. All the same, if those shops and businesses and public facilities that can take three days off were to do so, it could save lives. It would certainly show that we're taking the threat seriously and that might help keep the lid on the pressure cooker. If it can be done I think it would be a good idea.'

After a brief pause Dick Travis nodded. After a longer one, Donald Chivers did too.

'All right,' said Tyler, satisfied. 'I'll tell Seattle what we're doing. I suggest we meet here again on Wednesday morning and review the position. If the police still haven't caught this maniac and the body count's rising, I'll ask my head office to reconsider their opposition to a pay-off.'

He looked round them again, a man of action trying hard to play the diplomat. 'OK?'

There was muttering, some grunting, but in the end every one of them, willingly or unwillingly, consented to Tyler's proposal.

'Wednesday, then,' grunted Chivers. 'Assuming we're all still standing by then.'

As Shapiro showed them out, Tyler hung back. 'You're wrong. I don't think this is a hick town. I think it's probably a decent place to live. I hope you can keep it that way.'

'You've made your contribution,' said Shapiro. 'At least we're not going to be known as the place where you get kicked to death for having both a drug habit and a sweet tooth.'

'Frightened people do stupid things,' said Tyler. 'That won't be the last unless we find this man and stop him.'

EIGHT

IT WAS LIKE Twelfth Night, watching the decorations come off the Christmas tree. As the word spread, first one shop closed, drawing down the blinds and turning off the lights, then another. Owens Electricals in Bridgewater Street was about the first: all the televisions in the window went suddenly blank. Then Mr Reubenstein put up the steel lattice in front of Rubens the Jewellers in Castle Place. The leisure centre off Cambridge Road took longer to clear, but first admissions were stopped and then a succession of disgruntled swimmers, still damp and trailing towels, began to emerge. The bowlers were evicted from the municipal green at Belvedere Park, some of the old guard complaining that the place hadn't closed even during the Blitz and trying to drum up support for retaking it by force.

On the whole, though, the reasons for the decision had been understood by the people inconvenienced by it, and on the whole they thought it was a good idea. The car-parks that would be gridlocked on a normal Saturday steadily emptied from about eleven o'clock onwards. By noon the town looked as if it had been hit by a neutron bomb, the sort that wipes out populations but leaves buildings intact.

At Queen's Street Superintendent Giles was addressing the briefing room. 'The town may look quiet now but we'll have trouble enough before today is out. All those people who should be safely occupied shopping, taking the kids swimming or propping up the bar at The Fen Tiger'—he raised an interrogatory eye-brow: Sergeant Bolsover astonished him by nodding that yes, even The Fen Tiger had closed—'will have time on their hands and a good proportion of them will get up to mischief.

'Wherever possible, I want to catch the trouble while it's still brewing. I want every available body on patrol, every car out, and if we still have bicycles we'll use those too. I want us to be seen; and I want us to know who else is out and about. We can't afford another incident like the one under the castle. If the alternative is a few wrongful arrests, so be it—there'll be time to process the paperwork after this is over. Until then we must maintain order. Responsible citizens will recognize that: they'll all be home by now. Anyone still on the street is probably up to mischief. This is as good a time as any to try our hand at Zero Tolerance Policing.'

Upstairs, Shapiro was searching through the reports and witness statements for The Clue—the important one, the one he'd missed, the one that would topple the dominoes and let him use the time bought at such expense to good effect. Tyler's moratorium was brave and imaginative and would keep a lot of people safe. But it could only be a short-term measure. He had until Wednesday to repay the trust placed in him.

He found himself looking again at the letter: the second one, the tetchy one, the one that read like an overdue gas bill and was posted in Cambridge. Why?

Well, because he couldn't do what he did before, which was slip it under the wiper of a temporarily unoccupied police car. It worked beautifully once, but now they'd be watching for him. The post was good, it was anonymous and innocuous, but of course it was slower. If he mailed it at a main post office at six o'clock last night it would probably be delivered this morning, but he couldn't absolutely count on it, first-class stamp notwithstanding. It could have been another day on the way; it could conceivably have been longer.

So time wasn't the primary consideration. Of course he wanted his money, of course he wanted to be finished with this, but another day here or there wasn't vital to him. Which seemed to fit in with the long gap since the last booby trap was laid. Probably the last thing he did was the school showers on Monday afternoon. No, he really wasn't in much of a rush, was he?

Or was there some reason he couldn't do more than send threatening letters since then? Because—because—he was busy at work? It wasn't impossible. A man this clever could have an important job, a job he couldn't take time off from without being missed. It was important he stick to his usual routine.

Perhaps he had work in Cambridge. Or maybe not Cambridge itself but somewhere beyond, that made it easy to post his letter on the way through. If Shapiro got close enough to him to ask his employer whether he was in Cambridge on Friday the answer would be no: if he'd been working in Cambridge he'd have posted the letter in St Neots or Saffron Walden. But not in Castlemere. People here were too twitchy: the postman who emptied the pillar box would spot that distinctive writing and it would be possible to put the blackmailer on a certain street corner in a certain portion of a single day. And he wouldn't want that.

Shapiro sat back in his chair and looked at the dog-eared map on his wall. Newmarket, Norwich, Great Yarmouth, King's Lynn, Peterborough—or any of several hundred small towns and villages stretching across East Anglia to the North Sea coast. Without knowing what he did for a living it was impossible to say where he might do it. Shapiro needed more. He needed The Clue.

But if it was there he couldn't spot it. So—back to square one. Re-interview the witnesses. It was a tedious business, but it was always worth doing when all the trails had gone cold. Someone might remember something they hadn't mentioned before; or an inconsistency in someone's story might highlight a new suspect.

Perhaps; and perhaps it wouldn't. But the case wasn't going to solve itself and he couldn't think of anything more likely to kick-start the process again. Unfortunately, to redo all the interviews he needed a full team.

Liz's mobile was engaged. A moment later his own phone rang, and when he answered it was her. She passed on the news about Donovan's dog.

One of Frank Shapiro's strengths was an uncanny ability to say the right thing. 'He'll be sorry when he hears about that.'

Liz smiled. 'Yes, he will.'

'Any luck yet?'

'No. We doorstepped the whole of the north bank, we're

about halfway along the south bank now. Nobody saw anything, heard anything, knows, thinks or suspects anything. I suppose we could still get lucky...'

Shapiro sighed. 'I'm sorry, Liz, I need you back here. Both of you. We have to redo the interviews.'

She'd counted on having the rest of today and tomorrow. But he wouldn't have pulled the plug if there'd been any choice. 'We're on our way in.'

KENNETH SIMPSON, Miranda Hopkins, Sheila Crosbie, Tony Woodall, Miss Simmons the sports mistress, Mr Duffy the caretaker, Brian Graham. 'I'll take Brian,' Liz volunteered. 'I'll interview him over lunch. It's the only way I'm going to see him this weekend.'

They divided the rest between them. Shapiro took Woodall, Simpson and Miranda Hopkins; Liz took Sheila Crosbie and the people from school. She held on to Dick Morgan; Shapiro was going to take Mary Wilson, at the last minute changed his mind and called Scobie. If the lad was finally beginning to show promise as a detective Shapiro wanted to give him every encouragement.

As they headed out to the cars SOCO missed them by a whisker. Another officer might have given chase but not Sergeant Tripp. In his experience there wasn't much that couldn't wait an hour, including the mildly surprising results of a forensic test.

'YOU THINK IT'S ME. I know you think it's me.' Tony Woodall looked at Shapiro as though he might have brought a rope with him. 'You're wrong. I can see why you'd think it, but you're wrong.'

'Mr Woodall, I'm not here to charge you. I'm not ready to charge anyone.' Shapiro kept his words ambivalent, his tone non-committal. If the man had something to hide there was enough there for him to worry about; if he hadn't there wasn't enough for him to complain. 'But you're right, your youthful indiscretion is a bit of a problem in the present circumstances.'

'I can't turn the clock back!' said Woodall in despair. 'I wish I could.'

'I'm sure you do,' nodded Shapiro. 'But the best you can do now is help us get at the truth.'

'I'm helping, I'm helping,' whined Woodall. 'At least, I'm trying to.'

'Your son,' said Shapiro. 'James? How long has he been playing rugby?'

Woodall blew out his cheeks, surprised. 'He's fourteen now. Three years, I suppose.'

'And how long has he been playing for the school?'

'Since they went back after the summer holiday.'

Shapiro was nodding again, thoughtfully. 'So I dare say Monday was the first chance you'd had to go and see him play?'

Something seemed to warn Woodall the question was loaded. He picked it up carefully, checked the breach and the chamber, and put it down where he thought it couldn't do any harm. 'Actually, no.'

An elevated eyebrow marked Shapiro's surprise. 'Really?'

The under-manager of Sav-U-Mor thought he was digging himself out of a hole. There was a note of faintly tremulous satisfaction in his voice. 'They played their first home match three weeks ago. I was there for that one too.'

SHEILA CROSBIE HAD a flat at the top of Arrow House, sand-wiched between the Brick Lane timber yard and a monumental mason's. The lift worked on alternate Thursdays. Four flights of stairs left Liz breathing hard and all she was carrying was her handbag. She imagined doing it with a pram and bags of shopping. Whatever the government's view, being a single parent was not the easy option.

For a moment, when no one answered the bell, she thought it was all for nothing and they'd have to come back later. Then she heard footsteps, the thump of wheels and a breathless monotone swearing on the stairs: Sheila and the baby on their way home. Still red-faced and sweating himself, Morgan trudged back down the last flight to help her with the pram.

Sheila remembered Liz, assumed there'd been developments.

Fiddling with the front-door key she demanded, 'Have you got him? Did you get the bastard?'

Liz shook her head. 'Not yet.'

'Then—?' The door opened and Sheila pushed the pram inside. After a second she stood aside to admit the police officers.

'We're trying to make sure we haven't missed anything. We're talking again to everyone involved. I wondered if anything else had come back to you. If you saw anything odd in the chemist's. Someone acting suspiciously—watching you, leaving in a hurry, watching from a car or across the road? Anything out of the ordinary.'

'If I'd seen anything suspicious,' the girl growled, lifting the baby from his pram, 'I'd have said so before now.'

'Probably,' agreed Liz. 'But people do forget things. They're concentrating on what's just happened, they report what seems important; later they remember some detail that turns out to be what we were waiting for. Can we go through it again? Make sure there's nothing you've missed, or that we have?'

The girl gave a grudging shrug. 'All right. But you'll have to wait while I change Jason.'

'No problem.' Liz followed her into the tiny second bedroom, watched her busy expertly with wipes and powder and nappies and doll-sized clothes with improbable openings. Liz had never changed a baby in her life. She told herself she was an intelligent woman, she could drive a car and operate a computer, she could even programme the video: she could master the controls on a baby if the need arose. But the careless efficiency of this young girl left her wide-eyed with admiration.

In fact, looking around her, taking in the fresh paint, the bright curtains and the gently prancing animals of the wooden mobile, Liz found herself warming to Sheila Crosbie. She was doing a good job of raising this child. She'd made him a nice home, inexpensively but comfortably furnished; but more important than the decor, she was nice with him. Even a detective watching over her shoulder didn't make her impatient. She manoeuvred him deftly into his clean clothes; then she made him a bottle, and only when he was nursing contentedly in her arms did she raise her eyes to Liz again. 'So what did you want to know?'

The Mystery Library Reader Service™ — Here's how it works:

Accepting your 2 free books and gift places you under no obligation to buy anything. You may keep the books and gift and return the shipping statement marked "cancel." If you do not cancel, about a month later we'll send you 3 additional novels and bill you just $4.69 each plus 25¢ shipping & handling per book and applicable sales tax, if any.* You may cancel at any time, but if you choose to continue, every month we'll send you 3 more books, which you may either purchase at our great low price...or return to us and cancel your subscription.

*Terms and prices subject to change without notice. Sales tax applicable in N.Y.

If offer card is missing write to: Mystery Library Reader Service, 3010 Walden Ave., P.O. Box 1867, Buffalo NY 14240-1867

NO POSTAGE
NECESSARY
IF MAILED
IN THE
UNITED STATES

BUSINESS REPLY MAIL
FIRST-CLASS MAIL   PERMIT NO. 717-003   BUFFALO, NY

POSTAGE WILL BE PAID BY ADDRESSEE

MYSTERY LIBRARY READER SERVICE
3010 WALDEN AVE
PO BOX 1867
BUFFALO NY 14240-9952

Play The

Lucky Hearts Game

and get...

FREE BOOKS & a FREE GIFT...
YOURS to KEEP!

Yes! I have scratched off the silver card. Please send me my **2 FREE BOOKS** and **FREE GIFT**. I understand that I am under no obligation to purchase any books as explained on the back of this card.

Scratch Here!
then look below to see what your cards get you...

415 WDL DH5S

NAME   (PLEASE PRINT CLEARLY)

ADDRESS

APT.#   CITY

STATE   ZIP

Twenty-one gets you
2 FREE BOOKS and
a **FREE GIFT!**

Twenty gets you
2 FREE BOOKS!

Nineteen gets you
1 FREE BOOK!

TRY AGAIN!

Offer limited to one per household and not valid to current
Mystery Library™ subscribers. All orders subject to approval.

Liz had her go over it all again. There were no surprises.
When they first spoke Sheila was running on a high-octane mix
of shock and anger: now they had dissipated she wanted to forget the episode. Her hands had healed, Jason was safe, the man
who hurt her had gone on to do worse things to other people.
She would repeat what she knew as often as Liz asked but the
passion was gone. She didn't remember anything new. She
didn't think there was anything new to remember.

'That was a wasted effort,' said Liz, heading back down four
flights of stairs.

Morgan shrugged philosophically. 'Never know, though, do
you? Not till it's done. You have to finish the jigsaw before you
know which bits belong and which were found down the back
of the couch and put in the wrong box.'

Liz liked Dick Morgan. When he wasn't trying to hide the
fact he was a thoughtful, perceptive individual with an engaging
turn of phrase. 'You've got kids, haven't you, Dick?'

He nodded lugubriously. 'Famine, War and Pestilence.'

Liz laughed. 'What sort of an attitude is that?'

'It's not an attitude, it's a survival strategy. The first thing a
parent learns is that kids are trouble. They're going to dump you
in it at regular intervals. You're not allowed to strangle them at
birth, and soon after that you love them too much to leave them
on the church steps, so you have to get used to the idea. Recognize that their function in life is not to make you proud, it's
to build your character. Then every day that you don't commit
grievous bodily harm on them is a triumph.'

Liz had know DC Morgan for three years now, she didn't for
a moment believe that his children lived in fear of their lives. It
was part of the persona it amused him to have created for himself. He pretended to be slow and a shade dim and not terribly
efficient so no one would threaten him with promotion; but behind the smokescreen he was an effective, insightful police officer. She suspected that behind the mock bitterness he was probably a good father as well.

'Sheila Crosbie doesn't seem too disappointed with Jason.'

Morgan shook his head sadly. 'Give her time.'

AS HE DROVE Shapiro thought aloud about Miranda Hopkins. Whatever Liz thought of her as a person, he could not ignore the fact that Hopkins had the knowledge and the facilities to culture cholera. Uniquely among those involved; unless you counted Kenneth Simpson, and that really would be paranoid.

Scobie listened politely—DCs always listen politely to Detective Superintendents—but he plainly had doubts. 'A laboratory like that, you'd think *somebody'd* notice she was cooking up a deadly disease.'

'They work with deadly diseases all the time.'

'All right then, a different deadly disease to everyone else.'

It was a point. 'So maybe she didn't do it at the lab. Maybe she took what she needed home.'

'Kitchen table germ warfare?' said Scobie with a rising inflection.

Shapiro shrugged. 'This is not a fragile specimen, constable. This is a bug which can devastate whole communities, which can sidestep most of the defences raised against it and only be stopped by high-tech modern medicine. It kills five million people every year. It can't be so delicate as to need expert handling and optimal facilities to remain viable.'

Scobie scratched his misshapen nose. 'I wasn't thinking about the bug, sir, I was thinking about her. This is the mother of a kid. Would she keep something that lethal in her fridge? She'd be afraid of contaminating their food.'

'She'd know what precautions were necessary.'

'The kid wouldn't.'

Shapiro was saved the search for a convincing rebuttal by the ringing of his phone. He pulled over and answered it; he listened a lot, thanked the caller then rang off. Scobie waited for him to drive on, but Shapiro just kept sitting there. 'Sir?'

Shapiro drew a deep breath. 'I don't think I'd better arrest Ms Hopkins after all, constable. Maybe she does work with botulism, maybe she could get hold of cholera if she wanted, but unless she also moonlights at a greengrocer's she's not responsible for what happened to Mr Wingrave.'

He'd lost Scobie entirely. 'Wingrave?'

'The man who bought the bottle of flu remedy. Whatever the

label said, he never had cholera. He had a nasty case of food-poisoning caused by an inedible mushroom. That was the fever hospital. The results of their tests just came through. They took a while because, naturally enough, they were looking for cholera.'

Scobie was digesting it. 'So—basically—it could be anybody again.'

'Well, anybody with an *Observer's Book of Fungi.*'

There was a long silence while they considered the implications. Finally Scobie asked, 'So why did he say it was cholera?'

'To spread alarm and despondency,' said Shapiro. 'You can't start an epidemic with a dodgy mushroom. But you can make it look as if you have.'

'He still had to get the stuff into the bottle.'

'Yes. But he didn't need a Home Office licence to get hold of it. He could find it on a leisurely walk through the woods.'

'This mushroom: was it actually poisonous? Or just—you know—not very good for you?'

The hospital pathology department had identified the source of Mr Wingrave's illness as the fungus *Russula emetica:* the classic red-capped toadstool commonly known as the Sickener and found in mixed woodlands from July to October. 'It's inedible, it was always going to make someone ill. But unless they had a particular allergy to it, it shouldn't have killed anyone.'

They returned to Queen's Street. Sergeant Tripp was listening out for the Superintendent, caught him at the back door. 'That call from Forensics, sir. They've found something a bit weird.'

'Weird, sergeant?'

'That bottle we sent them, that the paramedics picked up at Mr Wingrave's flat? Seems it wasn't contaminated with cholera after all.'

Shapiro couldn't resist the temptation. He smiled knowingly. 'Do you know, sergeant, I wondered about that. It didn't seem like cholera to me. I'm no expert, mind, but I considered the possibility of mushroom poisoning.'

Normally SOCO's expression was all but impenetrable; now sheer astonishment got under his guard. 'Mushrooms?' he said faintly.

Shapiro nodded, straight-faced. 'Nothing too lethal, of course. Maybe—oh, I don't know—*Russula emetica?* You can find it in the mixed woodlands round here any time from July to October. It's known as the Sickener, you know.'

Tripp nodded too, hypnotically. 'That's what Forensics said, sir.'

Shapiro gave him a sunny smile. 'Lucky guess, then.' He continued upstairs feeling positively restored by the infantile deception.

NINE

LIZ WAS STILL TRYING to make sense of the new development as she drove home at lunchtime. So...*nobody* ever had cholera. Donovan had a cold, Wingrave had a close encounter with a toadstool. Sheila Crosbie burnt her hands on caustic soda, the hockey team took a shower in raspberry jelly, and lime jelly was the secret ingredient in Sav-U-Mor's yoghurt special.

The man who was holding Castlemere to ransom hadn't made a seriously life-threatening move yet.

Maybe he didn't intend to. Maybe he hoped—expected—to be able to frighten them into paying him off purely on the basis of what he might do if they didn't. Which, actually, is the bottom line in blackmail anyway. He'd got their pulses racing, now he expected them to reach for their wallets.

But the threat had to be credible. If he wasn't prepared to endanger life in any circumstances he wasn't going to get paid. He'd cross that Rubicon if he had to, he wouldn't have started all this otherwise. But he was cool enough and smart enough to realize that the longer he delayed that moment, the fewer boats he'd have to burn. If they caught him today, the worst that could be said at his trial was that he'd given a young mother a nasty case of washday hands.

The school. The school shower block was the one scene they could place him within a narrow time frame—between mid and late afternoon on Monday. At one point they'd wondered if he could have managed that too without actually being there; but that would have meant involving other people in his scheme, and the drawbacks that attended adult co-conspirators went quadruple for children. No, he'd both laid and primed the trap in person. He'd been up in that roof space on Monday afternoon—not under cover of darkness, with no certainty of avoiding witnesses; and therefore presumably with some kind of a cover story.

In the event Mr Duffy had seen no one. But if he had chanced that way at the material time, the blackmailer would have needed some tale that would convince even the caretaker. Oh, and something to cover his face. When the police came to investigate what happened they would ask Duffy for a description of anyone he'd seen. Before this man ventured on to the school campus he'd have had that angle covered. A face mask. One of those dust masks that workmen use. Everyone was used to seeing those, the caretaker's suspicions wouldn't be aroused if the man seemed to have a proper reason for being up there.

Well, there were workmen at the school. If he was attired as one of them, complete with face mask, and carrying a bag of tools with Sidgwick & Mellors logo on it, and he said—for instance—he'd been sent to check the roof battens for signs of rot while the builders were on site, Duffy would have seen no reason to raise the alarm. All right, in the event it didn't happen, Duffy was busy elsewhere at the critical moment. But this man wouldn't have counted on that. He would have had a story prepared just in case.

It might be just enough to start jogging memories. If she asked people who were at the sports field that afternoon if they'd noticed any of the workmen watching, or else heading back to the school buildings as if from that direction, somebody just might remember. She'd start with Brian. If she got no useful information, at least she could expect a portion of vegetarian stew and a chance to sit down with her husband.

She was almost in time to prevent it. As she drove up the hill towards Belvedere Park she could see the fawn car sitting at an angle in her drive, nose to the road. She frowned. She didn't recognize it, and there was something odd about the way it was just sitting there, not so much parked as abandoned.

She couldn't get in while it was there so she parked by the kerb and went to see what was happening. But as she turned around the gatepost four men were coming the other way, and they were in a hurry. They elbowed her aside so violently she ended up, openmouthed with surprise, in the hedge; before she could extricate herself they were in the car and roaring down the hill back into town.

Liz had no idea what it meant, but it wasn't Hallowe'en yet and anyway they were too big for trick or treating. Her first thought was for Polly. It was already too late to give chase— her car was locked and facing the wrong way, her visitors were halfway home by now—so she hurried to check the most vulnerable and, by a small margin, most easily frightened member of her family. But the mare was fine, still lipping up her morning hay, unaware of the drama at the front of the house.

Belatedly, she thought of Brian. She headed for the back door, calling his name. There was no reply. But he should have been there: the town was shut up, and anyway he had no transport. She called again; still silence.

It wasn't open-door weather but that's what she found: the kitchen door standing wide. She stepped inside.

There was blood on the kitchen tiles. Hesitantly, afraid of what she would find, she reached for the door into the hall.

He'd almost made it to the phone before the damage he'd sustained overwhelmed him. Blood pouring from his nose, his broken mouth and one ear had pooled under his face where he lay in a foetal curl on the parquet flooring.

WITHOUT ELPHIE the Turner house was quiet. Donovan could hear Sarah in the kitchen but he didn't want to go back in there. He needed to keep trying the phone, and somehow Sarah made him feel guilty about that. Anyway, he'd been under her feet long enough—she must be ready for a break from him too.

He wandered round the hall, soft-footed, opening doors. There was a sitting room, a proper dining room for when the company was too smart to eat in the kitchen, and a study lined with books. Presumably that was Turner's office, he was bound to feel trespassed upon if Donovan poked round in there. He went into the sitting room instead, sinking into deep chintzy upholstery. He thought he'd try the phone again in a few minutes. Instead, tired from his early morning exercise, with nothing to occupy his attention, listening to the distant rattle of pots in the kitchen he nodded off again.

His first thought, stirring dimly half an hour later, was that the family had gathered round to stare at him some more. But it was the photograph: Sarah's wedding photograph, taking pride of place on a pie-crust table beside his chair. Sarah and Robert and Simon and Jonathan, and the woman who wasn't Elphie's mother.

Looking at them Donovan began to see why Elphie had picked this particular young woman as a mother-substitute. It wasn't just that she was pretty, although she was—a girl of about twenty in a sprigged dress, with a mass of fair curls under a straw hat. There was something about her which the child must have found familiar. She *could* have been Elphie's mother. There was a kind of likeness there—not close, because Elphie's little pointy face was a thing all its own, but enough to make you wonder. Though of course Sarah said...

Sarah. *That* was what Donovan was seeing, the family likeness he'd recognized. It wasn't so obvious now that Sarah was twenty years older, but in the photograph Sarah and her bridesmaid, despite the years between them, looked like sisters. That was why Elphie was drawn to the girl in the picture. She was a younger version of the face she knew best in the world.

He thought he'd solved the mystery, went on regarding the little family group with a tolerant eye. And a certain sadness too, because they didn't stay like this for very long. The big man with the expansive smile and more expansive waistcoat was dead. So was the boy at his side. The girl in the sprigged dress must have gone her own way too or it would have been necessary to explain to Elphie about her mistake. Only Sarah and Simon remained at The Flower Mill, at a fly speck on a map of the fens that even a canal groupie like Donovan had never found his way to before.

But as he went on looking at it, something about the photograph began to trouble him. There was something wrong with it and he couldn't for the life of him work out what. His eye kept returning to the scowling boy by Robert Turner's side. There was nothing odd about that. Any photographs of the Donovan family would have shown a teenage Caolan scowling too; it's what teenagers do at family gatherings. And when that was taken Sarah's son had no idea what the future held for him. He might have hated The Flower Mill, hated his stepfather and brother, and would have been trapped until he was old enough to leave.

In the event, of course, Jonathan was to make his home at The Flower Mill while Simon went away. College wasn't an escape, it was just an interlude until he was back here walking in his stepfather's footsteps. So his misgivings had not been justified by events; or at least, not the way he feared.

Donovan looked from Sarah's son to Robert's. No worries for the future had spoiled his day: already the relationship that would blossom between him and his stepmother, to the benefit of The Flower Mill and all of East Beckham, was evident in the comfortable way they stood together. Perhaps that was what finally brought him back from his travels: the knowledge that, if he no longer had family at the Mill, he had the next best thing.

Donovan tried the phone again. It was still dead. He wished he had his mobile. He supposed it was still in his jacket pocket, and his jacket was still on *Tara* and *Tara* was in Posset. Though never entirely reliable, at least it worked sometimes. That was more than could be said for the phone at The Flower Mill.

Which raised the question of how anyone could run a business in the middle of a fen when their phone never worked.

THE AMBULANCE arrived within ten minutes, ten minutes after that Brian Graham was in radiography at Castle General. As soon as the plates were developed the A&E registrar, leaving his nurse to clean up the patient, hurried back to reception. It was a matter of urgency not because of what the X-rays showed but because DI Graham looked about ready to rip the drinks machine off the wall.

Dr Voss came straight to the point. 'There's a fair bit of damage but it's all superficial. He'll be fine. He'll be in here a few days, then you can take him home. What happened?—do you know?'

Brian had drifted in and out of consciousness during the ambulance ride. But even without his hazy recollections mumbled through broken teeth Liz could have pieced it together. 'They thought he was the blackmailer. They tried to beat a confession out of him.' Now the shock was dissipating and the worst of the fear had passed she was literally panting with fury.

'Why?' The doctor stared at her in astonishment. There were eighty thousand people in Castlemere: most of them had to be more promising suspects than a middle-aged art teacher.

'Because this town is the brain-death capital of Europe!' Liz exclaimed bitterly. 'Because everyone here responds to a crisis by kicking the living daylights out of someone else! Because tolerance is a dirty word in Castlemere, and thinking is a hobby for people with nothing better to do, and someone being reasonable in public is always asking for trouble. They were talking about it at school—criticizing my lack of success, actually. Brian pointed out the scale of the problem when most of what was known about the blackmailer applied to him too. It was absolutely true, but in the current climate it was more than enough. Or maybe'—she remembered the earlier warning, that she hadn't taken seriously until the paint-stripper attack—'someone else was talking out of turn. One way or another Brian's name got coupled with this, and four of the ignorant bastards thought they'd come round and get the truth out of him. Unfortunately, they didn't recognize it when they heard it.'

'Do you know who they were?'

'Not yet,' she said tightly. 'But if four big men come in here with split knuckles and stubbed toes, call me.'

Voss nodded. 'They gave him a drubbing, right enough. There's a couple of cracked ribs: we'll strap those but they shouldn't bother him as long as he takes things quietly for a bit. He's concussed but there's no skull fracture—we'll monitor him for a couple of days but I don't think there's anything to worry about. He'll need some stitches in his face, and an appointment with a good dentist, and he'll be as stiff as a board for a week, but after that he'll be as right as rain.' He smiled wryly. 'To use the technical terminology.'

When they arrived here Liz was too anxious even for anger. Reassurance freed her to give it a loose rein now, and if she couldn't avenge herself on the men directly responsible she could at least give a piece of her mind to someone who had, however inadvertently, helped arm them for the task. 'Look after him,' she said in her teeth. 'I'll be back in a couple of hours. There's something I have to do.'

TEN

UNSUCCESSFUL AT Sav-U-Mor, Liz drove round the oddly quiet streets expecting that sooner or later she'd chance on a trouble spot and Mitchell Tyler would be at the heart of it. But even the regular troublemakers, and Castlemere had its fair share of them, were somehow too uneasy to start anything just now. Most of them had lived in this town all their lives, but today it was like a film set—unreal, two-dimensional, too quiet. If someone else had started some trouble they'd have joined in with relief and enthusiasm, but nobody felt like being the first to break that oppressive stillness.

Liz drove up Brick Lane and round The Jubilee—even here people were staying inside with the doors shut—before admitting that she wasn't going to find Tyler this way. She turned the car back towards Queen's Street.

At that point she saw him, on foot, his sturdy figure distinctive in its unEnglish light grey suit, coming up Brick Lane. She didn't pause to ask herself where he was going. She drove at him, diving into the kerb to cut him off.

Tyler broke his stride like a surprised horse, bent on her a look to make strong men quail. But Liz was too angry to back off, and when he saw who was accosting him he took a deep breath and left his hands where they were. 'Are you all right?'

'Me?' She couldn't stop her voice from soaring. 'I'm fine. But Brian looks as if he's gone ten rounds with Frank Bruno.'

'Is he going to be all right?'

'Well, that depends on how you define all right, doesn't it?' snarled Liz. 'If you mean, is his life in danger or will he be permanently disabled then I guess the answer is no, he's going to be all right. Give or take a couple of teeth, some cracked ribs and a concussion, and even the doctor said it was nothing to worry about. Couple of weeks and he'll be as good as new.

'Only actually he won't. Because he isn't like you. Violence isn't a way of life to him; it isn't even a last resort. Something he couldn't get without violence he'd do without. So when men he doesn't know break into his house and beat him senseless for no better reason than they'd heard his name mentioned in connection with this blackmail business, that's going to make an impression. In fact, that's going to stay with him for the rest of his days. Knowing that, even in his own home, he wasn't safe from the thugs. If you're not safe there, you're not safe anywhere. Have you any idea what that's going to do to a gentle man?'

She was causing a twitching of curtains at the shut windows all around. Tyler ignored the attention they were attracting. His voice was low but not entirely sympathetic. 'Inspector Graham, I realize you've been upset by this—'

'Upset!' she interjected explosively, eyebrows rocketing.

He hung on to his patience—if she'd known him better she'd have recognized that as a Herculean effort—and ploughed on. 'I understand that: it doesn't matter how much you've seen professionally, it's different when it's someone you care about. What I don't understand is why you're yelling at me.'

'Because you're to blame for this!'

She'd managed to surprise him. 'Me?'

'I want to know who you talked to. After Tony Woodall offered you Brian as an alternative suspect. I want to know where you planted that venomous little thought.'

Tyler breathed heavily at her. 'I talked to you. No one else.'

'If you didn't spread it around, Woodall did.' She was heading back to her car. He stopped her with his hand: it was like walking into a wall.

'Calm down, Inspector. Woodall saw what was in front of his face: anyone who knows this town could see it too. Your husband's a teacher, an automatic hate-figure to a thousand kids. A thousand little amateur detectives. Any one of them could have fingered him as a suspect.'

'It wasn't kids who knocked me into the hedge!'

'Kids talk. They fantasize, and they talk. Somebody's father has taken the fantasy at face value. It's unfortunate—'

'Unfortunate!!'

'—Unfortunate,' he said again, in his teeth, 'but it's nobody's fault fate's playing games with Brian. I warned you this could happen. I thought you'd get him out of town until the dust settled. You didn't, and he paid the price. I'm sorry but I don't feel responsible.' He let go of her arm.

Liz went on standing there. Of course he was right. The facts were there for anyone to see. A minimum of research would have shown that Brian Graham had been there or thereabouts for every incident. In the current mood it was enough. The heroin junkie in the hospital had only his syringe and a bar of chocolate to incriminate him: Brian had been at the school, in the store and in the chemist's. Of course, only a simple mind would infer guilt from the elements of a coincidence; but when a mob is in the ascendant it's the simple minds that rule. They aren't inconvenienced by common sense.

Liz drew the first deep, steady breath she'd managed in some time. She looked Mitchell Tyler in the eye. His were the pale blue found in the hearts of glaciers. 'I'm sorry,' she said. 'You're right, I let emotion get the better of me. It was—unprofessional.'

Tyler shrugged. 'You're entitled to your emotions.'

But she wasn't an emotional woman. She prided herself on it. Cool, calm, rational: you could say what you liked about Liz Graham but you had to admit she was a pro. When things went wrong she didn't burst into tears, she swore with the rest of CID. Normally she'd have argued bitterly if someone had accused her of emotion.

But he was right about that too. The events of the last few days had left her angry and afraid and sickened. She felt out of control, spinning her wheels. In reality, this wasn't even about what had happened to Brian, or at least not entirely. She was blaming Tyler because she didn't know who else to blame, either for Brian or for Donovan. Looked at dispassionately, it was doubtful if she should have been working at all: if there'd been anyone to hand over to she'd have gone home. But she couldn't leave Shapiro to cope alone.

She drew a shaky breath. Tyler took her arm again, steered her back to her car and into the passenger seat. At first she thought it was a mistake—he'd forgotten about driving on the left. But he got in beside her. 'Where do you want to go?'

She wanted to be with Brian, but there wasn't much point: if they'd finished cleaning him up by now he was probably asleep. That left work.

'Where were you going?'

He did something with his nose that she'd noticed before when someone asked him a question. Half a sniff and half a sneer, it consisted of flaring one nostril, with a consequent narrowing of the eye above and curling of the lip below; a little like taking a pinch of invisible snuff. It was as if he knew the question was reasonable but his basic instinct was to resent it. It reminded Liz of the way Donovan rounded his shoulders and shoved his hands deep into his pockets so that he looked like six foot of sulky schoolboy. Tyler looked more like a circus tiger who's worked out that three metres of whip are all that stand between him and the best-dressed lunch he's ever had, but the sentiment was recognizably the same.

She was too slow to hide her grin. Tyler frowned. 'What?'

'I'm sorry. I was thinking about Donovan.'

She saw his expression flicker as he weighed that and found it wanting. She was amused by the thought of a colleague who was missing, possibly dead? But she hadn't the energy to go into it any further, and Tyler seemed wary of doing. Perhaps he thought she was verging on a nervous breakdown. Perhaps she was. But she'd worked her way through crises before, she would do it again. She waited for an answer to her question.

Tyler blinked and remembered what it was. 'I was going to see Sheila Crosbie, the girl who got her hands burnt. I haven't seen her yet.'

Liz was surprised. 'You want to?'

Tyler shrugged broad shoulders. 'If you've got a prime suspect you haven't told me about I'll go talk to him instead.'

But she hadn't. 'I've already interviewed her,' said Liz. 'Twice.'

He did the nose thing again. 'Nothing useful?'

'No. But don't let that stop you. She's happy enough to talk about it.'

'If she's that happy,' said Tyler, 'there's probably not much point.' He looked at his watch. 'Listen, I haven't eaten yet and I don't suppose you got much of a chance. Where can we get some lunch?'

Liz hadn't realized she was hungry, but in fact she last ate at six thirty that morning. She'd been on her way home when someone pushed her into the hedge. 'I remember lunch. That's the one where you put nice things in your mouth and go yum.'

She was just getting in the mood when she remembered that the restaurants, and even Fast Edna's under the castle, would be closed. 'Come on, Mr Tyler, I'll introduce you to the culinary delights of the British police canteen.'

WHEN PEOPLE WORK together for a long time, one of two things happens. Either they start hating one another's guts, or their thought processes start to converge. The same ideas occur to them and they process them in similar ways.

In CID this is a mixed blessing. It saves a lot of time and argument, but what you really need is people who think of things no one else has. It was Donovan's great strength, as Shapiro had often reflected. However long he spent in CID his thought processes remained resolutely individual.

Right now, though, Shapiro was reflecting on something else, and though he didn't know that Liz had been thinking along the same lines it wouldn't have surprised him. On this occasion, however, he went one step further. Of course, he wasn't side-tracked by being blown up.

He too was considering how effectively the blackmailer had succeeded in panicking Castlemere with the contents of the average kitchen cupboard. Jelly, caustic soda, an inedible mushroom... Shapiro knew you could blow up a city with a few household chemicals in the right proportions, but still, there was something quite deliberate about the way this man was using fear itself as his weapon. Fear of what?—nothing very much. Only the possibility of something worse.

A tap at his door and Sergeant Tripp appeared. He always looked morose: now he looked puzzled as well.

'*Now* what?' demanded Shapiro.

'I'm not sure, sir. Forensics have been back to me about the caustic soda in the baby lotion.'

'Yes. And?'

'Well, there *was* caustic soda in the baby lotion.'

'*Yes?*' said Shapiro again, heavily.

'But they don't think there was enough. Not to cause burning. The emollients in the lotion itself would near as damn it have neutralized the soda. It just might have caused a minor irritation, but they don't understand the actual burning Dr Greaves says he saw.'

Greaves hadn't been the only one to see it. And Sheila Crosbie had been in obvious pain when she came to Queen's Street. 'And there *was* caustic soda in the lotion,' repeated Shapiro pensively, 'just not enough to cause visible damage.' He took a deep breath. 'Sergeant, somebody's telling me porkies.'

Sergeant Tripp looked affronted. 'Well, it isn't me.'

'Of course it isn't,' said Shapiro cheerfully, 'of course it isn't.'

He called for Mary Wilson and reached for his hat. He didn't quite say, 'The game's afoot,' but it was tacit in the way he moved, suddenly much more positive, creaks and twinges forgotten.

'Where are we going, sir?' asked Wilson breathlessly.

'Arrow House,' said Shapiro, 'Brick Lane.'

'Sheila Crosbie?'

'I understand that's where she lives.'

Wilson wasn't quite sure how to put this. 'She lives on the second storey.'

Shapiro looked her up and down. 'Never mind, constable, you look tolerably fit to me.'

Nevertheless, they went in his car. Brick Lane was an easy walk, but not for someone still recovering from a bullet wound.

Shapiro drove. Wilson tried to find out what he was on to.

There are senior detectives who think it's good for their image

to keep junior detectives in the dark. Shapiro wasn't one of
them. He didn't see how anyone was expected to learn without
being taught. 'Think about the timing, constable.'

'The timing?'

'The first note we got from the blackmailer was—let's call it
left, shall we?—around two o'clock on Wednesday. Four hours
after Sheila Crosbie burnt her hands, and a day after she bought
the contaminated lotion. Yes?'

'Yes...' She still didn't see where he was going with this.

'Then think about how hard this man has tried to avoid actually harming anyone. Not because of his sensitive soul, of
course, but because if it goes wrong he doesn't want to have
too many real injuries to explain. While unsupported threats
would do, he settled for making threats. Why then would he
decide to injure someone before he'd even made contact with
us?'

'To concentrate minds?'

'Our minds were wonderfully concentrated already.'

'Sir—are you saying he *didn't* put caustic soda in that bottle
of baby lotion?'

'Let's say I'm wondering.'

Wilson stared at him. 'Well—somebody did.'

'Yes.'

'Who else?'

Shapiro squinted sidelong at his new DC. 'Constable, what
do you know about Munchausen's Syndrome?'

If he'd thought to throw her it was a miscalculation. Wilson
paused just long enough to sort the information. 'It's a psychological condition where people crave the attention that being ill
brings them. They get themselves admitted to hospital for a succession of imaginary ailments. They may even undergo surgery
because they'd rather have treatment, any treatment, than not.
There's a variation, called Munchausen's By Proxy, where patients, usually women, claim their children—'

Shapiro stopped her with a wave of the hand. 'Constable,
constable—if you don't know, just say so.'

They traded a grin.

'Suppose,' said Shapiro, 'just suppose, that Sheila Crosbie

found the note on the bottom of the bottle just as she says she did. But there was nothing inside except what was meant to be there. She could report it—it was obviously part of the blackmail campaign and so something we needed to know about. And we'd thank her, and take a note of her address, and that would be the end of that.

'Now suppose also that Miss Crosbie is that particular type of hysterical personality that needs to be at the centre of whatever's going on. Why be just another hoax victim when she could be the first victim of an actual attack? That would get our attention. All it took was a solution of caustic soda just strong enough to turn her hands red; then she put some more of the stuff in the bottle with the label on it and raced round to Queen's Street. Attention, sympathy, involvement—all for the price of a self-inflicted injury about as painful as sunburn.'

Wilson went on watching Shapiro and Shapiro watched the road. Neither spoke. There was no proof, and it was hard to see how there could be any—a box of soda crystals under Sheila's sink would prove nothing at all. Brian Graham's kitchen was undoubtedly full of the stuff.

But if Sheila Crosbie was the author of her own misfortune, the blackmailer hadn't done half what they'd originally thought. He hadn't introduced either a tropical disease or caustic soda into a sealed bottle. He'd bought some jelly and picked some woodland fungi. 'But in that case...' said Shapiro pensively.

Wilson waited a moment, but not too long. She wanted to know. 'What, sir?'

'Why did he change the wording? On the labels. At first he wrote, "This could have been" whatever. Later, he wrote, "This *was*". Why?'

'To pile on the pressure? The threats were causing panic; pretending to escalate would cause hysteria. *Did* cause hysteria.'

'Yes,' agreed Shapiro slowly. 'All the same, how lucky can a man get? He pretended to put caustic soda in a bottle of baby lotion—and it was bought by someone with the precise sort of psychological disorder that made her want to play along? We're not buying that.'

'Aren't we, sir?'

'I don't know,' said Shapiro. 'Are we?'

They'd reached Arrow House. He parked the car in Brick Lane, sat for a moment longer then got out. 'Let's put it this way. There's *something* rum about all this. Let's see if Sheila Crosbie can tell us what it is.'

ELEVEN

LUNCH AT The Flower Mill was a pile of sandwiches and a pot of soup kept simmering for people to help themselves as the opportunity arose. Simon Turner ate on the run, without taking his boots off; so, fifteen minutes later, did Jim Vickery the foreman. Each of them nodded a greeting to Donovan, then ignored him. There was no attempt at conversation with Sarah either. It was in-flight refuelling: as soon as the tanks were full they disengaged and returned to their duties.

The phoned went on not working. Donovan asked if anyone had a mobile: they looked at him blankly and shook their heads.

Elphie did not reappear. Returning to his room, Donovan heard a sound like puppies mewling and found her sitting on her bed, bare arms hugging her bare knees, sobbing rebelliously.

'Elphie? What's wrong?'

But she buried her face in her arms, hidden beneath the floss of ash-fair hair.

'Elphie. What's happened?'

The thin high voice was reedier than ever, disconsolate, issuing from a gap between her elbow and her knee. 'I'm not allowed to talk to you.'

Donovan was genuinely astonished. 'Me? What have I done?'

Without looking up Elphie shook her head again. 'Nana was cross about her picture. She said I shouldn't have taken it.'

Before he had the words out, Donovan knew the answer. 'What picture?'

'The one with Mummy in. I was only looking. I put it back afterwards.'

Donovan had always thought of children as an alien species,

disruptive and unpredictable; if the cost of perpetuating his genes was raising one he thought he could let the Donovan line die out without much regret. But something about this particular child touched him in unexpected ways. Her unhappiness troubled him.

He shoved his hands deep into his pockets, rounding his shoulders. 'Don't worry about it. I'll go see what I can sort out.'

He found Sarah in the kitchen, as usual. It seemed to be from choice: nobody sent her there when she was bad, the way they sent Elphie to her room. He pulled out a chair, sat awkwardly sideways on it. He wasn't sure how to broach the subject. When the woman looked at him, oddly, with a half-fearful expectancy, he just shrugged and came out with it. 'Elphie says you're angry at her for showing me your wedding photo.'

Sarah snapped back to the sink as if he'd struck her. Donovan unfolded quickly from his chair and came up behind her. A more confident man would have put his hands about her shoulders. Donovan, though he sensed her misery and wanted to help, found it hard to touch people. He always expected to be rebuffed.

'Sarah, what is it?' His voice veered between impatience and compassion. 'What's troubling you? It can't just be that Elphie borrowed your picture. It came to no harm—I saw it in the sitting room an hour ago. So what is it? Why's everyone here so—twitchy?'

She wouldn't face him. 'Cal, stay out of it. These are family matters and none of your business. Don't get involved.'

'But I *am* involved, aren't I?' Though he trusted his instincts, this wasn't really intuition: it was the only way to interpret how they looked at him. 'This isn't something I've wandered into— it happened because I came. Why—because I'm a policeman? Is there something going on that you reckon you can handle as long as the police don't get to know about it?'

'Of course not,' she insisted. But her voice lacked the conviction to persuade a much less suspicious man than Detective Sergeant Donovan. 'There's nothing going on. Just—get well and go home. Forget about us. There's nothing here to concern you.'

'I've been trying to get home since I woke up!' he exclaimed. 'Nobody thought it was a good idea, you included. *Tara*'s been moved, the phone's dead, I can't raise my office, I can't even check if my dog's all right, and now Elphie's been told not to talk to me. And I don't know what the hell's going on but something is! Tell me what. Maybe I can help.'

Finally Sarah looked at him, and it was in her face that she wanted to—perhaps, wanted desperately. But she was afraid. 'Please,' she murmured. 'Please, Cal—leave it alone. It's ancient history: don't start digging it up.'

She was talking to the wrong person. Donovan hadn't the right to walk away. There was something wrong and he felt a duty to find out what.

'It's to do with that photograph, isn't it? The girl—your bridesmaid—she really is Elphie's mother.'

'Cal—'

'But that's not it. She is, but that's not the problem. What is it you don't want me to know? That she's a relative of yours? Big deal. Who is she, your sister?'

Sarah Turner neither confirmed nor denied it. But a pulse of electricity flickered between them like tiny lightning, making the pots rattle in Sarah's hands and raising hairs on the back of Donovan's neck, and he knew then he was on the right track. It didn't explain much, but he knew now that he hadn't imagined any of this. There was a mystery, and it centred on a girl in a flowered dress in a twenty-year-old photograph.

He pressed on. Interviewing someone who isn't giving you any answers is like building a bridge: you throw out the construction ahead of you in the hope that when you reach the point where it ceases to be self-sustaining there'll be something waiting out there to connect it to.

'That's it? Your kid sister and your husband's son had a child? OK, I can see that might raise a few eyebrows. But it was eight years ago, and she doesn't even live here any more. Why is it still casting a shadow over all your lives?'

His voice dropped as the fingers of presentiment stroked his spine. 'Elphie? This is about Elphie, and what's wrong with her. What is it? Sarah, tell me.'

Sarah shook her head. 'You'll never have heard of it. Almost no one has. All the same, your ancestors knew about it. They thought children like Elphie were changelings. That they were fairies and goblins left in the place of human children. In your part of the world they called them the Little People. But it's not supernatural, it's just a genetic flaw, it could happen anywhere...'

But it *had* happened in East Beckham, in a small, isolated community that had hardly changed since the time when people believed in fairies. Donovan knew about small communities, he came from one himself. He knew about the iron fist of local opinion. The smaller the community, the less room there was in it for the individual; and communities didn't come much smaller than East Beckham.

But this had gone beyond raised eyebrows and sniggering behind the bulk sheds. A girl had abandoned her baby because of it.

'I don't understand,' he growled. 'Why did it matter to people? They were only related by marriage, they were free to marry if they wanted. In London, even in Castlemere, nobody'd give a damn. It was bad luck about the baby, but that was all it was. They're not the first couple ever to have a damaged child. For obvious reasons, remote villages like this see more than their fair share. Mostly they're tolerated pretty well. But not here. Here they resented Elphie enough to drive her mother out.

'Didn't they? They hounded her. They needed Simon to safeguard their jobs, but they wanted her out. Never mind that she had a new baby—a handicapped baby—never mind the anxiety she must have been feeling right then. The people of this village blamed her for bringing a changeling into their midst, and they turned on her. They made her life a torment. And Simon let them, and so did you.'

Sarah Turner was crying. Hunched over the sink, unable to shield her face for the pots she was too upset to put down, she let the tears flow down her cheeks and drip from her chin. 'You don't understand,' she whispered raggedly; 'you don't understand.'

Donovan shook his head. Scorn dripped from his voice. 'Yes,

I do. Places like East Beckham, like Glencurran, they're the last stronghold of fascism. People who'd be laughed off their soap-box anywhere else can still manage to grab a little power in a place like this. Who was it, stirring it up? Making damn sure the misgivings turned to outrage and everyone knew where to direct it?'

But actually he found he knew. 'It was Chapel, wasn't it?— the good doctor. Pointing the finger, making sure everyone knew what it meant—what the implications were of a genetic flaw in that particular baby. ''What's the place coming to when some smart little madam with her city clothes and her city morals can come in here and seduce her own sister's stepson? Is that the sort of person we want to live with—that we want our children to grow up around? When they ask why Elphie's the way she is, what are we going to tell them? It's because her mother's a harlot?'''

'Please,' sobbed Sarah. 'Please—'

But his compassion was not for her. 'And you let them. If you'd stood by her, you and Simon, they couldn't have hurt her. But you disapproved too. You weren't going to brave the con-tempt of your friends and neighbours to dignify a relationship you too believed was wrong. You turned your back on her, and they drove her out.

'Whatever Elphie's problem is, it could only be a coincidence. Your stepson and your sister have no genes in common. But to a place like East Beckham, to people like these, it looked like a judgement. They wanted someone to pay. What was her name?'

He took her by surprise. She'd answered before she knew it. 'Rosemary.'

'Where is she now?'

'I don't know.'

His dark brows soared. 'Your own sister? Elphie's mother— you don't know where she is?'

'She went to London. I heard she went to the States. I never heard from her again.'

'Why didn't she take Elphie with her?'

'It would have been too difficult.' Sarah's voice was so low it was barely audible. 'A woman on her own with no home and a handicapped baby? Elphie was better off here. Rosemary was better off alone.'

'Do you know you're talking about her in the past tense?' Donovan waited, but apart from the tears on her cheek Sarah made no response.

He was getting a bad feeling about all this. He'd thought he was somewhere near the truth. He'd thought it was bad enough, and reason enough for shame, that this poor girl—or woman, rather, these events happened some twelve years after the wedding group posed self-consciously in front of the church—was driven from her home and family, and some of the people he'd met in the last couple of days were responsible and others had stood by and watched.

But it didn't explain their reaction to him, to his arrival in their midst. What they had done was monstrous but it probably wasn't illegal. Even if it was, without a complaint from Rosemary he couldn't pursue it. Yet they looked at him as if he had the power to pull The Flower Mill down about their ears. 'Does she visit Elphie?'

'No.'

'Does she write—birthday cards, Christmas presents?'

'No.'

He sucked in a deep breath. People do disappear without trace, but only two ways. Some of them vanish from choice—there's something in their lives that they're running away from. Was Elphie's mother the kind of woman to abandon a handicapped baby and never enquire how she was getting on? Or was this the other kind of diappearance?

'Sarah—is your sister still alive?'

The woman stared at him, appalled. 'Of course she is!'

'How do you know?'

'I—she—' She drew breath and started again. 'She went to London. I heard she went to live in America.'

The tall policeman with his dark eyes like coals in the illness-pallor of his skin was slowly nodding. 'Did she? Or was that just the cover story? The people responsible told you she'd gone to London, and it suited you to believe them. She vanished overnight, you never saw or heard from her again, but those who'd taken upon themselves the moral guardianship of this precious little village told you she'd gone to London and it was in everyone's best interests that you didn't enquire any further.

'I don't think she went to London, Sarah, and I don't think she went to the States. I think she's still here. I think she died here and was buried out on the fen.'

Her mouth opened but no sounds came out. Her face was ashen.

'Did they kill her, Sarah? Because she lay with her sister's stepson and gave birth to a changeling? Because she refused to apologize for that, to genuflect to local opinion—to Dr Chapel's opinions. He called her—what, Jezebel, the whore of Babylon? She laughed in his face. They accused her and she defied them. She dared them to do their worst.

'And they did. They killed her.'

ONE

SHAPIRO COMPLETED the last flight of stairs one at a time, his face rigid with pain. Mary Wilson followed him anxiously, wanting to help and afraid of hurting his feelings. She wondered what Liz would have done. Probably told him to stay where he was and brought Sheila Crosbie down to see him.

'Sir, why don't I—?' she began.

'Tell you what, constable,' he interrupted through gritted teeth, 'why don't you make a note in your pocketbook? Suggested new regulation for consideration by Division: officers of superintendent rank or above should only interview suspects living above the first floor if there's a reliable lift.'

'It'll get a lot of support, sir.'

'So it should,' grunted Shapiro, finally reaching the last landing. 'It'll make a lot of fat old men very happy.'

Wilson took a minute to get out her pocketbook, test her pen, even blow her nose before knocking at Sheila's door. Shapiro wasn't fooled for a moment—she was giving him time to get his breath back.

Ms Crosbie answered the door with the baby in her arms. He wasn't asleep: he looked at Shapiro as if enquiring as to his business.

Sheila reacted differently. Her face slammed shut. She waited for a warrant card to confirm that the stout man at her door was who he claimed to be, then she nodded brusquely. She didn't ask them in, remained in the doorway, blocking it with her slight body. 'Again?' she said testily.

Shapiro pretended not to understand. 'Sorry?'

'This is the third time. I told them at the police station what happened, and I told the woman detective who came here what happened. Why do you think I'll tell you something different?'

The superintendent appeared to give that some thought. 'Because,' he said at length, judiciously, 'I'm not sure you were telling the truth.'

In polite society one doesn't often call another a liar to his face. Frank Shapiro was clearly a polite man, a decent respectable middle-class man, a husband and father and pillar of his community. Sheila didn't believe he'd have said that to her without good reason. Something behind her expression shrank and fell inward; she hugged the baby as if for protection. Her lips pursed and her eyes dropped. Then they rose again, defiantly. 'I don't know what you mean.' But a thickness in her voice belied the words.

Wilson offered a sympathetic little smile. 'Ms Crosbie, why don't we go inside and sort this out? I don't expect you've done anything too dreadful—just embroidered the truth a little? Really, that's all we need to know. Then we won't waste time following up false leads. Put the record straight, then we'll all know where we stand.'

At last, still reluctantly, the girl let them inside. Jason continued to watch the encounter with interest.

'Now,' said Shapiro, 'about this baby lotion. We know you bought it at Simpson's; we know that the warning label was already attached. It matches the others we have, we know it was put there by the blackmailer. What I need you to be absolutely honest about is whether there actually was caustic soda in the bottle.'

His gaze was steady and he waited for her answer without further prompting. The next step she had to take alone, and if need be he'd wait all day.

She wasn't intimidated. If she was hiding something, she wasn't going to give it up just because he asked her. 'Your doctor saw the state of my hands. What do you think—I did that to myself?'

'People do,' Shapiro assured her.

'Jesus!' Sheila turned on her heel, into the nursery, and put the baby down. He gurgled and reached towards the wooden animals prancing their slow circle in the airs above his cot.

Her hands free, Sheila spread the palms under Shapiro's nose. 'Look at them! They're still not right. It hurt like hell at the time, and it still hurts if I forget when I'm cooking or washing up. You think I did that deliberately? Why, for God's sake? You think I'm some kind of a pain freak?'

'People who do this,' Shapiro answered carefully, 'do it because they need attention. They're depressed, or frightened, or maybe just bored, and even pain is an acceptable price if they can get people to take notice of them. It makes them feel alive. Being ignored is like being dead.'

Her eyes thought he was mad. She pointed one arm, shaking with anger, at the cot. 'See that? That's what we in the trade call a baby. They need your full attention, a hundred per cent, twenty-four hours a day. If they don't get it they grizzle. Then they cry, and after that they scream. The MOT people fail cars that make as much noise as a ratty baby. Ignored? Mr Shapiro, I'd give my income support for the chance of being ignored for a full hour every day. I don't need to burn myself in order to get noticed. I just need to take Jason into a busy supermarket and tell him he can't eat the mothballs.'

It was only a theory but it had been a good one, he'd had hopes of it. But it was the most basic error in criminal detection: to cling to a theory, even an elegant one, when the evidence starts to contradict it. Listening to Sheila Crosbie rant Shapiro felt his doubts growing. Maybe she was hiding something but it wasn't that. She wasn't seeking attention, so she hadn't applied caustic soda to her own hands. Which left her as a victim after all.

He gave it one last try. 'Do you have caustic soda in the flat, Miss Crosbie?'

She glared at him. 'No. I don't use it; I've never used it. I like my household cleaners in handy sprays.'

'You won't mind if I check under the sink?'

'Not if it'll get you to leave.'

After that he didn't expect to find the stuff, and he didn't.

She could have disposed of it. But his gut instinct was that he'd jumped to the wrong conclusion; again.

Standing in the nursery door, Mary Wilson said, 'I like this mobile. Where did you get it?'

'What?' snapped Sheila, without taking her eyes off Shapiro.

'The mobile. It's hand-carved, isn't it? Those balls-within-balls can't be made any other way. Did you make it?'

'No.'

'No, I couldn't either. It's clever work, that; someone's a real perfectionist. His father, was it?'

'No,' Sheila said again, sharper.

'No? Your father, perhaps.'

'My father's dead. Will you go now?'

'Sheila,' Wilson said quietly, 'I don't believe you bought this. If you got it in a shop—if you could find it in a shop—it would cost a fortune, and I don't think you have money to waste on decorations. I think somebody made it for Jason. And I can't imagine why you won't tell me who.'

'It's none of your business!'

Shapiro said, 'You're acting as if it is.'

'Who is Jason's father?' asked Wilson. It was impertinent but the way Sheila was behaving suggested it was relevant. Still, Shapiro was glad she'd asked and saved him having to.

'I don't know. All right?—I don't know. That month, the fun just never stopped. I don't know who Jason's father is, and he doesn't know he has a son. I found the mobile in a second-hand shop, and it cost me three pounds.'

'It's brand new. It's new, and beautifully made. Made with love.'

She couldn't stop herself. 'Oh no it wasn't!'

Shapiro regarded the girl with a degree of compassion. Whatever was going on here, whatever she was trying to hide, she was in deep trouble; and she knew it, and she didn't know what to do about it. 'Sheila, talk to us. I know you're involved in this somehow. You're not going to convince me otherwise. Do you know who's behind the blackmail? Jason's father—is that who it is? Is that who you're protecting?'

'He burnt me!' She thrust out her hands again. 'He would have burnt Jason! Why would I protect him?'

'Would have?' echoed Shapiro softly.

'What?' She didn't understand.

'Would have. Not "He could have burnt Jason"—he would have. Did he threaten your baby, Miss Crosbie? Is that why you agreed to help him? Why you put your hands in caustic soda and then came to us to complain about it?'

'No.' Just that: a blanket denial. He'd worn her down. She had no explanations, no alibi, nothing she could say in her own defence. All she could do was deny everything.

Shapiro sighed. 'All right, Miss Crosbie. Well, I know you're lying. I'm not sure what you're lying about, but I know you're not being honest with me. I think we need to talk about it, at length and without distractions. Do you have family locally?— if you want to call your mother, we can drop off Jason on the way.'

'No!'

Her vehemence took them both by surprise. Lots of people have issues with their mothers; lots of people, in defiance of the evidence, doubt their mother's ability to look after a baby. But it was as if Shapiro had suggested parking Jason on a high window ledge while they talked, and that wasn't normal. The girl was having to help police with their inquiries, but still she wasn't as worried for herself as she was for her baby.

'Miss Crosbie,' said Shapiro, 'it's obvious that you're worried sick about something, and I don't think it's me. So either you haven't done anything I can lock you up for, or someone else is threatening you with something worse than the judicial process. I'm right, aren't I? You know who's doing this, and you're afraid what he'll do to Jason if you tell me.' He made her look at him. 'Miss Crosbie, I can't help you, and I can't protect either of you, until I know who it is you're afraid of.'

She shook her head, the rats' tails of her fringe flying. 'I don't need any help,' she said, 'and I can't help you. And the only protection Jason needs is me. If you're going to take me away, *you* take the responsibility. Take him into care.'

Shapiro stared at her in astonishment. People do occasionally

put their own children into care, as a last resort. But Sheila
Crosbie would rather have social services look after her baby
for the time this was going to take rather than leave him with
her own mother? Shapiro had come here suspecting this girl of
exaggerating her involvement. He was beginning to think it
would be impossible to exaggerate her involvement.

'Are you sure that's what you want?'

Sheila nodded stubbornly. 'If I'm not with him, that's the only
place he'll be safe.'

'From your mother?'

She eyed him with overt scorn. 'Of course not from my
mother.'

'Then—from his father?'

Her lips tightened, and she shook her head once more, deci-
sively. 'I'm saying nothing more. You think I'm lying? Then
prove it.'

DONOVAN DEMANDED to know where Dr Chapel lived. He believed that Chapel, if asked a direct question, would disdain to
lie to him. He remembered the conversation between Simon
Turner and the doctor at dinner. He no longer believed they were
talking about pest control.

Sarah wouldn't tell him. She blocked the kitchen door with
her body. He could have moved her aside; but she was a woman
old enough to be his mother who'd been good to him. And she
was so afraid. He didn't think she was trying to protect herself
from the consequences of what happened eight years ago. She
must know that keeping him here would only delay the inevi-
table. No, what she feared was a still avoidable catastrophe.

And it wasn't Donovan she was afraid of. For a bizarre moment he thought she was afraid *for* him. That was absurd; but
the terror in her eyes was certainly for someone else. Someone
close to her, someone who mattered a damn sight more than an
itinerant policeman who'd been unwise enough to fall ill in the
vicinity of East Beckham. Simon or Elphie: no one else had the
power to tap her emotions like that.

He had to remind himself that this was a woman who'd allowed her sister to be hounded to death. She didn't deserve his

sympathy. 'Sarah,' he said gruffly, 'I *am* going to talk to Chapel.
I think he knows what happened here, and I think he's arrogant
enough to tell me. Now, either you can get out of my way or I
can move you.'

Clinging to the door handle behind her back she pleaded with
him. 'Cal, you don't know what you're doing! You're wrong
about Rosemary. I swear to God, she came to no harm here.'

'You know that? For a fact?'

'Yes! Listen: if you don't believe me, ask Simon. Let me call
him. Wait till he gets here.'

'Call him how?'

'On his mob—' She bit the word off short with a guilty start.
It was already too late. He'd been pretty sure they'd been
preventing him from communicating with the outside world:
now he knew. 'OK. But now: I'm not wasting any more time.'

'He'll be here in five minutes. God in heaven, Cal, you owe
us five minutes!'

It took four, and Turner arrived knowing what the situation
was. There was no need for explanations. So they'd talked about
this, discussed what they'd do if they couldn't keep the truth
from him.

Turner said brusquely, 'Come into the study. I don't want
anyone walking in on us.'

He sat down behind his desk; Sarah took the chair by the
window. Donovan stayed on his feet. All this was taking its toll
on him, he'd have to rest soon, but he thought that if he sat
down now he wouldn't be able to get up again quickly enough
if the need arose.

'This is about Rosemary,' Turner began.

'Yes.'

'You think she's dead?'

'Yes.'

'She isn't. The last time I saw her she was in London, packing
to leave for Boston. She was in perfect health.'

'I'm supposed to take your word for that.'

'I may be able to contact her. I know the firm she was working for: even if she's moved on they may have a forwarding
address.'

'And it might take some time to find out whether they have or not,' said Donovan sceptically. 'When it comes to delaying tactics, this family could play for England.'

A note of desperation was rising in Turner's voice. 'What more can I tell you? You suspect a woman was murdered here. I've told you you're wrong and I've offered to prove it: what more do you expect of me?'

'You could prove it back in Castlemere. I dare say my superintendent could get an answer from Boston rather faster than you could.'

Turner hesitated. Donovan showed his teeth in a feral smile. 'Yeah, right.'

'No, *listen* will you?' insisted Turner. 'Make this official and you're going to destroy my family; and for nothing. Nobody hurt Rosemary. Unless you count me.' He forced a grim chuckle. 'I wasn't the man she took me for. But she left here because she wanted to. Rosemary always did what she wanted.'

'You're doing it too,' said Donovan. Turner looked puzzled. 'Talking about her in the past tense.'

'These are past events we're talking about! It's more than six years since I saw Rosemary last, eight since Mum did. She went out of our lives, by her own choice. And she chose not to keep in touch.'

'Not even with her daughter?'

'Elphie's my daughter,' he said softly, obscurely.

'I know.' Donovan frowned. 'What do you mean?'

'What's wrong with Elphie,' Turner said quietly, 'it's my fault. Not Rosemary's; not even just bad luck. It could have been avoided. It happened because I wasn't honest with her. She never forgave me for that. I think she thought leaving Elphie with me was...not exactly a punishment, perhaps just deserts.'

'How the hell can you be responsible for something like that?'

'Please—just take my word for it.'

'I can't!'

'If you don't, you're going to destroy us all.'

Donovan shook his head crisply. 'Then you have a big problem, because nothing that's happened so far makes me willing to take your word for anything. You've lied to me from the moment I woke up. You didn't move my boat out of your way, you moved it to keep me here. You say you took it to Posset but that isn't true either: you didn't want anybody to know I was here and George Jackson was bound to ask. And what about my dog? You said he was all right, that he was being cared for; but if *Tara* isn't at the Posset Inn you didn't leave him with George. What's happened to him?

'You cut off the phone. You didn't want me calling George, and you certainly didn't want me calling my nick. That car I heard in the yard last night—that was someone looking for me, wasn't it? Nobody round here uses a car, you live too close to one another. Somebody came here looking for me, and you sent them away. You told them you hadn't seen me.

'And now all at once you don't want to keep me here any more, you want me to go—and you still haven't told me why! If I'm wrong about your sister,' he demanded of Sarah, 'what is it you're so desperate to hide?'

Turner and his stepmother traded a fast glance. For a split second it seemed they wavered on the precipice of the truth; but then Simon looked down and saw the rocks. His voice was thick. 'We saved your life, Sergeant Donovan. You owe us something for that. I'll tell you what it is. I'll get the Land Rover and drive you out of here right now. I can drop you at Posset, I can take you to the Sinkhole engine house: you can call for transport from either of them, you'll be in Castlemere within the hour. What you do after that is your decision. If you want to come back here with sirens and flashing lights there's nothing I can do to stop you.'

Obviously there was something he hadn't yet said, the hook beneath the bait. 'But...?' Donovan prompted heavily.

Simon Turner looked like a man forced to choose which arm to have ripped off. His round face was not designed for deceit, and he was no better at hiding the pain of this than the fact that he'd been lying for the last three days. 'I want you to take my daughter with you.'

Sarah lurched to her feet, a hand flying to her mouth, a cry of 'No!' torn from her as if by torture. They hadn't discussed this. Was this what she saw and dreaded when she looked in Donovan's face: the breaking of her family?

Simon came round the desk and grasped her wrists in both his hands. 'I have to. Don't you understand?—I have to. She isn't safe here any more.'

'Why not?' demanded Donovan, confusion turning to anger because everything they said, everything they did, far from helping him to understand only compounded the mystery further. 'Why is Elphie in danger? Whatever happened, it wasn't her fault. She's a child: when Rosemary—left—she was only a baby...'

And that was it. He saw it in their faces. He wasn't sure what he'd found, but he knew it was the answer. The dominoes were all standing there, ready to fall: he just needed to set the first one in motion. He backed up a pace or two. Elphie: she was only a baby when all this started. And it was Simon's fault she wasn't like other people's babies...

The photograph. The Turners' wedding photograph: he knew what was wrong with it. Glencurran folk were great marriers: he'd seen enough wedding snaps in his time to know what they should look like. His aunties, the last repository on Irish soil of the Donovan family history, practically papered the front room with them. And they all looked the same: bride and bridegroom arm in arm, his family grouped on one side, hers on the other.

A domino teetered and fell. He called her Mum. But this boy was in his mid-teens when his father remarried: why didn't he call her Sarah?

He was standing beside her in the photo, a happy smile on his young face, looking forward to the future. A new home, more money than perhaps they'd been used to, the chance to join a man he liked in a business that interested him.

But the other boy, dark and wary at the bridegroom's side, had as much to lose as his stepbrother had to gain. He was going to have to share his home and his father with strangers, and he was pretty sure he'd have to share his inheritance with them too. Alienated, disenfranchised, he packed his bags and hit the road as soon as he was old enough.

Looking up, hollow-eyed, Donovan couldn't believe how stu-

pid he'd been. Damn it, they even looked alike—the same fair
hair and light eyes, the same open expression. Call himself a
detective?—a child could have seen the family likeness in all
three of them. In fact, a child had. Sarah Turner, her sister Rosemary—and her son Jonathan.

'*Now* I understand,' he breathed. 'It wasn't Rosemary who
died, was it? It was Simon.'

TWO

THE MAN DONOVAN had known as Simon Turner exchanged a fast, desperate glance with the woman who was—now—so obviously his mother. Clearly it was in the minds of both of them to deny that too, to maintain the deceit until the DNA results turned an inspired guess into a scientific fact.

Donovan panted at them in frustration. He'd known a lot of criminals in his life—sometimes he seemed to know no one else—and a number of murderers. The Turners—for lack of a better term—didn't fit any pattern he was familiar with. It wasn't just that they'd been kind to him, they seemed genuinely decent people. Except that at some point in the last twenty years a young man had died and been supplanted, in every particular of his life, by his stepbrother. Everyone in this village must know it, and none of them had done anything about it.

'I don't *believe* you people!' he spat. 'You move into this man's home, you accept his protection and his generosity—and when he dies you murder his son so you can keep control of his business! The poor bloody kid might well have looked sour at the wedding. He must have had the second sight.'

Sarah reached for his sleeve. Tears were streaming down her face: he wasn't sure whom she was crying for. 'Cal, I promise you, it wasn't like that. It was an accident...'

Jonathan threw up a broad hand in despair, but after that there was no point in lying further. They could tell him the truth or they could tell him nothing, but there was no longer any mileage in claiming that Elphie's father was Simon Turner.

Elphie...

Donovan sucked in a sharp breath. '*That's* why Elphie's how she is. Rosemary thought you were Robert's son. But you aren't, you're Sarah's—Elphie's the product of an affair with your aunt! Jesus!' he said then. 'It was only an affair? You didn't actually marry her?'

Jonathan shut his eyes. Then he shook his head. 'No. Even my stupidity knew some bounds. It was hardly even an affair— not much more than a one-night stand. But as you say, there were consequences.'

'Tell me what happened.' Then, remembering what it was they were talking about, he added, 'You do not have to say anything. But I must caution you that if—'

Jonathan cut him off with a wave of the hand. 'I know my rights. And if you're expecting a confession to murder you're going to be disappointed. But I will tell you what happened. Only, to understand, you have to go back twenty years. To when Mum and Robert were married.'

THE DAY AT THE CHURCH was filled with such promise. Two lonely people had found one another and the auspices were good. Sarah said it was love, and the beam on the man in the picture said she could well have been right.

More than that, two teenage boys who had been managing on one parent each would now have a full set as well as built-in companionship; and the business with which a widower had struggled alone would benefit from new hands and fresh ideas.

And for six years the portents were justified. The marriage was happy, the business throve. Sarah's son Jonathan flourished under the tutelage of his stepfather and at eighteen went off to horticultural college in France. The plan was that when he qualified he could assume more and more responsibility for The Flower Mill until Robert was ready to retire and install him as manager.

The only discordant note was the life Simon Turner chose for himself. He had never had any interest in the business, nor was the extended family to his liking. His father put it down, probably correctly, to his age and facilitated his desire to travel instead of grow bulbs. He continued to hope, even as the years stretched and the postcards came less and less often, that one day Simon would come home.

Fourteen years ago, said Jonathan, aged twenty-one, he returned to The Flower Mill with a newly framed diploma and a heart full of ideas for improving the business. But six weeks later, sitting on a straw bale to catch his breath, Robert Turner succumbed to a stroke. He was dead before the ambulance arrived.

Their first thought was that when the shock and grief subsided, life in East Beckham would go on much as it had. They were fortunate that Jonathan had chosen to follow in Robert's footsteps when his own son had not. The transfer of power would be as smooth as could be hoped for.

The first indication they might have presumed too much came with the reading of Robert's will. Naturally he provided, and generously, for his widow and stepson. But The Flower Mill was a family business, built up by Turners before him, and he left it to his own son—expressing the perhaps naive hope that the returned wanderer and the qualified plantsman might together forge a team strong enough to carry the Mill into the next millennium.

It wasn't what Jonathan had hoped for, but he was too honest a man to deny Simon's entitlement and he readied himself to work with and if necessary under him.

But Simon had no more interest in owning a bulb field than living on one. He returned to arrange for the sale of The Flower Mill. Not the house, which was Sarah's, but the fields and the sheds and all the paraphernalia of a successful business.

SARAH TOOK UP THE STORY. 'I begged him, pleaded with him. Not for my sake, I was secure and always would be. Not even for Jonathan: he could have had a good job in any nursery in the country. It was the village people I was concerned for. The Flower Mill was and still is the only employer. If Simon had sold it as a going concern it would have been something. But the best offer he was getting was from a leisure consortium that wanted to build a golf club. There'd have been a few jobs on the domestic side, they'd have needed a couple of groundsmen, but generations of experience growing bulbs would suddenly have been worth nothing. It would have been the death of East Beckham.'

'We tried to buy him out,' said Jonathan. Fourteen years later it was in his face and his voice that this was important, that he wanted Donovan to understand they'd tried to do things properly. 'People in the village were going to put money in too, we'd have run it as a co-operative. But we couldn't match what the leisure people were offering, and Simon hadn't a sentimental bone in his body. He was never happy here, he didn't reckon to owe the place or the people anything. He just wanted the most money he could get for it, and we couldn't compete.'

He fell silent, sombre and pensive. This time Sarah made no effort to continue the tale. Donovan supplied an ending. 'So you killed him.'

'No!' insisted Jonathan, his head coming up with a jerk. 'It was an accident. A tractor turned over on him. He wasn't familiar with heavy machinery, he shouldn't even have been driving it.'

'Why was he?'

Jonathan shrugged. 'We don't know,' murmured Sarah.

'OK,' said Donovan ruthlessly, 'so what makes you think he *was* driving it? Did you see him?'

Sarah shook her head.

'Damn it,' snarled Jonathan, 'it was on top of him in a ditch when we found him! It seemed a pretty safe guess that was what happened. Maybe he saw it as his last chance to play with his father's toys—I don't know. But he turned it over and it killed him.'

For the moment Donovan was prepared to leave it at that. Now they were talking he didn't want to break the flow. There'd be time to go into the details later. Besides, he really needed to sit down. He gestured at the spare chair. 'Do you mind?'

Jonathan shook his head. 'Of course not.'

Sarah said, 'You're really not up to this yet.'

Donovan chuckled weakly. 'Don't worry about me. Just— let's get this sorted out.'

Turner—except his name wasn't even Turner—gave an uneasy shrug. 'I don't know if we've time for all this.'

Misunderstanding, Donovan raised an eyebrow. 'I'm not going anywhere. Do you have more pressing business?'

'I meant—' But he didn't explain what he meant. 'All right. Where were we?'

'Simon had conveniently killed himself in a tractor he'd no reason to be driving,' Donovan said, deadpan.

IT WAS HARD TO REMEMBER, this long after, who first put it into words. The same idea occurred to several people more or less simultaneously: they could see it in one another's eyes. Finally somebody said it out loud.

'They'd both been away, you see,' Sarah said softly. 'Jonathan in France, Simon all over the world. Outside East Beckham there was no one who'd recognize either of them. It was feasible, if we all agreed.'

'To switch identities. To bury Simon Turner as Jonathan—' Donovan realized he didn't know her previous name.

'Payne. Yes.'

There wasn't much time. They could leave it overnight, pretend it was morning before they found the tractor in the ditch with the body underneath, but that was about all. They couldn't discuss it for a week and still expect to be believed. It had to be done quickly if it were to be done at all.

'We sat round that table in the kitchen and talked till three in the morning,' Jonathan remembered. 'It was so difficult—it seemed terribly wrong, to take a man's name in order to get your hands on his inheritance. I kept thinking how hurt Robert would be. But the fact was, Robert was gone; and so was Simon. We weren't actually hurting anyone—unless you count a leisure conglomerate none of us knew or wanted to. We were protecting a community, a way of life, my stepfather thought the world of. We couldn't bring Simon back by telling the truth. And we didn't know who'd inherit, who'd have the last word on whether the Mill was sold.

'Whereas if Simon was still alive, he could change his mind. Nothing had been signed. I had it in my power to look after all these people, my mother included. I could have refused. They couldn't have gone ahead without me. But the more we talked about it, the more selfish that seemed.'

'You can't blame Jonathan for the decision we reached,' Sarah interjected, stern in defence of her cub. 'He was twenty-one years old—he was a boy. We put him in a position where he had to choose between our future and his honour. Since then, of course, we've all had our regrets. But Jonathan made the biggest sacrifice for the smallest gain.'

'So you called for an ambulance and told the authorities your son was dead.'

She nodded, her eyes tight shut. 'You have no idea how difficult that was. Identifying the body, making the funeral arrangements. We had him cremated, it seemed safest. I thought I'd have to try and cry, to make it look right. It was no effort at all. I never knew him well, and the last time we spoke we were shouting at one another because what he wanted was going to destroy what I wanted. But he was Robert's son, and he died in a ditch, and he wasn't even getting the respect of burial under his own name. I was ashamed. Crying came naturally.'

'Then you went home and called off the deal with the leisure company.'

Jonathan nodded. 'I thought that was where it would fall apart. Simon had met these people, shown them round. If they came back they'd know I wasn't Simon Turner. I wrote to them in the first instance, told them the recent death of my stepbrother made it impossible to go ahead at this time, that my stepmother couldn't be asked to cope with any more.

'I expected they'd make a fight of it—come over and try to persuade me. They'd already spent money on a feasibility study, it was going to be wasted for what was not much more than a whim. And anyone who knew him, even slightly, would know Simon wasn't sentimental.

'In the event that worked for us. The conglomerate realized it was an excuse, but they thought I was trying to push the price up. They played it cool and said they understood perfectly, I should contact them again when I was ready to proceed. They warned that, of course, by then they might have lined up another deal... Plainly they expected me to call them back inside twenty-four hours. But I didn't, and apart from a rather cool follow-up a month later, which I also parried, they weren't going to beg. They thought it was about money and they weren't going to up their offer. The thing was laid to rest with much less trouble than I'd been anticipating.'

'A bit like Simon,' observed Donovan brutally.

Indignation sparked in Jonathan Payne's eye. 'You reckon? Simon's been dead for fourteen years. In that time he's been back to haunt us twice.'

If Donovan himself represented the second manifestation then the first was... 'You're talking about Rosemary.'

Payne nodded, then looked away. He was sorry about what happened to Simon. He was ashamed of what happened to Rosemary.

IT HAD BEEN ELEVEN years since the wedding. They had met for the first time outside the church, parted the next day. In all that time Jonathan Payne might have addressed three remarks to his Aunt Rosemary. He just about noticed she was a lot younger than his mother, a bare five years older than himself. She noticed that he'd grown since last time she'd seen him, but since that was his Christening she was hardly surprised. Five years is still a lot at that age.

Five years is a lot less between a man of twenty-six and a woman of thirty-one. A career woman with the world at her feet, she was beautiful and strong and confident, and she knocked him off his feet.

He knew it was impossible, out of the question. But she didn't, and of the two she was the stronger. And no one had let her in on the secret, and she never suspected the deception that had occurred and the massive consequences it would have for her. Paying her sister her once-a-decade visit, Rosemary found herself in the company of an intelligent, sensitive, good-looking young man, strong and hard-bodied from physical toil, whom she believed to be her sister's stepson Simon Turner, aged twenty-eight, rightful owner of all she surveyed.

It wasn't greed: she had money of her own. But powerful

people gravitate together: they see themselves in the mirror of one another and self-love is a great aphrodisiac. She wanted him. Her sister's fury only added to the pleasure of the chase.

'I tried to warn him,' said Sarah, speaking into her lap. 'I knew what she was like. I was fond of Rosemary, but her dearest friends would have to admit she was wilful. And—predatory.' She looked up. 'Isn't that what they say these days? A sexual predator?'

Not in Glencurran they didn't, and not much in Castlemere. But Donovan knew what she meant. He'd known people like that too; had spent his heart on one. 'She made the running?'

'I could have stopped it,' gritted Payne. 'She didn't rape me. A man with an ounce of character would have walked away.'

'But you didn't.'

'Not in time. It only happened once. The next day I told her it had been a mistake, it couldn't happen again. I asked her to leave and she stormed off back to London. But it was already too late.'

'When did you know?'

'Thirteen months later,' said Sarah, a bitter edge on her voice. 'When a red sports car roared into the yard. I was in the kitchen: I looked to see who it was. Rosemary was the last person I was expecting. She took a small suitcase out of the boot and put it on the kitchen step. Then she lifted something off the passenger seat and put it on top of the suitcase. I couldn't make out what it was. It almost looked like a carrycot.'

IT ALMOST LOOKED like a carrycot. Intrigued, Sarah went to the door and opened it, a greeting on her lips with a question right behind. But Rosemary was already stalking across the yard towards the packing sheds. Puzzled, Sarah looked down at the basket on the steps. It *was* a carrycot, and there was a baby inside.

The man calling himself Simon Turner wasn't in the shed: Jim Vickery directed the angry young woman to his office at the front of the house. Sarah too was looking for her son, to tell him what she'd found, and he was looking for her to ask what all the noise was about. They came together in the hall.

Rosemary was so angry she was shaking, her face flushed, her eyes ablaze. Apart from a brief detour to her flat she'd come here direct from the London clinic where she'd had the DNA tests done. The ones that showed Elphie's father and her mother shared almost as many genes as siblings do; that explained the baby's strange appearance and erratic development; that proved that Simon Turner was in fact Jonathan Payne. She'd borne her nephew's child.

Looking back she felt so stupid. The signs were there, if she'd thought to look for them. Damn it, she'd even met him under his own name. But he was fifteen years old, she a sophisticated young woman—why should she have remembered him? When she looked at the wedding photos—she wasn't a sentimental woman but she'd always thought she looked good that day and so she'd kept the ones Sarah sent her—it was as plain as day. The two boys didn't even look alike. Simon was dark; Jonathan was fair, like his mother. Like her.

Almost, that was what distressed her most. That she'd been duped. He hadn't come on to her, she'd come on to him, his reluctance only making her the more determined. That was why, when her contraception failed, she was not inclined to tell him. She didn't need his help, and in all honesty he could not be considered responsible for the child.

Or, could not have been had all been well with Elizabeth. But it wasn't. From the moment of her birth there were problems. When the baby failed to thrive as she should have the doctors raised the possibility of blood testing. Rosemary agreed because she hoped it would help her baby. In the event it didn't—but it did explain her.

The moment she saw Jonathan, standing astonished in the hallway, she went for him. She went for his face with her nails and for his heart with the rapier of her tongue. Sarah would have intervened but for the precious burden in her arms; and Jonathan himself was too taken aback to respond, even when the blood-red talons scythed at him. He finally recoiled, too late, with shock in his eyes and bloody tracks across his cheekbone.

'You bastard!' she spat, her fury stoked rather than dampened by the miles she'd driven. 'You *bastard!* You animal.'

He had his hand to his face, fingers trembling in the slick blood. 'Rosemary—'

She swiped at him again; this time he backed out of range, stumbling against the hall table. 'Don't you *dare* speak to me! Have you any idea what you've done? Have you? You've brought into being a child with no place in the world, a child with no future. Nine months I carried her. For nine months there were things I'd rather have been doing, but I carried her because I owed her that much. I made a mistake, and you can't just walk away. I thought we could make it up to one another after she was born.'

She stabbed the taloned hand towards the cot. 'See that? That's your daughter. And that, more or less, is how she's going to be for the rest of her life. Bigger, but not a lot brighter. She may not walk. She may not talk. She may be in nappies all the years of her pointless existence. And you did that to her, and nothing you do now can ever make it right.'

Springing tears mixed with his blood on Jonathan Payne's cheek. 'I don't understand...'

Rosemary thrust her face into his. 'She's not right! Do you understand that? She's defective—retarded—mentally and physically handicapped. What's the latest euphemism?—she'll have learning difficulties. Jesus, will she have learning difficulties! Like, which hole in your face does your dinner go in? Somebody's going to be spoon-feeding her when she's twenty-five years old.'

She took a step back. 'But it isn't going to be me. This is your doing, Jonathan, not mine. You knew it was wrong, that it was dangerous, and you said *nothing!* You let me believe you were Simon Turner—that you were fair game! You let this happen rather than come clean with me.

'I don't know what you did to him. I presume he's dead, and that's what was worth concealing at any cost. Well, I hope you still feel that way in ten years' time. I hope you can look at your daughter and still think her suffering was not too great a price to pay.'

And with that she left. Stunned, frozen in the hallway, they heard the car roar and spit gravel, and then she was gone. And the bundle that was Elizabeth, that was going to be Elphie, was still lying in Sarah's arms, squinting up at her.

The child never saw her mother again, except in a photograph. Perhaps it was intuition that drew her to the pretty woman in the sprigged dress, perhaps an incautious word in front of a child supposedly too slow to understand pointed her in the right direction. Sarah never saw Rosemary again. There were no letters, no cards, not so much as a telephone call.

Jonathan saw her once more. Dr Chapel had found a specialist who seemed to offer Elphie the hope of enhanced development but wanted to speak to her mother first. Jonathan went to London.

He found Rosemary packing her bags. She noted with satisfaction the small scar remaining under his eye before returning to her task. She was going to a new job in Boston, she said. She had hoped never to see him again.

He explained the purpose of his visit.

Rosemary shrugged. 'Tell him you couldn't find me. Tell him I'm dead. I did my share, Jonathan: everything since then has been your problem. Deal with it.'

Downstairs a taxi honked, and she picked up her bags and left. He neither saw nor heard from her again. The specialist lost interest in the case and Elphie grew as best she could in the love of her family and the solitude of the fen. In the end, she didn't make too bad a job of it.

'I DON'T UNDERSTAND,' said Donovan. It wasn't the only thing, but it was the one bothering him now. 'Why do you want me to take Elphie away now? What are you afraid of?'

'Don't you see?—Elphie is living proof of what happened. That I'm not who I claim to be. All those involved are threatened by her existence. As long as everyone who knew about it lived within a stone's throw of this house there wasn't a problem— no one was going to betray the whole village. Then you came. If you began to suspect any of this, all you needed was a sample of Elphie's blood. All the information is there. If you'd died we'd have been safe, and so would she. Now—I don't know. I don't know if either of you is safe here any longer.'

'You think—' Donovan heard his voice crack with astonishment and tried again. 'You think the people here might want to *kill* her? Might want to kill me?'

Payne shrugged. 'It's a big fen out there, Sergeant Donovan. It's Elphie's playground, but it could easily become her grave. As for you, you're missing already. Your colleagues think you fell off your boat and drowned. A body in the canal would confirm it. Three men and a bucket is all it would take.'

Donovan was having trouble taking it in. But an instinct for survival warned him it really would be that easy. 'Would you be one of them?'

Payne shook his head. 'I told you: I want you to get Elphie away from here. Mum, go upstairs and put some things in a bag for her. We're going now, while there's nothing to stop us.'

Dead on cue the kitchen door opened and shut, slow footsteps sounded across the hall floor and the handle of the office door turned. A desiccated hand appeared in the opening, followed by the pickled-walnut face of Dr Chapel.

'Afternoon, everyone,' he greeted them equably. 'I said I'd pop round sometime today, and here I am.'

THREE

AFTER AN HOUR in the interview room Shapiro emerged rolling his eyes. 'I know she's involved. I can't for the life of me get her to open up.'

'Do you want me to try?' asked Liz. Her tone was subdued. Shapiro thought she was thinking about Brian; actually she was embarrassed that she'd talked to Sheila Crosbie, twice, and not realized she was implicated in this.

'By all means. But I don't think she's waiting to be asked nicely. It's like interrogating a POW: you get name, rank and serial number, and after that she just grits her teeth and sits there. She's not even denying it any more. She isn't saying anything at all.'

'She's protecting someone.'

'Yes. She isn't doing herself any good so that has to be it.'

Liz frowned. 'That was odd about her mother. Not wanting her to have the baby, I mean. I suppose she does live locally?'

Shapiro nodded. 'In The Jubilee, a few hundred yards from Sheila's flat. I don't understand it either.'

'Maybe we should try to,' said Liz. 'I'll go and see the mother. She may be so angry that her daughter doesn't trust her with her own grandson that she'll let something slip.'

The Jubilee was a strange place, a walled city at the heart of Castlemere. It was built in the closing years of the Victorian period, six streets of the last word in artisan accommodation. Two up and two down, in long terraces separated by cobbles at the front and back-to-back yards behind, the little houses celebrated the end of the war with new inside plumbing, then promptly entered a time bubble. They weren't exactly neglected but they never changed. Even the people were indistinguishable at first sight from their parents.

The Jubilee had a reputation in Castlemere as the place where all the town's ills were fermented. Certainly a good proportion of the households derived at least some of their income from crime or the black economy, but there were decent people in the six streets as well. Nothing Liz was able to pull off the computer, or learn from Sergeant Bolsover who probably knew more, suggested that Margaret Crosbie wasn't one of them. The widow of a dustman who died too young to become a refuse collector, she raised five children in the little house in Coronation Row. All seemed to have made some sort of a go of their lives, with jobs, partners and children of their own. Sheila was the youngest.

Liz knew she was doing Mrs Crosbie no favours by parking in front of the house. Whenever she changed her car The Jubilee knew what she'd got before Brian did. But if she parked on Brick Lane and walked, the same quietly observant eyes would note where she was going in just the same way. But nobody would throw stones at Mrs Crosbie's windows because she'd had the police round. On the contrary, it might raise her social cachet.

She didn't recognize Liz instantly, the way many of her neighbours would, but even a friendly visit from the police is unlike anything else. Mrs Crosbie didn't need to see Liz's warrant card. Her eyes grew alarmed and she wiped her hands nervously down the front of her apron. 'What's happened? Is it Sheila? Jason?'

'In a way,' nodded Liz. 'May I come in? Sheila's in a bit of trouble. I'm hoping you can help clear things up.'

She could have been more discreet about the precise nature of the trouble Sheila was in. But there was only one crime at the forefront of everyone's mind right now, and the idea that Castlemere's second most senior detective might be working on anything else wouldn't have fooled Mrs Crosbie for long.

'It's this business with the blackmailer,' Liz said simply. 'We think Sheila might know who it is.'

Mrs Crosbie stared at her in horror. She was a woman of

about fifty who spoke with the same fenland accent as Bolsover and Dick Morgan. 'Sheila? My Sheila?'

'I don't know how involved she is. She won't tell us. She's obviously protecting someone. But if she won't talk she'll end up taking the blame for this.' This was rather over-egging the pudding, but Liz felt justified by the gravity of the situation.

'But—Sheila got hurt, thanks to him. Our Jason could have been hurt.'

'Well, maybe,' said Liz. 'The other possibility is that she deliberately dipped her hands in caustic soda.'

'*Why?*' Mrs Crosbie clearly thought she was mad.

It was no more than a possibility, but it made a kind of twisted sense. 'Because the blackmailer asked her to. Because it was safer for him than having to plant the stuff in the chemist's. He'd have had to buy it, doctor it and put it back; and he had to do this with a couple of items, and there was the risk that Mr Simpson would remember him. He didn't want to take that risk. I think he bought the baby lotion, among other things, took them home and added some special ingredients. Caustic soda to the baby lotion, an inedible fungus to some cold remedy. The cold remedy he planted on Simpson's shelves when no one was looking, but he took the baby lotion round to Sheila's flat. He also took some soda crystals: he made up a solution with them and had Sheila put her hands in it.'

Put like that it sounded barely plausible. Liz would have forgiven Mrs Crosbie for laughing in her face. But it was too serious for that and both women knew it. Liz wasn't talking about what she could prove but about what she believed. She was desperately trying to stop a dangerous criminal.

'You're saying that Sheila's helping him.'

'He may be threatening her. Or Jason; I don't know.'

'You think I can tell you who he is?'

'I hope so. He's already hurt your daughter. If we don't stop him he'll do a lot more damage.' Liz waited.

'I don't know all her friends.'

'This man isn't a friend. He has a hold over her: a hold strong enough to make her risk going to prison.'

Margaret Crosbie thought in silence for perhaps half a minute.

Then she shook her head. 'There isn't anyone she cares that much about.'

'Really? No one?'

'Well, maybe two people. But I didn't do it, and I don't think Jason did either.'

'We wondered about Jason's father.'

Mrs Crosbie raised a sceptical eyebrow. 'Go to prison for him? She wouldn't cross the street for him; she wouldn't cross the room for him. Far as I know she hasn't seen him since before Jason was born. I'm sorry, Inspector, but you'll have to do better than that.'

But Liz shook her head despondently, all out of ideas. All that was left was the secret weapon. 'Mrs Crosbie, when we took Sheila in for questioning we asked if she wanted to drop the baby off here. She told us to leave him with social services instead. Why do you suppose that was?'

Margaret Crosbie's cheeks darkened, her eyes flicked down and she caught a ragged breath. Liz had thought that would hit her hard, and it did. And she wasn't expecting it. It wasn't that they never saw eye to eye, or they'd had a flaming row. She was hurt and astonished and mortified all at once. She floundered after words. 'I—I don't know—it makes no sense. She really said that? But she leaves him here all the time. He's my grandson, for God's sake! Why would she give him to social services?' Tears were audible in her voice; a moment later they were visible on her cheeks.

Liz winced. It would have been worth distressing her if it had got them anywhere; but it hadn't. 'Don't be upset, Mrs Crosbie. There will be a reason, if we can just work it out. And it won't be anything to do with you. It'll be to do with what she's got herself into.'

They'd moved into the living room. Mrs Crosbie sank into her easy chair, waved her visitor to the sofa.

'All right,' Liz said at length; 'all right. Sheila's afraid of something, and she's protecting someone. But the only people she cares that much about are you and Jason. So what if she acted as she did in order to protect you and Jason? She isn't helping the blackmailer from choice—she's afraid of what he might do to her family Is there anyone she's that afraid of?'

Mrs Crosbie was thinking too. 'Tell me something. When social services took our Jason, where did they take him to?'

Liz hazarded a guess. 'There's a big children's home on Cambridge Road. Dunstan House. It might have been there.'

Margaret Crosbie nodded slowly. 'A big place. Lots of staff?'

'Yes. What—?' Then she saw what difference that made. 'She's afraid of someone abducting him?'

'Maybe. Maybe that's what Social Services could offer that I can't. Staff, security locks, closed circuit TV. Here there's just me, and if someone was determined enough to get in I couldn't stop him.'

'The blackmailer? All right, he's a vicious, dangerous man, I wouldn't want him near any baby of mine either.' Liz was thinking aloud. 'Sheila knows him—she knows him well enough to be afraid of him. She helped him because he threatened to hurt Jason if she didn't.

'She did what he told her, we seemed to believe her story, she thought she'd got away with it. When we picked her up, shocked as she was, the thing that worried her most was that the man behind all this would find out. He'd blame her for letting him down. He can't get at her while she's in custody, but he could get at Jason. And if the baby was here when he caught up with him, you could be hurt as well.

'So she sent him to Dunstan House. She thought they could protect him. If Jason can't be with her, he's safer there than anywhere else. She wasn't doubting your ability to look after him, Mrs Crosbie. She was doing her best to look after both of you.'

Relief made the woman's voice shake. 'But—who—? How would my Sheila know somebody like that?'

'There's a mobile over Jason's cot. Somebody hand-carved it for him. Sheila put it up, but she didn't seem too pleased with it. We wondered if it was made by Jason's father.'

'The psycho?'

Liz breathed lightly. 'You call him The Psycho?'

'It's what she calls him. She wouldn't tell me his name. She said she never wanted to hear it again.'

'I mean—Sheila had a relationship with a man you both think of as a psychopath, and you didn't think to tell me?'

DR CHAPEL REMAINED in the doorway. His eyes went from one to the next of them, cooling as they travelled. Finally he said, 'You've told him, haven't you?' His voice crackled like ice. 'You stupid, stupid people.'

It was telling, Donovan thought, that neither of them objected to being the butt of his insults in their own home. It wasn't just the courtesy due to an old man, or even to a doctor. They were afraid of him. Events had conspired to invest this little man with far too much power in the lives of those around him. It was something else that could only have happened in a hamlet so small it looked like a fly speck on the map. The twentieth century had barely impinged on East Beckham at all.

Jonathan Payne gazed down at the buttons on his shirt front. 'Some of it he guessed,' he murmured. 'The rest... He thought we murdered Rosemary. It seemed better to tell him the truth.'

'Oh it did, did it?' Chapel shut the door behind him with a soft but very definite click. 'And you thought you were qualified to make that judgement.'

Payne's head came up and he seemed about to rebel against his diminutive oppressor. But the moment passed and his eyes dropped again. 'No one is more involved in this than I am.'

'That's true,' agreed Chapel, the creaky voice still managing to carry an edge. 'It'll be a great comfort to those of us who get ten years to hear that you got twelve.' He turned to Sarah. 'Did you even wonder what'll happen to Elphie when everyone she knows is in prison?'

That was designed to hurt and it did. Sarah Turner caught her breath in half a sob.

Donovan had no mandate to defend these people, but he did resent the way this vindictive little man was allowed to browbeat those around him. 'I can't begin to guess what a court will make of all this,' he said, 'I've never come across the like before. But

I know one thing. If Elphie needs looking after, she'll get it. You have my word.'

The old man laughed out loud. '*Your* word? Oh well, that's all right then, isn't it? She's going to lose her father, her grandmother and her home, but she's got the word of some mick detective that she'll be fine. I can't see her losing much sleep now.'

Finally Donovan understood why Payne wanted to get his daughter away from East Beckham. This man, this old and vicious man, this man he owed his life to, would do whatever was necessary to protect East Beckham's secret. He would punish anyone who challenged him, trample anyone who stood in his way, destroy without compunction anyone who posed a threat to his authority. Elphie? He wasn't concerned for the child. He'd use her when he needed leverage against the Turners, wash his hands of her as soon as it was expedient to do so.

In all his years at the heart of East Beckham society he'd accreted to himself a power that went far beyond the respect earned by his service here. People had learned to turn to him, then to defer to him; they'd sought his opinions, ended up doing his bidding. It was the only explanation for his presence in this room right now. Any of them, Sarah included, could have shouldered him aside. He was still telling them what to do because he knew that if they defied him he had the support of the entire village to whip them back into line.

Donovan stood up and, deliberately turning his back on the doctor, spoke quietly to Sarah. 'If Elphie's ready, I think we'll leave now.'

Chapel vented a loud cackle, as if he'd made a joke. 'Leave? You think you're leaving here? You think that now you know what the people here have lied about for fourteen years you can just walk out, start the wheels of justice in motion and never mind who gets crushed? You're only alive because of us. Because of me.'

'And I'm suitably grateful,' spat Donovan, rounding on him. 'In fact, I'm so grateful I can't wait to get back to town and tell everyone what a fine and noble example of the medical profession they've got themselves out here.'

'Sarcasm,' the old man observed acidly, 'is the lowest form of wit.'

Donovan shook his head in disgust and reached for the door. Chapel stayed where he was, blocking his way. It was plain that what he wanted, what he really wanted, was for Donovan to knock him down. But Cal Donovan only looked like a violent man. He wasn't one, and he never had been. He struggled with the quick temper of his Celtic forebears, but he was much more likely to say something he'd regret later than to do something. Except in self-defence he hadn't hit anyone since he was about fifteen years old, and he wasn't going to start with a geriatric thug. He reached out and moved the doctor aside. Then he opened the door and went into the hall.

'Elphie? Come down now. Get your coat—we're going for a drive.'

But Chapel wasn't finished. His voice lifted in bitter accusation behind Donovan's back. 'If you go through that door you'll regret it. You have *my* word on *that*. There may be a way round this. Let's talk. Before anyone else gets hurt.'

Elphie came down the stairs, wide-eyed, one arm in the sleeve of her red coat, one foot in its green welly. She sat on the bottom tread to pull on the other. 'We *never* go for a drive!' she announced breathlessly.

'Be a treat, then, won't it?' Donovan would have liked to take her by the hand and lead her out of the house and out of this place without any further delay. But he was waiting for his chauffeur, and Payne was still trying to edge through the door without Chapel noticing.

Donovan took a deep breath, tried to explain it simply. 'There's nothing to talk about. A crime was committed here: I *have* to report it, I don't have any choice. I don't know what'll happen next. Maybe it won't be that bad. You lied to the Coroner, and you stole Simon Turner's inheritance. But if his legitimate heirs haven't come calling on him in the last fourteen years maybe there was no one. The court will take that into account. You could be looking at—I don't know—a short sentence, maybe even a suspended sentence.

'I don't know what'll happen to the Mill. You're not allowed to profit from a crime so I don't see how anyone here could keep it. I don't know who'd be next in line. Hire yourself a good lawyer, see what he can work out for you.'

'You're talking about the lives and livelihoods of a dozen families!' shouted Dr Chapel. 'You have no right to destroy everything they've built!'

'They had no right to build it on somebody else's bones!' retorted Donovan savagely.

Payne finally made it through the door. He hurried across the hallway, shaking the key he wanted out of the bunch. Sarah stayed where she was in the study: she wasn't coming with them. Donovan wasn't surprised. He knew Payne was coming back here as soon as his daughter was safe.

'All right.' Donovan took Elphie by the shoulder of her coat and held her in front of him. He didn't know what he was expecting Chapel to do, but he felt better keeping his own body between the old madman and the child. He opened the front door.

Washing up against the house was a sea of faces. Most of East Beckham must have been here. They'd gathered in silence, and in silence they watched the big house, waiting for something to happen, for something to be decided. Some of them were armed with wooden staves and some with iron bars.

FOUR

DONOVAN CLOSED the front door quietly and turned. Jonathan Payne looked stricken, shock and fear mingling visibly in his round face. Sarah looked numb, as if the implications of what she'd just seen had yet to reach her.

Dr Chapel looked as if he'd read once that gloating was not a particularly attractive habit but he'd decided he didn't care.

Only Elphie thought they were still going anywhere. She tugged at Donovan's hand. 'Everybody's waiting for us.'

'I know,' he said softly.

'SO WHAT'S HIS NAME?' asked Liz.

But it was never going to be that simple. 'Honestly, I don't know,' said Margaret Crosbie. 'Sheila's hardly talked about him. The Child Support Agency wanted to know too and she wouldn't tell them either. She said Jason's father could be any one of half a dozen men, but I knew that wasn't true. She knew who he was. She just didn't want anything more to do with him.'

'Do you know why?'

Mrs Crosbie shrugged. 'She calls him The Psycho. Says it all, don't you think?'

'If she felt like that about him, why did she get involved with him in the first place?'

'Because he was clever and charming, and he had a bit of money, and she was flattered. I think he was older than her, and she was just young enough to find that attractive. She thought he was sophisticated. Maybe he was—I wouldn't know. If sophisticated means scaring people till they daren't say no to anything you want from them, I don't want to.'

'Did he rape her?'

'Do you know, I'm not sure. She was that terrified by then I couldn't be quite sure what happened. I think she was willing enough when he started; and by the time she realized what it was going to be like she was too scared to tell him to stop. Is that rape? Whether it is or not, it was reason enough for her to stay away from him afterwards. As far as I know, she hasn't seen him since.'

It was heavily circumstantial, the keenest of the old hanging judges would have raised both eyebrows at it, but it all made sense. Sheila helped the blackmailer because he threatened her baby and she knew enough about him to take the threat seriously. Liz still hadn't got a name. But she was sure now that Sheila could give her that final piece of information, if she could be persuaded to.

'IT'S SO DAMNED frustrating,' said Shapiro, raking thick fingers through his thinning hair. 'Sheila could tell us who this man is in a moment. And she won't.'

'She's afraid of him. He knows, or he soon will, that she's here. If we turn up on his doorstep he'll know why. We have to convince her that he can't hurt her if he's in prison.'

'This is a perfectionist,' Shapiro said again. 'A man who whittles away with infinite patience until the block of wood he started with is a beautiful, delicate mobile—not a child's toy, a minor work of art. If there's one thing this man can do, it's wait. So we send him to prison. But everybody comes out eventually; unless we get really lucky and he dies in there. Eight or ten years from now she's going to answer the door and he'll be back. And he won't have caustic soda this time, he'll have vitriol.'

Liz sighed. 'It's a bit hard to see what we can offer her that makes the risk worthwhile. A pride in doing the right thing?'

'It's going to wear a bit thin while she's waiting for the skin-grafts,' Shapiro agreed ruefully.

'If it was just her, perhaps we could talk her round. She'd give a lot to have this man out of her life. She might risk a lot too. But it isn't just her, it's Jason too. I don't think she'll take any risks with him.'

Shapiro shook his head with a kind of wonder. 'You never get used to it, do you? The depths some people will sink to. This is his own *baby* we're talking about, and he's prepared to hurt it to keep its mother in line.'

Liz shrugged. 'If he really is a psychopath, he doesn't think of it as his baby. He doesn't even think of it as *a* baby: he thinks of it as a piece on a chess board. He'll sacrifice it without compunction if that'll win him the end-game. It doesn't matter to him. He never wanted a son.'

Her voice petered out as her thought processes got ahead of what she was saying. Shapiro waited, unwilling to interrupt if there was any chance of her seeing a way through this. Sheila Crosbie was a woman and so was Liz: maybe there was something she could offer that he wouldn't think to.

'Frank,' she said after a minute, and she was getting up as she said it, 'I think I've got an idea. Let me talk to Sheila, see where it takes us.'

'You're not going to beat her up?' asked Shapiro doubtfully.

Liz laughed aloud. 'I'm hoping that won't be necessary.'

SHEILA CROSBIE COULD have given lessons to a clam. She just about looked up when the door opened, registered Liz's arrival, dropped her gaze back into her lap. Her eyes were dead.

She'd already given up, and that made it harder, not easier, to get through to her. She saw no future for herself. All her energies now were focused now on keeping her baby safe.

Liz sat down, introduced herself for the tape and put her hands on the table. 'Sheila, I know everything about this man except who he is, and I know that you know that. I also know why you aren't telling us. Not to protect him; not even to protect yourself. Because you're afraid he might get to Jason.

'Well, you're right to be afraid. He's a deeply dangerous man. A man who uses other people, even those closest to him, to get what he wants. He burnt your hands, didn't he? Because it was easier, and safer, than hurting a stranger. Then he sent you down here to play the injured innocent. He must have known we could suspect you; he didn't care. He knew you wouldn't give him away. He was holding something too valuable over your head. Jason. What did he say?—that if you didn't do as he asked he'd burn Jason instead? No wonder you were so convincing. You didn't have to pretend that your baby could have been hurt, it was a real possibility.

'So I understand why you acted as you did. I understand why you're still not prepared to help us. I'm talking about the threat to a town full of strangers: you're only interested in Jason.'

She breathed steadily for a moment, plotting her course. What she said next—perhaps, the precise words she used—were going to be critical. She was only going to get one shot at this: if she didn't strike home this man was going to win.

'So let's talk about Jason. He's in care now. Your mother would have taken him, but you weren't convinced she could protect him from his father. I have news for you, Sheila. I'm not sure Social Services will be able to either.'

That got the girl's attention. Her head snapped up like a curbed horse's.

'Oh, they'll try,' said Liz, 'of course they will. But if you insist on doing this, the point's going to come where you're in prison and he's free. And he *is* Jason's father, and the fact that we have our suspicions about him won't count for much if we can't convict him in court.

'So if he turns up at Dunstan House in twelve months' time, and says he's the child's father and he wants to apply for guardianship, and he volunteers a DNA sample and right enough, it checks out—Sheila, I don't know what would happen then. Social Services wouldn't just hand Jason over. But if an application was made to the court, and the facts were that the mother was in prison and the father was an apparently respectable man with a clear record who was offering to provide him with a permanent home, they'd have to take that offer seriously.

'They'd ask your opinion. You'd object. You might tell them what you won't tell me, that Jason's father was responsible for blackmailing Castlemere. But the evidence would be long gone. They'd want to know why you hadn't said anything at the time. You'd tell them, but how much credence would they give to a woman who, by her own admission, had lied before? They'd think you were trying to get an early release.

'They'd probably ask the police for our view. We'd say that we considered Jason's father as a suspect, but we didn't know who he was and anyway the evidence was so tenuous it could have applied equally to any man you'd been involved with. Sheila—in those circumstances I think he'd get the baby.'

She'd been willing to give up all of her life that was worthy of the name for that baby. Now someone was saying it wasn't enough. It was too much to take in, and her expression froze while underneath the cogs whirred and the wheels spun. She wasn't stupid. She'd understood Liz's argument, and it had resonated with her deepest fears. She believed—she could not help believing—that she'd been tricked into abandoning her son to his fate. In another moment the superheated mix of terror and rage would be enough for the geyser to blow.

She didn't shout: she screamed. The piercing, primeval howl penetrated every wall in the elderly building. Superintendent Giles looked up, startled, from the monthly accounts. Frank Shapiro hunched his shoulders and plunged his fists deep into his pockets in a gesture he recognized, belatedly, as having learnt from DS Donovan. Sergeant Bolsover heard it, and so did four members of the public waiting in the front office. Sergeant Formby the custody officer leapt from his seat at the sound of it and dived for the interview room door.

He had it open before he remembered it was DI Graham conducting the interview. He knew her for a determined, enthusiastic detective, but he'd never yet caught her using thumbscrews. He coughed to cover his confusion. 'Sorry, ma'am. Er—everything OK?'

Liz nodded calmly. 'Yes, thank you, Sergeant. Ms Crosbie's a little upset. I think she'll be all right now.'

Ms Crosbie was more than a little upset. She was shaking with tectonic emotion. She could hardly get out two coherent words. But her mind was crystal clear. She'd made a terrible mistake. For all the right reasons she'd done all the wrong things. There was time, if she acted now, to rectify that. But there might not be much time because—now or soon—he'd be on his way back.

'I'll tell you everything,' she stammered, tripping over the words they came out so fast. 'But you have to keep that animal away from my baby.'

'Yes,' Liz said simply.

'Promise?'

'Cross my heart and hope to die.'

AS THEY HURRIED DOWN to the cars Shapiro said sidelong, 'You realize we've been pretty dim?'

'The information was there,' admitted Liz. 'Should we have recognized it?'

'I think we should. Once we realized that Sheila Crosbie didn't buy the bottle with caustic soda already in it, she applied it to her own hands.'

'She says she didn't. She says he made up a solution in the sink and held her hands in it. She says he put on rubber gloves first.'

'Figures,' said Shapiro tightly. The car was waiting at the bottom of the steps. 'His hands are delicate instruments. Look what he can do with them.'

Liz rolled her eyes. '*That* should have rung a bell. He made that mobile for the baby. That was the first Sheila knew he'd come back into her life: she answered the door ten days ago and there he was, holding the mobile and smiling at her. Until then she hadn't spoken to him since the night Jason was conceived. She didn't know he knew she'd had a baby: she'd dodged into alleys to avoid meeting him in the street. But he hadn't forgotten her: he'd kept his eye on her, was just waiting until she could be of some use to him. When the moment came, he made it impossible for her to say no. He knew where she lived. He knew she'd had his son.'

'It was Wilson who spotted that mobile, you know,' said Shapiro, just a shade sourly. Scobie started the car before they were even inside, took off quickly enough to flatten them in their seats. 'Even then it didn't occur to me what it meant. That Jason's father was a skilled woodworker; that maybe it was something he did for a living.'

'It might just have been a hobby,' said Liz, soothingly, trying not to notice how quickly Queen's Street had been left behind.

'Yes, it might; but it wasn't, and it should have occurred to me to find out. The facts were all there, for heaven's sake! He's a carpenter. We *knew* that. He works for Sidgwick & Mellors—he's been at Castle High for six weeks refitting the school library. Plenty of time to work out how to make this work. The yoghurt was easy—no one was looking for him then. The school was easy—he had every right to be on the campus. The baby lotion and the cold remedy were a doddle: he bought them over the counter, did everything that needed doing in the privacy of his own home. He didn't even have to put them back on the shelves: he just gave one to his accomplice, took the other himself.'

'He didn't get cholera from the cold remedy,' grunted Shapiro, 'he didn't even get food poisoning from it. He picked himself some suitable mushrooms, put some in the opened bottle and had the rest for his tea. Then he waited to get sick and called the ambulance.'

A squeal of protest from the tyres and they were on to Cambridge Road. All that would stop Scobie now were the flashing lights of a level crossing; probably.

'And all the time we've been looking for him he's been in hospital, sipping rehydration salts and nibbling digestive biscuits!' exclaimed Liz.

'Which explains the delay,' shrugged Shapiro. 'The days where nothing was happening. He couldn't come looking for his money any sooner, he was sick. He set it all up—the yoghurt, the school, Sheila's contribution and the ransom note on the area car. "Get it and wait." Of course we'd have to wait: he was going to be sick for the next few days. It's the classic way to avoid suspicion: convince everyone that you're a victim.'

'The second note, the one posted in Cambridge on Friday,' said Liz. 'He must have written that as soon as he could sit up and sent someone out with it. Cambridge, for God's sake: we *knew* who was in Cambridge. We should have wrapped this up then.'

'Martin Wingrave,' said Shapiro disgustedly. 'Martin bloody Wingrave!'

FIVE

WITHOUT LOOKING at him Donovan asked Payne, 'Where's your mobile phone?'

There was no reply. Donovan turned on his heel, his eyes like coals. 'Where? I know you have one—Sarah called you on it. If you want Elphie to be safe, use it now. Call Queen's Street. They'll be here in fifteen minutes.'

Payne's voice was so low Donovan genuinely couldn't hear him. 'What?'

'I said, I left it in the Land Rover!'

Donovan let his eyes fall shut. 'And I don't suppose you can fix the land line from inside the house, can you?'

'We cut it back up the road. We thought you might try one of the other houses.'

'You were *that* determined to keep me here?'

'Until we were sure you were no threat to us,' said Dr Chapel, 'damn right we were.'

'You people are crazy,' said Donovan thickly. 'I'm a police officer. You can't really believe you can make me turn a blind eye to this?'

'No,' said Chapel.

'Then what do you hope to achieve? Maybe you can keep me a prisoner here—for a week, for a month even. But sooner or later either I give you the slip or you get tired of feeding me and let me go. Either way, when I leave here you're going to have to face the music. You *know* that.'

Chapel was nodding. 'Yes, that's pretty much how we read it too.'

'Then——?' And then he understood. The anger, the confusion drained out of his face, leaving it smooth. 'Ah.'

Even after all that had happened, finally it came as a shock. He'd been threatened before; attempts had been made on his life before. But there was something peculiarly sickening about being threatened in a place where, and by people among whom, he had once felt safe. The old man had saved his life; Sarah and her son had cared for him. But he'd been too curious, taken too much interest in their affairs, and now they would only be safe when Donovan was dead.

When they'd taken him from the boat it had been a calculated risk. They'd known that if they made no effort to help him they'd be asked to explain why not, and it seemed safer to bring him here, get him well and send him, suitably grateful, on his way. The phone was cut and *Tara* was moved to control his access to the outside world until he was fit to leave.

But before that he'd become interested in the Turner family history. Mere habit had led him to ask questions that rang alarm bells the length of East Beckham. Once he knew there was a mystery here—that a pattern of deceit involving everyone in the village had been woven around the events of fourteen years ago—and realized that a suspicious death was the only thing important enough to warrant that, they could never let him go.

And still the habit of inquiry was grained so deeply that he had to know why they needed him dead. 'This isn't because of a fourteen-year-old fraud, is it? Because a dozen families in East Beckham agreed to take advantage of a nasty accident to secure their future. Sure, you lied about it; but that isn't why the whole damn village is waiting on the front step to beat my head in. They're ready to do murder because they did it once before. Simon Turner didn't turn that tractor over. You killed him.'

He got no immediate response. He took the silence as consent. 'He threatened your way of life, so you killed him. You bust him up so badly the only story that would do was that a tractor landed on him.' His gaze raked round them, still more bitter than afraid. 'I'm right, aren't I?'

Sarah Turner said, 'No!' and Dr Chapel said, 'Yes.'

She stared at him; he shrugged carelessly. 'In all the relevant particulars. You weren't told everything, dear. You and Jonathan were going to have to lie about whose body it was—it seemed unwise to let you in on all the facts.'

Jonathan Payne looked as if he was watching the man grow horns; as if no suspicion of this had ever crossed his mind. 'You killed him? Simon? You *killed* him?'

'In a way,' said the doctor obliquely, 'it *was* an accident. At least, it wasn't premeditated. It was a fight that got out of hand. Some of the younger men wanted to have it out with him— persuade him, bully him, call it what you like, into selling the Mill to our cooperative. He wouldn't listen; they tried to make him listen; it came to blows. When it finished Simon was badly injured.'

'Not dead?' whispered Sarah.

'No. But he had head injuries he might not have recovered from.'

'Didn't get the chance, though, did he?' sneered Donovan. 'Because they did what people in this village had got in the habit of doing: they brought the problem to you.'

Chapel nodded calmly. 'Of course they did. I'm the doctor.'

'You were Simon's doctor too. Much good it did him.'

Chapel shrugged. 'A decision had to be made. If Simon lived, five decent lads were going to go to prison and their families would lose their homes. And there was no certainty that he'd recover, that he wouldn't die anyway, just too late to do anybody any good. A judgement had to be made. I decided the greatest good would best be served by withholding treatment.'

'You let him die,' said Donovan baldly.

'That's fair comment,' nodded Chapel.

'Who knew about this?' asked Payne.

'Well—everybody, really. No, not everybody—it had to be kept a secret, we didn't want the children growing up and leaving East Beckham with it. We didn't want some tearful woman unburdening herself over the phone to her mother. But I called in the five lads responsible, and their fathers, and I told them what I was prepared to do—*if* I could count on their absolute support. Not just then, while their blood was up, but all the years thereafter. I could save them all, but I wasn't going to put my head on a block to do it. They swore to me they'd keep the secret safe. And give them their due, they did. They made sure that all those who knew what had happened also knew the consequences for everyone if anyone had an attack of conscience.'

Donovan felt his jaw tighten as he listened. Simon Turner was still alive while they were debating the matter. He might still have been saved. But it was more expedient to let him die. It wasn't enough that they'd beaten him to bloody sherds: now they took him into the fields and dropped a tractor on him.

'Any way you cut it,' he grated, 'that boy was murdered. His life meant less to you than the trouble of moving house.'

Chapel frowned. 'That's unworthy of you, sergeant. What was at stake here was the survival of a community. The mere accident of birth put one man, one rather greedy man, in a position to end a way of life three centuries old. We tried to reason with him, we tried to buy him off. He wasn't interested. He was a vindictive young man: he was never happy here, now he had the chance to wipe the place off the map.'

'That didn't give you the right to murder him!'

'Perhaps not. But it gave us a reason.'

Donovan fought to keep his voice under control. 'And now you're going to do it again.'

'I'm afraid so.'

'And again?'

'If necessary.'

It was surreal. They could have been talking about scrapping a piece of machinery or replacing a leaky shed. About sacrificing a crop of bulbs to prevent a pest from spreading. Now he understood that too. They'd been talking about killing him that evening round the dinner table. The only one who wasn't aware of the fact was him.

He barked a little snort of irony. 'Oh, it will be. There's never a last time. Ask any serial killer: it gets easier. The first time you kill it's the most important thing in the world to you. You end up doing it because it's easier than arguing.'

Incredibly, Chapel managed to look offended. 'Young man, you don't know us well enough to judge us.'

That did it. Donovan started to laugh. It was the absolute

absurdity of it. He'd faced gangland bosses and homicidal maniacs; he'd faced guns and knives and fire and worse. And he was going to die at the behest of a retired family doctor and at the hands of a bunch of Morris Dancers. The situation was too ridiculous for tears, so he laughed until he started to cough. His damaged lungs spasmed and slivers of pain slipped under his ribs. He put one hand on the wall to steady himself, clasped the other hard against his side. His knees started to go and he slid down on to the hall chair, fighting for breath.

Sarah hurried to help him. He waved her away. 'Fundamental error,' he gritted. 'I guess it's different with flowers but the first thing you learn on a farm is, Never make friends with anything you're going to eat.'

She recoiled in anguish. 'Cal—I never thought this was going to happen. If I'd thought—'

'What? You'd have left me on the boat? You should have done, at least I had a chance there. Maybe I'd have beaten the pneumonia. Maybe someone else would have found me. Only then they'd have wanted to know why you hadn't tried to help, and you couldn't cope with people asking questions. I was dead from the moment Elphie found me. You weren't taking care of me, you were just managing my death. Making sure I couldn't do you more harm dead than alive.'

He'd made her cry again. Payne moved to his mother's side, put an arm about her. 'Don't blame her,' he said quietly. 'You've every right to be angry, but not with her. She thought it would be all right. She didn't know how high the stakes were.'

'I don't think you do, either.'

'No,' agreed Payne. 'Maybe it suited us to be deaf and blind, but neither of us knew that Simon was murdered. I thought the worst that could happen was that the fraud would come out, I'd go to prison and we'd lose the Mill. I never guessed how far they were prepared to go.'

Donovan shook his head. 'That's not what I meant. After me they'll kill Elphie.'

It shouldn't have come as such a shock. If they hadn't feared for the child, why ask him to take her away? But they still weren't able to confront the monster they'd helped to create.

Sarah's hands flew to her mouth as if to catch the little choked denial in her throat. Hollow with fear, Payne's eyes flicked between the policeman and the child as if Donovan were the one threatening her.

Elphie's little pointed chin dropped and her eyes saucered, and she clung to Donovan's hand as if she'd never let him go. He knew he'd frightened her. He couldn't help it. He wasn't making this up: he knew how events would proceed. If they got away with killing him, soon their eyes would turn to her.

'Don't be ridiculous,' snorted Dr Chapel. 'Elphie's one of us. She's safe here. This is the only place she *can* be entirely safe.'

Donovan didn't believe him. 'After I'm dead, she's the main threat to your security. You can count on one another to keep the secret—you all know what the consequences would be if anyone let it slip. But you can't count on Elphie, and you never will be able to. She talks to people. There's no guile with her— she couldn't lie to save her life. If the police come back here looking for me, and they ask Elphie what she knows, she'll tell them. She won't think she's avenging me, she'll just think it's interesting and they'd want to know. She's going to betray you all. You'll never be safe as long as she's alive.'

His eyes swivelled from Chapel to Payne. 'Right now I'm the only thing stopping them from killing her. There's no point while I'm the problem; but they won't risk leaving her alive once I'm gone.'

'Damn you!' cried Jonathan Payne in agony. 'That's my *daughter* you're talking about!'

'She's living proof of what happened here.'

'Don't listen to him,' Chapel warned gruffly. 'He's trying to save his own neck. Nobody's going to hurt Elphie. Yes, we killed Simon. It's the only reason any of us is here today. And now we have to deal with another threat. That should buy us another fourteen years; or forty. He's supposed to be dead already: when he turns up in the canal nobody'll suspect us. They'll think they know what happened. That'll be the end of it. I promise.'

'Believe him,' suggested Donovan negligently. 'Bet your daughter's life on it.'

Payne was standing beside the front door. It was shut: now he reached out and quietly locked it. 'Go,' he said softly. 'Go now. Take Elphie and get away. Take the Land Rover if you can reach it'—he proffered the keys—'otherwise I don't know what to suggest. I'll hold them here as long as I can.'

Chapel looked up at him, no match physically, infinitely tougher psychologically. 'If you do this,' he said in a low voice, 'I won't be able to help you. I won't be able to help any of you.'

Payne looked at him as if seeing him clearly for the first time. How small he was, how vicious. 'Do you know something, Doctor? I think my family might do better without your help.'

He was small, and he was vicious, but even his detractors had to admit he was as brave as a lion. He filled his narrow chest to call for help.

Donovan was too far away to stop him. Payne shook him, hard; which might have introduced an interesting tremolo into his yell but would have done nothing to muffle it.

Sarah Turner lifted the brass candlestick off the hall table and hit him over the back of the head with it.

Dr Chapel gave a choked little grunt of surprise and dropped where he stood. A spurt of blood painted bright splashes on Elphie's white cheeks.

'Go,' Sarah said, and her voice was hard. 'It'll be ten minutes before they get up the nerve to break in, and that's the only way they're getting in or he's getting out. Leave by the back door and stay close to the wall. If you're careful you can reach the sheds without anyone seeing you; unless they've put a guard on the Land Rover. If they have you'll have to fight your way out.'

Donovan nodded. He knew she wasn't doing this for him but because she saw in him Elphie's only salvation. Still, it would have been easier to do what they'd done before: believe Chapel when he said everything would be all right. She'd trusted a stranger with her most precious possession, and pushed the limits of her own character to buy a chance for both of them. Now wasn't the time to tell her he hadn't the strength to fight his way out of a wet paper bag. 'I'll do my best.'

'Remember this,' she said tersely. 'Nothing matters—*nothing*—besides getting that child safe.'

He nodded. He took Elphie's hand and stepped over the unconscious body on the hall floor, and went from the house.

THE DOCTOR WHO met them on the steps of the fever hospital looked both anxious and relieved. 'That was quick.'

Liz and Shapiro traded a puzzled frown. 'Sorry?'

'I can't be ten minutes since I phoned. I wasn't sure you'd come at all, let alone that quickly. I didn't think I was getting through to you about the seriousness of the situation.'

'Situation,' echoed Shapiro. He thought about it but no, it still didn't make any sense. 'This is the first time we've spoken.'

'It wasn't you on the phone?'

'It wasn't anyone at Queen's Street.'

'Queen's Street?'

Shapiro took a deep breath and started again. 'Queen's Street Police Station, Castlemere. That's where we're from.' Light dawned. 'You've been talking to the police in Cambridge? About Martin Wingrave? Why, what's happened?'

'He's gone!'

'Gone? You don't mean died?'

'There'd be nothing to worry about if he was dead,' said the doctor impatiently. 'He's not: he's a lot better. Well enough to have put his clothes on and walked out. He knocked one of my nurses down.'

Liz was frowning. 'I thought people had the right to discharge themselves.'

'They have; even from here, most of the time. They don't have the right to help themselves from the samples cabinet before they go.'

Liz stared at him. 'Samples of what?'

'Anything from E. coli to haemorrhagic fever, for God's sake! This is a fever unit: we deal with agents too dangerous to leave in the general hospitals. We're still working out exactly what he got away with, but there was nothing harmless in that cabinet.'

'Where did he go?' asked Shapiro.

The doctor shook his head. 'Nobody saw it happen—well, the

nurse he knocked down did, but by the time she was up to raising the alarm he'd vanished. We're searching the hospital right now, but nobody's seen him. I think he's gone.'

'How was he?' asked Liz. 'I mean, should we stake out the public conveniences?'

'He was fine. He was ready for home. Why would he suddenly do this? All right, he's an odd sort, there was a general consensus here that a dose of poisoning might have been God dropping hints, but still…'

'Mr Wingrave deceived us all,' said Shapiro. 'Nobody poisoned him: he poisoned himself. We think he's the blackmailer who's been holding Castlemere to ransom.'

The doctor went on staring at him as the implications fell slowly through his eyes and began to hit bottom. 'Then—what's he going to do with the samples he's taken?'

Right now that was the only important question. And it wasn't going to be resolved in Cambridge. Liz and Shapiro headed back to their car.

'He isn't going to win now, is he?' said Liz. 'It's too late for that. We know who he is, he can't take the money and disappear—he's lost.'

Shapiro thought then nodded. 'I suppose.'

'Then what he wants those samples for is vengeance. He's not going to get his money, he's probably going to prison—but by God he can make sure we've no cause to celebrate either. While he expected to succeed he was willing to see how far he could go on threats alone. Now he's lost he's going to show us what he's capable of. He's going to hurt as many people as he can before we catch up to him.'

'So he's heading for Castlemere.'

'I'm sure of it.'

'Even though that's where we'll catch him? Anywhere else he has a chance, but in Castlemere we will catch him. He must know that.'

'I don't think he cares. I think, if he can't have what he wants, the only thing left that matters to him is punishing those who got in his way. He'd rather go down in history as a mass murderer than someone who tried to blackmail a town and failed.'

'If it's a numbers game, I suppose the water supply would be a good place to start.' Shapiro called Queen's Street, despatched a patrol to the water treatment works on the edge of The Levels. 'Where else?'

'Anywhere.' Liz shook her head despairingly. '*Anywhere!* If he stands on the castle ramparts and smashes the bottles on the cobbles in the square he can be pretty sure of spreading something nasty. It might be a scattergun approach, but if all he wants is bodies...'

Her voice slowed down as her thought processes caught up. 'But that isn't all he wants, is it? He also wants to punish Sheila. He's worked out by now that she's in custody—maybe he's been trying to call her at home, when he couldn't get through he guessed she'd been picked up and we'd be after him next. That's why he left the hospital, and why he left it equipped to do some damage.'

'Sheila's safe enough,' said Shapiro. 'He can't get at her in the cells.'

'He doesn't need to.' Liz's eyes were wide and she took the phone from his hand. 'Frank, we *know* what matters most to Sheila, and it isn't her own safety. He's going for her baby.'

SIX

THEY'D HAVE HIM within the hour. Wingrave wouldn't be sure where Jason was: he might go to Sheila's flat first or he might go to her mother's house. Another phone call sent officers scurrying to both addresses.

He had a half-hour start on them. Even if he'd hijacked a Porsche he couldn't have got from Cambridge to Castlemere in under an hour so there was time to intercept him. When Shapiro had explained the situation to Superintendent Giles he took a deep breath and proposed that firearms officers be part of each group, at Arrow House and at Coronation Row.

Giles sounded shocked. 'Is that necessary?'

'Yes,' said Shapiro plainly. 'This is a deeply dangerous man. A psychopath equipped for germ warfare: it's hard to imagine a more lethal combination. He raided that hospital cabinet with the explicit intention of spreading fatal diseases. He doesn't care who falls sick, who dies, except that the longer the casualty list the more vindicated he'll feel. It's his way of paying us back for outmanoeuvring him: if he's not going to get his money he's going to create as much mayhem as he can before he's caught. He won't be stopped by the flash of a warrant card and a firm hand on his collar.'

'Can we prove he's behind the blackmail?'

'I'm sure we can,' said Shapiro. 'With Sheila Crosbie's testimony and a thorough search of his house I'm sure we'll put it beyond any doubt.'

'But not in the next half hour.'

'Well—no.'

'Frank, before we kill this man we have to be absolutely sure he is who we think he is.'

'I hope it won't be necessary to kill him,' growled Shapiro. 'But if we have to fight him to the ground, a lot of people are going to be in danger. Our people. It isn't reasonable to ask unprotected police officers to engage in a wrestling match with a plague carrier.'

Still Giles thought about it. But in the end he did the only thing he could: he agreed. 'Ask Inspector Graham if her reclassification is up to date.'

It was, but Liz wasn't carrying a weapon and going back to Queen's Street to check one out would take too long. 'If he wants my name on the sheet,' she said grimly, 'he'll have to send me something to fire.'

'He wants it as by-the-book as he can make it,' said Shapiro apologetically. 'If Wingrave ends up dead, it looks better for an inspector to have done it than a constable.'

'And better a woman than a man. If Jim Stark does it he's a police thug rampaging out of control. If I do it I'm a plucky heroine protecting a tiny baby.' Under the irony her voice was taut. She had no illusions about what lay ahead. This was not a man who would be deterred by threats. If he arrived at a scene where she was the authorized firearms officer, she would have to shoot him.

She could do it. That was what all the hours of training, practice and reclassification were all about: so that in an emergency, to protect lives, she could drive enough hot metal into a man's body to stop him. She'd done it once before. But it didn't make it any easier. For some AFOs, once was enough.

She sniffed. 'Well. There'll never be a better candidate, or a better cause.'

The car paused in Brick Lane long enough to let Liz out, then proceeded on into The Jubilee. 'If there's nothing doing at the flat I'll catch up with you at Sheila's mum's,' she called after it, and Shapiro waved a hand in acknowledgement.

Stark and WPC Flynn had been at the flat for half an hour but no one had come to bother them. Liz waited with them for perhaps ten minutes, but increasingly came to see it as futile. If

Wingrave came here she'd know within thirty seconds anyway, and Stark would deal with the situation until she could return. Probably, though, he would go to the house. With Sheila in custody he'd expect the flat to be empty and Jason at his grandmother's home.

'OK,' said Liz, 'I'm going over to Coronation Row. If he turns up here I can be back in two minutes. Just—don't take any chances with this man. I'd rather see him dead than either of you.'

As she walked up Brick Lane someone fell into step beside her. He came from nowhere, suddenly he was at her side, and her first thought was that somehow it was Martin Wingrave and she still didn't have her firearm.

But it was Mitchell Tyler. He said, 'Developments?' in a tone heavy with implied criticism. As if she should have told him before haring off to Cambridge.

She spared him an irritated glance. 'Yes. We know who's behind it. Hang around: he's on his way here now.'

'He?' The left eyebrow arched. 'So you were right—it wasn't Sheila Crosbie.'

Honesty piqued her. 'Right and wrong. She *was* involved, but only under duress. He threatened her baby. He's still threatening the baby.' She condensed the story into a few brief sentences.

Tyler heard her out in silence, a massive presence beside her. 'And do we know yet what samples he took?'

The hospital kept scrupulous records, they'd provided a full list within ten minutes. 'Typhoid, legionnaire's disease and hepatitis.'

His expression didn't flicker. But he'd understood well enough. 'Are your shots up to date?'

She managed a thin smile. 'Not against that lot. So be warned: if you do want to be in at the arrest our health authorities may turn you into a pin-cushion for the privilege.'

'Jeez!' he swore feelingly. 'I've only just got out of the last damned hospital!' That reminded him. 'How's your husband doing?'

It struck her with a pang like knives that, with everything that had happened in the last couple of hours, she hadn't had the time to find out. She hadn't even had the time to wonder. 'He'll be all right.'

'That's something, then.'

They turned the corner into Jubilee Terrace. Tyler said, 'At least the stupid girl got one thing right. She put the kid where he'll be safe.'

Liz nodded. 'It was the one thing she always knew: that she had to keep the baby away from his father. Everything she did was geared to that.' They continued half a dozen paces more, then she slowed and stopped, her face creased in a puzzled frown. 'Mitchell—I didn't tell you what we did with the baby.'

He shook his head, unaware that it mattered. 'The neighbour did.'

'Neighbour?'

'The flat next to Sheila's. When I got no answer I raised the neighbour. A black woman, mid-fifties? She told me you'd arrested Sheila and taken the baby to the children's home.' He was watching her closely, his gaze like needles. 'Why?'

Liz let out a long breath and shut her eyes for half a second. 'Because if you can know that, so can he. Wingrave. He wouldn't even have to go there. If he knew the neighbour's name he could phone her up and ask what was happening. If she'd tell you, a total stranger, she'd tell him.

'He's not going to the flat, and he's not going to Coronation Row. He doesn't have to. He knows where Jason is. He's on his way to Dunstan House. He's taking his bugs to a children's home!'

'Then we need to get there.'

It was too far to run. 'I have to tell Frank...'

'I'll drive, you call him.'

'Drive what?'

He strode back into Brick Lane. A white van was manoeuvring at the junction. It belonged to a rep who'd taken a wrong turn looking for the River Road. He was about to find out just how wrong.

Tyler stepped in front of the van and it stopped. There wasn't much choice: running him down would have been like driving into a brick privy. Nervously, the rep wound down an inch of window. 'Yes?'

Tyler smiled, not altogether reassuringly, and stepped round to his door. He yanked it open and hauled the rep outside. 'You can get it back from the police in an hour. By then it should have saved some lives.'

He got in behind the wheel; a moment later Liz swallowed her doubts and got in beside him. As they drove off she said reprovingly to the rep, 'If you'd had your seat-belt on that wouldn't have happened.' Then they were gone.

THE LAND ROVER was being watched. Donovan's heart sank. With it he wouldn't have needed a head start: he could have gone through the villagers and any obstacle they were likely to throw in front of him. He'd have done it, too. These were people who'd conspired in one murder and were set upon another. They had too much to lose: they wouldn't listen to reason. If they caught him they'd stamp him into the dust.

Nor was it only his own life at hazard. Whatever Dr Chapel said, whatever these people would say if they were asked. Donovan knew that the next thing they felt threatened by would suffer the same fate. Fourteen years ago they had embarked on a road by which there was no returning. When they'd killed two men and still didn't feel safe, in no time at all their gaze would turn towards the changeling child who could betray them.

In the circumstances he'd have had no compunction about flattening anyone who stood between him and the road out of here. But there were three of them, and even on a good day, even with surprise on his side, dealing with three men would have been a problem. Today it was a joke. They could have overpowered him and made corn dollies with their other hands.

No Land Rover then. He backed away cautiously, sliding out of sight round the corner. But he still needed transport. He couldn't have walked out of here if nobody had been after them.

Elphie could. Elphie could disappear into the fen and keep herself out of sight until she found help, and a search could pass within a metre of her and never find her if she wanted to stay hidden. But would she do it? She was eight years old; mentally she was less than that. These were people she'd known all her life. If they called to her that the game was over now, they were all going back for tea, she'd pop her head out of the sedges and join them. Frail as he was, Donovan still thought her best chance was with him.

And maybe she could help him in return. He squatted down, face to face with her, his voice an urgent whisper. 'Elphie—the quad bike. The thing your dad tows the trailer with. Where does he keep it?'

One red sleeve rose as she pointed. Just in time he slapped a hand over her mouth. 'Quietly!'

She nodded obligingly enough. 'The stable.' He followed her finger to the range of outbuildings across the yard. The stable was the last one and backed on to the first of the bulb fields. God knows what he'd do to next year's daffodils, but if he could get it out and started they could cover a lot of ground before a pursuit capable of following could be mustered.

And they'd have to, because the sound of the little engine would be like rifle fire ricocheting between the stone buildings. Their ten minutes head start would shrink to the time it takes a strong man to run fifty metres carrying an iron bar.

Even footsteps could betray them now. They tiptoed across the yard and opened the stable door just enough to slip inside.

Donovan didn't do a lot of praying. But he prayed now, and it seemed to work. The key for the bike was on Payne's ring along with the keys to the Land Rover. He made sure, half-turning it in the ignition; when there was no resistance he went to the back of the bike to disengage the trailer.

It was heavier than he expected, or he was weaker: the tow bar dropped to the cobbles with a crash that made his heart leap. Surely someone had heard that?—the men at the Land Rover if not those in front of the house. Instinct told him to freeze and listen. Common sense told him to keep moving, that whether or not he'd been heard this was his one chance of escape and the sooner he took it the better.

'Elphie,' he whispered. 'Open the stable door, then get up here in front of me.'

They were ready. It was now or never: he turned the key and

punched the starter. In the confines of the stable the engine roared like a B-52 taking off and the chunky machine shot out of the door like a cannonball.

Elphie shrieked in what Donovan, gob-smacked, recognized as exhilaration. The noise was immaterial now—everyone in East Beckham must have heard the engine fire—but it drove home what he constantly needed to remember. This was a child, and not a normal child. However often he told her they were in danger, she would forget; however much he impressed on her the need for quiet, however well she seemed to understand, she couldn't be relied on. If he was to save her it would be despite her best efforts.

The bulb fields opened before them, newly ploughed, the dark brown corduroy as yet unmisted by green. He had only the vaguest idea which way he was pointing, and right now it didn't seem to matter. All he cared about was putting distance between himself and East Beckham.

He had to stay off the road. It would have made for easier riding than the humps and furrows of the field, but on tarmac the Land Rover and whatever other vehicles they had would overhaul the bike in minutes. With only one road in and out they couldn't have missed him. He had to stick to ground too rough even for the Land Rover, or tracks too narrow for it.

The towpath. It didn't run, free and unbroken, all the way into Castlemere, but there were good stretches where the bike could maintain whatever its top speed was and others where he could drag it over, past or round assorted obstacles. They couldn't do that with the Land Rover. If they didn't catch up with him before the first spot where the path narrowed he'd be free and clear.

Besides, by the canal he might find help. It was too late in a bad season to hope the water might be crowded with boating parties, but there was always the chance of meeting the odd fanatic like himself. A boat would be good. Failing that, someone on horseback would do. He knew people rode the towpath, and more in winter than in summer when they had to pick their way past old men fishing and boys on bicycles. Donovan couldn't ride but he could heft the child up behind a rider and issue strict instructions to get as quickly as possible to the first house known to be safe. A horse could go places even the quad couldn't. Across fields broken by banks and ditches it could also go faster.

'The canal,' he shouted in Elphie's ear above the slipstream. 'Which way?'

The red sleeve pointed unhesitatingly. Unfortunately, it was pointing back the way they'd come.

'Figures,' growled Donovan. He wasn't turning back, not for anything. He put the bike into a sweeping curve that would bring it down to the towpath over the next half-mile or so. He was heading away from Castlemere all the time, but that didn't matter too much: if they reached the Sinkhole engine house they'd be safe enough. The main thing was to swap a geography which favoured his enemies for one which favoured him, and nobody knew the canal better than Donovan. If he was going to beat the odds and save both their lives, that was where.

They came to the corner of the field and a gate. Elphie climbed down to open it; but she couldn't manage alone, Donovan had to go and help. When he turned back, bitter disappointment jolted through him. He genuinely hadn't thought of that. It hadn't occurred to him that, if a quad bike was the ideal means of conveyance around the rough headlands and narrow tracks of the fen, The Flower Mill would have more than one.

As he watched first two, then another one, then another breasted the swell of the field and started down the long incline.

SEVEN

THE CALL WENT OUT as the borrowed van cornered hard—two wheels digging deep into the gravel, two spinning in air—into the drive of Dunstan House. Urgent: all available officers to Cambridge Road: intruder in the grounds of the children's home: consider armed and dangerous. Without her radio Liz didn't receive it; but then, it wasn't telling Liz anything she didn't already know.

They didn't have to hunt for Martin Wingrave: he was standing on the front steps, hammering at the glass door with a stone prised from the rockery. It was safety glass, designed to stop an over-excited ten-year-old running through it. It was never meant to withstand a determined attack by an adult with a brick.

Liz couldn't guess how long it would hold. It might delay him until the reinforcements arrived or the glass might shatter at any moment, admitting a man with no conscience and a burden of lethal bacteria into what should have been a place of safety.

She couldn't take the risk. She was out of the van a second before it stopped moving, racing across the lawn, wondering what the hell she could use to stop him. But this was a children's home: anything that could be used as a weapon was locked away. Hence the stone from the rockery: Wingrave would have used a sledgehammer if one had been lying about.

She shouted his name and he turned towards her, lowering the stone. For all that they had been at war for a week, this was their first actual meeting. Somehow, Liz was expecting more. A giant of a man, perhaps; or a man with evil branded indelibly on his face. But if evil men looked evil there'd be a limit to how much damage they could do. Martin Wingrave was a good-looking man, a little taller than most, a little broader, with the firm musculature of someone for whom physical fitness was not so much a hobby as a way of life. He was a carpenter, she remembered: his upper body strength would be considerable. If he wanted to punch a hole through that door, sooner or later he would.

'I know who you are,' said Martin Wingrave. At first she thought he was an incomer like herself. But it was a fenland accent until he'd worked at refining it. From early youth he'd had the innate conviction that he was better than those around him.

A faint tremor in his voice indicated how much effort had gone into this incomprehensible act of revenge. Three days ago he was dramatically, violently ill; it had passed, as he'd known it would, but not without leaving its mark on him. He'd been ready for home, but nobody'd said anything about protracted physical exertion. When his task here was accomplished the dregs of energy would fail and he would quite possibly fall over. But Liz couldn't wait for that.

'I know who you are, too.'

Wingrave raised one sandy eyebrow. In colouring he was on the foxy side of fair. Liz recognized an expensive haircut when she saw one, though working with policemen she didn't see one very often. 'I'm here to visit my son.'

'Most visitors ring the bell and wait for the staff to answer.'

'I did that,' said Wingrave, smiling slightly. 'They seem to have been held up.'

'You have no right of entry here, whatever your relationship to anyone inside. Also, you don't look well. Why don't you come with me while we get this sorted out?'

Wingrave looked disappointed. Clucking with disapproval he shook his head. 'Inspector Graham. Detective Inspector Elizabeth Graham, walking advertisement for the Equal Opportunities programme and all-round stupid cow. Even you can't be so totally braindead as to think I'm going anywhere with you.'

Liz was used to abuse. She'd had insults, and worse, thrown at her on a regular basis since she was twenty years old. She didn't take it personally. Mostly it wasn't even very alarming: people hurling obscenities were not usually hurling anything else. Violence tended to start when the verbal inventiveness ran out.

This was different because the man doing it was different. He wasn't drunk, or angry, or baiting her. Scorn dripped from his tongue like venom. With his back to the wall and a police officer blocking his exit, he still genuinely believed he was in control of the situation. He thought his natural superiority would enable him to succeed in whatever he attempted. He would never, under any circumstances, give up and come quietly.

Mitchell Tyler had reached the same conclusion. He looked away and said dismissively, 'Shoot the bastard.'

Liz spared him a furious glance. 'Mitchell, will you stay out of this!'

He understood. 'Oh yeah. This is Britain, isn't it?—you believe in tackling violent psychopaths with stern words and an appeal to their better natures. You haven't got a gun.'

Liz wasn't sure if he said it loud enough for Wingrave to hear. She hoped not. 'Are you trying to get me killed?' she gritted in her teeth.

He did the wolfish smile, fanning it between her and the man at the door, and reached under his coat. 'No sweat.'

She wasn't expecting a pocket Derringer—Tyler wasn't a man to do anything on a small scale—but she wasn't expecting a cannon either. She'd never seen a Colt .45 up close before, had no idea how much gun it actually was. She thought, If Tyler was pointing that gun at me I'd wet myself.

But Martin Wingrave had no imagination. He couldn't anticipate how it would feel to have a bullet that big punch through his flesh, or the devastating effects on the entire body of losing that amount of blood and tissue between one breath and the next. Perhaps he thought that if John Wayne could swap his gun into his other hand and go on shooting, he could do the same with his rock. He lacked the sense of personal vulnerability that should have warned him that real people shot with a .45 round fall on the floor, all their mental and physical processes pro-

foundly disrupted, and they don't get up again without a lot of
skilled medical intervention. If at all.

The carefully modulated voice was mocking. 'You're an
American! You've no authority here. You shouldn't even have
that gun. If you shoot me they'll put you in prison.'

'You're absolutely right,' Liz said firmly. 'He has no right to
carry a firearm in this country.' She put her hand out, palm up,
demanding.

Tyler looked at her, at first incredulously, then with an un-
characteristic uncertainty in his strong features. She raised her
eyebrows and snapped her fingers at him like Brian confiscating
a stink bomb.

He thought she hadn't understood the consequences of what
she was asking. 'Inspector Graham,' he began in a low, warning
voice.

'Now, please!' She held her hand out until, with deep reluctance, hardly able to credit what he was doing, he put the gun
into it.

The weight swung her arm down. But it didn't stay down.
With both men watching, one smugly, the other with profound
misgivings, she brought it up again and held it, rock steady, the
foresight on Martin Wingrave's chest.

'I, on the other hand,' she informed the wanted man coldly,
'am trained and authorized to use firearms when the need arises.
You're endangering a house full of children: I think that quali-
fies. They won't put me in prison for shooting you, they'll give
me a medal.'

For the first time Martin Wingrave appeared to consider the
possibility that he might get hurt. He looked at the gun. He
looked at Liz's face, then at Tyler's.

Then he smiled and turned back to what he was doing.
'You're not going to shoot me in the back. Stupid slag. How
would that look on your annual report?'

She breathed steadily. 'You've been watching too much television, Mr Wingrave. Nobody'll care how I shoot you, only that
the situation made it necessary. The rules of engagement are,
we don't shoot unless there's a serious risk to human life. But
if there is we end it as quickly as we can. We don't try to wound:

if you're lucky enough to escape with your life it's because that was the only shot available. We don't take up arms at all unless we're prepared to kill.'

He didn't believe her. He swung the rock again, hard. The glass rang and shook under the assault.

'Shoot him,' said Tyler, low and urgently. 'Now. If he gets in there, so do his bugs. Do it. You'll have to in the end. Finish it. Now.'

'Shut up, Mitchell,' she said briefly.

He thrust a broad hand at her. 'If you don't want to do it, let me. We can sort the paperwork out later. Nobody's going to be too upset that I was in a position to deal with a homicidal maniac. Shoot the animal, now, or I will.'

The rock rang again on the armoured glass. Lightning cracks spread out from where it struck.

'Liz!'

She didn't shift her eye from Wingrave's back but her fury was all for Tyler. 'Mitchell, if you don't get the hell out of my way I'll shoot you! This is my job, I know how to do it. Now watch or walk away, but don't presume to tell me what to do!'

'Somebody has to,' he flung back. 'Or we're going to have dead kids to explain.'

The rock fell again. The glass crackled from side to side.

'Mr Wingrave,' she said, her voice quaking with intensity, 'if that glass breaks it'll be the last sound you hear. I will shoot you. I will shoot you dead.'

Incredibly, his answer was to laugh. 'Stupid, stupid, stupid! You can't shoot me. My pockets are full of glass vials: if you shoot me with something that size the contents will go everywhere. I'm not sure what I've got here, but they all had biohazard markings on them. Release them into the air and it won't be me killing the children, it'll be you.' He laughed again, pleased with himself. 'Didn't think of that, did you?'

Her voice came back like ice. 'I'm a good shot, Mr Wingrave. I can drop you without going anywhere near your pockets.'

He didn't believe her. He wielded the rock once more.

The glass broke and fell out of the frame. With a snort of triumph Wingrave reached through and felt for the latch.

Tyler cast one last despairing look at Liz. He didn't think she'd fire either. Not everyone can. Training is one thing, actually shooting another human being is something else. Some people can never do it; some can do it once but never again.

And whoever Wingrave was, whatever he'd done, whatever he meant to do, he was an unarmed man with his back to her. The training programmes never envisaged that. They presented you with targets which were, figuratively as well as actually, black and white: scowling men, heavily armed, racing at you in a menacing crouch. Nothing ambivalent about a situation like that: it's kill or be killed. Most people could shoot someone like that.

It took a different mentality to shoot someone posing this more academic sort of threat. Harder, or perhaps just cooler. You had to see past the target's defencelessness to the threat posed by his very existence.

The trouble was, it wasn't a now-or-never situation. Liz didn't have to fire immediately because that would be the only chance. She could follow him inside, repeating her intention to shoot, and still be following him when he reached the children and started breaking the vials.

She'd given Tyler two choices: neither of them appealed to him. There was another option. He thought he could reach Wingrave before Wingrave could get inside. He knew he could bring him down. Ten years older than his opponent, carrying a couple of stones that his doctor disapproved of, Mitchell Tyler still met very few men he couldn't bring down. He'd never raise his head again if he couldn't beat a man who'd spent the last three days in bed with gyppy tummy.

That hit home. Typhoid, legionnaire's, hepatitis: nasty, messy, painful, dangerous, indignity-heaping diseases every one. Catching, too.

It didn't have to matter. There were bigger things at stake. Mitchell Tyler wasn't a sentimental man but he wasn't going to expose small children to something he wouldn't face himself. He launched himself at Martin Wingrave.

Who saw him coming and calmly pulled a wood-chisel out of his belt.

Tyler didn't make a lot of mistakes but that was one: assuming the man had only one offensive weapon. It was a rudimentary error, but he might not get the chance to kick himself for it. A hostage to his own impulsion, it was too late to back off. The only evasive action he could manage was to twist and hope the waiting blade buried itself in his shoulder rather than his heart or throat.

Pain shot him through, explosive, concussive. He gasped with the shock and curled into a ball around it. But that defensive ball exposed his skull and his spine to a man with a blade designed to penetrate hardwood: it took a real effort of will but he had to straighten out, find the man and the blade, fight his way clear of them. Whatever damage he'd sustained he had to absorb it, put it to the back of his mind for the next two or three minutes while he fought for survival. Nothing that could have been done to him was such a threat to his life as a psychopath armed with a wood chisel.

Ignoring the pain as best he could—a detached portion of his brain had traced it to the left side of his chest, was still puzzling over the noise in his ears and the blood in his eyes—he located a bit of his opponent and yanked hard. The next thing he knew they were tangled together on the ground. Shaking the blood out of his eyes Tyler groped for Wingrave's right hand. Typhoid be damned: if he didn't grab that chisel soon he wouldn't live long enough to get typhoid.

The sting of his skin parting told him better than his obstructed vision that he'd found it. One powerful hand closed over Wingrave's as Tyler struggled to free the other from under him. He wished he could see. At least the man was no match for him physically. It was as if Tyler's ill-judged assault had been the last straw and he'd given up.

Given up? Psychopaths don't give up.

A hand on his shoulder made Tyler squirm like a bulky snake; the voice in his ear stopped him. 'Mitchell, it's all right. It's over.'

Liz helped him out from under the still form. Even now he was reluctant to release the chisel. But when he did, and wiped his sleeve across his eyes, finally he understood that the danger had passed. Martin Wingrave was dead. There was a hole in the centre of his forehead and the back of his skull was gone. It was Wingrave's blood in Tyler's eyes, not his own. The momentum of his charge had carried him on to the chisel, but even then it was held in a dead hand.

'You shot him,' he grunted, pain suddenly clamping up his chest.

'I did,' Liz agreed. She sat him down on the steps and parted his clothes to find where the blade had cut him. An inch-wide wound pumped blood from his left side. Liz wadded a handkerchief against the injury and pressed his hand over it. 'Hold tight, help's on the way.'

'I didn't think you would.'

'I was always going to shoot him rather than let him inside. I didn't expect to have to get round you to do it.'

'Sorry,' he mumbled. The afternoon light was fading faster than it had any business doing.

'Don't worry about it. It's over. Everyone's safe now. Well, nearly everyone.'

Tyler looked at the man crumpled at the top of the steps. He was a long way away and receding by the moment.

Liz read the look, and the comment he lacked the strength to make. 'I wasn't thinking of him. He's in the only place he'd ever be safe. No parole; no gullible psychiatrist thinking he's cured because he says so. I was thinking of Donovan.'

But Tyler wasn't listening. Liz sat on the step beside him to spare him the indignity of toppling over and propped him up until a siren heralded the ambulance.

EIGHT

ON HIS OWN BIKE and on a level playing field—roads and tracks that he knew as well as those pursuing him—Donovan would have given anyone a run for his money. He'd ridden motorbikes, quite illegally, since he was twelve years old. The sense of proprioception which tells most people where the various bits of their bodies are and permits them to perform complex manoeuvres without conscious thought extended in Donovan's case to a pair of wheels. He could make a bike do things that the makers never thought of.

But not today. There were too many factors working against him. This wasn't his bike, or any bike: it was a hybrid whose dynamics and performance envelope were quite different. It wasn't a level playing field: the men behind him worked in these fields every day, they knew where the tracks ran, how wide and how rough they were. He had a passenger to look after. And the power of the engine throbbing between his knees could not totally compensate for his lack of physical strength. It was like coursing a three-legged hare: the poor little sod would give all it had but the outcome was a foregone conclusion.

The quad had seemed a good idea at the time. Donovan knew now that he wasn't going to make his escape on it.

In times of difficulty the psalmist lifted up his eyes unto the hills. In the same way Donovan looked for the canal. It drew him like home. Whatever hazards he faced, gut instinct always told him to put water at his back. It was his faithful friend and would not let him down.

But there were two fields and three fences still between him and the Thirty Foot Drain, and he couldn't stay ahead of the

pursuit long enough to get there. Even if by some fluke he did—
if two of the men behind him collided and the others turned
back to render first aid—he wasn't sure it would do much good.
There was no drawbridge he could cross and then pull up. There
was no bridge at all, and no roads, no dwellings, no phones.
The nearest sure help was at the Sinkhole engine house, five
miles east, or the Posset Inn four and a half miles west. With
or without Elphie to care for, he hadn't a hope in hell of reaching
either of them.

When he first saw it he thought he was hallucinating. That
his desperate need had conjured up a mirage. He wiped his
sleeve across his eyes and looked again. But it was still there:
a small narrowboat, black below and cornflower-blue above,
chuntering along between the sedgy banks at a steady three
knots.

It was October, well past the tourist season. A pleasant autumn might have tempted people out for a late holiday, but it
had hardly stopped raining since August. Come September, even
in a good year, the visitors thinned out and withdrew to the
cosier core of the inland waterways: the Grand Union, the Ashby
& North Oxford, the Avon Ring and the Thames above Reading.
The Castlemere Levels weren't picturesque in the same way,
were a long haul from any of the pleasure-boating centres, and
had a daunting, godforsaken look except at the height of summer. Mostly, only people like Donovan—boat owners, people
who lived on the water or kept their boats out year-round—
would be out here after mid-September. Which meant he should
have recognized the little cornflower-blue narrowboat; but he
didn't.

It didn't matter. He wasn't going to get so many chances that
he could afford to squander one. Whoever they were, they probably had a phone. Five minutes with a working phone and they
were safe. There was nothing to be gained by hurting either him
or Elphie once the police were on their way.

If he could reach the canal before the pursuit reached him.
Which he couldn't just by opening the throttle. If he tried to go
as fast as the men behind him, either he'd bounce Elphie clear
off the quad or he'd turn the damned thing over.

Which left dirty tricks. If he could lock the gate... Oddly enough he wasn't carrying a padlock today, but maybe he could find something that would serve. Barbed wire? You're never far from a loose bit of barbed wire in the country, and this field was no exception. A coil of the stuff, left from last time the fence was mended in anticipation of it needing mending again, had been thrust into the hedge beside the gate. Donovan hauled it out, found the end and began weaving. He took no care over it, ignoring the pain of his torn palms. Thirty seconds from now when the men got here the wire would have ravelled up tighter still, the in-built tension of the coil twisting it like a spring until the barbs meshed together. It would take longer to undo than it had taken him to do it; and because he was running for his life and they weren't the prospect of injury would worry them more. They'd waste a minute trying to find a way round; when there wasn't one they'd waste another minute deciding who should tackle the job and a third looking for gloves.

It might be enough. If he could turn a minute's lead into three it just might be enough. As the quads raced down the slope he dropped the wire and ran, blood on his hands, and chased the machine up through the gears as fast as he could.

As they fled Elphie looked back over Donovan's hunched shoulders and waved. 'That's Uncle Jim! Uncle Jim, Uncle Jim—it's me!'

Donovan couldn't think of a single comment he could make in front of an eight-year-old so he just gritted his teeth and drove.

PERIWINKLE WASN'T a hire boat but nor was she in the hands of experts. In an unguarded moment her owner had promised to lend her to his two nieces as long as they avoided the busy tourist season. They'd been out for three days now, had got the hang of stopping, starting and steering, were less familiar with the map.

'This is the Thirty Foot Drain,' said Stella Merrick with la-boured patience. 'Not the Sixteen Foot Drain. Look at it: it's thirty feet wide!'

'Not all the way,' said Sylvia; which was perfectly true. When the canals stopped carrying commercial traffic there was little incentive to maintain the banks. Consequently, the width of the Thirty Foot Drain varied between ten metres and about six. Interestingly enough, the Sixteen Foot Drain wasn't five metres wide all the way either. Sometimes it was wider.

'Look,' said Stella, shaking out the map on the coach-house roof. Then she turned it round. 'Look. We came through Sinkhole, and we followed the right-hand bank. If we'd followed the left-hand bank we'd have gone down the Sixteen Foot Drain. This is the Thirty Foot Drain.'

'Then why haven't we come to Posset yet?'

'Because we haven't gone far enough!'

'We came through Sinkhole yesterday afternoon! Four hours max should have got us into Posset.'

'You can't count the time we were tied up last night,' Stella said reasonably. 'Or the hour we spent with our nose stuck in the bank this morning. And untangling the mooring rope from the propeller must have taken another hour.'

'In that case,' snapped her sister, 'maybe you should be more careful!'

'And maybe you should do a bit of the work around here instead of posing at the tiller in the hope of impressing muscle-bound farmhands!'

'What was that splash?' asked Sylvia.

Quarrel forgotten, Stella went to *Periwinkle*'s side and peered over. 'An otter?'

Even a small narrowboat like *Periwinkle* is ten metres long, it doesn't move much with the weight of the people on board. So the first warning the sisters got that they were no longer alone was when something as wet as an otter and the same streamlined shape but bigger and with an Irish accent levered itself out of the dark water and slumped on the forepeak, shivering and coughing like a sixty-a-day smoker.

'Sorry to disturb you,' spluttered Donovan, his teeth chattering with cold and exhaustion, 'but I need your help.'

WITH THE GATE FINALLY behind them, the men on the quads didn't see Donovan dive from the bank and swim to the little blue narrowboat or drag himself on board, or the boat move over to the near bank so that a small figure in a bright red coat could spring sure-footedly into the well. But it was a reasonable assumption that that or something very like it had happened. 'God damn it!'

'Don't panic,' warned Jim Vickery. 'We don't know who that is. They may not be able to help them; they may not be willing to.'

'How well do you have to know somebody to let them use your phone? And he is a police officer.'

'We know that, but they don't and he can't prove it. The doctor has his wallet. As for the phone, those things are about as reliable as your missus's drop scones. Sometimes they work, sometimes they don't. This isn't over yet. Damn it, lads, we've nothing to lose!'

'I wish the doc was here,' whined Alan Hunsecker. 'He'd know what to do.'

'*I* know what to do,' growled Vickery. 'Come on—back to Cowslip Bend. We'll stop them there.'

Tyros on the Castlemere Ring always planned to picnic at Cowslip Bend. It sounded so charming, they imagined a water-meadow decked with wild flowers, the air full of the hum of bees and the occasional whistle and plop of a kingfisher.

Invariably they were disappointed and mostly they kept motoring. Cowslip Bend wasn't a good place to stop. It was a tight turn complicated by dense willow scrub on both banks, and it was named not for the meadow flower but for an ammunition barge which failed to make the turn back in the 1880s and blew up. Some of the debris landed in East Beckham a mile away.

Even without a hold full of nitroglycerine it was necessary to slow down to manoeuvre a narrowboat round Cowslip Bend. Even little *Periwinkle* would have to inch her way round, and as she did it her prow and stern would come within a few feet of the bank.

Even on straight stretches narrowboats travel at only walking speed. The quads had no difficulty in reaching Cowslip Bend first.

'Leave the talking to me,' said Jim Vickery. 'We don't know

what he's told them. He may not have told them anything; or they may not have believed him. We may be able to get them on our side.'

'I wish the doc was here,' whined Hunsecker.

SYLVIA WAS AT THE TILLER. The elder at nineteen, the boat's safety had been entrusted to her, and even without being quite sure where she was she could tell that the dark bend coming up was going to be tricky. She throttled the engine back to a notch above idle, and as the way came off the snub-nosed little vessel she steered towards the outside of the bend. When she was almost on the bank she put the tiller full over so that the bows swung across the turn. It was not an easy manoeuvre, particularly the first time of trying, but she judged both speed and angle accurately and *Periwinkle* made the awkward turn as if under the guidance of an expert.

It was not a misjudgement that made her brush against the willows on the northern bank, it was appropriate use of the space available. But it was what, cloaked by the canal-side vegetation, the men were waiting for. Hunsecker stepped calmly aboard at the bows, Vickery—tipping an imaginary cap to the astonished girls—at the stern. Within seconds they'd thrown the mooring warps to those waiting on the bank.

Vickery reached down and stopped *Periwinkle*'s engine. 'Don't be alarmed, girls,' he said in his most unthreatening voice. 'There's been some trouble but it's nothing to do with you. We're looking for a man with a child. A tall man, dark; a little girl wearing a red coat. He's abducted her. They were on the towpath five minutes since. Did you stop for them?'

Sylvia's jaw dropped and she turned horrified eyes on her sister. 'I *said* there was something strange about him! He abducted the little girl? My God!'

'You saw them then?'

'More than that. He was on board—he asked for help. He wanted us to hide them. He wouldn't explain why, or what from, just kept muttering about the police. I didn't trust him an inch.'

'You were dead right,' said Vickery with feeling. 'Tell me—have you got a phone on board.'

Stella shook her head. 'We brought one, but somebody'—she looked daggers at Sylvia—'didn't check the battery. It's dead.'

Vickery tried to hide his satisfaction. 'So where are they now? Below?'

'You think I let someone like that on my uncle's boat?' Sylvia raised a blonde eyebrow. 'I sent him packing. Last seen heading up the bank that way.' Her arm indicated the direction of Sink-hole.

They were two slender teenage girls. Donovan had been sick but he was still a six-foot police officer. 'How?'

'I asked him to leave, politely.' Sylvia gave a sly grin. 'Then I turned the fire extinguisher on him.'

If it was true it was probably all to the good. At least they wouldn't have to drag Donovan kicking and screaming off the boat and then decide what to do about the witnesses. On the other hand, it sounded a mite convenient. Vickery let his gaze fall. There were dribbles of foam on the deck. Maybe it was true.

He cleared his throat. 'Listen, girls, it's not that I don't believe you. It's just that a kid's safety is at stake, and ruthless people can make other people lie for them. Can I look round the boat?'

Stella was standing in the companionway, elbows resting on the roof. She made no immediate effort to move. 'Who are you people—where are you from?'

Vickery had thought this out. 'We're from Castlemere. The kid's my niece, my sister's girl. The man's her father. He's trying to take her to Ireland.'

'He did have an Irish accent,' nodded Sylvia.

'Right now it's a family matter,' said Vickery. 'We get her back and we don't need to involve the police. Which I'd rather not do, because they'll want to know why my sister left the kid alone in the house. She could end up in care.'

'I wish we could help,' said Sylvia. 'But honestly, the best thing you can do is go back the way you came. You're bound to catch them, it's miles to the next village.'

'I know,' nodded Vickery. 'That's what we'll do. But—I'm sorry but you understand, I have to do this—I want to search the boat first. I won't disturb anything and it won't take five minutes. But I can't risk him sneaking past us.'

For a moment nobody moved. The girls traded a glance; Stella shrugged. 'You're in charge.'

'All right,' decided Sylvia. 'God knows I don't want to be the reason a woman loses her child. Go ahead. Just be careful you don't do any damage.'

'I won't.'

Stella swung aside and Vickery vanished below. Hunsecker went with him; the other two remained on deck.

No two narrowboats are exactly alike. Within the basic shell a wide variety of layouts is possible, and great ingenuity goes into fitting the maximum facilities into the limited space. Particularly on smaller boats storage is the biggest problem, so cupboards and cubbyholes are built into every available niche. Even the spaces under the floorboards are used, accessed by hatches and ideal for keeping beer cold.

So a cursory search of the boat—a saloon, a sleeping cabin, the heads, the shower compartment and a hanging locker—was completed within thirty seconds. But a proper search took longer. Every door, however small, had to be opened and a torch flashed inside to be sure no one was hiding behind it. Every hatch had to be lifted, and this meant moving the furniture and even the carpets; then someone had to lie full length on the floor and stick his head inside. If he got lucky, that person could expect a fist to come rocketing out of the darkness, so the job was undertaken with more care than speed.

Then there was the chain locker under the forepeak. The last time Jim Vickery was on a boat like this the chain locker contained a spitting, snarling whirlwind of a dog. Again, he lifted the hatch cautiously and lowered his head inside an inch at a time.

But there was no one else on board. After seven minutes Vickery was sure enough to make his apologies to the girls and take his leave.

'By the way,' he said, 'the damage to your bilge-pump—that wasn't me. I found it like that.'

Stella looked at him interestedly. 'What's a bilge-pump?'

Vickery hadn't really time to explain. 'It's what stops you sinking. But it needs a hose between the pump and the outlet. Could cost a few quid; could save you thousands.'

'You'd think Uncle George'd know about things like that,' said Sylvia severely. 'Thank you. I'll make sure he gets one.'

'Get the fire extinguisher filled up again too. There's nothing worse than a fire on a boat.'

'Yes; thanks,' said Sylvia.

'Good luck,' called Stella after the departing backs.

BUT THE SEARCH PARTY never picked up the trail again. They found the quad, shoved out of sight into some willow-scrub. A little way down the bank they found where Donovan had boarded *Periwinkle,* breaking the sedges and leaving a mud-slide to the water's edge as he did. They could not find where he came out of the water again.

'Maybe he swam over to the far bank,' said Hunsecker. 'If he did we've lost him.'

'And leave the child? I don't think so.' The scorn in Vickery's voice was mostly to hide the worry. 'For one thing, we'd have found her by now.'

'Could she have swum over too?'

The water was cold and dark, the banks steep. Thirty feet doesn't sound far to swim, but every year people drown in canals. 'Maybe they didn't make it. Maybe they've solved the problem for us.'

'Jim. Come down here.'

It was invisible from the top of the bank. But Hunsecker had climbed carefully to the water's edge, and from there he had a view along the reeds. Something was caught among them. Something red.

'It's her,' whispered Vickery. 'That coat she was wearing: you could see it a mile away.'

'What do we do?'

Jim Vickery thought. If both the fugitives had drowned they were safe. If Elphie had drowned and Donovan had made the far bank, they had as long as it would take him to find a phone to dispose of the body. Maybe East Beckham could stare down the police as long as the child could not be cited as evidence. Dr Chapel would know what to do. There seemed no point in hunting further: either the policeman was safe or he was dead. Right now it was more important to use what might be the limited time left to help themselves.

'Give me your hand,' said Vickery, stepping down the bank. 'I can almost reach...'

The sodden bank gave way under him, and he found himself floundering in four feet of water. It was too late to care. He kept hold of Hunsecker's hand and waded, chest-deep, along the reed line until he could reach with his other hand for the floating hem of the red duffle coat. With a kind of reverence he pulled it towards him.

'Ah...'

There was no resistance. Not even Elphie could lie that lightly in the water. The coat was empty.

NINE

AT SEVEN THIRTY they were watching themselves on the television in Shapiro's office. Superintendent Giles had made a statement after the shooting at Dunstan House. Neither Liz nor Shapiro had added anything to it, but both had been filmed outside the hospital. Liz thought she was putting on weight. Shapiro thought he looked as if he'd wandered off from a day-care facility.

'We've had a busy week,' he said defensively.

She cast him a wan smile. 'We'll have another. There'll be a lot of questions to answer. A man ended up dead: somehow we have to justify that.'

He watched her with concern. 'Is that giving you a problem?'

Liz looked pensive for a moment before responding with a gesture that was half a shrug, half a shake of her head. 'I don't think I had any choice. Whether Internal Investigations will see it that way is another matter.'

'Why wouldn't they? There'll be a fatal shooting inquiry but I can't see why it wouldn't support your actions. The man who died had been terrorizing this town for a week. He'd burned Sheila Crosbie and stabbed Mitchell Tyler and was trying to infect a children's home with typhoid. No one's going to think you should have given it a bit more thought first. The people of this town will feel you did them a great favour.'

'That'll be a comfort when I'm looking for a job as a night-club bouncer!'

Shapiro was dismissive. 'Don't worry about your career. It won't damage you to have it on record that, when the alternative was watching other people get hurt, you took a difficult decision and did what was necessary.'

'Assuming the record agrees it *was* necessary.' She sighed. 'It seemed so at the time. Now—I don't know. Maybe there was something else I could have done. Maybe I *should* have shot to wound. Maybe I could have talked him down.'

'You tried. It didn't work. A man like that, it was never going to work.'

'Maybe someone else could have made it work. You could.'

He shook his head, more annoyed than flattered. 'Liz, I'm not SuperCop! I do the best I can, but I can't work miracles and I couldn't have turned Martin Wingrave into a reasonable man. He was a psychopath. It doesn't matter what you or I think, he didn't believe he could be stopped. There was only the one way.'

'Tyler thought he could take him. Maybe if I'd helped...'

'Tyler only tried to take him because you'd got his gun! And he got three inches of wood chisel in his chest. If you hadn't shot when you did Wingrave would have killed him. Then he'd have gone on to infect twenty-two children and eight members of staff with dangerous diseases. You did the right thing, Liz.'

'Then why doesn't it feel like that?'

'Because good and decent people hate the idea of damaging other people, even those who're neither good nor decent. What you're feeling now, it's about you not Wingrave. It doesn't hurt because there was a spark of human decency left in him that was worth saving. It hurts because of who and what you are. Let's be honest here: Martin Wingrave is no loss. I'm only sorry you were the one who had to do it.'

'It was your idea,' she reminded him, troubled enough to be unkind.

'I know. On paper that was a good decision too. Here'—he tapped his chest—'it feels like a mistake. Next time this comes up, be damned to how it looks!'

Liz sighed and shook her head. 'No, that matters too. And if you weren't sitting here commiserating with me you'd be doing it with Jim Stark, and quite possibly he'd have a tougher time ahead.

'If I wasn't prepared to shoot people I shouldn't have done

the firearms course. I knew what it meant. I accepted that, just sometimes, shooting someone is the right and necessary thing to do. I still do. It's just—you can't help wondering. Logically, killing Martin Wingrave was both vital and urgent. So why don't I feel—vindicated? Why does it feel so bad, so wrong?'

'You have to wonder,' said Shapiro sombrely. 'To be unsure. It's a necessary safeguard. You couldn't give a gun to someone who was comfortable about using it.'

They sat in silence, lacking the energy to go home.

The phone rang. Shapiro picked it up. He listened without speaking for a minute, then he held it out. 'Sorry, Liz,' he said with an odd ring in his voice, 'it seems today hasn't finished throwing surprises at us yet.'

She took it, scowling. She really didn't need anything more to deal with. 'Yes?'

Shapiro watched, feeling the tiredness roll back, feeling a little warmth creep back into his heart, watching astonishment and then delight burst across her face like a sunrise. For a minute her lips moved, sketching questions and essaying responses, and no words came. Finally the pressure built up enough to burst the dam, and all the emotions whirling through her—shock, regret, relief, anger, incredulity, amazement, suspicion and impatience—erupted in one great geyser of a cry that filled the upper storey like a cheer and made the people downstairs look up in alarm.

'DONOVAN!!???'

JUST ABOUT THEN Dr Chapel was sitting on Sarah Turner's sofa, holding a bag of frozen peas to his head and listening to Jim Vickery recount the events of the last hour. He did it in great detail, concluding with what he'd found floating in the reeds and what he hoped it meant. Chapel listened patiently because it was too late to do anything else.

'So we came back here,' finished Vickery. 'We couldn't see any bodies but that doesn't mean they aren't there somewhere. What do you think?—maybe we should make a proper search of the bank at first light?'

'I think,' said Dr Chapel carefully, 'the police will be here in about half an hour. I think, if you want to kiss your children goodbye, now would be a good time.'

Vickery stared at him, appalled. 'You mean it? You think he got away?'

'I think he got away,' nodded Chapel.

'But—*how?* He couldn't have swum the canal, not with the child in tow.'

'He didn't have to. They were on the boat.'

The foreman shook his head firmly. 'I'm sorry, Doc, but you weren't there. We searched that boat from stem to stern. No way could we have missed them.'

Chapel was still nodding—carefully because his head hurt. 'You checked everywhere?'

'I told you. The cabins, the lockers, the cupboards—even under the goddamned floorboards. They weren't there.'

'You looked underneath?'

Vickery stared at him as if only now beginning to doubt his sanity. 'Underneath what?'

Chapel sighed. 'Underneath the boat. Jim, what do you suppose happened to the hose from the bilge-pump?'

THEY WERE AT the Posset Inn. It was the first place *Periwinkle* arrived that Donovan could count on getting help. He no longer expected to find his boat there, or his dog. But he found people he knew would protect him and Elphie if the East Beckham militia made a last desperate sortie this far, and he finally found a working phone.

Liz didn't park the car: she abandoned it at the front door. She abandoned Shapiro too. She felt badly about leaving him to unfold creakily from the passenger seat, but not badly enough to wait for him.

George Jackson, the publican, checked who it was before admitting her. He nodded towards his back parlour. 'In there.'

Her first impression was that sitting round a roaring fire in the grate were two Indians, a big one and a little one. Jackson had raided his hope chest for something to get them warm, and these large and rather colourful blankets were the best he could come up with. The tall Indian was hunched over the fire with his back to the door and a faint steam rising from him. The small Indian appeared to have gone to sleep on his knee.

So Liz tiptoed over and laid a soft hand on his shoulder. 'Donovan. I am so glad to see you. Now—what the hell's been going on?'

When he turned and she saw him properly she was a little shocked. Not because he was wet and dirty and smelled of the canal, but at how white and drawn he looked. He might not have had cholera but he'd obviously been ill. His chest rattled as he spoke. 'Ambulance?'

'On its way. They'll sort you out.'

'Not for me,' he said scathingly, 'for her. She needs looking after. She probably needs shots: she swallowed half the canal. I swallowed the other half.'

Shapiro had found them. He wasn't an effusive man, didn't go in for hugging and kissing. He regarded Donovan levelly for a moment, then he shook his hand. 'I was beginning to think you'd got yourself into some kind of trouble.'

Donovan snorted a weary little chuckle. 'Me? Chief, whatever would make you think that?'

Shapiro was too old for sitting cross-legged round fires. He found himself an armchair. 'Tell us what happened.'

So he did. With the changeling child asleep in the hollow of his side, he related enough of her family history to make sense of the things that had been done, of his own actions and those of others.

Liz listened in amazement. 'You think they'd have hurt her?' Lying against him Elphie looked so small and frail it was impossible to imagine anyone feeling threatened by her.

'Boss, they'd have killed her. They'd have killed me; and then they'd have had two murders to cover up, and a fey child standing between them and safety. Damn right they'd have killed her, and sooner rather than later.'

'And the doctor was behind it all?'

Donovan nodded. 'I think Simon Turner would be alive today if East Beckham hadn't had its own doctor. It's possible to be too damned self-sufficient. People think it's some kind of an idyll, a little rural community miles from anywhere where everyone knows everyone else and the village is more important than the people who live in it. It isn't: it's a monster. Sure, you can blame Chapel, he orchestrated the ill-feeling and then channelled it. It would likely have stopped at a black eye or a broken window, except he was clever enough to see how they could salvage the situation.

'But Chapel wasn't the reason it happened. The reason was East Beckham.'

'Explain,' said Shapiro.

'Something like that couldn't happen in Castlemere. But it happened just ten miles away in East Beckham, because the people there aren't individuals, they're ants in a colony. They lived together, they worked together, what was good for one was good for all. That village gave them birth and nurtured them, and in return it expected them to protect it. Whatever the cost. They weren't afraid of the consequences. They were all in it together, it never occurred to them they might have to answer to a wider world. They thought they could get away with murder.'

'They almost did,' murmured Shapiro. 'But for the fluke of you having to spend long enough among them to start piecing it together, they might never have been found out.'

'That's what they reckoned,' said Donovan grimly. 'That's why they thought it was worth killing again.'

'What would you have done,' wondered Liz, 'if that boat hadn't appeared when it did?'

Donovan looked at her askance. 'I'd have been caught and had my head beat in, that's what! I was all out of options.'

'But not ingenuity,' observed Shapiro, chin on his chest, smiling to himself. 'You realize that'll go down in police mythology: the detective who hid out underwater?'

Donovan shrugged ruefully. 'There was nowhere else. They couldn't miss seeing the boat, they were bound to stop and search it. Me, two girls and a child weren't going to fight them off. The canal was the only place left. The hose from the bilge-pump gave us an air supply. It tasted foul but it kept us alive until they left.'

'They never looked over the side?' asked Liz.

'They wouldn't have seen us if they had. We stayed hard against the hull, under the rubbing strake—they'd have had to hang out over the water to spot us. Any time someone leaned on the rail we dropped down under the boat and breathed by tube. Someone on the far bank might have seen us but the men on the boat would have had to know we were there.'

Liz looked at the sleeping Elphie. 'It was a lot to ask of a child. How did you know she could do it—that she wouldn't panic and give you away?'

He shrugged, embarrassed. 'I didn't. I made sure she couldn't. I strapped her against my chest: when I went down she came too. I kept my hand over her mouth, and the air-pipe in it except when I needed to breathe. It wasn't very long. We were only in the water fifteen minutes, under it for maybe five.'

'I bet it felt longer.'

'Bloody forever,' admitted Donovan.

The ambulance arrived. Elphie just about stirred as Donovan handed her to the paramedics.

'Go with her, Sergeant,' said Shapiro. 'If she wakes up surrounded by strange faces she'll be afraid. Plus, somebody ought to look at you too.'

'No way,' grunted Donovan, obstinacy in every line of his body. 'She'll be all right—she likes strange faces. And I'm going back to East Beckham. You want me to see a doctor? That's what I want too.'

EAST BECKHAM WAS DESERTED. Not a soul was visible on the street, in the gardens or as the twitch of a drawn curtain. It was dark now so they weren't making up for lost time out in the bulb fields, nor were they still gathered at The Flower Mill. Only a pitchfork lying in the drive told Donovan he hadn't imagined the events of two hours ago.

He wasn't sure what he'd find at the house, was relieved when Jonathan Payne opened the door. Sarah Turner was in the living room, on the sofa, her hands across her mouth as if she was afraid what would happen if she tried to speak. Her eyes, desperately anxious, watched him over the top of them.

'Elphie's safe,' he said briefly.

'Thank God,' whispered Payne. 'Oh, thank God.'

Behind her hands Sarah began to cry.

'Chapel?' asked Donovan.

He was speaking in monosyllables, Liz realized, because his feelings about these people were confused. They saved his life, twice. But they were also part of a conspiracy that robbed a man of his life and his inheritance, and would have killed again to protect the secret.

They'd also killed his dog. On the scale of criminal enterprises it came pretty low, but it was personal in a way that the murder of Simon Turner was not. When she told him about Brian Boru his reaction had been so slow in coming she wondered if he'd understood and was about to repeat it. But he understood well enough. He just didn't know how to feel. He was alive, the dog was dead. It seemed a good trade. He wasn't a very nice dog—now he was dead it was safe to admit he was a pit bull terrier, an animal with as much charm as a chainsaw. But the dog too had saved his life once. He couldn't just bin the DoggyNosh and forget.

Liz cleared her throat and translated. 'You have to tell us where we can find Dr Chapel.'

'He left here half an hour ago,' said Payne. 'I suppose he went home.'

'Everyone else?' asked Donovan, his voice gritty.

'The same. We knew you'd come back. People thought they'd wait at home.'

'Everybody? Nobody thought of running away?'

'Run where?' asked Payne. 'This is the only place they know. Where could they possibly run to?'

'Where does Dr Chapel live?' asked Liz.

The house reminded Shapiro of his own, stone-built, hunched low against the weather, thick-walled to endure. If the village died now, that little house could stand empty for a hundred years and still be habitable for the cost of a new roof. Stone flags led to the front door, painted a magisterial black and flanked by a pair of dark shrubs trimmed into clever spirals.

'I want to see him alone,' said Donovan.

Liz's eyes widened. Shapiro shook his head once, crisply. 'No.'

Donovan's sharp jaw came up, thin and bloodless lips curling with the same scorn that sparked in his dark hooded eyes. 'Why not? What do you think I'm going to do in there?'

'I don't know, Sergeant,' said Shapiro plainly. 'What do *you* think you're going to do in there?'

Now he was safe and so was the child, and even the less pressing task of getting justice for Simon Turner was all but accomplished, only anger was keeping Donovan on his feet. When it dissipated he'd sleep for twenty-four hours. Liz thought he was stoking the anger as other men might swig coffee.

'He tried to kill me,' he grated. 'If things panned out differently he'd have done it. I want to arrest him. That's all. But I want to do it myself, and alone. I've earned it.'

Though it didn't quite work like that both of them felt churlish arguing. Liz looked at Shapiro and shrugged. 'It's your decision.'

Shapiro breathed heavily. He knew he was beaten, the only issue now was terms. 'All right. But Donovan, don't make me regret this.'

'I won't,' said Donovan, terse with satisfaction. He raised one bony hand to the knocker.

Unlatched, the door swung inward.

'I think he's expecting you,' said Liz.

Donovan set his jaw and stepped inside. He half-expected to be followed but when he glanced back, true to their word his inspector and superintendent were waiting on the doorstep. He proceeded alone.

Dr Chapel was waiting for him in the little kitchen at the back. Somehow he'd guessed it would be Donovan. There was a teapot on the hob, two cups and saucers on the table.

Donovan stood in the doorway, his eyes disbelieving. Chapel beckoned him inside. 'Sit down, sit down. We might as well do this like gentlemen.'

Even after all that had happened, all that would have happened if Chapel had had his way, Donovan had to admire the old man's gall. He was going to spend the rest of his life in prison. But he wasn't behaving like a man who'd been defeated, more like someone who'd taken a gamble and lost. Never mind, old chap, can't win them all; shake hands; it isn't whether you win or lose but how you play the game...

Donovan couldn't think of it as a game. It had cost one man his life; if it had gone on much longer it would have cost Elphie hers. He found that harder to forgive than his own close call. It's the nature of the job that criminals daydream about murdering policemen. But Elphie was a child, an innocent in every sense of the word, and they'd have killed her because she hadn't the wit to keep their secret.

He shook his head. 'I'm not a gentleman, Dr Chapel; neither are you. You're the man who organized the murder of Simon Turner, and I'm the policeman arresting you for it. You do not have to say anything, but I must caution you—'

Chapel waved a hand dismissively. 'I know; I know. God, you're a humourless fellow! Aren't you even going to have a little gloat? You won, I lost. Come on, Sergeant Donovan, enjoy your victory.' He poured the tea, raised a cup to his lips. 'If I can toast it, I'm sure you can.'

Donovan stared at the other cup but made no move towards it. 'I don't understand you.' Always when he was tired or under pressure, the accent thickened until he sounded as if he'd just stepped off a potato boat. 'It mattered enough to kill people for. Now it's more important that we part as friends? I have news for you, Dr Chapel. We're not going to part friends.'

Chapel sniffed and arched an eyebrow before finishing his tea. 'Perhaps it's a matter of breeding,' he observed snidely. 'Go on then—caution away.'

Donovan made no pretence about his background. His family hadn't been out of the top drawer even in Glencurran: everywhere he'd travelled since his accent had earned him the scorn of those who put store in these matters. So it didn't worry him if people thought him rough. He just didn't understand why a man who'd spent most of his life in a village you could fit on a football pitch and talked as if through a mouthful of peat considered himself better.

But he wasn't going to bicker with a man he was arresting

for conspiracy to murder. 'I must caution you that if you do not mention when questioned something which you later rely on in court, it may harm your defence. If you do say anything it may be given in evidence.'

When he'd finished Dr Chapel nodded. An expression almost like pain flickered across his face. 'If that's the formalities complete, you might want to call a senior officer about now.'

Donovan frowned. 'Detective Superintendent Shapiro's outside. Don't worry, he'll be—interested—to make your acquaintance.'

'Only if he hurries,' said Dr Chapel faintly. Then he bent suddenly forward in his chair, and then he fell off it.

TEN

'THE SHRUBS AT THE FRONT door are yew trees,' said Liz. 'He made the tea with the berries. He'd no intention of going to prison. He'd have killed you too if he could have done.'

Donovan was sitting in the back of her car. Shock had finally overwhelmed him: even with the blanket around him he was shaking like an aspen.

She turned to Shapiro. 'Look, I've got to get him to hospital.'

Shapiro nodded. 'I'll tidy up here. It's mostly a matter of paperwork; that, and finding enough cells to bang up all the people I'm going to arrest.'

He watched the car leave. A minute later another arrived with the Forensic Medical Examiner. 'What have you got for me?'

'Suicide by yew berry,' said Shapiro succinctly.

Dr Crowe raised an eyebrow. 'If you people keep doing my job like this I'm going to try my hand at traffic control.'

They went inside.

In fact the signs were pretty clear, right down to the yew berries steeping in the teapot. But Dr Crowe was on his dignity and wouldn't admit it until he'd made a thorough assessment of the scene.

Constable Stark came over to Shapiro with an odd expression on his face. 'Letter for you, sir.'

Stark was holding it through rubber gloves so Shapiro took the same precaution. 'You found that here?'

'On top of the desk in the parlour.'

When he'd read it he put it carefully back in its envelope and then in an evidence bag. He sucked his front teeth. 'You sneaky sod.'

'Sir?'

'It's a suicide note.'

It wasn't just a suicide note. It was partly an explanation, partly a justification, substantially a shifting of the blame to where, now, it could do no harm.

'I don't know how much Detective Sergeant Donovan will have told you of events here,' Dr Chapel had written in the last hour of his life. 'I also don't know whether he'll be able to elucidate further. Either way you should know that his understanding of what happened may be unreliable. For much of his time here he was ill; which may explain his willingness to believe what he was told by a mentally retarded child. It was clear to me that he suspected a conspiracy where none existed.

'I was wholly and solely responsible for the death of Simon Turner. He was brought to me with minor injuries from a fight, and I took the opportunity to end his life. No one in East Beckham knew what I intended until it was done, although other people then assisted me in passing off the corpse as Jonathan Payne. In particular, this could not have been achieved without the co-operation of Payne himself and his mother.

'My motive was the preservation of a community and a way of life which would have been destroyed had Simon Turner lived. I regret his death but it was the lesser of two evils. In a very real sense he paid the price for his own greed. If he'd been prepared to sell to us he'd be alive today.

'If I did not persuade him to share a last drink with me, tell Detective Sergeant Donovan that he is a deeply suspicious young man. I don't mean that as an insult: in his line of work it's probably a good thing. I don't think he'll accept my best wishes; but tell him I'm sorry about his dog.'

WHEN LIZ PHONED later from the hospital Shapiro told her about the note. The contents were burned into his memory.

There was a long silence while she absorbed what he was saying. 'He thought he could give them a way out. So what can we actually prove?'

'That Elphie's father is Sarah Turner's son and not the man he's been impersonating for fourteen years. And that Simon

Turner was murdered. We have Chapel's confession; we can't prove he had any accomplices.'

'There were a dozen of them,' said Liz. 'Chapel told Donovan as much.'

'Of course he did, and of course that's what happened. But Chapel's dead now, and has said his last word on the subject. And Donovan was sick: a good brief will cast huge doubts on the accuracy of his recollection.'

'He said it in front of the Turners. And the Turners weren't involved in the murder: they'll tell the truth.'

'I dare say they will,' nodded Shapiro, 'but can we prove it's the truth? If they *were* involved in the murder, it's in their interests to lie. They had as much as anyone to lose if the business was sold, and they were the only people whose co-operation was vital. Quite a moderate brief would make it look as if they were lying to hide the extent of their own involvement.'

'But they did it again. The villagers. When they were threatened with discovery, they took up arms again. They went after Donovan with farm implements!'

'Did they? Or were these honest country-folk on their way home at the end of the day when they heard a disturbance at the big house?—in which case what more natural than that they should gather in the front yard to see what it was all about. When a man they hardly knew appeared to have kidnapped a village child, of course they gave chase. It was only later they learned her father had asked Donovan to take Elphie with him. At the time they thought she was being abducted.'

'There have certainly been some unfortunate misunderstandings, M'lud,' he went on, poker-faced, 'but all the people before you today are guilty of was failing to blow the whistle on a deception which preserved their way of life fourteen years ago. They didn't know Simon Turner was murdered—Dr Chapel's dying confession accepts the blame for that. Your Honour may take the view that Sarah Turner and her son have more to answer for, but as far as my clients are concerned, the interests of justice might best be served by binding them over to keep the peace...'

Liz stared at her phone in horror. She was on the hospital steps, had wanted an update without going back to Queen's

Street. She knew if she put her head through the door she'd be there until the early hours, and she desperately needed some sleep.

'You mean, that's it? The people who killed Simon Turner, who tried to kill Donovan, are going to get away with it? Get their wrists slapped, and then go home?'

'It looks that way.'

'Is it me,' she asked after a moment, 'or has the justice system gone quite mad?'

'It's you,' Shapiro said without hesitation. 'The justice system has always been three clauses short of a Traffic Act. It's trying to perform two conflicting functions: to punish the guilty and protect the innocent. Sometimes it has to compromise. Stick with the essentials: the truth, or at least the greater part of it, is known now. Elphie's safe, and no one else is going to stumble on to East Beckham's murky secret and pay for it with his life. If that's not a total success, at least it's worth something.'

'You'd better explain it to Donovan,' said Liz. 'You make it sound quite reasonable. Whereas if I try and tell him, he'll think he went through all that for nothing.'

'How is he?'

'Asleep. They put him on a drip and he went out like a light. They say they'll probably hold on to him for two or three days but there's nothing to worry about.'

'What about Tyler?'

'A bad enough injury. He lost a lot of blood before they got him stitched up. If it doesn't sound too mean, I was quite pleased about that. If I hadn't dropped Wingrave when I did, Tyler'd have bled to death.'

'And Brian?' Shapiro was ticking off the casualties on mental fingers.

'Also on the mend. He'll be home tomorrow. He's going to need some expensive dentistry but everything else'll heal itself.'

'Was he able to describe his attackers?'

'Not yet. But he's been on painkillers since it happened: I think if I showed him a publicity shot from *The Wizard of Oz* he'd finger Judy Garland.' She sniffed and her voice dropped and hardened. 'But I saw them too. I didn't recognize any of them, but that doesn't mean they're not in the files somewhere. Tomorrow I'll start looking. And if I don't find them there, sooner or later I'll see one of them on the street. It may take time, but they're not going anywhere and neither am I.'

'Go home, Liz,' said Shapiro wearily. 'Go home and go to bed. Tomorrow is another day.'

'There'll be loads to get organized. We'd better make an early start.'

'*I'll* make an early start,' he said sternly. 'You will have breakfast in bed, then visit Brian. Then you can go see Donovan, and after that you can take some flowers to Mr Tyler. And any of the day that's left after *that* you can take off. Put your feet up, get your head straight. I don't want to see you in the office before Monday.'

There was a lengthy silence at her end. Then: 'Isn't tomorrow Monday?'

'Tomorrow is Sunday,' Shapiro said heavily. 'Liz, for heaven's sake go to bed. What earthly use is a detective who doesn't even know what day of the week it is?'

She murmured apologies and rang off.

Shapiro sat alone in his office, alone in fact on the top floor, listening. But there was nothing to hear. No trouble on the street, no querulous voices rising up the stairwell, no running feet in the corridors. He smiled gently to himself. It was over. Peace was restored.

Though not for long. Soon enough they'd all be back in the old routine. A couple of days from now Castlemere would have caught its breath and be back in business, and thieves and thief-takers would once again be trying to out-smart each other against the looming backdrop of Castle Mount. But for today at least they could all relax.

His eye narrowed and after a moment he opened a drawer, took out his diary and traced down the pages with a stubby fingernail. Then he leaned back, satisfied. 'Sunday. I knew that.'

A Great Day for Dying

Jonathan Harrington

**A DANNY
O'FLAHERTY
MYSTERY**

An assassin wearing a leprechaun mask shoots the grand marshal of New York's St. Patrick's Day parade, and Danny O'Flaherty is the only witness. But when police accuse Danny's friend and IRA activist Brendan Grady, Danny is determined to prove Grady's innocence.

While juggling teaching at an inner city high school, romance with a feisty Irish beauty, and threats that go beyond politics into the world of hard drugs and danger, Danny must reach back to his own past, to a woman he once loved, and the caprices of fate that can both bless and shatter lives.

Available March 2002 at your favorite retail outlet.

WORLDWIDE LIBRARY®

WJH413

Take 2 books and a surprise gift FREE!

SPECIAL LIMITED-TIME OFFER

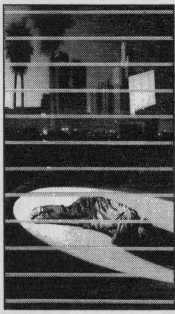

DEATH
OF THE
PARTY

A FAITH CASSIDY
MYSTERY

Catherine Dain

Actress-turned-therapist Faith Cassidy knows that dreams are born and broken every day in Los Angeles, and only the strong survive. So when her bungalow is burglarized, and an impromptu block party gets an uninvited guest—a corpse wearing her stolen bomber jacket—she fights back.

The only eyewitness leads Faith back to a past she left behind: the world of hard partying and drugs. As a former lover tries to seduce her into returning to a dangerous lifestyle, she wonders if his reappearance in her life plus another dead body is more than a coincidence....

"A pleasant series addition of easy-to-read prose and intriguing characters."
—*Library Journal*

Available March 2002 at your favorite retail outlet.

MEMORIES CAN BE MURDER

A Charlie Parker Mystery

CONNIE SHELTON

While stowing boxes away in her attic, Albuquerque CPA
Charlie Parker uncovers chilling information about her
father—and his work as a scientist during the Cold War
years. Worse, she now suspects the fatal plane crash that
killed both her parents was murder.

Determined to solve the fifteen-year-old crime, Charlie
quickly learns that asking questions is dangerous. Soon
dead ends—and dead bodies—have her worried she's
next on the hit list. But what secret is worth killing for
after all this time?

"Charlie is slick, appealing, and nobody's fool—just what
readers want in an amateur sleuth."
—*Booklist*

Available March 2002 at your favorite retail outlet.

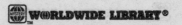 **WORLDWIDE LIBRARY®**

WCS414

THE PUMPKIN SEED MASSACRE

Native American psychologist Ben Pecos has returned to New Mexico as an intern with the Indian Health Service. Still struggling with the demons of his past, he is plunged into the nightmare rampage of a mysterious virus that is killing the residents of the pueblo, including his own grandmother.

One of the victims, the powerful tribal governor, opposed the construction of a proposed gambling casino on pueblo land. Ben suspects his murder was premeditated—but that doesn't explain the insidious killer now stalking the innocent.

"...great plot...a gripping novel."
—Tony Hillerman

Available February 2002 at your favorite retail outlet.

SUSAN SLATER
A BEN PECOS MYSTERY

WORLDWIDE LIBRARY®   WSS411

TIP A CANOE

Peter Abresch

A JAMES P DANDY ELDERHOSTEL MYSTERY

LIKE A CORPSE OUT OF WATER

Maryland physical therapist James P. Dandy embarks upon his third Elderhostel vacation, eager to reunite with his ladylove Dodee Swisher for some romance and outdoor adventure in South Carolina's lovely Santee Dam lakes.

At first, nobody was calling the accidental drowning of a local man murder, or worrying about ecoterrorism at the discovery of an empty box of dynamite. Then the body of a fellow Elderhosteler is found feeding fish in the swamp, and soon Jim is wading into the muddy waters of murder. But when Jim's clever reasoning unravels the shocking true motive for murder, it leaves him up the proverbial creek—with a killer holding the paddle.

Available February 2002 at your favorite retail outlet.

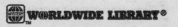